For Martin Benkkover —
Do we miss you!
Thanks, for the memories.
All the best,
always,
Henry & Jean Hofer
LA/CA   5/25/99

The Ebola Factor

THE EBOLA FACTOR

A NOVEL OF SUSPENSE

G. HENRY HOFER

ENGLAND • USA • SCOTLAND

PUBLISHED BY PENTLAND PRESS, INC.
5124 Bur Oak Circle, Raleigh, North Carolina 27612
United States of America
919-782-0281

ISBN 1-57197-010-X
Library of Congress Catalog Card Number 95-071346

Hofer, Gunter Henry
The Ebola Factor / by G. Henry Hofer

This is a work of fiction. Names, places, incidents and characters either are used fictitiously or are products of the author's imagination. Any resemblance to actual events or places or persons, living or dead, is entirely coincidental.

Copyright © 1996 Gunter Henry Hofer
All rights reserved, which includes the right to reproduce this book or portions thereof in any form whatsoever except as provided by the U.S. Copyright Law.

Printed in the United States of America

With Love,
To Vera, who walked with me Per Aspera Ad Astra,
And with Hope,
To our young who will straddle the millenia:
Keep the Faith!

ACKNOWLEDGMENTS

Thanks are due, in great measure, to a number of people who shall not go unmentioned:

To Bill Fremont and to Harold Colin, my best readers and critics who keep nudging me on; To the real Thad Montgomery (Semper Fi!) who gladly lent his name to a fictional character; To Kurt, who kept asking and finally has a real book to take home.

And yet, all would have been for naught had it not been for Vera, my love, my life, my friend, my wife.

Nettie

It felt unseasonably cool for a Fourth of July morning, and immediately as he thought so Tom had to smile. This was cool only when you came from the humid pressure cooker of the East, of Washington and of Baltimore. For Los Angeles such early morning overcast was par for the course this time of the year. It would be eleven o'clock or later before the sun had burned through it. That would be just fine with him. By that time he would be at the boat in Ventura harbor, ready to cast off. And Nettie would have the coffee brewing.

Aaah, Nettie . . . and coffee . . . and a long weekend . . .

Tom zipped up his windbreaker, gripped his canvas bag and stepped over the airport roadway to the island where the stops were for the rental car vans. His was the third one down, Avis. The thunder of take-offs towards the ocean was like a distant roar and rumble, intermittent but steady. He plunked down his bag and sank his hands into his pockets. It had been a long night, for he had worked at the Institute all day Friday well past eight in the evening, then showered and changed out of the uniform into his civvies. On the way to Dulles International airport, he had the Army carpool driver stop at a Howard Johnson and bought dinner for both of them. The driver's name happened to be Howard, too, and they had grinned about that across the table. This Howard was about his own age; Tom wondered what it would be like to be in your mid-thirties and still only be a sergeant in the Army. He immediately chided himself for unfairness. He himself was only a major in the US Army Medical Corps, and Tom knew damn well that many if not most of his classmates were by now well ensconced in highly lucrative specialty practices and would look down on him working for a salary that was not much more than what they were paying their office nurses.

He was tooling along on the Pacific Coast Highway, disdaining the crowded freeway for the no less busy beach traffic along the coast, but here at least he had the ocean to his left, and a horizon that just wouldn't quit whenever he caught a glimpse of it between houses and businesses that rimmed the shoreline. Soon he and Nettie would be together again, and for one lustful moment he wondered if they would make love the minute he stepped onto the boat. He could see himself doing it, jumping from the dock into the cockpit, and before she had time to notice swing himself down the hatch into the cabin, pulling the cover shut above; they would kiss and hug, wouldn't they? And desire each other? After all, it had been six weeks since they had been together last. By God, he loved this woman, this great, big earthy blonde, all roundness and softness in bountiful measure, with those trusting dark blue eyes that, as much as her body, had first attracted him to her.

Tom sighed. Of course they wouldn't make love right away. For one thing, they would still be at dockside, with weekend sailors in boats next to theirs; Nettie was a very private person. For another reason, too. He wondered if she was feeling well—her period, perhaps? When they had talked last, on Wednesday she had sounded distracted, citing a headache. This was one excuse she had never used against his amorous advances. But she refused to tell him, her husband—and not only that but a doctor as well—exactly what her symptoms were. They had left it at that, with her saying, somewhat irritably, that she knew what to do. Okay, she had her degree in veterinary medicine and she knew her body best. Besides when they got married they had promised not to "ply their trades" on each other.

Tom sighed again. So, it would have to wait until the evening probably, when they were anchored offshore somewhere and had had a drink and the waves would slap mutedly at the hull of their boat.

It looked as if the weather would be on their side. He searched the blue wedge of ocean now coming into view as the highway bore down from Malibu's Pepperdine University hills. All right; no white caps and hardly any waves to entice surfers. He liked it that way; he never pretended to be a sailor, that was Nettie's business, her "distant Viking genes" as she called it. For him, the water was something best flown over, or plunged into for a swim or for surfing. Still, when Nettie had found this one-time opportunity to buy a boat, a "MacGregor 25, practically all new," from a departing colleague, he had quickly agreed with her that they should buy it. It would be used. They would soon be permanently established on the West Coast, Nettie was already there working for an animal testing laboratory in Goleta near Santa Barbara. Tom would be resigning from the Army and joining some organization—governmental or academic—that could use his skills as an epidemiologist. Nettie's mother, the cranky, formidable, fiftyish Mrs. Carla Goldsmith, once divorced and once widowed, had already sold her Minneapolis home and "joined" them in an apartment near their rented Goleta house. Very convenient for baby-sitting purposes, as she did not fail to point out. She "just loved little Bertie, my one and only grandchild so far. Hint, hint." It was with her that their son, just turned three years of age, was spending this weekend.

Bertie, the apple of his eye, their only child, "so far," but surely not their last. For the boy's sake alone moving to Santa Barbara was a good idea. Good climate, good schools, nice people. So different from the suburban Maryland of their early married years. Yes, this would be a future worth pursuing, even though truth be told, he would miss the Army.

He was passing through Oxnard now. Soon he would have to watch for the cutoff to the road leading to the Ventura marina. And then, Nettie.

Visions of Nettie danced in front of his mind's eyes, Nettie in short-shorts and T-shirt clambering over the deck to untangle the spinnaker line; Nettie in the cabin, later, sans everything and all delectable womanhood. Loose hair, pink nipples, round buns, long legs. Stop it, Tom, he told himself, as he wondered again for the umpteenth time how he could have been so lucky to lure beautiful Natalie Goldsmith into marriage when he knew that there were others, men richer and more powerful then he. Men Mother Carla would have preferred for her daughter, but Nettie turned them all away, saying she only loved him, and soon walked down the aisle, two months pregnant, all in demure white but radiant with joy. And then later, being wild, absolutely wild in bed with him that first married night, teasing him, the prim Episcopalian, with a naughty story about some Protestant prick. He remembering, between tongue-wrestled kisses, the famous European surgeon at his medical school who upon his appointment, added an "e" to change his name to Perick, which convulsed them into giggly laughter, with Nettie henceforth giving him the intimate nickname "Perry." Ah, Nettie, my love, my life, here I am! He looked at his watch; he was within minutes of 1300 hours ETA!

He left the car at a gated parking lot, putting the ticket into his wallet. The wallet itself was in a waterproof cover, in case he got dunked. Then he took his bag and walked towards the mooring slips. Their boat was towards the end of the last row. They had been lucky at that to retain the slip from the previous owner. Sailing was a booming business in California.

He saw the boat, the Helena, lying still in the water, tied to the floating dock. The immediate neighbor slots were already empty, those boats early at sea this holiday weekend.

Walking more briskly, he strained to sight Nettie somewhere. In the cockpit? Sunning herself on the cabin roof? He could not see her, and as he came closer it was clear that Nettie was not outside. Wouldn't she know that he would arrive just about now? Tom fought down a feeling of annoyance; she was probably ashore, getting some last minute supplies.

As he came to the boat he threw his bag into the cockpit and jumped in after it. "Hello, pet!" The cabin roof was pulled shut. "I'm here! Hello?" He bumped his nose against the vertical Plexiglas insert when he tried to look down into the cabin. "Nettie? Hello?"

Dimly he saw someone stirring, a person reclining on the starboard berth, her back against the kitchen sink, hair wildly disheveled, dressed in a sleeveless dress, head lolling, eyes unfocused. Good Lord!

"Nettie?" he cried, unbelieving, and banged his fist on the cabin roof.

The person feebly raised a revolver towards him, her arm wavering, then with another arm brought a tape player to her lips. The gun in her hand made a brief pointing movement, as her lips formed words spoken into the microphone. It was then that he saw a pair of earphones dangling from the rim of the cabin door. He recognized the "tape player." It was the sound detector they had bought for their infant son's nursery, with a cord long enough to reach their adjacent bedroom, for easy monitoring of their baby's sleep.

Deeply shocked now, he recognized the person as his wife

He grabbed the earphones and put them on. "Nettie!" he shouted against the glass barrier, "Sweetheart, what's going on?" Had she been drinking?

There was a raspy breathing sound, a phlegmy cough. "I . . . arrh . . . love you, Tom . . . we . . . both . . . love Bertie . . . " A blood-tinged bubble formed on her lips.

"Yes, yes darling, we do." He tried the cabin door; it was locked. "What is happening, dearest? Tell me!" He would have to break the door down.

"Arrh . . . do not come in, I beg you!" Tears, bloody tears rolled out of her eyes. "Do . . . as I say . . . if you love me . . . "

He stared in stupefied horror. "Oh my God!" he groaned, uncomprehending. Nettie was bleeding! "What happened? You are hurt! Let me help you!"

He saw her lift herself up, painfully slowly, to retch into the sink. As she slumped back onto the berth, her gown had hitched up to reveal black spots on her thighs, spots the size of silver dollars. Her chest was heaving. Her eyes were closed. Her hands, still clutching the gun and the microphone, rested limply by her sides.

"Nettie!" He banged his fist against the roof again. "Nettie, speak to me!" He felt cold stark terror creep up his veins.

She opened her eyes and lifted the microphone. Her voice was just above a whisper but more steady now.

"I want you to take us out to sea. Please. Now. Then . . . we will talk . . . "

It suddenly came to him that he was confronted with a situation that he could only control if he went along with it. His wife was seriously ill, that was chillingly clear, and she would need help. Her repeated pleas for him not to come into the cabin would have a reason that, for the moment, he would have to honor. And taking the boat out to sea made sense; they would have to move somewhere. He could put in to Santa Barbara harbor, alert the Coast Guard and have Nettie transferred to nearby Cottage Hospital. In that manner, within the hour she would be in competent medical hands, for whatever ailed her.

He decided that one hour was an acceptable time frame under the circumstances. He was a physician himself, albeit more of a research scientist than a practicing doctor. Even during the Gulf War his unit was not concerned with patching up the wounded but centered on the prevention of mass disease, of epidemics. His wife's obvious acute illness would need a specialist's attention. And that, he swore silently, she would get.

With swift, purposeful action he untied the boat, started the outboard motor and steered the vessel out of the channel into the open sea. The sun had come out, he took off his windbreaker and put on his Desert Storm hat. Every minute or so he peered through the Plexiglas into the cabin. Nettie was lying in deep sleep, her chest heaving regularly. He wondered if she had fresh air, until he saw that the small side windows had been slid partially open. The windows were part of the outside structure of the cabin, flush with the body of the boat; there was no way for him to poke his head through the narrow opening, even if he could stretch to reach them from the cockpit.

The physical activity had returned a measure of calm to his mind. It became apparent now that Nettie must be suffering from an infection; he recalled their telephone conversation earlier in the week when she had complained of not being well. He wished he had taken it seriously then, instead of presuming menstrual discomforts. Also, it would seem that the disease had reached more alarming proportions since Nettie had come to the boat. Why else would she have come here otherwise? She was a reasonable woman, a caring mother who would have availed herself of timely medical attention without having to be prodded into it.

And if it was an infectious disease, would he not be the perfect doctor to render a diagnosis? He would need to examine her.

Tom recognized the gun with which she had threatened him as his father's old service revolver, a Mauser, kept at home hidden away, but on which he had trained her on an Army shooting range because they had both felt she ought to be familiar with it for self-defense reasons.

He took a quick peek into the cabin, to see if the safety was on or off. It was on, he could determine, just next to her thumb resting inertly below it. Why? Why have the gun along at all, on a weekend sailing trip?

Then he looked at the table close to her bunk bed; had she brought any medication? There was a water bottle and a glass, some banana peels, and yes, a bottle of aspirin, her watch in an ashtray, next to a bright red lighter - why the lighter? She had quit smoking when she married him; he had begged her. And she had obliged him, or had rather obliged the baby that was coming.

He also noticed, now that he looked at her more intently and with a clearer mind, that the black spots on her legs were bleedings under the skin. Petechiae. Nettie's dress had slipped up revealing her pubic area, and there was blood seeping out from her labia. Good God! With those pink tears, and the red froth around her mouth—multiple hemorrhagia! How could that be in a perfectly healthy woman? What had happened?

He sat back, badly shaken, as he was steering the boat over a calm sea, unaware of how he was doing it. Tom's mind was a jumble of confusing and anguished thoughts. He had to command himself with all the willpower of which he was capable, to assess the situation, to call forward his own scientific training. There had to be a solution to this horror.

If he were called in on this "case," he asked himself, which he easily could be owing to his specialty, was he not trained in highly infectious diseases that could become epidemic? And had he not just attended a four-day seminar at the Centers for Disease Control in Atlanta, to research the mysterious outbreak of vague symptoms of ill health now being experienced by Gulf War veterans? "Get on with it," he shouted at himself against the wind.

Yes. All right, doctor. First step: Patient history. This patient was Nettie, his dear wife. He knew her as well as any person can know another. A well-nourished, physically and mentally normally developed 33-year old female, married, with no history of major diseases or injuries. Except for occasional colds, he had not ever seen her ill.

Next—the patient's primary complaint. Tom let out an agonized curse: Look at her, her whole body, her obvious suffering was one huge outcry of pain, of physical and perhaps mental disorder! There was no need for her to tell him. Nettie, his beloved, the mother of his son, was gravely and acutely ill!

Examination of patient? She had prevented him from entering the cabin by barricading herself inside. Why, in heaven's name? Why would a patient do that, against all instincts of self-preservation? This patient would. Nettie, graduated in veterinary medicine, was as fully conversant with medical terms and conditions as he was; sometimes more so, as he had noticed on occasion that her mind was more clinically analytical than his own. Her work was in a research laboratory, where wild animals were received and housed for use in pharmaceutical research and in preparation of cell cultures for vaccines. Those animals were mostly monkeys, brought in from Southeast Asia. Her working conditions reflected the latest in technical development, with security levels one through four. The fourth level, the last, was where Nettie worked frequently, being almost astronaut-like in sterility of environment. That elaborate security setup was geared to prevent accidental infection with often highly virulent agents always present in laboratory cultures.

Wait a minute! Good Lord, no! Had Nettie become infected there? Was that why she isolated herself so completely—to prevent the spread of her infection to her husband, and through him her baby? Because she knew that she was an acute danger to the two people she loved the most!

Damn it, Nettie, what are you doing? Talk to me! I love you, too!

He slumped down onto the floor of the cockpit, burying his face in his hands. Anguish and pity overwhelmed him, he felt helpless. He cursed himself for possibly being too late. Or was it? He had to try something!

Rising from the floor back up to the cockpit bench, he took stock of the present situation. Where was the boat right now, and where was it headed? Damn it, he hadn't paid any attention to the job of sailing.

He looked at his watch. Since coming to Ventura harbor, two, two and a half hours had elapsed. One of the promises they had made each other when they started sailing was that they would always stay within sight of land; another, that they would always reach a safe harbor by nightfall. Anxiously he scanned the horizon. There was land visible abeam, but was it the California coastline or one of the Channel Islands? He decided he would steer closer to it, that being safe either way.

How far had he traveled? He knew the boat was capable of doing twelve knots, but that was under sail. How much could he have done with the outboard? He had not run it full throttle. Maybe only half? Six knots? Six knots times two or more hours, say fifteen knots total. Remembering his sailing class arithmetic, one knot being equal to one nautical mile per hour, that would give him fifteen nautical miles, and a nautical mile being fifteen percent longer than a mile, that would mean, say seventeen miles as the seagull flies. That strip of land there had to be Santa Barbara, or was he passing Santa Cruz Island on the leeward side, towards the open ocean? Either way, he would hold more to starboard.

Then he decided to do two things. First, he hoisted the mainsail, a relatively simple matter on this boat. As he clambered onto the cabin deck to uncover the sail, he was looking through the window. Nettie's position had not changed. The sail deployed easily with an audible snap, and gave instant push to the boat. He turned off the outboard; he knew there were two extra cans of fuel in the forward hold but wondered if he would have access to them.

Next, he pulled the inflatable dinghy out of the stern locker, pumped it up with the bellows and, having secured it to a line, heaved it overboard. There were two life jackets, or personal flotation devices as required by law, in the locker also. He put on one of them, keeping the other on the floor of the cockpit. For Nettie, once he got to her.

All this activity suddenly made him aware of how thirsty he was. His throat was parched. He remembered that the previous owner had freshwater containers built into both sides of the cockpit, underneath the seat benches. Nettie had remarked how important it would be to have these constantly refilled. He tore off the seat cushions, first on the starboard, then on the port side that he was sitting on. Yes! Two gallon plastic bottles stood upright in each bench space. All four were full. He lifted one out, unscrewed the top and sniffed. The smell was a bit stale. He gave it a taste, found it acceptable and hiked the bottle up to his mouth on the crook of his arm and drank so eagerly, some of the water was running in dribbles over his lips down his chin and throat.

Having slaked his thirst, he zipped open his canvas bag and pulled out his small medical emergency kit. He opened it: bandages, iodine, collapsible splints, syringe packets, (no drugs—they would be in his regular medical bag for security reasons), and a set of instruments for emergency tracheotomies and suturing. Wonderfully inadequate for his present purpose. He did find a stick of gum; and his airplane breakfast croissant. Maybe he'd be able to give it to Nettie.

These diversions made him feel better, as though he was gaining a measure of control. The initial horror would now have to give way to rational thought. Nettie would have to be brought to expert care, regardless of whether her condition was hopeless or not; the Coast Guard would have to be alerted first. He checked the boats direction by keeping the distant shoreline straight abeam. Soon, help would be available.

Securing the tiller, he crept forward to the cabin entrance and peered through the Plexiglas. Nettie was lying motionless on her bunk, and for a moment his heart stood still thinking she had died, until he saw a faint heaving of her chest. She looked bad. Her mouth was half open, blood oozing down from her gums, joining the trickle that came out of her nose, running in rivulets down her cheeks onto the already dark-stained pillow. Pink concentric circles had formed on the front of her gown over her nipples. Another dark puddle of blood had gathered underneath her thighs. This looked worse than just an hour or two before! Textbook knowledge: Rapid physical disintegration, owing to viral profusion overwhelming the body's defense mechanism! A particularly bad virus.

He stumbled back onto his seat. A hemorrhagic fever of this magnitude, what could it be, Dengue, Lassa? Nettie hadn't traveled anywhere to acquire these exotic infections.

Then it hit him. She hadn't traveled, but the animals at her laboratory had! She must have acquired the virus by handling the animals! But how could that be, when the security measures at the lab were of the latest design, not to mention the strict rules of worker-to-worker support, a true buddy system that would spring into action at the slightest mistake or accident. Would her colleagues not have become alerted to her? Also, there is an incubation period of three to seven days before symptoms appear, plenty of time in a manner of speaking, what with general supportive measures being the only therapy, but time enough in that sense to begin counter action? Why was his wife not immediately tended to by her colleagues and fellow workers?

Because Nettie hadn't told them? If not, why not? Because this smart, bright woman had obviously recognized the seriousness of her situation, by isolating herself most effectively, by keeping herself away from her home environment and her baby, and lastly, by relying on him, her physician husband, to understand the circumstances. Hence the gun—a shock symbol underlining graphically her command not to be approached. Crude, but effective. And the microphone setup, the same smart thinking.

But why, in all her smartness did she not immediately commit herself to the isolation ward of a hospital? She would have a fighting chance there, and even though there is no cure for these fevers, some people do recover from it with proper supportive care. Why didn't she do that!? Why, why, and why again? The questions pressed on his mind. The answers would eventually present themselves. But first, he had to attend to Nettie.

Securing the tiller once more, he went over to the cabin and began banging on its roof, looking down to see if she heard him. He banged and knocked again, until she began to stir.

"Nettie!" he shouted. "Nettie!"

Wincing as he watched her struggle with her failing senses, he saw her lift her arm and bring to her face the microphone her hand was still clutching. She wanted to talk, but it seemed a superhuman effort for her to form words. Her tongue had swollen and her voice had become a mumble. He put on the earphones, and the magnification of what he heard made it more gruesome. Badly shaken, he tried to make sense of what words he could catch.

Slowly a picture was beginning to emerge. He was reasonably sure what Nettie was trying to tell him. She had been "jabbed" with a "needle," that he should check with "Jack" or "Mac," and that he should not think it was her fault. "Ack!" she tried to blurt out, "Ack!" Then, with a sudden surge of strength she rose from her bed, the revolver cluttering to the floor, and stumbling like an eerie bloody ghost she came to the Plexiglas partition.

There was no need for the microphone to hear her crying, stammering, "I love you and the baby . . . take care . . . promise . . . Mack . . . do . . . promise!"

"Nettie!" he cried back, "I love you, darling, please hang in there!"

"Promise . . . !" She whispered once more and pressed her lips to the glass leaving a bloody kiss as he watched her crawl back to her bunk, half fall down sideways, then lie inertly still. Tom felt tears rolling down his cheeks. After a moment when he feared that she might have expired, he saw her roll herself on her back, her chest heaving with great gulps for air.

He kept his eyes on her for long minutes, thoughts racing through his head as to what he could do. He cursed his medical knowledge that prevented him from being foolhardy, from bursting into the cabin and holding her hand, comforting her. Why could he not be ignorant of the consequences and do the impulsively human thing? He groaned, because he knew that that way he would become infected himself and that they would both die. That was what Nettie was trying to tell him when she begged him to take care of the baby. He had to survive.

When he finally returned to the tiller, he noticed that the sky had become darker, that the sun was hidden above a thick blanket of fog. The coastline had disappeared into the gray mass of moist air all around him.

Where was he? There was no radio on board; that was one item they had planned on adding, while in the meantime they would use the boat only for easy cruising just off the marina. He had no idea whether the wind had changed, and with it his direction.

One fact was obvious—he was lost. The other pleasure boats he had seen distantly before, had all vanished. He and Nettie were alone, at sea.

Slowly as that thought sank in, a sense of peace came over him. This was what was in store for them both, a journey into the unknown. They were in the hands of God, truly and irrevocably. Thy Will Be Done.

He let the boat find its own way.

Later, when it had become dark, he heard the sound of what seemed like waves breaking against a shore. With nightfall the fog had lifted, revealing a clear star-studded sky. Peering out, he could discern the glistening white of the breakers not more than a hundred yards away, and a steep cliff darkly behind. He quickly dropped the sail, found the anchor and threw it overboard. It caught fairly quickly below the flat bottom of the boat, and he pulled the line tight. The boat turned with the waves, then held steady with a constant bobbing motion. He hoped it would hold for the night. There was no sign of habitation on the strip of land he was facing, no lights, no human sounds. It became clear to him that he was at one of the islands, presumably Santa Cruz. That was all right. They were safe, for now. By the crack of dawn he would sail the boat in the opposite direction, towards the California coast towards help and sanity.

He looked in on Nettie. She lay prostrate on her bunk, in a different position than before; he wondered if she had gotten up again and crawled around, perhaps looking for him. The thought gave him a jab of pain. Dear God, was he doing all that could be done at the moment? He asked himself, if he were not a medically trained person, if he were ignorant of the consequences, would he not already have broken down that door and knelt by the side of his wife, giving her some comfort, and would that have not been right?

Touching the side of the cabin, where the narrow window was, he could feel that it had been slid shut. Feeling the other side, that one, too, was shut. He wondered why she had done that and if it was meant to protect him? But the cause of her bleeding fever—if a virus—did not travel the air and survive to infect anew. Blood and body fluids were the mode of transmission. She knew that well when she isolated herself so completely from him.

Once more he knocked on the Plexiglas window of the cabin door, rattling it, banging, making noise until Nettie raised her head. He trained his flashlight on her. Slowly, she struggled up into a sitting position. He saw that her tongue had so swollen that she could not close her mouth. Now, agonizingly, she brought a bloody hand up to the table. With a superhuman effort she moved her index finger over the white table cloth, brought the finger again and again to her mouth and back onto the table, until Tom was able to comprehend the purpose of the ghoulish exercise—a message, written with the blood oozing out of her. His dying wife was leaving him a message. As he followed her finger with the beam of his flashlight he was able to discern letters. First, what? An E? Then an 8 or a B; a circle, a zero, the letter O?; an L now, and yes, an A. Five symbols, numbers or letters. What did she mean, what was the message? Dear Nettie, what are you saying?

Numbed and shocked, he switched off his light and retreated. He sat back against the tiller and closed his eyes. He silently said the Lord's Prayer. The gentle rocking motion of the boat, the slap of the waves against the hull, the darkness of the night—at last the beneficent grace of sleep. But then a blinding flash, a whooshing sound with the force of a hurricane wind, and at the same instant he felt himself propelled through the air, until a long second or two later he splashed hard onto the water. He landed on his back, but he was too stunned to move; the impact had knocked the wind out of him. His life jacket kept him afloat. He was bobbing around senselessly like a cork, until a wave splashed over his face. When he opened his eyes again, he saw and felt the heat of the huge fireball that in white-hot fury was consuming the boat. The heat was so intense he paddled frantically to get away from it. That made him bump against the dinghy, still tied by a twenty-foot line to the stern of the boat. He labored hard to heave his water-logged self into the dinghy, then quickly untied the line. The short oars of the inflatable were where they should be. He unclasped them and stuck them through the rowlocks, scrambling to row away from the inferno as fast as possible. Another explosion wracked the flaming hull. He remembered the cans of gasoline stacked in the forward compartment. The water around the boat was lit brightly by the flames, an eerie sight as he rowed aimlessly around, searching for Nettie? Good Lord, Nettie was in that roaring inferno!

A mighty wave heaved the dinghy onto a rocky landfall, at such speed that all he could do to hang on was clutch the oarlocks, dipping the oars now and again to keep the blunt snout of the inflatable pointed to shore. He heard a scraping sound, felt it through the floorboard, and jumped out of the boat immediately, holding on to the dinghy by its side straps against the pull of the receding wave. He dragged it up onto the stony beach, his feet sinking to the top of his sneakers into the soft wet gravel, until he was on drier ground. Instinctively, he stumbled up the short beach, pulling the dinghy behind him as he groped in the dark for a stone or a tree trunk against which he could anchor it. He realized as he came closer that what was looming dark and high just ahead was a steep cliff, impossible to climb in the dark. There was at the foot of it, an arm-thick root sticking out of the ground, making a hitching post perfect for tying up his precious float, his link back to civilization. He heaved the dinghy up over the gravel as far as he could, and stuck the bow ring firmly over the root. Only then did he stop and look back.

The bright red whoosh of flames that had been his constant, terrible beacon as he paddled shoreward was reduced to a flicker now. He watched transfixed until the last lick had ceased, darkness engulfing the deathly scene as if a final curtain had fallen on it.

And so it was—deathly and final. With a groan, he fell to his knees and then prostrated himself like a penitent, clawing at the stones. His head turning from side to side, unintelligible moans bursting from his lips with each breath until he lay quiet and turned himself over, his eyes to the stars. He brought his hands together and clasped them in prayer to the omnipresent power of the universe to whom he had prayed all his life in childlike reverence so that he had never felt shaken, even now. He prayed for the salvation of the soul of his beloved; he gave thanks for the love they had for each other and for the child they had created. He asked for strength, for himself and for his child, for the child's health and happiness. For himself he asked for the grace of truth about what had happened to them, for the wisdom to know right from wrong and the loathing of the comfort of cowardice. He then said amen and rose up shaking the sand from his clothes. His mind was at peace.

There was a waterproof cover sheet on the bottom of the little boat. He unfolded it, crawled into the dinghy and covered himself. Staring into the void of the night, he kept his heart in check. He must be strong now, stronger than ever. His eyes closed.

"Sir!" Somebody was shaking him by the shoulders, again and again. He did not want to wake up. He had a dream—a weird, wonderful, golden dream. "Sir, are you all right?" He felt his eyelids being pried open and a flash of light pierce the darkness. He blinked, hard, stared. The night had passed and a milky daylight of fog had spread itself over the sky above him.

Tom jerked his head up with a jolt and tried to focus. A uniformed man was bending over him across the tube of the inflatable. Sitting up, he saw a flat bottom motorboat down at the water's edge. Another uniformed man was straining to hold it in place against the waves. Off shore, a cutter hove to. Coast Guard. He recognized them. Reality was coming back.

"Yes," he croaked hoarsely.

"Sir—can you understand what I am saying to you? Is that burned-out boat out there yours?"

"Yes."

He said yes to all the other questions put to him. Could he get up? What was his name? Was he thirsty? Were there any other passengers on that boat?

"Yes, one. My wife."

"What happened to her?"

"She . . . there was an explosion . . . she was in the cabin . . . I was outside, at the tiller . . . couldn't save her, it all happened so fast . . . "

"An explosion? How did it happen?"

"I don't know . . . Oh my God." Tom's bewildered anguish was genuine. He buried his face in his hands.

The officer touched him by the shoulder: "Sir, you will have to come with us to make a statement. Please, get up. Easy, now." The Coast Guard officer led him away.

They put him onto a bunk on the Coast Guard cutter, gave him hot coffee and covered him with a blanket, telling him to take it easy.

On the trip to shore, Tom, left alone, forced his mind to go back over the last moments he had seen Nettie alive. He recreated her frantic efforts of leaving him a message. Clear as her spoken word it came to him: E-B-O-L-A

Ebola, a deadly virus named after a river in Zaire. Nobody infected by it had survived, humans and animals alike. Monkeys were the carriers.

Monkeys! Nettie worked with monkeys! Had she infected herself? No, not Nettie. If she had, she would have acted differently. Instead, she kept silent, until it was too late. Why? What was she trying to tell him?

Tom

"Name?" The jovial booking sergeant had not lost his patience.

Tom was morose. "It's all there, in the Boating Accident Report."

"I want you to give it to me, just the same. Okay?"

Tom nodded wearily. This was the third time he was doing this, first at the Coast Guard who provided him with the "C-BAR" report form, had him fill it out and then turned him over to the Ventura County sheriff's office. The people there transferred him, reds light flashing and all, to the Santa Barbara police headquarters. Because the boat owners' address was in Goleta, Santa Barbara, and one had died in the accident; and more to the point because he, the operator of the boat, the husband, had been the only other passenger who was very much alive now, a bit scruffy and unshaven but otherwise miraculously unhurt. Because of all that he was taken to the police; under suspicion, no doubt.

Tom made the effort. "Campe, with an 'e' at the end, as in Porsche."

"Okay." A sideways look. This a wiseguy? "First name?"

"Thomas."

"Thomas." The police sergeant nodded, making the wisps of hair atop his bald pate undulate like seaweed. T-h-o-m-a-s, he typed onto the keyboard.

"Middle initial, or name?"

"V for Vonder. V-o-n-d-e-r. One word. As in Wonder Bread, but with a German accent." *Come on, Tom, don't be an ass . . .*

Another look. "Yeah. I get it." Vonder, tap-tap-tap.

"Address? Home first "

"Until recently, and mine still, Five Mockingbird Lane, Chevy Chase, Maryland. Two-oh-eight-one-five. My wife and child have moved here ahead of me."

More tapping. "Okay. Business?"

"It's an acronym, sergeant, and a long one. I don't want you to think I am putting you on. USAMRIID," he wrote the letters on a sheet of paper and handed it to him. "It stands for U. S. Army Medical Research Institute for Infectious Diseases. In Frederick, Maryland."

The policeman took the paper from him and put the letters into the computer. This was a Sunday night, almost the end of his shift and he longed to go home but here he was wasting his time. The guy the sheriff had brought in wasn't your usual weirdo, of which there were plenty in Santa Barbara, especially on a long holiday weekend. Hell, on the contrary, this fellow was straight and sober (he could tell when they were not especially if drugs were involved), six feet tall, muscular, flat-bellied, hair neatly trimmed and combed back without a part, and wearing glasses of the kind that tie behind the ears, for when you do sports and stuff.

The computer screen now came up with information, eight, nine lines until the end blip. He nodded. Things were falling into place. Piece o' cake.

"Tell me what you do, Mister, uh, Campee."

"I am a major, in the Army Medical Corps."

"A doctor?"

"That's right."

"Your Social Security number."

"Five-five-six, six-oh, two-one two-oh." The answers came without hesitation.

"All right." The policeman leaned back in his chair. It all jibed with what he had on the screen. He'd go talk to the senior duty officer. Let him handle it. "Please stay where you are for a moment, sir. I'll be right back."

He wasn't away long, and when he came back he brought his boss with him, a short man with a round head and a gray crewcut. They both craned their necks to read the screen. Then the short man spoke.

"I'm detective Perez. Look, major, we have no right to hold you. This is a matter for the Army. The sheriffs shouldn't have brought you in here."

"They probably didn't know he was Army," said the sergeant.

The short man nodded. "Of course they didn't know." Turning to Campe again, he said, "Sir, we have to let you go. No charges have been filed, and won't be unless the Coast Guard investigation comes up with something. Even then, we'd have no authority over you, because you fall under the Uniform Code of Military Justice. But I must inform you that we will forward the information we have here to the proper authorities. It would be wise if you returned immediately to your base and reported to your superior officer. It'll be up to the Army then." He shrugged his thick shoulders.

"File charges? For what?" Campe's face looked flushed as he rose from the chair. "For having survived the explosion and fire on our boat?"

"It says here in the accident report that your wife died in that explosion." The short man fingered the sheet of paper and let it drop back on the desk. "The circumstances of the fire and her death will have to be investigated, no matter what." Then he added, "I'm sorry your wife died, major."

Campe waved his hand, half a salute. "Thanks," he said, and turned to leave. "I won't go back to Maryland just yet. My wife's funeral . . . and my little boy is here . . . you know where to find me if you need me."

"Sure thing." The detective picked up the accident report. "This has to be filed within forty-eight hours of death occurring. I can forward it to Sacramento for you, and you take a Xerox copy with you."

"I'd appreciate it."

"No problem. And Doug here can drop you off at your house. His shift is over. Okay, Doug?"

"Okay."

"Thanks," Campe said again. "Thanks a lot."

The house Nettie had found and rented at first sight was in the university section where the streets were named after Ivy League colleges. It was on Dartmouth Lane, just a half mile off the freeway towards the mountains. From the upstairs rooms it was possible to catch a view of the ocean. Night had not yet settled in when the police car pulled up in front of his driveway. Campe said, "Thank you, officer. Much appreciated, really," and walked across the little square of lawn towards the front door. He had seen his mother-in-law and his son in the brightly lit living room, Carla scooping up the boy in her arms and rushing to the window, making Bertie's arm wave at him. He took him from her when he was inside the door.

"Hi, Bertie!" Campe nuzzled the boy's cheek. "Hi! How are you? Did you have a nice time with grandma?"

"The poor boy." Carla came up and wrested him away from Campe. "What are we going to do? How are we going to tell him?"

"The first thing we won't do is talk about it in his presence." Campe wasn't surprised that Carla already knew. One of the first things the police would have done was to go to the victim's home bearing the message, and not only for compassionate reasons. It paid, sometimes, the see the reaction of the next-of-kin crowd. This information he had gleaned from the many detective stories he had read, cast-offs from Nettie's reading list who was a real fan of that genre. "I am going to sit with him for a while, Carla." He gently pried the child loose and cooing softly, carried him down the hall to the nursery. It was almost an hour before he came back into the living room. "Bertie is asleep now," he said.

"Did you give him something?" Carla asked. There was suspicion in her voice, too strongly accented to sound genuine. "The poor kid."

He knew what she meant. "Yes," he replied sharply. "Lots of love." He went to the kitchen and took a beer out of the fridge. When he came back he saw Carla slumped in the high-back chair, her hand covering her eyes. Her shoulders were twitching. She stayed that way as he sat down in the opposite chair, on the other side of the fireplace.

He just knew that she was faking sorrow. She had never been very close to Nettie, or to her other two daughters for that matter. For Carla, it was Carla who came first, last and always. Almost from the moment he had first met her—they were introduced on the day that Nettie announced their engagement at Thanksgiving at her apartment in Los Altos, with all of Nettie's other family and close friends attending—he had felt an antipathy towards Carla. There was something about that woman that struck him as wrong, the way she was overly friendly while at the same time making catty remarks about people when their backs were turned. He had chided himself for being unfair; after all, he had only just met her, and he was giving in to prejudice. But then a word came to his mind: False. One of two ways his father would judge the core of a person's being, false or genuine. "Genuine" being tantamount to a stamp of approval that would last a lifetime. "Echt, oder falsch," his father's nasal voice was still echoing in his mind, "True or false. That's what it comes down to with people and you'd do well to remember that, lad." Hugo von der Campe rarely brooked dissent, and Thomas his only son would certainly not have dared to disagree. He was not yet eight when his father was "taken from us," words that were also etched in his mind. His mother was holding him in her arms when she said that. He learned as he grew older that his father's death was caused by an entirely preventable accident. Hugo von der Campe, formerly of the fledgling West-German diplomatic service and lately an executive of the Badische Anilin and Soda Fabriken BASF/USA in Trenton, New Jersey, was easily annoyed by petty failings, be they human or mechanical. One busy December afternoon, when his car broke down on the New Jersey Turnpike he stepped out to check the cause. He was promptly sideswiped by traffic. His body was found a hundred feet down the lane, his hand still clinging to the door handle. He was aged forty-one.

Thomas von der Campe, or "V for Vonder" as he petitioned to have his name changed when he came of age, grew to realize that he owed his own more malleable nature to the practical-minded, tough-love approach of his Yankee mother Eleanor, who had the foresight and the money to send him to the best private and prep schools in the Northeast. His sister Betts, three years older, was claimed by her English grandmother and went to live in the Old Country when Eleanor remarried. "Mom," he remembered crying, "why did you send Betts away?" It was then that he learned that Bettina, under whose covers he had crawled many a night during frightening thunderstorms, to be embraced and comforted by her, was not his mother's child. "Betts is English, darling, from your father's first marriage. She has family there, you know, and they love her and she wants to go there." Bettina was thirteen then, and almost a head taller than her half-brother who was about to enter the Brownley School in Manhattan, just around the corner from where the man his mother had married owned a townhouse. It was a confusing time, and to keep himself from crying Thomas the boy threw himself into two passions: Science at school, where he excelled much to the surprise of his mother and his teachers, and riding horses on weekends and during holidays, at a riding academy up the Hudson river near West Point. Foster "Fos" Watson, his mother's new husband, was most supportive of both endeavors.

It had all worked out, over time, but the shadow of his father's death never quite receded from Tom's horizon. He had missed him, even after the pain had gone. And now, little Bertie was to grow up motherless.

Tom noticed that Carla was observing him through the slats of her fingers. Her shoulders had stopped shaking. He knew that he would have to say something, but the words, "I am so sorry" seemed totally inadequate. "We have both lost Nettie" was too banal and stuck in his craw. He couldn't bring them out.

In the end, he did say them, "Carla, I am so sorry. We have both lost Nettie." Shit, he thought. I shouldn't have said anything.

She dropped her hand from her face. Her eyes were dry. "What happened?" she hissed at him. "Why didn't you save her?"

That question, and the tone of her voice, made his hackles rise. "Do you think I wouldn't have saved her if I could have?" He felt his eyes burning.

"Look at you!" Carla was getting worked up. "Nothing happened to you, not a scratch on you! You are just fine! And my baby is dead!" Tears were now pouring out of her eyes as if she had ordered them, a copious flow accompanied by a wailing sound that stopped as abruptly as it had started by a stentorian blowing of her nose into the corner of the apron she was wearing.

Tom sat there watching the spectacle. At the beginning he had wanted to rush over to her chair and comfort her. After all, she was Nettie's mother and Nettie was her child, in a manner of speaking. But then he remembered that he had seen the show before, at the same intensity for lesser, often trivial reasons. They always seemed to center on a perceived slight against her person no matter whether there were any factual causes for it or not, and there seldom were. Her three daughters, at one time or another were the selected accused. She had succeeded in preventing her middle daughter Laura, a gentle and loving woman, from marrying "a Jew." Laura had defied her by living with her man anyway, and had not been talked to by her mother since. The youngest daughter, April, had withdrawn voluntarily by choosing to live with her father and by following in his footsteps studying dentistry. Carla had divorced her husband in a spectacularly spiteful emotional rampage when the girls were in their teens. Nettie had confided to Tom once that she hated her mother, something that so shocked her that she was overwhelmed with guilt. She needed to balance the scale, she said, and be especially compassionate towards her mother. That was reinforced when Carla's second husband died a wretched death of a postoperative infection, pneumonia, after removal of a cancerous stomach. Now, Nettie told Tom in tears, she had to invite her to their wedding a year later, even though that meant disinviting her father who was to have given her away, and with him her sister April. Laura came, defiantly, with "her Jew"—by now a successful Los Angeles lawyer—and into the breach to fill the missing bridesmaid slot jumped Tom's sister Betts who was flying in from London a couple of days early for the rehearsals. Tom's mother only arched a well-bred eyebrow at these goings-on. The wedding took place at her—the Watson's—Palm Beach house and was catered entirely by the in-house staff. There were over one hundred guests, and Eleanor was busy doing the right thing for her boy and only child. As it happened, Carla behaved herself, perhaps intimidated by the opulence of the surroundings. It must have occurred to her that "her baby" was not just marrying an impecunious Army officer but the scion of an old and presumably wealthy family. Tom and Nettie had privately laughed at that; the joke of it was that Tom had used up his father's inheritance by paying his own way through college and medical school, and that the Watsons had hit hard times, through bad investments compounded by Foster's increasing medical bills for his eye problems and prostate cancer. There was still real estate, yes, but that was eroding at an alarming rate, too. The Watsons return to New York, trading the Palm Beach estate for a cooperative apartment in the East sixties, was officially proclaimed to be for the proximity of top medical specialists; but the family knew better. It was the last hurrah. And Tom and Nettie knew that they were on their own, as they truly had hoped they would be when they married, in personal and financial matters. They and little Bertram who came along eight months after the wedding—the three of them would be one family. A fresh start, with all the jinxes wiped clean off their slate, and with some luck there would be another child . . .

Tom was beginning to feel overwhelmed by sadness. He stood up. "I will sleep in Bertie's room. I'll roll out the cot."

"You are leaving me? No condolences for my loss, my grief? What kind of heartless person are you? I curse the day I let you marry my baby!" She screamed these last words at him.

There we go, Tom thought, the old Carla coming to the fore. Turning to leave the room he said curtly, "We all need some sleep. Please let yourself out, Carla."

But Carla wasn't through yet. Lunging at Tom with her fisted hands, she pounded his arms and chest. "You bastard!" she screamed. "You killed her! You wanted to get rid of her all along, I know your kind!"

"Carla, please!" Tom caught her wrists and turned down her arms. "You'll wake the baby. We'll talk tomorrow. We've all been under a terrible strain."

But Carla would have none of it. She wrested herself free, giving him a furious look, and stormed out the door. Tom was glad that her car was parked in the rear of the driveway and she had to use the back exit from the kitchen, away from public view. Even though the neighborhood was laid-back Californian where people minded their own business, it was enough that he had been brought home in a police car. He would not have wanted Carla, shouting and banging car doors, to draw more attention to him.

It was dark out, and after Carla's departure all was still. Monday was a working day, and after the ten o'clock news it was bedtime for most people around here. As Tom prepared for bed—showering, brushing his teeth, getting out some sheets and pillows for the folding bed—he became aware of a growing feeling of heaviness in the pit of his stomach. He diagnosed it as an impending panic attack and immediately resolved to combat it; it would be important to suppress his increasing anxiety, bring it down to a manageable level if he wanted to be able to function. "For Bertie's sake," he murmured through clenched teeth. He took a mild soporific from the upper shelf of the medicine cabinet. Both he and Nettie resorted to sleeping pills so seldom that when they did one tablet would usually knock them out for the night.

He looked over the boy in his crib, sleeping like an angel. He gave a silent prayer and then a vow: I shall be there for you, Bertie, always. I know what it is like to lose a parent as a small child. We will work this out together.

He awoke once during the night, his ears were itching. When he touched them they were wet. It dimly puzzled him, until he realized that tears had collected in them; lying on his back as he had fallen asleep, the deep sadness within him had overflowed his eyes. He did nothing about it. He knew this would not be the last time it would happen. With quiet resignation he went back to sleep again.

Ping-bong . . . ping-bong . . . and again ping-bong . . .

He sat up with a jolt. The door bell! Peering at his watch in the semi-darkness he could make out the time—a quarter past five in the morning. Who would come to his house this early? Fearing the worst, he padded to the door. He didn't bother to use the peephole. "Yes?" he said.

A man and a woman, Nettie's sister from Los Angeles, and "her Al" as he was known in the family. The man waved and the woman fell around his neck saying in a choked voice, "Tom, oh my God, we are so sorry!" then looked at him with tears in her eyes. She kissed him on both cheeks.

Tom said, "Laura! Thank you," and going over to the man, "thank you, Al. Thank you both for coming." The two men embraced briefly, patting each other on the back. "Come in, come in, Bertie is still sleeping."

Keeping her voice low but wringing her hands, Laura kept repeating, "It's so sad, so terribly sad!" dabbing her tears away.

"Let me put on some coffee," Tom said.

"No, no, you don't! I will look after it, Tom. We are here to help, especially with the baby." Laura was beginning to catch herself.

"Bertie is not so much a baby anymore. Nettie got him potty-trained since you saw him last, and you should hear him talk! A blue streak, all day."

Laura waved him down and went into the kitchen. It was dawn out now, and Tom still in his pajamas, told Al that he wanted to get dressed.

Al said, "Before you go, let's talk for a minute. Okay?"

Tom nodded. "How did you know about Nettie?"

"Now you are waking up. Good. Siddown!" Al, who Tom thought had lost some weight since he had seen him last—and that was last Christmas—was still a heavy man, and if he were any smaller than six-foot-two he would be overweight, as Laura was fond of saying. He was in blue jeans and an alligator shirt, both of which strained over his chest and waist. His bright blue eyes under those dark bushy brows and the high forehead "a precursor of baldness" as he called it—shone with sharp intelligence. He and Laura made an impressive pair, she also tall for a woman, and blond and bosomy. When they walked arm-in-arm the earth shook.

"Okay. How do we know, you ask. One word: Carla. She called last night, which she has never done before, day or night, and in such high hysterics that I could hear from the receiver, on Laura's side of the bed mind you. She was crying that her baby got killed, but that that monster—that's you, Tom—got away without a scratch, and on and on. She hardly gave Laura a chance to say anything, or ask some questions. But she said that you had been arrested by the police and then they let you go, but she would go file a report and have you put away for good. Words to that effect."

"My God," said Tom.

"Yeah. Well, it's not for nothing that I am a lawyer. Which is exactly what you need right now. I'm available."

Tom felt dazed. "Available for what?"

"To protect your interests, and those of your son."

"Protect them against whom, Al?"

"Generally and potentially, against The People, as we officers-of-the-court call the prosecuting powers. More specifically, against Carla."

"Wait a minute, Al! Hold on just a minute there! This sounds to me as though you are saying that I killed Nettie! Is that what you believe?"

"Hey, Tom, easy. I neither said nor believe such a thing. But what I believe is neither here nor there if push comes to shove. The operative word here is "if"! What I am trying to get across is that it is possible that charges will be brought, if the coroner's inquest raises any doubt, and if the Santa Barbara county DA gets fed any incriminating or suspicious material. Laura and I talked about it after Carla's harangue, and we came to the conclusion that Carla is entirely capable of being a major shit disturber here, for various and sundry reasons none of which, mind you, will have anything to do with your actual culpability! Am I getting through to you? Huh?" He reached over and put his hairy hand on Tom's neck, squeezing it.

Tom nodded. He liked Al, he always had. He liked his easy humor and his booming laugh at the end of almost any good story, his own or someone else's. When Al spoke, his Noo-Yoack accent Tom always felt transported back to his youth, to baseball diamonds, and soda fountains, and movie lobbies on Saturday afternoons when he would hang out with the guys as a kid. His own speech had his mother's bland Yankee pitch, and he envied people their rich twang or drawl, that it came natural to them, that it gave them character and color.

"Good. Now Tommy my boy, I want you to get dressed and to pack all that you need. Laura is already doing that for Baldwin, I hear."

"Bertram."

Al grinned. "Just checking if you're awake. Then we leave, for our house in Santa Monica. Then we talk. Okay?"

An hour later they were on the road, Al driving his new Mercedes. His law practice was "goin' good," he grinned. Tom sat next to him, Laura in the back with Bertie, who was wide awake and enjoying the outing. The car trunk was stuffed full with clothing and toys. Both pockets of Tom's windbreaker jacket were stuffed full with 3.5" computer diskettes that he had taken at the last minute from Nettie's work table. He had remembered what Nettie had tried to tell him about "Jack" or "Mac," which he now took to mean, possibly, her computer. When he saw the little box with floppy discs next to her "Mac" it suddenly came him that she could have taken these home from her lab. Without thinking further he scooped them up.

As they were leaving, Tom explained that they would have to pick up the rental car from the marina, as well as Nettie's Buick station wagon that she would have parked near the boat docks somewhere at Ventura harbor.

"Okay," said Al, "so we'll have a caravan. You drive the rental, Laura the Buick—there is a car seat for the baby in it, right? We don't want to get a ticket—and I'll stay with this one. No freeway, we'll take the coast highway, it's safer and closer to where we live, anyhow. Let's all make an effort to keep each other in sight. And now, we're going get out of here! I bet Carla's antennae are already telling her something."

They did find both cars without any trouble. Al insisted on getting receipts from the attendants, with the exact in and out times. Laura used the stop to take the boy to the washroom. Potty-training, in times of stress, goes only so far. Tom, watching her, thought that Nettie couldn't have done it more lovingly. He gave both of them a hug when they came back.

It was a lovely drive along the ocean, the surfers at county line already out there craning their necks for the perfect wave. Tom thought of all the beaches he had tried at one time or another during his medical school years—Carillo, Trancas, Zuma, Point Dume, Pepperdine, Malibu, Pacific Palisades. It seemed ages ago, in a carefree sun-dappled past; would he have a chance to teach Bertie to swim, to surf? Of course he would. From the rearview mirror Tom watched his little boy in the car seat of the Buick, content and happy next to the blond woman driving—the blond woman who wasn't Nettie.

Tom slammed a fist against the steering wheel. Nettie! She was gone, and he would have to come to terms with that. He would have to think forward from now on, for Bertie's sake; and even though he would never be able to erase those gruesome images of her dying hours, he would have to keep them to himself, and for very urgent reasons at that. Under no circumstances could he let the true story come out. If Nettie was right, if she was deliberately infected by someone, then whoever it was who perpetrated such a heinous act could reasonably assume that he, Tom, would be on to him, if not now than later. Beyond that, little Bertie could also be in danger.

No, he could not let that happen—he would have to outsmart that unknown adversary. That was his only defense. So, first of all he would have to give the appearance of being ignorant, of being unsuspecting. That would not only be necessary in dealing with the authorities, where he had given that impression already, but it would also allow him the time he would need to gather his facts, to ascertain exactly what had happened—and then to take action. What action? He didn't know, yet. All he knew was that Nettie was the victim of a deliberate attack by persons unknown. Nettie was killed, murdered . . .

"All right, Tom, you are officially my client now, with all the appurtenances of such an exalted state, including but not limited to Confidentiality and Privilege." Al sucked on his pipe, smiling. They were sitting in his corner office of the law firm of Smedley and Becker, Attorneys at Law. Reginald Smedley, a suave Londoner, was a former Q. C.—Queen's Counsel—who had come West to expose himself to the rigors of the California Bar examination which he overcame on the second try. Alfred Becker, Esq., himself a refugee from New York, had coached him. He and Reg and Laura and Reg's wife, Doreen, had met at amateur theatricals.

Laura in whose serious CPA body resided an actress wanting to come out, and Alfred the assistant DA who thought that acting would improve his trial mannerisms, had taken the English couple under their wings. It was not long after that the men hit on the idea of opening their own law firm. It had been a lucky hit from the word go. They soon could afford the prestige of being in Santa Monica's most acclaimed office building, a structure that sat cantilevered to Ocean Boulevard so that the windows would catch the early morning to the late afternoon sun, with a panoramic view from Catalina Island to Malibu that impressed even the most jaded client.

Tom sat with his back to the window. He had moved his chair that way; he told Al that he had no desire to look out over the ocean where his wife had lost her life so recently.

"Yes, Al. I'm all yours."

"Good. I'm delighted. Can you write me a check for, say, a thousand dollars? Just a formality. We have to get something down on paper. A retainer. Consideration, as it's called. Makes a contract binding."

"Sure." Tom went to his wallet and pulled out a check. He always carried a couple of blank checks. He wrote out the sum and gave it to Al. "Here."

"Thank you. I'm pleased to have you as a client, Tom, and that's a fact.

Now, let's start with what happened on that boat. Step by step." He pressed a button. "I'm recording this, tape and video. D'you mind?"

Tom did, vaguely, but he said, "No, I don't." He leaned back, his hands folded over his stomach. "I don't know what to tell you. There was the explosion I mentioned before . . ."

"What kind of an explosion? Can you describe it?"

"Well, an explosion is always very sudden, and violent, isn't it. I was not prepared for it."

"Where were you, exactly, when it happened?"

"In the cockpit of the boat, at the rudder. It was getting late, in fact it was dark already. We were trying to make for Smuggler's Cove to lie at anchor overnight."

"You said you were at the rudder; you mean the tiller, don't you?"

"Yeah. The one you steer the boat with."

"Are you an experienced sailor, Tom?"

"No, in fact I am rather inexperienced. Sailing is not my sport. I am more land-based."

"Then why did you buy a sailboat?"

"Actually, it was Nettie's idea. She was crazy about it. The boat was a bargain, it was easy to tow and to maneuver and was very safe because it had self-righting water ballasts, simple sails, and an outboard motor."

"Did you take a course of instruction in sailing?"

"We both took a boating safety class offered by the Coast Guard, in Santa Barbara last April. Nettie was an accomplished amateur sailor, she had sailed a lot in San Francisco Bay. I was picking up some pointers from her."

"Even on this last trip?"

"Well—yes. Off and on. There wasn't much to do, actually, the boat almost sails itself, and the weather was good, and the sea smooth."

"You said you were looking for a safe harbor for the night. With Nettie being the more experienced sailor, why wasn't she at the tiller?"

"She was kind of tired, she had been on the boat all night and the previous day, making it ready, lugging the groceries and supplies, cleaning up and so on; sailing is a lot of work. I myself was unable to help her, because I didn't get on board until late in the morning, having taken the red-eye from Washington and then driving up to Ventura from L. A."

"When you cast off, from the Ventura Marina, who was at the tiller?"

"I was. We had agreed that I would do most of the sailing. If this was to be our main hobby, I needed all the practice I could get."

"Were you in a good mood? Was there any tension between you?"

"We loved each other. We had looked forward to this weekend very much, separated as we are—were—by twenty-five hundred miles, plus weeks at a time without seeing each other. We were going to discuss how we would change that. I would quit the Army and would practice medicine in California or get a position with UCLA in their Department of Public Health. We were going to discuss all that, the pros and cons, also where to buy a house, we had to think about school for Bertie. It was to be a happy weekend, Al."

"Happy—a key word. What overall adjective would you use to describe your marriage, Tom?"

"Happy, is certainly one of them."

"You were married, how long? Three years?"

"This coming Christmas Eve would have been our third anniversary."

"In those three years that you have been together, how did it go, did you have any fights?"

"Fights—in the pugilistic sense of the word, certainly not!"

"Altercations. Disagreements."

"No, to the former, some, to the latter, but then only in terms of what would be best for our child, or our respective careers, and even that, rarely. What are you fishing for, Al? We loved each other!" Tom glared at him.

"Easy!" Al reamed out the bowl of his pipe and tapped the ash into a container that opened by pressing down a button and closed when the button was released. "I merely want to get at some basic facts. I'm on your side. If you think I'm obnoxious, let's hope you'll never get grilled by a prosecutor."

"Grilled for what, Al? I didn't do anything!"

"Yeah. Let me clue you in as to what is most likely to happen. There will be an inquest, to determine if the circumstances of the person's death were such as to require further investigation. I would guess that the answer will be in the affirmative, in which case there will be a battle as to who has jurisdiction. As an active member of the Armed Forces you fall under the Uniform Code of Military Justice. The Army will get involved, as they must when a member of the Armed Forces or a dependent of such—wife, child—dies under questionable circumstances. That would require the appointment of a summary court-martial officer. All this is irrespective of your guilt or innocence, and absent the normal protection of the law that the rest of us civilian folk enjoy. Am I making myself clear?"

Tom sat stunned, silent. He barely nodded.

Al turned off the recorders. He leaned forward on his elbows, clasped his hands and spoke in a deep, low voice. "You are in potentially deep shit trouble, Tom, is what I am trying to get across to you. What I can do is to be your back-up, your legal counsel, because you do have rights that go beyond your uniform. And you have other problems, civilian ones, for which I can be of real help. Custody, for instance. Carla will try to get you on that one."

"I appreciate all you are doing, Al," Tom said tonelessly.

"Okay. I have three questions to ask you, and I want absolutely honest answers. Nothing is being recorded, this is strictly between your ears and mine. I take client privilege seriously. Ready?"

"Go ahead."

"Number One: Do you have a lover?"

Tom was taken aback. "What?" he asked, his voice almost a shout. Al kept a steady gaze on him. "Are you asking if there is another woman?"

"Or man."

"Are you crazy? What are you taking me for, an adulterer? A queer?"

"Just yes or no, will do, Tom."

"No! No!"

"Okay. Take it easy. Now think carefully. Are you in any way responsible for the death of your wife, accidentally or intentionally?"

Tom slumped back into his chair. He threw his head back and stared at the ceiling. After a long moment he said, "If I could have prevented Nettie's death, or taken her place, I would have gladly done so, without any hesitation." Then he looked at Al, "Nettie and I were the only ones on that boat, and Nettie died a horrible death. Not only did I not cause her death, but I was utterly helpless to prevent it. If it had not been for our child, I would have chosen to die with her. That is the truth, I swear to God."

Al nodded, and nodded again. He unclasped his hands, and went for his pipe, filling it from his humidor. Striking a match with his thumbnail and gliding the flame over the bowl, he drew the first puff. Then he said: "The last question is more in the nature of a request, commensurate with our client-counsel relationship. I want your assurance that anything that comes up that relates to this case, that comes to mind later or develops later you will tell me, without delay. Can you give me that assurance?"

"Yes, of course." Tom had caught himself again. "But I want a counter assurance from you—anything that comes up that threatens my custody of Bertie I want you to vigorously defend."

Al smiled. "You mean, you want me to vigorously defend your rights to custody of your son."

"Yes."

Al waved the check Tom had written. "That's what you are paying me for, isn't it?" He grinned and rose from his desk. "Let's go do lunch, as we say here. You look as though you haven't eaten much lately. That's part of your interests I am defending, that you stay healthy."

Al took him to Schatzie, an Italian-Mexican-Austrian restaurant Arnold Schwarzenegger had bought and named for his wife, Maria. It was a busy place near the beach, but there was always a table held for Smedley & Becker; Reg was Arnold's "solicitor" for certain U.K. rights that needed looking after. Al grinned when he explained that. "All Reggie does is fly over a couple of times and use his connections. But what the hell, it pays the rent."

They ordered pizza. Al recommended it, along with a carafe of red wine.

Halfway through the meal Al said, "Tom, this is a business lunch. Okay? So we'll talk business. Okay with you?"

Tom nodded, okay. He was chewing hard. There were chunks of bacon in his pizza.

"First, let me tell you about myself, or Laura and me. I don't suppose you know we are married?"

Tom looked up, surprised. "No!"

"Yeah. Carla harping about me being a Jew, and my family telling me not to marry a shicksah—we got tired of all that crap. So Laura had this brilliant idea. She goes to University Synagogue for instruction, first without telling me, but I got wise to her. I told her she wouldn't last, but she did. She converted, with bat mitzvah and all. Can you imagine." Al was shaking his head. "Remember we were in Israel just when the Gulf War started? That was our honeymoon. At a nice little hotel in Haifa. Saw a couple of Scuds, too." Al shook his head again, at the wonder of it all.

"Congratulations!" said Tom.

"Thank you. I tell you this for two reasons. Three, to be exact. One, it's time you knew. Laura was going to tell Nettie pretty soon, anyway. Second, we are a married couple. When you consider giving custody, temporarily or partially—a problem that may arise, and that we shall discuss in due course—that will be important. So, Laura is a married woman, a sister of the deceased, and a blood relative of the infant in question. No problem."

"You sound as if you see me in jail already, tried and convicted."

"Nonsense. You'll never go to jail, there isn't enough evidence to convict. But we are in this for the long haul, and shit happens. You gotta think of the kid. It may take a while before this is all worked out. And there is our beloved Grandma Carla. She, too, can make a strong case for custody."

"I see what you mean. Let's talk about it when I get back from Maryland. I want to go there as soon as possible, wind up things, one way or the other."

"No hurry. I just want to make sure it's on the agenda. Now, there's number three."

"You always go by threes, Al?"

"I'm just a lawyer. After that, it's higher math. Hey, here's a question for you, the doctor. All right?"

Tom smiled. "Shoot."

"Laura and I—we've been trying to get pregnant. Everything checks out fine—the plumbing, the ingredients, the works. Okay? But nothing happens, and it's not for lack of trying, believe me. What do you make of that?"

"My specialty is infectious diseases, Al. I haven't done gynecology since my intern days."

"Yeah, but you know more about the human body than I do. Could it be up here?" He tapped his forehead.

"Possibly. Maybe you are concentrating on it too much. Maybe being uptight causes the fallopian tubes to constrict, and by the time the egg has traveled down the eager little buggers waiting down in the uterus are all pooped out." Tom smiled again. "Just a wild guess, Al. Don't pay any attention to it."

"No, no, you may have something there. We had an adoption case a couple of years back where the woman could not conceive, so after eight years of marriage they adopted. As soon as the new baby was in the house—bingo, she gets pregnant. I've been thinking—it could work for us. Laura looking after your baby—she's really good with him, isn't she? Imagine. . ." he left it there.

"Could be. Of course, if she conceives, I expect a reduction in your fees."

"It's on the house, brother, it's on the house."

On Thursday morning Tom received a call from the Santa Barbara sheriff's department. They, he with Al and Laura, had spent all day Wednesday setting up a memorial service for Nettie, securing a time slot for early Saturday afternoon with Father Stacy of the Good Shepherd in the Fields Episcopal church in Goleta. It was a painful exercise, as many of the people to be invited had no idea that Nettie had died. Tom's mother was particularly out of sorts at the news—she had liked Nettie from the first time she had met her. She promised to come, immediately, but Tom managed to persuade her that Friday would be early enough; he would pick her up at Los Angeles airport and drive her to Santa Barbara. "I want a hotel, Thomas," she said. "I hear the Biltmore is a good one."

"Yes, Mum," Tom said. He had already thought along those lines. The Biltmore should also be the venue for the after-service reception.

So here, early Thursday morning, out of the blue, comes that male, all business police voice. They would like to inspect the premises of the deceased and could Tom be present? He had the right to refuse but they could get a court order and a warrant.

"No need for that, sheriff," said Tom. "Go ahead, please."

"We'd like you to be present, sir."

"Sure. When do you want to meet?"

"Right now, sir."

"Sheriff, I'm in Santa Monica. It's going to take me at least two hours to make it to Santa Barbara. More, depending on traffic."

"I'll be at your house at ten o'clock, sir. I'll understand if you can't be right on time." He hung up.

Tom cursed. It was just half past seven. He'd have to leave right away. He went upstairs to hug Bertie, who was sitting on his bed—Laura had rushed out on Monday to buy a bed!—and was playing with toy cars. He kissed him on the forehead and tousled the little boy's hair. "Daddy has to go to work now, Bertie, so you have a nice time with Aunt Laura, okay? I'll be back right after your nap time, and we'll play." He kissed him again.

Al was not too thrilled to hear about the house search. "Comply, but don't volunteer anything. Remember your rights. Call me if they are giving you a hard time." Laura gave him coffee in a styrofoam cup and a glazed donut to take along. "Junk food, but you'll need it. Here, take this multivitamin with your orange juice." Laura was mothering everybody.

He was only a few minutes late. There was a car parked in his driveway, but he was relieved to see that it was without police markings. A man in a business suit got out of the driver's seat when Tom had parked his car.

"Doctor Campee? I am Elvon Harris, with the sheriff's department. Thanks for coming up. Sorry for the inconvenience."

"Hi." They shook hands. "Glad to be of assistance. Please show me your credentials when we are in the house." The neighbors, Tom was sure someone was watching.

Elvon Harris was an investigator. Tom scrutinized his picture—a light-skinned black, about fifty, with a thin mustache and graying temples—and the official seal and markings. Unquestionably genuine. He handed it back.

"Now, Doctor Campee—am I pronouncing your name correctly, sir?"

"Close enough, sergeant."

"Thank you. I want you to know that I am recording my findings as I go along." He pointed to a small microphone that was pinned to his lapel. "I'd like you to come along as we go through your house, sir, but you may remain silent if you wish."

"No problem."

"Okay. Let's start with the kitchen." Tom pointed the way. "All right. When have you been in the house last?"

"Monday morning, when my wife's sister and her husband picked me and my son up. We have stayed at their house in Santa Monica since. You called me there."

Harris nodded. He looked around the kitchen. "See anything different? Anything disturbed, not in it's usual place?"

"No. But then, I haven't spent much time in the kitchen."

"A woman's preserve. Right?" He opened the refrigerator door. "Have a look. Anything missing?"

There were cartons of milk in there, soft drinks, cottage cheese, eggs, butter, salad dressings. "Looks all right to me . . ." Tom shrugged his shoulders.

"Do you keep drugs in here, injectibles?"

"Drugs? Certainly not! Whatever for? None of us is diabetic."

Harris closed the door. "The stove is gas, I see. Do you prefer gas over electricity?"

"I don't know. It came with the house. We are renting here, sergeant."

It was a meticulous room by room search that Harris was conducting. Tom had no idea what he was looking or fishing for.

When they came to the room upstairs next to the nursery that Nettie had set up as her office Harris perked up. He removed the cover from the Mac and having asked Tom's permission turned on the computer. He called up the hard disk and went to the system folder. The last entry was for Wednesday, June 30, at 9:22 A.M. He recorded that information into his lapel mike. Then he wanted to know if there was a gun in the house. No, said Tom. Did Tom own a gun? Yes, but he kept it in the Chevy Chase apartment.

"Would that be in Los Angeles, sir, or in Maryland?"

"Maryland. Near Washington, DC. We used to live there until my wife got this job with Goleta Research Labs. I am still with the Army, Medical Corps, for the time being."

"You an active duty officer, sir? What rank?"

"Major."

"Did you see service in the Gulf War?"

"Yes. And in Panama."

"My son's a Marine. Spent six month in the Persian Gulf as a crew chief on an assault carrier. Helicopter pilot." There was pride in his voice.

"Good man. It was six months for me, too."

Harris nodded. A bond had been established.

When they trooped downstairs Harris said, "Can I see the garage, now?"

"Sure. This way."

They went in through the kitchen. Tom switched on the light. The garage was empty except for Bertie's tricycle. He would have to take that back with him. Laura's back yard had a large paved patio. Bertie could ride it there.

"What's this?" Harris pointed to a contraption in the corner that had a black cover over it.

Tom went over and pulled it off. "A barbecue." He had not seen it before but he remembered that Nettie had said they should get one now that summer was coming. The price tag was still on it, from Builder's Emporium. $129.95 reduced to $99.95. "My wife must have bought it."

"You have never seen it before?"

"No. I only come out on weekends and we usually have something planned."

"It won't work without the LPG."

"The what?"

"The propane gas container. See? It fits in here." Harris pointed to an indentation on the bottom shelf of the barbecue. He opened the lid. The grill was pristinely clean. "Never been used."

"I see."

"The LPG container comes with the unit, but it is empty. It has to be filled."

"Yeah."

"There are various places where you can get that done. Most marinas have one. But you got to be careful. It's highly flammable."

"Yeah. I don't know what happened to it. Maybe it's around here somewhere." Tom opened the doors of the workbench cabinet that lined the wall.

Harris gave him a look, and then said, "Okay, I think that does it."

When they were outside, Harris shook his hand. "Thank you, major. I'm sorry I brought you all the way up here, but it was necessary. For your own good."

"I was a pleasure meeting you, sergeant. I appreciate your professionalism."

On his way back to Santa Monica, Tom pondered the significance of his encounter with Sergeant Harris. The investigation appeared routine, but it was thorough, nonetheless. The purpose of it would be to determine if any culpability existed on his part. Did he kill his wife, or did he cause her to be killed? He had better report the whole thing to Al. Might as well drive right through to his office; it was still early in the day.

"Well," said Al when Tom had finished rehashing the Harris interview into the tape recorder, "that's it! There's your answer!"

"What is?"

"The propane gas! Nettie must have taken the propane gas tank aboard, and being careless, or inexperienced, or both, off it went. Whoosh! The gas is under pressure, and generates enormous heat. Everything in that cabin would catch fire immediately, plus don't forget the reserve tanks of gasoline for your outboard. That's it, all right."

"Why?"

"Why, what?"

"Why would Nettie take a gas canister on board?"

"What are you cooking with in the galley? Has to be gas! Who is the maker of your boat, do you know?"

Tom told him; a yacht builder in Costa Mesa, near Newport Beach down there in Orange County. Al called in his paralegal and told her to get right on it, specifications, brochures, everything. "We've got that one licked, my boy. The inquest will come to nothing. We should have the death certificate next week."

The memorial service at the modern little church in Goleta was a dignified if sad affair, the sorrow of mourners genuine even if Carla's sobs were too audible at times. The whole family was there, including Dr. Walter Goldsmith, the father-in-law Tom had never met. He had come at the insistence of his daughter Laura, Nettie's favorite sister who had also been one of the bridesmaids at their wedding. Little Bertie was kept busy in the church nursery by Mrs. Stacy; Tom had insisted that he not be present at the ceremony. Father Stacy asked Tom to read the 90th Psalm, which he did, hesitantly at first, from his mother's Book of Common Prayer. Gradually, with the organ playing softly from Brahms' "Requiem," he found strength and succor when he came to the line "So teach us the number of our days, that we may apply our hearts unto wisdom." The priest then recited from the I Corinthians, in a near-whispering voice "Behold, I shall show you a mystery," and bellowing, "Death, where is thy sting?"

There was no urn and no interment. The service closed with the Lord's Prayer, and the Benediction. As Tom and his mother filed out first, he saw a man sitting in the rear of the pews, in a business suit, who seemed no to belong to any group. He was bald, had wire-rimmed glasses, and avoided Tom's glance. Afterwards, he did not see him again.

The reception, hosted by Mrs. Eleanor Watson at the Biltmore, was a relief. "You know," Eleanor said to her son, "I am so sorry your sister

Bettina couldn't be here. She would have wanted to come. But being on a walking tour of Nepal, there's no way of knowing when she gets the news. I sent a wire to her magazine in London." She caressed a lock of hair from Bertie's forehead.

"Thank you, Mum. I'm sure Betts would have come if she had known." Tom was carrying Bertie on his arm, feeding him tidbits from the table. Later, when Carla came to claim the child for a while, he let her have him. Laura, who had seen that, said to Tom that she would get him next.

Dr. Goldsmith turned out to be an interesting character. Tall and big-boned, with a full head of hair and bushy eyebrows, fleshy nose and lips. Tom had offered him and April the use of the house, while he and Bertie were keeping Eleanor company in adjoining rooms at the hotel. They had barely exchanged a word on Friday night, with everybody in a rush. Now he came up to Tom, smiling, offering his hand. "What a sad, sad occasion for us to meet, Tom. May I call you Tom?" He had a deep but melodious voice, pleasant on the ear.

"Certainly. What should I—what did Nettie call you?"

"Father—the last time we spoke. A good generic term." A wan smile, "I suppose you know we didn't talk much. Natalie being the oldest of the girls, she was thirteen when I divorced her mother. I don't think she ever really forgave me. Even though she knew that our marriage was hell."

"Nettie told me. But to me, she always spoke highly of you and April."

"Yes. April wasn't the problem. It was Carla."

"Carla is a problem to me, too. I think she wants custody of my son. On grounds that I am an unfit father, as I have been an unfit husband."

"Don't let her get away with that, Tom! You have no idea how wicked that woman can be. I don't know—it's like she has a defective gene or something. She fabricates an issue out of thin air, usually involving her fragile and suffering ego that can be placated only by the offenders offering abject apologies. I used to do that, just to put the matter behind us. But I began to realize that put me on a different plateau, and now the next 'insult' had a history of past offenses that were never forgotten, and the punishment rose by increments." Dr. Goldsmith sighed. "The girls suffered, too. Natalie the most."

"I know," Tom said softly. Then Dr. Goldsmith abruptly changed the subject, "You know who those people are, don't you, Tom?"

"What people?" Tom said, and followed the pointed nod. "That group over there? Yes. They are Nettie's colleagues from the lab."

"I meant, the company, the lab. I'm an investor now—haven't practiced in over ten years—and I do a lot of research on the companies I want to put money into. You have to these days, if you don't want to get suckered, what with all the mergers and acquisitions and stock swaps. Anyway, when I heard that Natalie was going to work for Goleta Research

Laboratories it kind of rang a bell. Two years ago, someone broke in there and 'liberated' a bunch of animals, causing a loss of valuable research material. The parent company of Goleta is White Cross Veterinary, which in turn is a wholly owned subsidiary of New Brunswick Pharmaceutical, a health care giant traded on the New York stock exchange. NB Pharm lost two points, and would have lost more but they wisely did not engage the animal rights groups in litigation. Those animal rights fanatics were behind that break-in."

Tom frowned. "Were they? Can you send me something on that?"

"Sure. I have it on file. I was going to call Natalie about it—but then I didn't. It would have sounded being critical of her job choice."

"Thanks, I appreciate the input, uh, doctor."

"Hell, call me Mike." They pumped hands, smiling, then exchanged addresses and phone numbers. They patted each other on the arm when they parted. That evening, as they sat on the couch in the hotel room, Tom and his mother and Bertie between them watching a cartoon on TV, there was a knock on the door. Tom got up. That would be room service; he had ordered hot dogs and popcorn, and some tea.

A man stood there, in a business suit, bald head, wire-rim glasses.

"Good evening, Dr. Campe." A polite voice, pronouncing his name correctly. "I apologize for the intrusion, but I wonder if you could spare me just a moment?"

Tom was taken aback. The man from the back pew in the church. "Who are you, and what do you want?" Another investigator?

"I am a private citizen, and I volunteer for an important humanitarian organization. I am here to express to you our profound regrets at the untimely death of your wife."

"Give me your name, please."

"My name is not important. My mission is." The man craned his neck, to look into the room. Bertie stood up leaning over the back of the sofa, waving. Eleanor was holding him by the seat of his pants.

"Your mission? What do you mean?"

The man smiled, "I can see this is the wrong time to talk. Sorry."

Tom had the sudden feeling that this was an important contact. In an even tone of voice he said, "It'll always be the wrong time unless you identify yourself." He moved the door as if to shut it.

The man, still apologetic, said, "Of course. There'll be another time."

He inclined his head towards Tom, waved at the boy, turned and walked back down the hall, the sound of his footsteps swallowed up by the thick carpeting.

Tom, fighting the urge to run and grab him to shake his name out of him, watched him disappear around the corner. It would be better this way; let them play their cards first. Whoever they were. He had no doubt he'd hear from them again.

Quietly he closed the door and went back to his son and his mother.

"Who was that?" asked Eleanor.

"A salesman, probably," Tom shrugged, and put Bertie on his lap.

"Really!" said Eleanor.

On Sunday night Thomas Campe caught the red-eye to Washington. His mother had opted to stay on in Santa Barbara for a couple more days, spending time with her only grandchild. There was talk that Bertie would come to her New York place at Christmas time, with Al and Laura bringing him; unless, of course, Tom had found a way by then to rearrange his life in such a way that his son could live with him permanently, and he would bring him himself.

Sitting in the frequent flyer lounge drinking coffee, Tom shook his head: He doubted that the mess his life had become would have been cleared up by then. There were too many open ends, too many ifs and buts to be normal that soon.

He sighed. Over the rim of his cup he became aware of a woman he'd been watching, unseeingly, since she'd walked in and sat down opposite him. About Nettie's age, he guessed, all fresh and firm, but taller, and darker-haired, and oh-so self-contained and sure of herself, and rich, too, judging by the style of her clothes and her leather bag. Classy broad; Manhattanite, probably. She looked at him now, green eyes. So, was he staring? Sorry . . .

She got up when the New York flight was called. He was right; also about the fact that it would be ages before he would talk to a woman like that again, ever . . .

Emily

On the Saturday morning of the memorial service for Natalie Campe, Father Stacy of the Church of the Good Shepherd had sat in his study trying very hard to parse just the right phrases from "The Order of the Burial of the Dead" to make it fit a situation where there was no body to commit to the earth, not even an urn of ashes—with the doughty priest wondering if it would not have been possible for the authorities to scoop up a handful of ashes from the boat and declare it to be those of the deceased. He sighed. He well remembered the young woman, a Roman Catholic, coming to him with a wish to convert, and he telling her that it was not such a giant step to become an Anglican Catholic, and her answer, "I don't care, Father, I am doing it for my husband and my son!" Father Stacy had nodded to that, although he knew that that was fuzzy theology. And now she had gone to Heaven to be with the saints. He sighed again. As he looked out the window from the second floor study of the manse, to the distant right he could see the rooftops of the buildings on the campus of the University of California. Students from that hallowed place of learning had, some twenty years before, stormed in righteous fury the nearby branch of the Bank of America and burned it to the ground. Young Edgar Stacy, a student there at the time and deeply into Nietzsche, saw in the event a manifestation of the Antichrist and resolved right then to become a priest. It had made him find his life's calling, struggle though he must with the meaning of it all, again and again.

Equidistant from Father Stacy's window, but more to the left as the crow flies and in every other sense in the opposite direction lay the exclusive community of Steadman Ranch, stretching from the freeway to the ocean. At a cul-de-sac ending just above the beach there stood not a manse but a mansion where at that moment a young woman dove headlong into a swimming pool. She parted the water with a few quick strokes until she touched the rim at the end of the basin, then with an expert kick turned around for a return to the other end, repeating the exercise until she had swum thirty laps. "One for each year of my life," she said to herself as she climbed out of the pool. Grabbing a towel that barely covered her nakedness she padded back leaving wet footprints on the flagstone terrace, entering the annex of the house through a door she had left ajar. She walked with the whipping, long-legged strides of the aerobic exerciser, pulling a towel across her back.

Some time later, having showered and leaving her light brown hair in wet strands, she dressed in a white shift with bold plumeria print that said Las Brisas, stepped into a pair of wooden clogs and made her way through the length of the house until she reached a small patio that was protected from the sea winds by a multicolored hedge of bougainvilleae. There, under a white umbrella a breakfast table was set for two. "Good morning, Mother!" she said to an older woman already seated, who eyed her over her morning paper but held out her cheek for a kiss. "Lovely day, isn't it?"

"Emily, I don't like it, your swimming naked!" The disapproval expressed did not match the motherly fondness in her eyes. Angelique Dessauer had never been able to deny her only child anything. Within reason, of course, but reason stretched conveniently far. And Emily was always so reasonable.

"Oh Mom," Emily smiled and pulled up a chair at the table. "There is nobody here! Just the two of us! Besides, I didn't bring a swimsuit." She cheerfully sprinkled sugar over her grapefruit.

"What about the servants?"

Emily laughed, "Servants! Is that what they are, old Felicia in the kitchen—who, by the way, used to change my diapers—and Alba and her husband who live over the garage with no view of anything except the driveway!"

"The forecourt," her mother corrected her. "And the caterers could arrive at any moment. Besides, a good-looking girl like you must always be circumspect."

Emily spooned up some grapefruit and nodded, "I am, Mom, in New York and everywhere else. Believe me. But this is your home, totally private."

"Nothing and nobody is that private, Em, not anymore." Her mother sighed and then changed the subject. "Did you have a chance to look at the papers I left in your room?"

"Yes, briefly, last night. I went over the whole folder. Do you want to discuss it now?"

"You eat first. Help yourself to the omelet, it's made from low-cholesterol eggs. And the bacon is low-fat lamb."

"Really? And it tastes just like the real stuff? Amazing. Of course, my normal breakfast at home is cereal and yogurt. And bran toast with fruit spread. We'll all live to be a hundred." Emily made a face.

"You're not forgetting your vitamins, I hope."

"Never! Mother, one question, I noticed Nick on your guest list. Was that necessary? You know that we broke up, and I don't think it's a good idea to have him come up here. It can only be embarrassing."

"First of all, Nick is driving poor old Mary. I think it was very kind of him to come all the way up from Los Angeles to take his mother from her house to mine."

"Mother, Mary Grady lives in Montecito! A half-hour away! And she has a live-in nurse who drives her everywhere."

Mrs. Dessauer ignored that. "Secondly, Nicholas' firm is involved in the project. This is also a business trip for him. Besides, there was a time when you were all hepped up about Nick. Remember the almost-engagement?"

Emily laughed, "Hepped up! Where'd you get that expression? As for the almost-engagement, let's not forget who broke it!"

"Not who," her mother looked at her sternly, "but what! Poor Mary's stroke—it almost killed her! And then your move to New York."

"You make it sound like a one-two whammy! I had nothing to do with either. Not with Mary Grady's stroke, and my bank didn't give me that big promotion just because of my blue eyes."

"Your eyes are green."

"A figure of speech, Mother."

"And besides, the fact that your mother maintains a million-plus deposit with your bank didn't hurt, either."

"Now, wait a minute!" Emily put her knife and fork down. "I got that promotion at MuniBank strictly on merit! I worked hard in the trenches for five years!"

"And you have a summa cum from Stanford and an MBA from Harvard."

"Sure, but so have many others. There's a lot of competition out there. Although I admit, maybe being a woman helped. Some."

"And your father's smarts. You got your father's smarts."

Watch it, Emily told herself, theme number one coming up. The unspeakable, undeservedly early death of Morrie Dessauer. Dead of a heart attack, at not yet sixty-five. On a business trip. Emily remembered it well, she was twenty years old and was on a spring break from Stanford when the phone rang. She picked up the kitchen extension and heard a strange man tell her mother that he had "bad news." Then the scream—the shrill, unearthly wail emanating from the upstairs bedroom where Angelique Dessauer had taken the call.

"I know, Mother," she said mildly. "I inherited his genes, but you—you learned from him. Look what you did with the money he left you!" She made a sweeping gesture taking in the visible estate. "You, what, tripled your net worth?"

She had struck the right chord. Her mother looked pleased.

"Quintupled, according to last year's statements. Not so big a deal. The Dow Jones alone would have tripled it. All this here," mother imitating daughter's gesture, "cost me one year's earnings, and it's financed at seven percent simple from the Dessauer Trust. Morrie would be proud, huh?"

Emily chose just to nod, with her mouth full. The building of this castle, this chateau had been a mystery to everyone who had known quiet, busy, ever friendly Angie Dessauer, wife—correction—second wife of Big Morrie Dessauer, best known for being his hostess and for her fabulous French cooking, and lately—Patroness of the Arts, benefactress of a dozen charities. What in the world could have possessed her to leave Beverly Hills and move out to the boonies—that's what it is, dear, let's be frank, Santa Barbara does not measure up, no matter how pricey it gets—and build this monstrosity—just like one of those super-mansions the dreadful Persians have saddled us with all around here—five bedroom suites, all with ocean views, ten bathrooms, a vestibule the size of a hotel lobby, and a sculpture garden. . .

Emily could almost hear the bridge-party chatter. Some of the gossip had in fact reached her via her girlfriends' letters, old Marlborough school chums who wouldn't lie to her. And even though her mother had not kept it a secret from her, on the contrary, involving her with it constantly in her almost daily telephone calls, she was still shocked when she first saw it during her Easter visit. So big—what was her mother going to do with all those rooms! And so isolated, on a cul-de-sac rimmed by the ocean, with no visible neighbors right or left! A sudden anxiety had gripped her. Was this some kind of incipient illness? She had read about brain tumors making people crazy. On the sly she broached the question to an old family friend, a neurologist. He had laughed, "We should all be so crazy! No, no, old Angie is all right. She has all this money, and she is spending it the way she wants to spend it. Your dad would have approved. Over time, the property will appreciate and be worth even more. Think of it as your inheritance going up in value!"

Emily flew back to New York, much relieved. She loved her mother, as much as she had loved and admired her father. Here were these two people, a penniless immigrant from Canada and an even more impecunious nanny from the Alsace, getting together and building this empire! She, Emily, with all her advantages and education, would be lucky if she did half as well. And if she did, she wouldn't be doing it for herself or her family, she would be enriching the already rich coffers of her employer, Municipal Pennsylvania Bank and Trust, also referred to as Money-Penny. But at least she was doing what she liked, especially now that she was in the international department.

"You are not saying anything, Emily!" Angelique Dessauer was not a woman to tolerate idle thought.

"You are right, Mom. Dad would have been proud of you." She leaned over and gave her mother a kiss. "Have you decided finally what you are going to call this place?"

"Les Parages."

"'The Neighborhood'?" Emily looked puzzled. "I don't get it."

Her mother nodded. "It's a private name. Your father always said to me, when we were not together, we would always be toujours dans les parages, in our hearts. Always nearby."

"Oh Mother!" Tears were welling up in Emily's eyes. "How fitting!"

"Yes. I'm glad you think so, too. Now, I'd like to discuss the folder with you when you are ready to go over the figures before I present them at the meeting tonight. Come up to my room, in about fifteen minutes? And put on something warmer, Em, the fog is rolling in already." She rose and walked into the house.

Emily followed her with her eyes, wondering yet again how her mother could look so different from herself. Angelique Dessauer nee Falck was an Alsatian country girl, from a small town near the Swiss border. Everything about her was big and voluptuous, reminiscent of the women idealized by the painters of the Baroque. Thighs and calves round and muscular, buttocks strong and bosom full, blond hair worn braided around her head—even now that she was in her mid-fifties her hair was still blond with nary a gray strand. The only outward trait mother and daughter shared was their height of nearly six feet, and the strong jaws, the generous mouth and the truly pretty nose, straight and not quite upturned at the end, which gave them both a face pleasant to look at.

Emily's figure was more of a slimmed-down version of her mother's, with a lighter bone structure that imparted some natural gracefulness to her movements. She wore clothes awfully well, and since she could afford to buy the best in style and material, she was quietly, often enviously admired by the sophisticates of New York society. Her hair, in a rich light-brown, was cut to fall perfectly into place after the wind had ruffled it, or more often, when she would comb through it with wide-spread fingers, a habit which she had acquired since school days when she was thinking hard. This gesture, innocently though it was made by Emily, together with that intense look from her bright gray-green eyes, seldom failed to have an electrifying effect on her business partners or colleagues at meetings, and it wouldn't matter if she was not the only female present—the others just wouldn't count. Her hands contributed to "the look," fingers long without being bony, ending in flesh-pink nails, and without adornment except an emerald ring worn on her right ring finger. Yes, many a man had taken note of the fact that this infuriatingly attractive female was still single, and seemingly unapproachable. How and with whom did she get her kicks?

Emily wandered back through the house, on a private inspection tour in bright daylight to see what Angelique and her money had wrought.

When she was here last in April, workmen were still scurrying about and some rooms were still scaffolded. Now all was done, and the place made a peaceful and lived-in impression. She liked what she saw, assuming of course that what was there was needed and functional. The huge vestibule, with sunlight pouring in through a glass dome, had a center table that held a large flower arrangement coming out of a bowl of fruit. She pinched a leaf—it was real—and when she took an apple she found that also to be fresh and crisp to the bite. Curious as to how one would keep the fruits attractive through the day, she found that the base held an ingenious cooling and watering system. Clever.

Large French doors, now closed, would open to the outside terrace where no doubt that night cocktails would be served to her mother's party. And the long rectangular reflecting pool would be illuminated, vying with the orange sun setting over the far horizon. Yes—her mother's "folly" would be impressive even to the most jaded tastes.

Munching her apple, Emily wandered on. A door was half open to a darkened room. She stepped in and pressed a light switch. She stood, stunned.

The room, half circular and in dark wood paneling, was an exact replica of her father's study in the Beverly Hills house. The big leather club chairs were there, where she had sat many a time talking with Daddy, and the fireplace was the same, and there over the mantelpiece was that painting of the Laurentian winter scene!

"Oh!" she moaned.

Carefully, as if not to disturb the ghosts of the past, she walked around, switching on the lights over the writing desk, the cabinets, the bookshelves. The photographs came to life, familiar to her and now new again. All of the family of Morris Dessauer, from his somber-looking parents, father in the uniform of a Canadian Pacific train conductor, mother frail and thin with the same aquiline nose she gave to her son—her paternal grandparents, long gone and never known to her. Her father was in his forties when he married her mother. And there were photos of all the various Dessauers at this or that occasion, her half-brothers Rick and Ben with their mother at the beach, at a Dodger baseball game, as school boys. A favorite of her father's—a silver framed double portrait of his first family with Miriam and the boys, all four of them nicely dressed up, and an older and still happily smiling Morris with Angie standing around the piano where she, Emily, then about ten, was seated at the keyboard. Miriam had suffered from breast cancer and when her condition worsened Morris had hired away from his friend, the French consul, a sturdy young Alsatian woman who seemed to him to be strong enough to cope with two rambunctious boys, and could teach them French in the bargain, a point of importance to Morris who as a Montrealer was bilingual himself. As it happened, young Angelique came to stay, accepting Morrie's proposal of marriage and in due course presenting him with his only daughter. Morris Dessauer couldn't have been more delighted. One day, when she was in her teens and unsure of herself, Emily asked her father if he wouldn't have rather had a boy. He had roared with laughter, "Your mother would have had a fit! She told me that no baby boy of hers would have the skin cut off his peewee! Those pious Calvinists, you know, they have their own rules! Just like us Jews. Ha-ha! Religion—it's good only for weddings and funerals." Then he had turned serious, "You know, Emmy," he had stroked her head saying that, "you are the best thing that ever happened to me in my whole life. Bar none. Just between you and me, okay?" And he had taken her face in her hands and kissed her.

"Oh Dad," Emily groaned, putting down the frame. She had always loved her father, with an adoring intensity that she did not feel for her mother. As in turn her father, she knew, adored her. That was put to the test one day—and there was that photograph, Emily Dessauer winning fifth place at the Van Cliburn Piano Competition in Dallas. She had chosen Mozart's Piano Concerto No. 23 in A, which she had practiced with such mixture of emotion—loving the music and hating the mindless repetition of rote learning—that she could play it with her eyes closed.

Her father had hovered backstage, and embraced her when she came by him after taking the customary bows. "You were magnificent, Emmy! You are going to the top, believe me. You have the talent, and I have the money. We'll do it!"

Emily cried when she heard that, "Daddy, please, I don't want to be a pianist! I hate it!" And then she had blurted out, "I want to be like you! I want to be in business, doing something important—more lasting!"

A hug from her father, "So—you want to be a Dessauer? It's a tough choice, kid, but it's your call. Go to it!"

And Emily did, enrolling at Stanford that fall. There was one piece of advice her father had given her that had stayed with her: Keep going; never look back. "Regrets, Em, are for party invitations only."

Slowly, quietly, she turned off all the lights and left the room.

"Where have you been, dear?" Her mother was sitting at her desk, peering at her over her half-glasses. "At least you are wearing something more sensible. Nice sweater—cashmere, yes?" She fingered the material.

"Yes." It was a beige cashmere, over a brown tartan skirt. "From Saks. It was on sale." That was true; Emily always looked for bargains, not only because she enjoyed doing that but mainly because she lived entirely on her salary, not an easy feat in expensive Manhattan. Her mother felt the same way; for her trip to California she had sent Emily frequent flyer certificates.

"Come sit here." Her mother patted the chair next to her. "Have some tea." She poured a cupful from a teapot and gave it to her.

Emily sat down and took the cup. It was then that she noticed the details of her mother's workplace. What had looked, upon entering the cozily furnished room, like a traditional if rather large rosewood desk in secretary style, was in reality an intricately designed control station, with everything at the user's fingertips. Computer with printer, telephone with fax machine, and a bank of closed-circuit monitors that at the flick of a switch would show the front entrance, the vestibule, the kitchen, the terrace.

"Very impressive," said Emily. "Is my room bugged, too?"

"No, of course not, dear. None of the living quarters are. But here—let me show you something else." Angelique pulled open a drawer and turned a key in a heavy socket. "Did you hear that?" A clicking sound could be heard, from the door and the balcony. "This locks everything down, including the entrance to this wing of the house. Then all I have to do is press this button, and the alarm rings at the Steadman Ranch guard house."

"Well, Mom, that makes sense. You are awfully isolated here. I'm glad you took care of this problem. Really, it's a relief."

"Yes. I'm not a little old lady any fool burglar can knock over."

"I don't think anybody will ever mistake you for a little old lady," Emily smiled. She sipped from her tea. "Now, can we go to work?"

"Yes, Miss Businesswoman. Talking just like your father." She opened a folder. "Now, even if you only had time to glance at it, you must have seen what this is all about."

"About the creation of a new symphony orchestra?" Emily asked carefully.

"Exactly. Now, Emily," Angelique Dessauer hesitated, looking out over the rim of the balcony balustrade into the gray milkiness of the seaborne fog, "I ask you to bear with me as I go over this with you step by step. In the end, we may disagree but we will not have misunderstood each other. D'accord?"

"D'accord," Emily smiled. This was going to be like one of those school day tête-à-têtes when her mother wanted to coax an extra effort out of her.

"So, tell me. You are still going to Philharmonic concerts, aren't you. Even in New York, from the program notes and newspaper clippings you are sending me. What percentage of people your age are attending, would you say?"

"Of the audience, you mean; twenty percent—maybe less, sometimes."

"And what percentage of people my age do you see?"

Emily laughed, "Obviously, the reverse! What is this, Jeopardy?"

"Jeopardy! Good word. The whole system of classical music presentation is in jeopardy, all right. Why is that, Em? When huge amounts of money are spent on symphony orchestras, on concert halls, on administration, on advertising and promotion? And look at the money we lavish on conductors, most of whom are kapellmeisters from Europe, with unpronounceable names yet. And they are in such demand they are booked years in advance, just like the few star soloists. So, tell me, how many really big orchestras do we have?"

"Ten—or is it six? I forget."

"Let's say ten. Ten orchestras, and each have about a hundred musicians. Musicians with tenure, aging before our very eyes, and they can do a standard repertoire in their sleep, which they seem to be doing, anyhow. Is that all we can do, a people of two hundred fifty million?"

"Certainly not!" Emily exclaimed. She was beginning to enjoy this.

Her mother nodded. "Right now, all the orchestras depend heavily on private donations. Your father and I have been very generous with the Los Angeles Philharmonic, and also with the Montreal Symphony. No problem there. But it is never enough! The more you give them, the more they want from you. They tell you it's not enough to cover the cost, even if they sell every seat in the house—which most of the time they don't, by the way. There's a deficit, they tell you, and they go grovel before the government for grants and allowances."

"Who is 'they'?"

"The administrators. The leeches. And what do they think of next? They go and build a new concert hall. Fifty million bucks from Mrs. Disney—and that is 'just seed money'. Can you imagine, the waste?"

Emily shook her head.

"So I ask you—what about the music? The people? They get lost in the shuffle. But that's what it's all about, isn't it? People making music for people?"

"It certainly is."

"Tell me, Emily, have you been to rock concerts?"

"Uh—yes, of course. Not a lot, though."

"And where did those concerts take place—at the New York Rock Concert Hall? At The Beatles Auditorium in London? At The Sting Pavillion in El-Ay?"

"Sting, Mother."

"That's what I said."

"There is no 'the' in 'Sting', Mom."

"Whatever! You get the point, don't you. These bands are all self-supporting, profit-making enterprises. They rent the venues where they make music and the people buy the tickets without government assistance, and the masses come in droves, don't they. I have seen pictures. Amazing, simply amazing. And you know something? That's the way it used to be, with what we call classical music! People had standing room only when

Mendelssohn conducted his music in London, or in Leipzig, and the same with Strauss, all of them, and so on down the line. What's happened here, Emily? Is your beloved Mozart only for the elite few? And if so, why should every taxpayer subsidize your hobby?"

"What's your point, Mom?"

"Forgive me, Em, I haven't come to my point yet. Here is what I want to show you." Angelique got up and went to a side table on which lay several stacks of booklets bound by twine. She wrestled one of the booklets out and came back, slamming it down on the desk top. "Look at this."

Emily pulled it towards her and flipped it open. "A prospectus!"

"Yes indeed! A prospectus for a profit-making venture called 'The South California Symphony Orchestra'. I want you to go over the figures for me."

Emily leaned back. "I'm surprised, Mom!" She looked at the booklet again, glanced at a page or two, then said, "Extraordinary!"

"'Extraordinary' is not a business word, Emily. Give me your professional opinion. Be frank."

"All right. The way I read this, you want to raise twenty-five thousand shares at a thousand dollars par value, to start an orchestra that has no year-round home but travels from venue to venue."

"That's part of it. You have to read the whole prospectus."

"First of all, you need an underwriter. Secondly, the thing may have no practical merit. The kind of money you need cannot be raised from little old ladies in Montecito or Pasadena. That's what you are trying to do tonight, isn't it? You are going to try to raise some money?"

"Pledges. I myself will buy two thousand five hundred shares."

"Mother! That's two-and-a-half million dollars!"

"I know. About a one-month return on my Dessauer holdings."

"Whatever! It's money down the drain if this thing doesn't fly!"

"It will fly. D'you know why?"

Emily sighed. "I know you'll tell me."

"Because there is more to it than just an orchestra. You didn't read the 'Remarks' pages. Let me summarize them for you. First of all, I want an All-American orchestra, with no gender or race barriers. Just the most talented musicians coming out of our colleges and universities, who now get rejected ninety-five out of a hundred by the orchestras they apply to. Secondly, I want conductors to match. Yes, I mean plural. Two of them initially, and they must be top instrumentalists themselves. Thirdly, our concerts will feature one contemporary piece of music, and I mean really contemporary, not some aging Penderecki or Boulez. Have you any idea how much music is being created in America right now, stuff that has no chance of ever seeing the light of day? What a waste! Our orchestra will be free to play it, beholden to no one except the artists. And furthermore, we will pay a decent wage to our musicians. Do you know how much a French horn or a viola makes in salary with the, say, Honolulu Symphony? They are dickering over twenty thousand a year!"

"That's not a fair example, Mom. Those small orchestras only play a three or four month season."

"True. Our orchestra members will be full-time salaried people, with a bonus incentive. No lifetime tenure but promotions on merit."

"What about the people who start it, the shareholders?"

"Dividends, of course! We'll be running a business!"

"What about competition, Mother? The big boys in their award-winning, super-acoustic palaces of culture—my God, you already have me talking like you—won't they try to suppress you with ridicule and worse?"

"Yes, they will ridicule us. And on occasion, we will ask them to rent their pavilion or hall to us, and you know—they will rent it to us— because they'll need the money, and because we'll have the crowds. Paying crowds, not the paper ones. And money talks, all the time."

Emily sat there, contemplating her mother. She nodded, "I'm impressed. That's a business expression, Mother, and it usually means we'll seriously look at it, and if it checks out, we'll talk again. In that context, let me ask you if you have run this past the boys?"

"The boys," in family lingo, were Morrie Dessauer's sons by his first marriage, Angelique's erstwhile charges. Both had been well provided for under their father's will. Rick, the older, had gone into computer science and was scarcely interested in anything his stepmother did with her money. Benjamin, the younger and more sentimental of the two, after he got his law degree at Georgetown University had married into a Milwaukee family, become the father of two boys himself and called Angelique "Mother." He was rumored to have political ambitions, but he, too, usually left Angelique to her own affairs.

"No, Em, I haven't. It's really none of their business."

"You're right. I rarely hear from them, myself." There was no hostility, just a gradual estrangement, natural if regrettable under the circumstances. The initial shock of having a baby half-sister come into their lives, so soon after their mother's death, had mellowed. The old scar, if it was still there, did not hurt anymore. "Still, it might be a good idea."

"I will send them a prospectus, don't worry." She smiled, "Maybe they will want to invest."

"Yeah, maybe! But shouldn't you get somebody to check this all out for you? You can't fly this by the seat of your pants, Mom!"

"I have had it checked, thoroughly. At Sheridan, Grady and Post."

"I might have known. Nicholas Wilson Grady, Junior. At your service."

"Not like that, the way you make it sound, Emily. Nicholas just took it to the Senior Partners Committee. They came back with a cautiously optimistic approval. They also suggested very strongly to keep the project under wraps until it is launched. They took steps, legal steps, to protect the idea."

"For a hefty fee?"

"A fee, yes, of course. But not hefty; their remuneration comes when the business end of it starts rolling."

"Well, Mom, what can I say. You have thought of everything. So tonight we'll toast the new Southern California Symphony."

"The South California Symphony Orchestra. I anticipate the state splitting into two. North California and South California. Like North and South Carolina. Or the two Dakotas. We here are definitely South."

"Good heavens, Mother! You're not going around touting that, are you?"

"Of course not. I'm no fool, Emily. I'm not making an issue of it. But if it happens that California splits, it won't be necessary to change our name. We'll be right there, already. Can't hurt, can it?"

Emily laughed. "As I was saying—you've thought of everything, Mom! Congratulations, and here's to your complete success." She clinked her tea cup to her mother's.

The caterers arrived at noon, in three vans. They unloaded, carried their boxes to the side entrance of the house, parked their cars out of sight and went to work. It was an eye-popping experience for Emily. Instead of bringing the usual folding chairs and tables necessary for a party of close to two hundred people, they went to the storage room behind the garage, brought forward some fifteen round wooden tables with matching chairs and set them up in the salle á manger alongside the existing rectangular sets of dining tables and chairs. The room was large enough to hold them all.

"Where did you get the extra tables?" Emily marveled.

"Oh," her mother flapped a wrist, "at an auction of a bankrupt furniture store. So much more practical than card tables, don't you think?"

And the caterers descended into the kitchen, but not to the regular, modern yet cozy one next to the "small" dining room, rather the one with the heated floor tiles "to keep your bare feet warm when you come padding in for your morning coffee." No, their kitchen was in the half basement with outside access, where large amounts of food could be prepared and lifted up, piping hot, by a dumb-waiter directly to the serving alcove of the large dining room. Emily guessed that this contraption was a streamlined American version of the kind found in the Alsatian villas where her mother's mother had served the haute bourgeoisie. "Good for you, Mom," she thought. "It's your turn, all right." Even as a girl, Emily had never been unaware of the humble origins of both her parents, and had taken a silent pride in it.

Banners were strung across the main entrance to the house, and a balcony above was manned by two musicians, a French horn and a trumpet. A valet car parking service set themselves up at the rotunda, and a special detachment of Steadman Ranch security people took up their posts unobtrusively. At six o'clock five tuxedoed musicians came, rolled the Bechstein onto the terrace into a wind-protected spot, set up their chairs and music stands and began tuning up—violin, cello, flute, drums and piano. Emily could tell they weren't going to noodle chamber music into the cool ocean air. This would be more like the Palm Court schmaltz at the Plaza in New York.

By seven o'clock, among the very first of the guests to arrive to a trumpet blast and horn fanfare, was Nicholas Grady chauffeuring his mother and her nurse in his Mercedes. Emily followed her mother to step outside to greet them. There were embraces and air kisses, except when Nicholas got hold of her he kissed her neck and, ever so slightly, pinched her bottom. "Hi, Em," he said when she disengaged herself from him. "Long time no see." He grinned, "Et cetera." He wore a dark gray suit so well tailored it fit his muscular body like a second skin. Nicholas Grady was not tall—about the same height as Emily, which made her tower over him when she wore her really high heels; but he was compact and agile, with an intelligent face. The first impression he gave people was that of a man supremely confident of his abilities both physical and mental. When he flashed his toothy, thin-lipped grin and winked with both eyes, one knew one wanted to be his friend, if for no other reason than to avoid his scowl, for Nicholas Grady, Esquire, could also be a formidable foe.

"I see you are letting your hair grow." Emily ruffled his dark blond mane as they were walking into the house. "Over the ears, even!"

"You like it?" He hugged her waist with one arm. With the other arm he carried a clothes bag slung over his shoulder. "I'm finished with the Marine Reserve. I can be a civilian now."

"Emily!" Angelique called after them. "Show Nicholas to the suite opposite yours. I am taking Mary upstairs to mine."

"We are staying the night!" Nicholas flipped his eyebrows up and down looking at Emily. "My tux is not all I have in this bag!"

"Don't get your hopes up, Nicky."

"And my hopes is not all I am getting up!"

Emily just gave him a look back and shook her head. Then she walked on ahead, through the vestibule, left down the hall towards the guest annex.

"Great!" Nicholas made enthusiastic noises as they went. "Look at this! Fabulous! Your mother and her decorator have really done a great job!"

Another turn, to the right this time, and they had reached their rooms. Emily pushed open the door to the one opposite hers, and said, "I guess this is yours. Wouldn't matter, they're all the same."

Nicholas stepped past her into the room, flung his bag onto the bed, said, "Nice, very nice!" and turned. He was ten or more feet away from her.

"Emily," he said, without a trace of mockery or jest in his voice, "I . . . want you to know something . . ."

"Yes?"

"You are—gosh, I hope this doesn't sound screwy—you look fabulous. Scrumptious. I mean—really well, and all together. Absolutely great. Yeah—great. You look great, Emily."

"Why, thank you, Nick!" She smiled, "And, no, it didn't sound screwy, and I presume it isn't just my dress you are referring to."

"Your dress?" He seemed to look at it for the first time now. Emily was wearing "a simple black number" according to the sales lady at Bergdorf Goodman, with the round neckline stopping just above her cleavage. She liked showing off her neck—it had a graceful swoop. "In another life, you must have been a swan!" her father once said admiringly. It lent itself well to showing off pearls, a double strand of which she was wearing now. Her hair was cut and combed pageboy style, and with the high-heeled black silk pumps she resembled one of those tall fashion models, except that she did not throw her hips when she walked. "Your dress," said Nicholas again. "Sure. You always dress well, Em. Nothing new there. It looks great, though."

"Okay, Nick. Stop while you're ahead. Thanks for the compliment. See you out on the terrace for cocktails when you are ready." Still smiling, Emily closed the door. "This Nick," she thought as she walked back to the party, "what am I going to do with him?" One thing she knew she would not do was to tell him off, to discourage his obvious advances. The chemistry that was once there, was still there; she could feel it, to her own surprise. By the same token—she took a deep breath at that—she could not lead him on, encourage him. For—another deep breath—what about telling her mother? If MuniBank came through with the plans they had for her—"we believe you'd be perfectly well suited for the European market, Ms. Dessauer. Our London office looks after that, as you know. Do you think you'd be able to transfer, if it came to that? On rather short notice?" She had said yes to both questions, coolly but inwardly excited, but then what about Nick here in California?

The terrace had begun to fill up quickly, tuxedoed and bejeweled long-gowned people were milling about talking loudly, waiters were carrying trays with delicious little snacks and were taking orders for drinks, the quintet was doing imitation Schrammelmusik, and through it all there was Angelique trying to talk to everybody. When on her next turn she bumped into Emily, almost spilling her champagne, she laughed loudly. "See? Almost ruined my new dress. Do you like it, Em? You haven't said anything!"

"I do!" Her mother was wearing a black chiffon pantsuit, the collarless jacket in bold black and gold stripes. "I thought I had said so!"

"Very nice, Mrs. Dessauer." Nick weighed in with his judgment. "Very stylish."

Angelique laughed again. "These large buttons? People think they're rhinestone, but guess what!" She waited for an answer.

"They're not?" Nick took the bait. "Well, I must say, very stylish!"

"Thank you, Nicholas!" Angelique swirled off into another direction.

"'Very stylish'," Emily mimicked. "Really, Nick, you don't have to butter up my mother!"

Nicholas put an arm around her waist. "Wouldn't dream of buttering up your mother, Emmy. It was the firm's client I was buttering up."

"Sucking up is more like it!"

He gave her the toothy, USC-football kind of grin that she had come to like about him because, when she was still at Marlborough, all the girls were in love with Robert Redford and when she had first met Nick she thought he looked like Robert Redford. "What's wrong with sucking up?" he asked.

"Oh, you!" She boxed him on the arm. "Just do me a favor. Mother has asked me to host a table, an important table. That means we both host that table, Nick, and I want you to be at your best waspish behavior."

"Does that mean, no limericks?"

"No limericks, no politics, no religion."

He nodded. "Just the plain vanilla. I get you."

"You hope!" she said.

The dinner was excellent. Five courses—nouvelle cuisine be damned—including chateaubriand and truite bleue. There was no musical entertainment, and even without it the decibel level rose proportionately with the number of empty wine bottles sent back down to the kitchen.

After the coffee and the fruit, the caterers were excused and the doors to the hallway shut. Fresh ocean air wafted in from the opened windows. Then Angelique Dessauer rose and launched into her speech.

It was an impassioned speech, if the declarations and exclamations of a strong-willed woman can be so called. And it made an impression. The idea was clearly understood, the newness of it—to own a symphony orchestra, instead of donating to one—did not fail to impress, after a few initial giggles. Then Dick Tertunian, chairman of the Senior Partners Board of Sheridan, Grady and Post, rose to announce his firm's endorsement of the business side of the proposed enterprise. He added a note of caution, "You may avail yourselves, ladies and gentlemen, of a prospectus before you leave this room. They are in those boxes underneath each of your tables, that you may already have stubbed your toes against. Let me add quickly that the pain you have felt is not symbolic of what lies ahead." Under rising laughter, he sat down. A scramble ensued to pull out the boxes and take out a brochure. It had the effect of breaking up the party. Angelique announced in a loud voice that more coffee and tea was being served in the library, "to keep you wide awake on your return home. And thank you, thank you all so very much for coming."

"It went quite well, don't you think?" Nicholas Grady had his arm around Emily's waist as they were walking back to the guest wing.

"Yes, I do. Of course, it's a long way yet to the finished product."

"True. But a journey of a thousand miles, and all that. I thought it was a good beginning."

"How much did you have to do with it?"

"Personally? I was hardly consulted. The senior partners think of me as a jock. Not really quite there yet, in the brains department."

"Oh come on, Nick! You are kidding!"

"I kid you not. I have this image—football, the Marine Corps, girls—you know."

"Girls? Am I one of your girls? Never mind, don't answer that. Besides, you graduated magna cum, made the Order of the Coif, you are no dummy, Nick."

"Thank you. I needed that. And in answer to your question—no, you are not one of my girls. I hope you will be my woman." The had reached their corridor. Nicholas put his hand on his doorknob. "What next, Em? You call the shots."

"Wow, that's not fair! Am I not supposed to be wooed?"

"Well, it's been some time, and you may not be in the mood, have a headache, or your period or something. I wouldn't want to ruin anything."

Emily laughed out loud. "That's a new one, Nick! I can remember when you couldn't take your hands off me! What happened—cat got your tongue, or something? Okay, never mind that. And for your information," she counted it out on the fingers of her hand, "if I were having my period I would have already hinted at it; secondly, I never use the stupid 'I've got a headache' cop-out; and thirdly, you are the one who's supposed to put me in the mood."

Nicholas smiled and pulled down his black tie. "I'll be in your room in five minutes."

"Make it six. I've got to go to the bathroom first."

"Ah yes. The diaphragm?"

"And then some. How about you?"

"Don't worry. I play fair."

Emily came up close to him and pulled his chin. "You are a bit of a jock, Nicky." Then she kissed him.

It was an entirely satisfactory night. Truth be told, Emily had not had sex for quite some time, what with the generally unappealing circle of her male acquaintances in New York, not to mention the ever present specter of AIDS hanging over all intimate encounters. And Nicholas had done his best, snuffling and grunting, throwing his all into the exercise, not once but twice. As she finally fell asleep, her last drowsy thought was wondering if this was love, and if it was, if that was all there was to it.

The next morning, Angelique insisted on driving her daughter to the Los Angeles airport. Nicholas had offered to do so, eagerly, but was firmly rebuked with a soothing smile from Emily thrown in, and told to take his mother home and spend the rest of the day attending to his filial duties. Emily's plane was not due out until the early evening, and even allowing for summer holiday traffic it would not have been necessary to leave Santa Barbara until after lunch. But Angelique got her way, to no one's surprise, and by mid morning, Emily still grumpy about it, they were on the road tooling south.

There was a reason, of course, for leaving early, as Emily had half suspected, so she was not too surprised when her mother slowed for a left turn and gunned the Cadillac up a steep side road when the traffic had cleared. They were at the southern end of Malibu city limits, close to the intersection of Toganga Canyon Road with Pacific Coast Highway.

"Mother," she asked, mildly curious, "what are we doing?"

Angelique smiled, "You'll see in a moment."

The narrow road turned sharply right and became a broad parking place, with a garage building against the hillside. Angelique braked the car to a halt and got out. "Come, let me show you something." Obediently, Emily climbed out and joined her mother who had walked to the rim of the lot.

Still smiling, Angelique made a sweeping gesture with her right arm, "Look, there is Malibu, behind that bend in the road. And to the left, Santa Monica. And in between and to the far horizon, the blue Pacific. On a clear day you can see Catalina Island. Now, turn around." She took her daughter by the shoulder and made her face the mountain side. "See those palm trees on your right? Behind them, and the bougainvilleae hedge, is a house. More about that later. To your left, there, the road goes up to another lot, and there is a house on it, small but nice, a guest house, you might call it. It is currently occupied by the people who look after the property. A nice couple, middle-aged, he's a screenwriter, she a nurse. You'll like them when you meet them."

"Meet them? Why would I want to meet them?"

Angelique ignored that question. "Come, let's have a look at that house here." She took Emily by the arm and led her around the hedge. The house now came into view, a simple California ranch house with overhanging eaves to shade the porch and the interior. It was set to face the ocean and to catch the sun from noon to evening. Angelique pulled a key ring from her purse and unlocked the door.

The house was unoccupied and bare of furniture. Emily stepped over the transom into a large room that would be called a living room if there had been another room from which to set it apart but there was none; it was just a large room with a stone fireplace, pegged wood floor and high beamed ceiling. It adjoined a kitchen to its left, and Emily, stepping along, noticed that it was also large, with rustic cabinets and a breakfast counter and windows to the porch and the ocean below. "Mother?" she said. "Who's house is this?"

"Mine. It came with the property. If you go through that door," she pointed to the one at the end of the kitchen, "you'll be in the hallway with a bedroom and a bathroom on either side. Go on, the tour isn't over yet."

Emily looked at her mother, shook her head and followed Angelique who had opened the door. She found what she knew she would, two bedrooms, one bright with an ocean view, the other cozy but just as large, with windows that opened onto a purple-red hedge and palm trees and a stone wall rising steeply against mountain slope. The two bathrooms had standard equipment, tub and shower, toilet and sink. She liked the sink area, it had been tiled in Mexican glazed terra-cotta. And the fixtures, while not modern, were certainly not of the same pre-war vintage as the ones she had in her Manhattan apartment which probably meant they functioned better and did not make that clanking noise when they were turned on. "Nice," she said. "Real nice. Do you intend to rent this out, Mom?"

"Yes," Angelique deadpanned, "to you, dear."

"To me? Mother! I live in New York! What would I want with a house in Malibu?"

"You come here so often, you need your own four walls. Not that you aren't welcome at my place anytime, you understand, but a person must have something to call her own, where she can be completely herself." She waited for an objection, and when none came said, "Besides, think of all your nice things you put into storage, that ancient four-poster bed you love so much, and the Chippendale dining set, and your Sevres china. Not to mention your grand piano. There'd be no neighbors to worry about when you practice!"

Emily came up and put an arm around her mother. "Oh Mom, did you go to all this trouble just so that I can have a place of my own?"

"Actually," Angelique replied dryly, "it was the price that caught my attention first. One hundred and thirty-two acres, with three flat pads and a private road close to the highway but a hundred twenty feet above it, all that for four million dollars! That's half the price per livable acre as compared to what you have to pay in Malibu or the Pacific Palisades! And the financing was dirt cheap! And deductible as a second home! How can you lose?"

"Oh! I see. And here I thought it was meant for me." Emily smiled at her mother when she said that.

Her mother smiled back. "Well, of course, I knew I would have a tenant. One smart enough to see the business and personal advantages in the deal."

Emily laughed out loud, "Mom, you have a deal! If the rent is not too high, that is. I'm not touching my principal."

"We'll work something out. I'm so glad you like the idea."

The two women embraced, swaying back and forth, patting their backs. They had tears in their eyes when they looked at each other again.

"Wait," Angelique said. "I brought us a bottle of champagne. I'll get it." She came back carrying a little leather pouch that, when zipped open, revealed an insulated holder for a bottle and two glasses. Veuve Clicquot, and two crystal flutes. Emily popped the cork and poured the foaming liquid. "Santé, Mom," she raised her glass, "and bonne chance!"

"Et bonne fortune!" said her mother.

They drank, and kissed each other. Then Emily took the bottle, ran outside, sprinkling the champagne as she ran. "I christen thee," she shouted into the hillside, "Dessauerland! Yahoo!" She flung the empty bottle into the chaparral with a wide-armed pitch. "Yahoo!"

There was a lot on her mind when she flew back to New York that night.

Scrub

There was a note Thomas Campe made to himself on the night flight to Washington. He had bought a drink of Scotch from the beverage trolley as it came down the aisle, poured the contents of the little bottle over the ice in the plastic glass the attendant had put down on his tray, and swirling the ice cubes in the golden liquid, had taken his first long sip. It went down warm like a mother's touch, he felt it almost instantly reach his blood stream, and as it coursed to his brain it set off a stir in his still benumbed mind, craving action, an urgent desire to do something, anything that would allow him to regain control over his life. Where would he go from here? What would be the priorities from now on? He needed a Mission Statement.

He pulled the pen from his breast pocket, turned the little cocktail napkin around and wrote:

> Bertram—Preserve and Protect, at all costs!
> Nettie—Research and Explain! (Murder??)
> WHO??—Hunt and Destroy. No mercy.
> Do it alone—Observe Strict Secrecy—Trust no one!

He knew it sounded primitive when he read it over, but he couldn't help that; the first step in any new direction is awkward, he remembered having been told in a Basic Research class he had taken, but the important thing was the first step, and the second, the third, until a firm goal would emerge, unmistakably. He nodded to himself, then tore the written piece from the napkin, folded it over, and put it in his wallet. With one more gulp he finished his drink. He turned off his seat light and leaned back, closing his eyes.

He knew now that the first step was over and that he must take the second step and the third.

The Monday morning staff meeting at the Institute began at 0800 sharp because Colonel Snyder, Officer Commanding, wanted it that way.

Tom, with all the others, was there as usual, a few minutes before. They were in uniform—no white coats permitted, also on orders of Colonel Snyder. On the dot of eight the colonel entered the meeting room from a side entrance, like a judge in a courtroom, the senior officer of the week shouted "tenSION!" all rose, faced the flag in the corner and recited the pledge of allegiance, another of Colonel Snyder's sine qua nons. He had made it very clear, at the beginning of his tenure, that he considered the pledge, recited once a week, a necessary and not burdensome duty.

From all that, however, it did not follow that the colonel was the very picture of a martinet. Quite the contrary, he was a smallish, roundish man with the ruddy face of the North Dakota farm boy that he was, who bounced along when he walked like a circus clown in oversized shoes. But nobody laughed at him, not even behind his back. It was well known that Bill Snyder had performed acts of true heroism in Nam, especially when he headed a Medi-Vac team during the Tet Offensive, rescuing the wounded and the dying from fates worse than death. That he was also an outstanding epidemiologist whose papers commanded respect in scientific circles was almost a given.

"At ease!" he commanded, and when the shuffling noise of chairs had ceased he continued. "Major Campel!"

"Sir!" Tom, just seated, rose again.

"I speak not only for myself but for all of us here when I express to you our heartfelt condolences at the sudden death of your wife."

"Thank you, colonel. And thank you for the flowers. Very thoughtful and much appreciated."

"We all liked Nettie around here. Lovely young woman, wonderful mother. I'd like to see you in my office after the meeting, major."

"Yessir." Tom sat down.

The meeting ran longer than usual, there were new regs from the Centers for Disease Control and with the Gulf War disease scare having reached Capitol Hill, there were predictable repercussions from the Pentagon. Tom, hungry and tired, had trouble staying alert during the meeting. Afterwards, he dashed down to the cafeteria to grab a donut and slurp some hot coffee with cream and sugar before he reported to Colonel Snyder's office.

"Siddown, siddown." The colonel motioned him to a chair at the side of his desk. "You look like hell, Tom. Terrible ordeal, I know. Sue-Ellen says to tell you she's saddened, deeply saddened."

Tom, who was actually beginning to feel better after the sugar rush, said, "Thank you. Please tell her thank you for me."

Snyder nodded and looked at him with narrowed eyes. "What happened, Tom? Can you tell me? Can you talk about it?"

Tom glanced past him out the window. The gentle rain from the early morning had changed to a downpour. How many times has he been telling his tale now? How many more times lay ahead? "It all happened very fast," he said slowly. "I've been giving extensive reports to all kinds of official people."

"I bet you have. I'm sure it's very painful to you each time you do." Snyder leaned back in his armchair and folded his pudgy hands over his stomach, "But I need to know, from you directly, in your own words and as you look me in the eye, exactly what happened, Tom."

"Sure. I understand."

"I don't think you do, Tom. The shit's already hit the fan." He fumbled for something on his desk and came up with a piece of paper. "Got a fax last Friday from the Pentagon, the Judge Advocate General's office, ordering me as your commanding officer to commence investigating the circumstances of your wife's death." He was holding the fax, then dropped the paper back contemptuously. "I have no choice there, Tom. And neither have you."

"I understand."

"Stop saying that, goddamn it! You understand diddly squat! I have to order an autopsy."

"There couldn't be one, the remains were just ashes. But there is a report, the Santa Barbara county coroner's investigation."

"Great. No autopsy. Maybe the Armed Forces Medical Examiner will consent to accept the county coroner's findings. Do you know what's in it?"

"I've not yet been informed, colonel."

"Bill! Call me Bill. We're buddies here, Tom."

"Bill. Everything burned up, down to the boat's hull. In an intense fire flash. They identified Nettie by dental records and charred bone fragments. You know how that's done."

Snyder reached over to the end of his desk and got hold of a wood-framed photograph. He looked at it, then waved it at Tom. "Sue-Ellen. Been married going on thirty years. She is the dearest person in my life. I'm asking myself what I would do, how I would feel if what happened to Nettie had happened to her." He whipped the frame in his hands. "I don't presume to know what I would do, and I won't presume to tell you what you should do. But I tell you what I'd think." He looked at Tom, who returned his gaze but remained silent. "I'd think, in that case—fuck the Army."

Tom, unflinching, said nothing.

"I tell you why. This fax here, that's the opening shot of the bureaucracy getting itself geared up. They're going to look at this from every angle, and the presumption is not of your innocence but of your guilt. We have the MacDonald case to thank for that, the Green Beret doctor who killed his wife and two little girls. Remember? The Army at first gave the guy a clean bill of health. No more. Oh no. Now our ass is in the sling until we can prove it wasn't our ass. So brace yourself, my boy."

"Bill, I appreciate what you are saying. My brother-in-law has already been telling me the same thing. He's a lawyer. He's been checking me out from day one. Every piece of evidence, all my movements. I'm clean."

Snyder carefully put his wife's picture back and leaned forward. "Know what that sounds like to me? Like typical lawyer crap. Won't mean bugger if the JAGs start sqeezin' you by the nuts."

"Colonel—Bill, with all due respect, I don't agree. They can't pin something on me that isn't there. And there is nothing there. I had no idea how the day would end, a week ago Saturday, when I stepped aboard that boat and we made for the open sea. I loved Nettie. We had no problems, no little nooky-nooky on the side, either of us. We had Bertram, and a wonderful future ahead. I still have Bertie, thank God, but the rest of our future is gone." He clenched his fists on the armrests. "And I tell you something else, they can have my commission back if they want to."

"So? That's not a big deal. You are already on record, with me anyway, of desiring to resign from the Army, moving to California to join your family. That's not going to cut any mustard with them. Don't tell them that, Tom." He made a negating gesture with his pudgy hands. "Motive. Let's talk about motive as if you were guilty. Money. Who benefits?"

"Bertie. A trust my brother-in-law is setting up for him. I will make an irrevocable assignment in my son's favor."

"How much?"

"About a hundred fifty thou, from insurance. That'll increase by fifty thou if the ruling of accidental death is accepted by the insurance company."

"Two hundred thou. People have killed for less."

"Bill, dammit, you talk as if I killed her!"

"Easy, boy. I'm not accusing you of anything. In fact, I believe you, and I will make a statement to that effect to the JAGs. I'm just trying to prep you for the way these guys are thinking. You know what they say about lawyers. A whole ferry full of them, sinking in the ocean? Too little, too late."

"I'm sorry. It's so—I don't know—frustrating. What can I say?"

"They'll give you a lie detector test."

"I'll take it."

"Sodium pentothal."

"That, too."

Colonel Snyder leaned back in his chair, folding his hands over his stomach again, and eyed Tom for a long moment. Then he said, "Okay. We'll see how it goes." He nodded.

Tom took that as a sign of dismissal. He was already out of his chair and about to salute, when Snyder spoke up again.

"Tom, one more thing. Your career in the Army is kaput. You know that, don't you? This will be on your fitness report. There goes the bird colonel, which you would have had maybe next year. In my opinion, if this had not happened and if you had stayed on for the duration, you would have had a clear shot to general officer. I would have liked to see that. One of my boys making the grade."

"How about you, sir? Making general?"

"Naw. I'm pushing sixty. By that time I'll be teaching at Johns Hopkins. Career change. They say it's good for you."

"Well, thank you, sir."

Snyder gave a snappy return of Tom's salute.

It was not until he got home that evening, to the apartment that was quietly gathering dust balls under the bed and the dresser and probably everywhere else, too, that Tom became aware of the loneliness that was now his. He felt not just the temporary separation kind of loneliness that he had endured since Nettie and the baby had moved to California in the spring, but the sudden awareness of his widowerhood. It was like a vise clamping down on his heart, oppressing him, making him suck in air in big heaving gulps. He grabbed the back of a kitchen chair and held on to it until his knuckles shone white. He told himself, actually speaking the words through clenched teeth, "Get a grip on it, dammit, and think of Bertie!" To combat the turmoil of grief and panic that was besetting him he decided to do something that was useful, even necessary. Was there any food in the house? No; he would go, immediately, to the all-night food market and stock up. Without even changing out of his uniform he turned on his heels and dashed down to the underground parking garage.

The tires were squealing as he floored the white T-Bird up the street ramp. At the Grand Union he pushed the shopping cart through every aisle, plopping things in the basket as he went: milk, butter, eggs, packages of cheese, ham, turkey breast (buying the low-fat, low-salt kind of each, following a diet regimen that Nettie had set up for them), cereals, pasta, lamb chops (their favorite meat), kipper (his, and only his, favorite Sunday brunch item), and bread, thick-sliced, hefty loaves of bread. The whole procedure had a curiously calming effect on him. On the way back he stopped to buy some take-out tacos and beans, then pulled over and ate it all in the car when he became involved listening to a Mets game. He had always liked the Mets; hard-luck players like himself. Deserved better than they got, hung in there just the same.

Back in his apartment, after he had stowed everything away, he picked up the phone and dialed Santa Monica. It was still before 7:00 P.M. there in

California, and he got Laura on the first ring. Al wasn't home yet, and she was in the kitchen giving Bertie his supper.

"He loves chicken! Did you know that? And hot dogs. He just gobbles it up." There seemed to be a sense of wonderment in Laura's voice. "I can't feed him that every day, can I, Tom?"

"No," he laughed, "not together, anyway."

They chatted some more, Laura giving him a complete rundown of what the day had been like—she and the boy had spent nearly every minute together.

"I hope it's not too much for you?" Tom inquired.

"Oh no, I love it. He is such a neat kid. D'you want to talk to him?"

Of course Tom wanted to talk to Bertie. They spent the next ten minutes exchanging incomprehensible words, saying in the end, "love you!" and smacking air kisses. When Laura came on the line again, they agreed that Tom would call every evening at about this time—"maybe a little later when you want to catch Al, too"—and that Tom would try to fly out to the coast every weekend that was possible. "Of course, you'll stay with us," Laura said.

Tom caught the nine o'clock news on CNN, then channel-hopped when Larry King came on. He felt restless again, the pictures from Bosnia deeply disturbing. The relentless political grind in Washington, with the budget problems and the forthcoming national health plan, made him vaguely anxious. How would he fare if he went from the Army to private practice—such as that would be—would he be able to make the transition? He would have to provide a home for Bertie, somewhere permanent. Probably in California, because that's where he was licensed. And he'd have to hire a housekeeper, a nanny-type.

He woke up that night, drenched in sweat, from a bad dream that he couldn't remember. He took a cold, then hot shower, and sat down on the living room couch eating a banana. Nettie's advice—when you can't sleep, get up, take a shower, eat a banana and read, then take an aspirin when you go back to bed. He'd have to remember to take the aspirin. As for reading, there were three novels on Nettie's night stand. Her bookmark was in one of them, a novel by A. Alvarez. She had started reading it when she was here last, before her move to California. He wondered what the book was about, and why Nettie would have liked it enough to nearly finish it. He picked it up and began the first page. It was not about Mexico or the Southwest, as he had assumed from the author's last name. In fact, it played in London, England . . . interesting . . .

He made it through the night.

The office of the Army Judge Advocate General's Corps called shortly after eight in the morning on Wednesday, just as Tom had reached his desk. The call had been put through from the Institute switchboard, so when Tom picked up the receiver he knew it was the "JAGs."

"Major Thomas V. Campe?" A female voice.

"Speaking. Major Campe here."

"Major, this is Captain Shoeman, S-h-o-e-m-a-n?"

"Shoeman. Yes, captain."

"I am with the Judge Advocate General's Corps, major. I would like to set up an appointment to see you."

"Yes. Certainly. Any time would be okay, assuming your interview will not take too much time away from my duties."

"Okay, great. You are in Frederick, Maryland, right? If I leave now, I can be at your office at between half past ten and eleven o'clock?"

"Fine. D'you need directions?"

"No, thank you, major. That's all taken care of." There was a click.

Tom held the receiver away from his ear, and shook his head. This would not be an easy encounter. He had detected an edge to the woman's voice, but from what? Hostility? Prejudice? He was a man, he outranked her, he was suspected of having caused his wife's death, and what do you want to bet she's black. He sighed. He would have to take it as it came.

The phone rang again. Colonel Snyder. "I just had a call from the JAGs. You, too, I guess. When she arrives, I want the meeting to take place in my office, Tom. I am the CO here, I would be the one to convene a court-martial, and nobody talks to you without me being in on it. You understand?"

"Yessir," said Tom. He would not have wanted to be interviewed—interrogated?—in this place that he called his office which was no more than a cubicle in the general laboratory area. On any working day, the lab was a beehive of activity, people all around busy at computers and laboratory benches, at sinks, titration stands, autoclaves, ovens and centrifuges. There was a certain distance, a wariness in Tom's character, friendly and gregarious though he appeared socially. Since they had learned of Nettie's death, his coworkers had been very thoughtful, and respectful of the privacy of his mourning. They had begun to bring him little gifts, a cake, a potted plant, an invitation to "come have dinner at the house when you are up to it." Tom appreciated that. Still, he doubted than any of them knew the ramifications of his wife's death. Nor would they ever, if he could help it.

The "JAG" arrived shortly before eleven o'clock, Tom promptly being summoned to the colonel's office. There she was, getting up when Tom entered, a tall blond woman whose gray-green uniform jacket closed tightly over an ample bosom. She gave an almost chic appearance, from her intelligent face down to her non-regulation black oxfords. The Corps' insignia—quill and sword crossed over a laurel wreath—looked almost like jewelry on her lapels.

They were introduced by Snyder and shook hands. It was only then that Tom noticed the third person in the room, a man in civilian clothes who mumbled his name and flipped open his credentials wallet: Federal Bureau of Investigation. Tom, a bit nonplused, shook hands with the FBI man also, who had a strong, almost hurtful grip, accompanied by a thin-lipped smile on a face that vaguely reminded Tom of the stern visage of a former drill sergeant.

They all sat down in front of Colonel Snyder's desk. An orderly brought coffee in styrofoam cups. Tom helped himself to two packets of sugar and one of milk powder, stirring the liquid until it turned light brown.

Snyder opened the proceedings by asking that the purpose of the meeting be clearly stated beforehand. Captain Shoeman replied that the Corps was merely following procedure relating to the violent death of a military dependent. Interviewing the husband, who in this case was present at the occurrence and had escaped unharmed, was a necessary part of it. She pulled a small tape recorder from her briefcase and put it on the table.

"Is this a deposition, Captain Shoeman?" Tom asked. He had heard the term when Al had mentioned it to him, with the advisory to insist on the presence of counsel if it should come up.

"No sir, Major Campe. An interview. You are not under oath, but of course we expect your statements to be just as truthful."

"Of course," Tom nodded.

She then took him over the same ground he had trod before, so many times before. Tom answered all her questions quietly and without hesitation. There was nothing new in her questions, and nothing different in his answers. It had been an accident, the boat caught fire from an explosion inside the cabin when he was outside at the tiller. Captain Shoeman seemed satisfied. "I'm all through, colonel," she said, switching off the tape and looking at Snyder.

"Okay. Thank you, captain. Now, Mr.—uh, sorry, I forgot your name."

"Montgomery." The FBI man, who had sat listening and occasionally hitting the keys of his notebook computer, leaned forward.

"Mr. Montgomery. Do you have anything to say?"

Montgomery cleared his throat. "I want to explain my presence here to the major. If I may ask some questions after, colonel."

"Fire away," said Snyder.

"Major Campe, we work in conjunction with the Judge Advocate General's office when members of the military are involved in matters touching on federal laws and internal security." He spoke with a slight Southern drawl.

"I see," said Tom. Then he added hastily, "Actually, I take that back. I don't see what that has to do with me."

Montgomery nodded. He slung one thin long leg over the other and rested his notebook on his thigh. He said, "What do you know about your wife's employer, major?"

"Her boss? I have never even met the man."

"The company. Goleta Research Laboratories. Why was your wife hired?"

"Why? She is—was—a veterinarian. The lab imports animals that have to be properly cared for. That's what veterinarians do."

"What kind of animals?"

"Monkeys, mostly. Also some domestic animals. Beagles. Cats. Rats."

"What do you know about Goleta Labs as a company?"

"Nothing, actually, until quite recently. They are apparently a division of a major Eastern pharmaceutical house."

"How recently did you learn that?"

"At the memorial service, last weekend. My father-in-law mentioned it to me. He is a retired dentist who invests in the market, and he looked it up when Nettie joined the company. NB Pharma, I believe. It rang a bell because we use some of their diagnostic sera here."

"Your wife had not mentioned the connection to you?"

"The parent company? No."

"You never discussed her career prospects, where she could move up in the company?"

"Mr. Montgomery, my wife and son moved to California in March. I am stationed here. We got together on weekends as often as we could. Her career prospects were definitely NOT what we discussed when we got together."

Captain Shoeman smiled and looked down at her hands. Tom saw that she wore a nice-sized diamond on her left ring finger.

Montgomery was unperturbed. "Did your wife ever mention trouble at her work place?"

"No. What kind of trouble?"

"Commotion. Unrest. Picketing. Security measures."

Tom shook his head. "No."

"Let me ask you something, agent Montgomery," Snyder cut in. "What are you driving at here with this line of questioning?"

"Sir, we are looking at a sabotage angle here. The possibility of the event not being an accident. Of a deliberate attack on two people who are identified as working at laboratories where animals are used for experiments. The fact that the employers of both Major Campe and his wife—the government and the pharmaceutical industry—are identified as the enemy by certain animal rights groups. And finally, the probability that the major would have been in the cabin with his wife, and would have perished with her, if they had not been late in reaching their overnight anchoring spot." He turned to Tom, "Major, let me ask you this question. Did you or your wife smoke?"

"No sir. Never have, either of us, as long as we were married."

"Yet, the remnants of a cigarette lighter were found in the ashes."

"Could have come from the previous owner," Snyder grumbled. "Didn't you say you bought the boat second-hand, Tom?"

"Yes." Tom nodded.

Montgomery said, "The lighter which has a flint, was found almost fused, by the heat of the fire, to the remnants of a handgun. It could have been part of a simple timing device—the details of which need not be disclosed here—aimed at the propane gas container."

Captain Shoeman said, "That device could also have been set by a husband intent on murdering his wife. A husband who conveniently remains on deck as the explosion occurs. A husband who happens to wear a life vest, and has a dinghy trailing the boat, a boat that happens to be anchored at a desolate spot of a deserted island." She looked at Tom with clear blue eyes.

Tom shrugged his shoulders and said nothing.

"Are you going to prefer charges against Major Campe?" Snyder asked.

"Our investigation is not finished yet, colonel. But we ask that the major report all his movements to us until our investigation is completed."

Tom spoke up, "Wait a minute! I intend to visit my son in California, this weekend and any other that I can manage to do so!"

"Yes. We are aware of that. That's why we ask that you report to us your movements. Otherwise we would order you confined to base."

"We are not a base," Snyder interjected. "We are a scientific institute."

"There are still bases in California," Shoeman smiled.

"Let's summarize what's happening here," said Snyder. "Major Campe is being investigated by the Judge Advocate General's Corps as a suspect in his wife's death. Right, captain?"

"At this point, technically the major is not a suspect. And personally, I hope he never will be. He is more of a material witness."

"But you are not ruling it out that he could become a suspect?"

"Our investigation is ongoing, colonel."

"Okay. I hear you, captain. Now agent Montgomery. What is your case, the FBI's case, against Major Campe?"

"We have no case against him. If he has committed a crime, it would not fall under our jurisdiction. We are checking his case out to see if there is any connection to animal rights terrorism." Montgomery closed his notebook.

"So you are out of the picture, Montgomery. Thank you for coming."

Montgomery rose and said, "You are welcome, colonel." Passing Tom, he gave him his card. "Keep this, major. Call me if something comes to mind." Then he left the room, closing the door quietly behind him.

"You didn't tell me about this guy," Snyder said to Shoeman.

"I didn't know he was coming here until I got a call from him, just as I was leaving Charlottesville."

"What do you make of his theory?"

"Interesting. If they can prove it."

"What about Tom, here? Don't you believe his story?"

Captain Shoeman smiled, "What are you doing, colonel? Leading me down the garden path?"

"I'm trying to get this crap behind me, that's what I am doing, captain. We are engaged in serious work here, and Tom is an integral part of the team."

"I take it you believe in the major's innocence?" She was still smiling.

"You give me proof, and I'll direct a summary court-martial."

"That's what I am trying to do, colonel." Turning to Tom she said, "I would hate to have to prosecute a brother officer. Particularly one with your record, major." She pointed to the bars of ribbons on his uniform. "But make no mistake about it. If I have to, I will do it. All the way." Then she took her card out of her briefcase and handed it to Tom, "Are you planning to go back to California this weekend? Okay, no problem. Where can you be reached?"

Tom wrote Al's name, address, business and home phone numbers on a sheet of paper he took from Snyder's desk and handed it to her. Captain Shoeman thanked the colonel for his time, saluted, and left the room.

"Shit," said Snyder. "Sheeyit. You know what a scrub is, Tom? That's what you look like to me. A scrub. Either way this comes out."

No Grounds

It was like waiting for the other shoe to drop, a very high drop of a very big shoe, and a very long wait at that.

Tom, increasingly fidgety and restless, tried to make the best of it. He established a routine of activities that would carry him through the day with a minimum of time left for contemplating what lay ahead. He would get up at the crack of dawn, slurp a blend of fruit juices and vitamins, and go outside to run. He did not particularly like running—it never gave him the "high" that aficionados claimed to get from it; he would have preferred riding, but there was no stable nearby, and in any case, it would not have fit into his schedule. Riding, being a more complicated sport, involved two parties, man and animal, the latter requiring its own attention. Tom didn't have time for that. He needed exercise to wake up his body. Running was it.

The coffee would be perking by the time he got back to his apartment, he would drink some, put pop-up tarts into the toaster and go shower and shave. He was a firm believer in the "Five Ss" inculcated in him since his upper form days: a Shave, a Shower, a Shit, a Shirt and a Shine. The only thing extra he had added was to slap on some after-shave lotion, the more astringent the better. A man had to be alert and awake. He wondered sometimes, when he saw jet contrails streaking a high blue sky, if he would have been happier if he had gone to the Air Force Academy and become a pilot, instead of making his living peering into people's innards. Almost instantly he would scold himself. Medicine was his métier, and there wasn't a damn thing wrong with that.

Without fail recently, by the time he was leaving his apartment the door would open from the condo across, and a blond young woman would step out with her little daughter in a stroller, both dressed in matching warm-up suits.

"Good morning, Tom," a wave and a greeting from the woman, as she would bounce the stroller down the few steps to the sidewalk

"Hi, Phyllis, Margie," and he'd be off, down the stairs into the parking garage. Phyllis and Nettie had been friendly, each expecting their first child at about the same time. With both husbands being in the military as medical officers, Phyllis's on an aircraft carrier half the time of the year, the two women had felt drawn to each other, and would often sit and talk. Since Nettie's death, Phyllis had kept her distance, looking at him with dark round eyes as if she were afraid to stir his sorrow. That was all right with Tom. The last thing he needed was chitchat with an across-the-hall neighbor.

By eight o'clock Tom would be at his desk in his cubicle, downloading his computer of what had come in overnight. There had been plenty in recent weeks, from all kinds of sources. It was Tom's job to take it down, channel it to the appropriate work stations and oversee the statistical evaluation of each of the categories. Worrisome statistics—an ominous increase in TB cases that were resistant to known antibiotics. The unexplained mass deaths of deer in the Pacific Northwest had finally been traced to an adenovirus, a virus routinely if harmlessly found in humans as well; why did it kill deer and not people? Or had it begun to kill people in the guise of an as yet unexplained syndrome? And what about that hantavirus, spread by the droppings of infected rodents that had started an epidemic on Indian reservations in the Southwest?

There was also lots of stuff from the CDC; Atlanta was never silent. Seldom was there anything really new from the Centers for Disease Control and Prevention—the CDC was more reactive than proactive, in the jargon of the activist crowd, but it certainly promulgated policy, with the clout of the force of law behind it. Policies which frequently riled Colonel Snyder.

"Get this, Tom," he slapped his hand down hard on a piece of paper lying on his desk. "Look at what these clowns are doing now."

Tom craned his neck. It didn't look very unusual, just the report for the quarter ended June 30th. Routine statistical information.

"I can't quite see, colonel, with your hand over it."

"Yeah. Well," the hand was withdrawn, "it's no surprise, actually. Just more HIV arrows in the AIDS quiver. All venereal infections—see? Pelvic inflammatory disease. Cervical dysplasia. Genital warts. And so on. What do they all have in common? You tell me. You're the smart one around here."

"Sexually transmitted?" It was too obvious an answer, and Tom knew it. He also knew what Snyder was driving at, but he wasn't going to say it first. Ever since the CDC had revised the definition of what should be on the palette of acquired immune deficiency syndromes the colonel had been seething. "Politics!" he would hiss through clenched teeth. "Science be damned!"

Snyder was still mad. "Women, Tom, women! We're getting a new bell curve for women! Just when the one for men was nicely declining, obeying Farr's Law. Right? What goes up, must come down. Remember, Epidemics 101? Now we are mixing new ingredients into the AIDS pot, getting another rise out of it." He was shaking his head. "You are still keeping separate track of things for us, though, aren't you?"

"Frank Potter's group is working on it, most of the time now, colonel."

"But you are still supervising!"

"Yessir, I am."

"Keep it up. I want you fully involved."

"I am trying to delegate the work, so that when I'm not here anymore it can go on without interruption. Sir."

"Geez, Tom, you make it sound as if you're going to croak or something."

Snyder sighed. "I know what you mean. What have you heard from the JAGs lately? They haven't gotten back to me since I gave them my statement and sent them your performance report."

"I haven't heard either." Tom shrugged his shoulders. "I suppose my case is grinding its way through the system."

"Yeah. No shit is going to hit the fan if there is no shit to begin with. Is there any fucking shit, major? Tell me there's no shit."

"No shit, colonel," Tom smiled.

The visits to California were becoming more stressful. Not so much for the physical aspect of flying back and forth on the same weekend—Tom rather relished the private, very inward-looking hours on the airplane that gave him a chance to think, regroup and think again about what his future plans should be. Unalterably, however, on the top of his list remained his son, Bertie. And it was leaving him behind, the youngster becoming more and more aware of their parting and often bursting into tears at the final hug, that tried Tom's soul.

And then there was Al, of Smedley and Becker, Attorneys at Law, who would make demands on his time. For very good reasons, granted, and mostly at night when the boy had been put to bed by Laura and Laura alone—"we don't want him to get accustomed to being tucked in by his father, do we, Tom, when you can't be here every night." Tom saw the point.

"I've been in touch with your buddy Captain Shoeman, Tom," Al said one evening. They had gone over to the law office, after hours a quiet place, with the windows showing the slate-dark expanse of the ocean that swallowed the far horizon. The room was redolent with the pungent smell of pipes smoked past.

"She is not my buddy, Al, and wouldn't be even if she weren't prosecuting me."

"Not your type, huh?" Al laughed and stuffed tobacco from the humidor into his pipe. "When I had you describe her to me she sounded quite zaftig." He had to stop grinning because he needed to close his lips over the pipe stem to draw in fire from the match.

"Tell me what you have been in touch with her about." Tom was helping himself to two fingers of Grant's, the Scotch standing next to a mouthwash in the little fridge under the corner sink. Al liked all his drinks cold.

"I've been plying her with information. Fax after fax. Daily. Everything about you I could lay my hands on. Even got your mother into the act. College transcripts. Sports, awards—hey, I didn't know you won ribbons as a junior at the Madison Square Gardens Horse Show! Dressage, huh? Hoity-toity! Then, names and addresses of colleagues, friends, from med school on, as character witnesses. Your bank records. I guess the Army will give out your performance records to the JAG woman directly. She sounded very grateful. We are 'Al' and 'Carol' now. Next I'll shove Nettie's stuff over to her."

"To what end, Al? This has nothing to do with the accident."

"She is looking at it from the angle that it wasn't an accident, which means she will have to prove intent. Premeditation. Remember M-O-M? Method, Opportunity, Motive? You certainly had the opportunity, and as a military man you are not unfamiliar with explosives. It's motive they are stuck on. If we can prove there was no motive for you to kill your wife, the whole case being circumstantial to begin with, they have too weak a case to prosecute on. That's what I'm shootin' for, see? That they'll throw in the towel and say aw shucks. No prosecutor likes to take on a weak case, it doesn't reflect well on him or her. So here I am, telling her about Thomas the Good, weakening her case like crazy. Fortunately for her it's all long distance. Otherwise I might even be weakening her knees. Does she look a lot like Laura?"

Tom smiled. "I am much reassured by your zest, Al. By the way, how is it going, in the fertility game?"

"Goin' good, brother, goin' good!" His Cheshire cat grin disappeared behind a burst of blue smoke.

During the Labor Day weekend, Al, Tom, Laura and Bertie were together again. They were riding bikes on the beach bike path, Al and Laura on their ten-speeds and Tom on a rental with a baby seat on the back. Bertie was getting almost too big for the seat, and the helmet too small, giving the kid a jaunty look.

"I don't think they are going for court-martial, Tom. Carol almost said as much." Al was on the lead bike and turned his head, shouting to Tom who was bringing up the rear.

"Carol!" Laura, in the middle, gave a mock alarm. "It's Carol now, have you noticed, Tom?" She was shouting over her shoulder.

They were riding single file. "If we want to talk," Tom shouted back, "let's stop somewhere. We could all do with a Coke, and maybe a hot dog for Bertie."

They pulled in to a refreshment stand on the Venice boardwalk, and dismounted. Venice, California was at its busiest, zaniest best. People, people everywhere, forming clusters around sidewalk acrobats, musicians, hawkers and beggars, bathing beauties on roller-skates zooming by, their blond or black pony tails whipping from side to side, curiously ignored by muscular young men on the latest in-line blades wearing helmets and kneepads. Tom wondered why that was so, this deliberate ignoring each other of the sexes. Was that the new trend, or was he getting too old? He still followed beautiful women with his eyes, as if by reflex, and took vicarious pleasure in it.

Bertie didn't want a hot dog when Tom handed it to him. He wanted ice cream on a stick. Laura got it for him. Tom heaped some mustard on the bun and ate it himself.

Al was slurping some Coke. "You heard about Clara, Tom? Tell him, Laura. She's your mother."

"Gee, thanks." Laura made a face. She said to Tom, "She's disappeared. It was her birthday last week, and I made a phone call to her at her number in Santa Barbara. It was disconnected."

"Oh?" Tom raised his eyebrows. "She must have moved back East."

"No such luck," Al said. "I made some inquiries. She broke her lease in Santa Barbara, paying the penalty. And moved, all right. Guess where to."

"Don't keep me on pins and needles, Al. Tell me."

"Brentwood. Less than five miles from our house, as the crow flies."

Laura grimaced again. "Nice, huh? Moving real close, but not telling us. Al found out where she lives. It's a townhouse, three bedrooms, two baths, close to schools and transportation, as they say in the ads. What's a little old lady going to do with all that space? Huh?"

Al didn't give Tom a chance to answer. "Not so little, not so old, and no lady, if you don't mind my saying so, Laura. Anyway, in my business I have ways to find out things. Carla bought the condo with a hundred thousand cash down, and a four-week escrow."

"I see," said Tom.

"No you don't," said Al. "Two questions. One, where did she get that kind of money, and two, why relatively pricey Brentwood? For a hundred thou she could have bought a ranch in Idaho. What's she doing here, next to us?"

"Good Lord. I see what you mean!"

"Do you?" Al gestured silently over Bertie's head. "Do you now?" When Tom nodded, he continued, "We gotta talk. Tonight. Okay?"

Laura said, "I know what she's after."

Al said, "We all know that. But she may not know that we know, already. Let's the three of us talk about it tonight. Laura, wipe the boy's fingers? He is sticky all over."

They had beer and pretzels on the patio after Bertie had been put to bed. Laura had brought the city guide from the glove compartment of her car. They poured over the page map that Al said was Carla's new vicinity.

"See? This is Galway Lane, nicely tucked away in a side street off San Vicente Boulevard. Meaning? Safety, from big-city traffic. But close to three churches, Catholic, Presbyterian, Methodist. A synagogue too, for that matter. What else? Schools? Brentwood Public, which happens to be a magnet school, and the private Collingwood Academy. And what else? Hospitals? UCLA Med School, with its first-rate emergency facilities, less than two miles away. Very important, that one, from a court's point of view. Not to mention shopping, police, fire stations—all close by. An ideal place for what, Tom? Go ahead, say it."

Tom didn't need to spell it out. He had thought about it since they had pedaled back from the beach. "Carla is after Bertie, I suppose is what you are trying to say."

"You bet. And not just for a while, as we are, taking care of Bertie for you temporarily. No, she wants your son for keeps."

"Tom is still the legal father and guardian, Al!" Laura's face was flushed and she had folded her paper napkin into its smallest triangle. "Carla can't just lay a claim to the boy and get away with it!"

"Don't be fooled about that. Let's not be complacent. If she can prove that Tom is an unfit father, she can very well lay claim to her daughter's child. Carla is young enough—early fifties? Fifty four, okay. And she is ruthless and cunning enough to go after Tom."

"First of all," said Tom, "I have no intention of giving up my boy. In due course I will be out of the Army, and I will establish a home for the both of us."

"Excuse me, Tom, but first you will have to go out and earn a living. And unless you remarry right away quick, you will be a single parent."

"I'll hire a housekeeper, Al, and I'll be the best damn father a kid ever had! All I need is a little time to put my affairs in order, and for that period I am enormously grateful to you two for taking Bertie into your home!"

Laura put her hand over his and squeezed it. "We love him, Tom!"

"Sure we do," said Al. "No problem there. But you should give us some temporary power of attorney, Tom. Let's go to my office tomorrow, before I take you back to the airport, and sign some papers. I'll also look into the Carla move; there has to have been a lawyer involved. I hate being kept in the dark, and then whammo, get hit with a custody suit. Leave it to me. I'm an old boy scout. Flatbush Troop Six. Always prepared!" Al raised his beer bottle against Tom's and made a toast, "To Bertie!"

Laura clinked her bottle to the men's, "Bertie!"

"My son," vowed Tom, and chugalugged his beer. He wiped his mouth with the back of his hand. "As the Marines say—don't tread on me!" There was a hard glint in his eye when he put the empty bottle down.

Later, when they were bringing the dishes back into the kitchen, and there was a moment to speak to Laura privately, Tom asked, "What do you hear from your father, Laurie? You keep in touch?"

"Oh, yeah, I guess. Not more than normally. Birthdays, holidays." She looked at him, "Why d'you ask?"

"I had kind of hoped to hear from him. We spoke at the funeral, and seemed to hit it off. And he is, after all, Bertie's real live grandfather."

"You are comparing him to Carla, in that regard, aren't you?" Laura shook her head. "If you are hoping he will intervene, against his former wife's intentions, you're barking up the wrong tree. The divorce was so bad, so hateful, it made him withdraw from us completely. We are all adults now, he has no obligations to his daughters anymore, so he is living his own life. Gave up his practice. Invests his money. Travels a lot." She shrugged again. "We are not a normal family, Tom. My mother queered it for all of us."

"Okay. With your permission, Laura, I would like to phone him. He gave me his number, and I'd like to make the effort. If you don't mind."

Laura grimaced, "Good luck. Want to use the kitchen phone?"

Tom said thank you and went to his wallet to extract the card Dr. Goldsmith had given him. There was a good chance that nobody would be home on a holiday weekend, but the phone was picked up on the third ring. A male voice.

"Dr. Goldsmith?" Tom made an okay sign to Laura. "It's Tom, here, Thomas Campe, your son-in law. I am standing in Laura's kitchen, and we were just talking about you. How are you, sir?"

"Tom! Nice to hear from you! I am fine. And by the way, it's Mike. Okay? How are you yourself, getting back to normal? How's your little boy?"

"I sure am, Mike. And Bertie is fine. Laura and Al are looking after him while I am winding up my Army days back East. They are wonderful people, your daughter and her husband. Laura says she wants to talk to you, too," he grinned and nodded against a frantic "No!" wave with both hands from Laura. "But before she does, let me ask you something D'you remember, at the memorial service, you said you would send me some information on that New Jersey company that you are investing in. I am still interested in receiving it, and I am wondering if perhaps you sent it to the wrong address?"

There was a moment's pause before the reply came, "Yeah, sure, I remember. I, uh, haven't sent it to you. I am sorry, I usually keep my promises. Tom?"

"Yes, I'm here."

"Is someone . . . uh, or maybe . . . is there a number I can call you back on? Later, when you are back home?"

"Sure." Tom gave him the Maryland number of his condo. "I'll be back there tomorrow night, Mike. Look forward to hearing from you. Here's Laura." He handed the phone to Laura, and left the kitchen.

He found Al in the den, and before he could say anything about talking to the father-in-law of the both of them, which he felt obliged to do, Al looked up and said, pointing to the TV screen, "Arafat and Rabin are both coming to Washington. Can you imagine that? Shaking hands with that son-of-a-bitch?"

There was no doubt who the son-of-a-bitch was. "No I can't," said Tom. And settled down next to Al, strangely relieved not to have to mention his talk with Mike Goldsmith. No doubt Laura would mention it eventually, but by then it would be old hat, and he might not be here anymore.

Mike Goldsmith did keep his promise to call. It was past ten in the evening, and Tom had arrived at his apartment just an hour before.

"Tom, I apologize. I was going to send you that stuff on NB Pharm's run-in with the animal liberation front, but before I got around to it I had a visit from the FBI."

"The what?"

"The FBI. I don't know if your apartment is bugged, and frankly I don't care. It's my daughter and your wife we're talking about here. As Americans, you and I, we have a right to talk about her. And if they don't like it, they can stuff it up you know where!" He spat that out vehemently.

Tom's knees went weak. He sat down. "Mike, I don't understand."

"Sure you do. They came to you, too, didn't they? At least that's what the agent here said to me. 'In the course of an ongoing investigation', as he put it. About animal rights terrorists. He made it sound as if Natalie's death was somehow connected to the terrorists. I really got mad when he seemed to imply that Natalie was involved with the terrorists, and something went wrong and she was killed by them. But he kept saying it was 'just routine'."

Tom felt shock rise inside him. He didn't know what to say.

"Tom, you there?"

"Yes, Mike. I can't believe what I am hearing."

"Yes, neither could I, at the time. About a month ago, it was. They made me promise to keep their visit confidential. And I have done that, until now. I am really glad you called me, Tom."

"Thank you for telling me."

"What did they tell you when they interviewed you?"

"Well, actually, I didn't think of it as an interview. There was an FBI agent present when the JAGs took my deposition."

"The who?"

"The Army lawyer. I am being investigated for possible court-martial."

"You? For what, for Christ's sake!" Mike's voice rose again.

"Suspicion of having murdered my wife. Of course I didn't. I couldn't. So eventually, the JAGs will probably drop the case."

"Now I am speechless."

"Anyway, an FBI agent took part in the interview, and he asked me some questions about what Nettie was doing at Goleta Research, and if I was aware of her complaining about outside interference from activists, and so on. I said no. And it's true, Nettie never mentioned anything of the sort." As he said that, Tom had the eerie sensation of seeing Nettie's madly distorted face, forming the words "Mack" or "Jack," that he had taken to mean Macintosh disks. He had gone over all of the ones he had taken from her desk; they were all about computing, none of them personal.

"My God, Tom. I had no idea they were suspecting you! Were—past tense correct? You said they are dropping the case?"

"That's what Al says, Laura's husband. He is acting as my lawyer."

"Of course they will drop the case. This whole thing is insane. Neither you nor Natalie did anything wrong. But once the Feds get their hands into your affairs, they are hard to get rid of. It's like a mechanic fixing your car. There's always some dirt or oil they leave on your seat, or the steering wheel. Know what I mean? Wipe it off, and forget about it."

"The whole thing will be hard to forget, Mike."

"Time will take care of that, Tom. Believe me. Time is a great healer."

Tom wondered, after they had hung up, what significance he could reasonably attribute to the fact that Mike Goldsmith, Nettie's father, had been visited by the FBI. Were the Feds on a fishing expedition, or were they on the trail of something specific, with Nettie's death fitting, or seeming to be similar to events that had been occurring elsewhere. If the latter applied, why didn't they make an effort to contact him, Tom, directly? That could only be for one of two reasons. He himself, was the object, that is to say one of the suspects, of their investigation; or, having considered that, they had found that notion to be without merit. Tom's contention, that he was an unsuspecting witness to an explosion that killed his wife and very nearly him as well, a story to which he had stuck from the beginning, had found acceptance; at least must have sounded more credible than alternative theories. Hence, he was left alone. Soon Colonel Snyder would hear that no court-martial should be convened. In consequence of which, Tom would be free to resign from the Army. He would also be free to pursue, as he had vowed, the perpetrators of Nettie's death, the killers, on his own. From that position there was now no safe return, at least none that he could see that would make his position more credible. On the contrary, he could expect to be asked, and reasonably so, why he hadn't come forward with that information, this version of Nettie's death that he now claimed to be the true one. Why had he withheld that information until now, and why had he prevaricated, indeed perjured himself in a deposition? The spotlight of suspicion would be turned on him; no telling where that would lead. It would certainly not help his efforts to retain custody of his child. In effect, both solemn promises he had made to a dying Nettie, that he would take care of Bertie and that he would avenge her death, would be jeopardized. Foolish though that may seem to an observer, Tom felt that he could consider no other choice but to continue on his path. These promises were his covenant to his wife, the woman he loved, and to her child, his son. He would honor them. In the best, the most determined, and if need be, the most devious way he knew how.

Except for the timing, Tom's hunch about how his case would develop was borne out. It was not until the end of the month that Snyder summoned him to his office to inform him officially that no charges would be preferred against him, hence no convening of a summary court-martial.

"That's it, Tom," the colonel said after he had harrumphed through the reading of the fax he had just received. "Bloody nonsense is all over. Took the JAGs two months to figure that out. Well, anyway. Congratulations."

"Thank you, sir." Tom was standing in front of the colonel's desk.

"Don't thank me. I am sorry it took so long. Siddown, siddown." He gestured to a chair. "So what are you going to do now? Still want to resign?"

"Yes, colonel. More so than before. I have to reorder my life. It wouldn't be fair to my son, and not to the Army, either, if I stayed on. Sooner or later a problem of priorities would come up, that I'd have to deal with. It's better to make a clean break, now."

Snyder nodded. "I see your point. Sorry to see you go, just the same."

He picked up some forms. "Get these filled out. You still have some leave coming, don't you? Take it. And, Tom? Let's work on the transition now, Okay?"

Discoveries

Time crept slowly. The "transition," as the colonel called it, was an exercise in redundancy, as Tom had handed over most of his work to Captain Potter during the past two months. New projects were no longer routed to Tom, who found himself in the unaccustomed position of frequent idleness. On the dot of four in the afternoon, when the official workday at the institute ended he would race to the parking lot and head home, there to shower and change when a dinner invitation was looming, as was frequently the case. Most of his colleagues, from Snyder on down, had insisted on "having him over at the house," instead of giving him one big farewell party, that idea having been quashed because he was "in mourning". Other evenings he did what he hadn't done in a long time, not since Nettie had moved to California. He went to the movies. He was astonished at the breadth of themes that the multi-screen cinematic emporia were presenting, and while he didn't like everything he saw, he was fascinated and stimulated nearly all the time. It made for good, deep sleeping back in his lonely, empty apartment that was becoming emptier by the day, because he was selling off every stick of furniture, pots and pans, most books and pictures, records and CDs. His footsteps began to echo in his place, as he moved from the kitchen counter that now held his computer and a telephone alongside the percolator and the blender, to the single bed now in the master bedroom underneath a remaining wall lamp.

The selling off of his belongings was accomplished largely by the energetic initiative of his neighbor across the hall, Phyllis Cole, who had volunteered for the job over Tom's protestations.

"Hey Tom, no problem! It's fun for me, all right? What else do I have to do all day, with Winston still on carrier duty and Margie in pre-kindergarten now. Heck, I'd love to sell your stuff for you. You just pay for the ads, and I take care of the rest!"

There was no point in arguing. Phyllis was right. And every other day or so, when she had sold something, she'd leave a note and he'd go over to her apartment and collect the checks. For the cash purchases Tom suggested she put the money in Margie's piggybank. "My token of appreciation," he said. Phyllis, a tall bosomy woman with a head of curly blond hair, put her arm around his neck and hugged him. Her warm breath, by his ear, caused a tickle than ran down his back like goose pimples. He shuddered; it was too early for desire.

Coming home one evening—he had unexpectedly worked late—Tom found a note stuck to the screen of his computer monitor.

> Tom—
> I got a package for you. Fed-Ex. I signed for it. OK? Come pick it up. Anytime.
> —Phyllis.

He plunked down his briefcase on the one remaining stool, ripped the yellow piece of paper from the screen and went out again, knocking on the door across the hall. It was opened before he could knock again.

Phyllis, whom he had never seen in anything but casual "get-ups," as she described her daily wardrobe, was in a black low-cut dress. Her hair was done up and lipstick, rouge and mascara put accents onto her plain face that made it look interesting. Even her eyelids were shaded in some light purple.

"Oh, Tom. Come in!" She smiled broadly. Phyllis had big healthy teeth.

He noticed a table set in the dining room, with candelesticks and wine glasses. "Uh, I just came for the parcel," he peered past her. "You are expecting guests?"

"You bet." Phyllis gave a nervous laugh and pulled him inside, closing the door. She walked ahead of him. She was wearing no shoes, he saw. And more than that, she had round, sturdy calves. He had never seen her legs before.

Her apartment was a mirror image of his own—the entrance through the living room, dogleg to the dining area, breakfast counter, kitchen beyond it.

Over her shoulder she said, "I haven't gotten around yet to putting on shoes. You don't mind, do you?"

"Heck, no. I'm sorry to be barging in on you. I should have waited till morning or called first."

"Barging in!" Phyllis went around the sofa one end, he the other. "You are never barging in here, Tom."

At the dining table she stopped. "Will you do the honors?" She handed him a book of matches and pointed to the candle sticks. Only two places were set, but the china gleamed ivory-elegant and the crystal glasses seemed heavy.

"Me?" he asked, and knew instantly it was a dumb question. Still, he went on, "I mean, shouldn't you wait until. . ."

She come over and stroked his cheek with the back of her fingers. "Yes, you, Tom. I am giving you a farewell dinner. For old times sake."

"Phyllis, that's great, and you look very nice, but here I am, still in my uniform, smelling of formaldehyde, probably." More stupid words, he thought. She is trying to be nice, so be nice, yourself! Still, he hesitated, and before he could act she took the matchbook away from him and began lighting the candles, bruskly, breaking two matches before she got a flame. He saw that she avoided his eyes. The second candle's wick didn't seem to want to catch, and he wasn't sure if it was impatience or something else that made her hand shake.

He said, "Here, Phyllis—let me. I am sorry if I seem rude. This is very nice of you. You set a lovely table. It's just that I wasn't prepared for it. I would have brought some wine."

She blew out the match just before it had burned down to her fingers.

"Okay, it's all yours." She gave him the matches back. When he took them, her toothsome smile returned.

"Hey, Phyllis?" He laughed, jokingly. "Is this some heavy symbolism here, or what? You light my candle, and I light yours! All right!" The flame cought with a bluish flicker.

Phyllis closed her lips over her teeth, and he became aware of how large—and not unattractive—a mouth she had. She sounded embarrassed, "I don't know. I am such an idiot!" She shook her head so hard some of the long strands of locks she had combed up came loose, making her hair look like a fallen souffle. "When your parcel came this afternoon," she motioned to the kitchen counter towards a wrapped carton, the size of a shoe box, with colorful express labels stuck on it, "I thought, hey, this is probably the last time I'll have reason to speak to you, and I came up with this idea that I would cook us a dinner. As I said, for old times sake, and with Margie still at her grandparents house in Bernardsville—it was my mom-in-law's sixtieth birthday last Friday, and I went up to New Jersey with Margie, I bet you didn't even notice we were away, but I don't mind that, really I don't, Tom, please, don't look so embarrassed—anyway, you have always been so nice to us, and it means a lot to me to have a man around now and again, what with Win still off the coast of Somalia, and before he gets back it'll be March," she stopped and slid a finger across her eyelids, and then across her nostrils.

"Phyl, you need this." Tom pulled out not a handkerchief, for he never carried one, but a square piece of gauze and gave it to her. "Clean. Never used. Might even still be sterile. Now blow!" When she did, noisily, he patted her on the back. "There!" His hand had landed on warm skin, and he withdrew it quickly. "Phyllis, forgive me. I have been very thoughtless."

"It's okay. I understand. You have a lot on your mind." She crumpled up the gauze tissue. She smiled, "Don't you want to know what's for dinner?"

"Sure! What's for dinner? My favorite question. Second favorite, maybe."

"All American. Lobster bisque. Green Salad. Filet mignon. So what's your first favorite?"

"Uh—depends, on the occasion," now he was embarrassed.

"Uhuh. And how do you like your steak?"

"Medium well, thank you. I do wish I had brought a bottle of wine."

"No need. We got plenty. Winston built a wine cellar into one of the closets, you know, the one that was a broom closet?" She took his hand and led him into the kitchen. Only when she unlocked the closet door—"it's climate controlled!"—did she release his hand.

There was rack upon rack of wine bottles stacked into the small space, with necks of yellow, olive, red and gold foils protruding from their slots.

"My goodness, Phyllis, what a collection! I can't possibly make a choice. I might pick one of Winston's treasures, and then where would we be?"

"Win would never know. He is not fussy, keeping track of every bottle of wine. Go ahead, take what you like. A good, hearty red is what I like."

"Bordeaux, then." He pulled one out. "Saint Emilion. No way. Winston would definitely miss this one."

"For heaven's sake, Tom, don't be so timid! I am offering it to you!" Stooping, she yanked the bottle out. When she straightened up they were very close, face to face, breast to breast, and for a moment their eyes met.

Tom quickly bent forward and pecked a kiss on her cheek. "Thank you, Phyllis. A generous offer." They stepped away, and Phyllis locked the closet.

Tom uncorked the wine near the kitchen sink and said casually, "We should let it breathe a little before we drink it." He put the bottle on the countertop, next to the parcel.

"Right. I never understood what breathing means for a wine, but never mind. Want a wee Scotch to wet your whistle, Tom?" She affected a brogue that sounded almost genuine, and when Tom commented on that she said, "My father was a Scot. He used to talk like that."

"Was? Past tense?"

"He died, when I was ten."

"Mine, too, when I was about that age."

"I know. Nettie told me. We used to talk a lot when we were very pregnant."

"Did you? I never knew you were close."

She handed him a glass with the golden liquid. "If you want ice, you are on your own. Cheers." They raised their glasses to each other.

Then she said. "We weren't what you would call close. Good neighbors. Companions in pregnancy. Nettie was . . ." she hesitated, then shrugged.

"Nettie was what?"

"Too beautiful, if you must know!" She sounded almost furious. "And too educated! A doctorate, to my measly B.A. from Ohio State."

"Oh, come on. You make Nettie out to be a snob. She was not that, was she? To you?"

"No, she wasn't, Tom. But that's not the point. It was my feelings I am telling you about. Thats what people live by, their feelings, don't they?"

Tom smiled. "Tempered by rational thought, if we are lucky. Besides, you may be putting yourself down. You are a woman of beauty in your own right."

She slammed her glass down on the counter. "Don't be an ass, Tom! Nobody has ever called me a beauty, not in high school, not in college, and certainly not now!"

"Whoa, easy, there! Come here." He pulled her towards him and put his arms around her waist. "Now listen up. Phyllis Cole, you are a true, genuine beauty in mind and body. And I kid you not." He hugged her tight. "So, from now on you can't go around saying that nobody called you a beauty."

She groaned and put her head on his shoulder. "Oh, geez. We better stop while we are ahead." She looked up and began to smile. "You are something else, you know, Tom. I'll miss you."

She composed herself by walking over to the box of tissues, ripping one out and blowing her nose heavily into it. She came back and poured more Scotch into their glasses. She walked back, picked up a loaf of bread and put it in the warmer oven. She started the gas underneath a pot on the range and began stirring gently. All the while, Tom watched her, arms crossed over his chest, leaning against the sink, sipping his drink.

"Do something," she said.

"Gladly. What?"

"Open your parcel. Anything. Just don't watch me all the time."

"Okay." He turned around and picked up the parcel. It was heavy. The label said "Seidel Verlag Frankfurt a/Main". A well known medical science publisher. "Medical books," he said. "Just what the doctor ordered. The latest handbook on bacteriology probably. How's that grab you?" Actually, he could not remember ordering anything, but perhaps the institute had done that for him. He put the parcel back.

She shrugged, "Whatever. I had better put my shoes on. We can eat in five minutes. After the soup, I'll make the salad, while you cook the steaks, if you don't mind? Get them done to your taste."

They sat down on opposite sides of the small round table. Phyllis had ladled out the soup in the kitchen, and they had each carried in their bowl. The french bread was crisp and hot. Tom waited to see if Phyllis was accustomed to saying grace, but when that was not forthcoming he took his first spoonful. He pronounced it excellent, and asked what the spice was she had used. "Oregano," was the answer. Phyllis plonked pieces of bread into her soup and said to him, "I love it this way. Bread and soup. My dad used to take us camping, three girls and my mother, and we'd always have soup and bread. Or beans and bread. He said you can't go wrong with your basics. I was just a little kid, but I never forgot it."

"The basics," Tom nodded. Then he said, "I think the wine has done enough breathing," and got up to fetch the bottle and to pour. "To you, Phyl, a great dinner, a great idea. My compliments." They drank. It was a good wine.

They spooned their soup in silence for a while. They looked at each other and smiled. There was a certain awkwardness that seemed to have descended on them. A fear, perhaps, to say the wrong words, to offend unwittingly.

Phyllis broke the spell. "Did you really mean that—about this being a great idea?" She leaned back in her chair and put a piece of dry bread in her mouth, then took a swig from her wine glass.

"Absolutely. In fact, I'm ready for seconds."

"I wasn't talking about the soup, Tom. I'm talking about the idea of the two of us sitting here, alone, at a candlelight dinner. Do you honestly think that is a good idea? After all . . ." She let the phrase hang.

"After all what, Phyllis?"

"Don't be so dense, Tom. I, a married woman whose husband is away serving his country, am entertaining a gentleman in my private quarters, alone."

Tom made light of it. "I think your privates are perfectly safe from this gentleman, Phyllis." He smiled.

"Uh." She got up, with his soup plate, and went to the kitchen for his second helping. When she got back she refilled their wine glasses, too. She looked flushed in her face.

"One thing I can't stand, Tom, is dishonesty. I'm allergic to it, to the weaseling around," her hands snaked over the table cloth, "around certain delicate subjects."

"Like what subjects, Phyl?"

"That's just it. I can't say it. I'm doing the weaseling here."

"Maybe I can help you put it into words?"

"You probably could, but this is my ticket. I've got to say it."

"All right." He put down his spoon and looked at her. "Say it."

"This phrase meant to be funny—about my privates being safe from you—I know they are. Seriously, you are not the kind of man a woman had better be on guard against. On the contrary, you are the proverbial nice guy, considerate, polite, caring."

Tom grimaced, "This is a compliment? I'm not gay, Phyllis."

She laughed, her horsy laugh, "I know that, too! That's the first thing a woman can tell about a man." She put her hand on his arm. "Look. Here we are, the two of us, you without your woman and I without a man. Know what I mean?"

"You are still doing the weaseling, Phyllis. And yes, I know what you mean. May I say it?"

"Be my guest."

"Number one, I already am your guest, Phyllis! Number two, what you are getting at is that I also become your lover. For tonight. How am I doing?"

"Bingo."

"Right." He nodded. "End of weaseling. Now we can talk."

"Talk?" She made a face. "These things can be talked to death, Tom."

They were still in a semi-jocular mood, and a little bit drunk. Tom replied, "Phyllis, we have to know our parameters. I mean, you don't expect me to get up and carry you to the bedroom, do you? You're tall, I'd stagger, I'd bump your head, or skin your knees before we even got there. Pooped out, too." He demonstrated with exaggerated body language, finally dropping his arms down.

"Christ!" She laughed out loud. "I like you, Tom. Really, you're a kick-and-a-half." She said, "Eat your soup. We got some cookin' to do."

But he shook his head, "I'd rather skip this, if you don't mind. I can't cook on a full stomach."

They went back into the kitchen, Phyllis wagging her finger at him, "Oh you!" And Tom carrying his soup plate and emptying it into the pot on the stove. Phyllis got busy tearing and cutting lettuce, endives, arugula, green onions, mushrooms, bell peppers and tomatoes into a colander, washing the salad and drying it in paper towels, rubbing the wooden bowl with a clove of garlic and dumping the salad into it. She put the steaks in the oven, along with some precooked spuds, set the timer and told Tom to watch them and not let them burn. She turned her attention to the salad dressing. "How do you like it, tart and lean or hot and sweet?" she asked him. Tom grinned, "How about lean and sweet?" She retorted quickly, "You can't have it both ways, Tom."

He grabbed her by the waist and pulled her towards him, "Why not? I am lean and you are sweet. You tellin' me it don't go together?"

"Oh geez. Perfect timing, Tom. Just great." They stood close, unmoving for a moment before she freed herself from him.

There was some Scotch left in their glasses; he brought them over and said, "Let's finish this. In fact, Scotch goes very well with steak, why don't we stick with it. I'd hate to take another one of Winston's finest."

She took her glass, emptied it with one quick sip and said, "Will you leave Winston out of this, please? What we are doing here has nothing to do with him." There was an angry edge to her voice.

"Phyllis, it has a lot to do with him. You are his wife and I am his brother officer."

"So?" She returned to her furious mixing of ingredients, with her back to him. Her hair was working itself loose some more.

"So, we've got to watch it, Phyl! So far we are safe. Beyond that, well, you know the boundaries as well as I do."

She turned around. "Would you admit to an attraction for me? Be honest!"

"Of course."

"Thank you. Because I've already made enough of a fool of myself going gaga over you." She turned back and let some honey drip from a wooden spoon into her concoction. "I don't know where this is going, Tom. All I know is that there is a gender bias at work here. The little woman sitting at home, minding the kids and her knitting. Totally reliable. Sex life put on hold, for months at a time. Come menopause—ten years down the pike for me, Tom!—we won't miss it anymore anyhow. And the men? Do I know what Winston is doing when the fleet puts in at Naples? Is he going to stay aboard in his cubbyhole, writing love letters to me?" She continued, not expecting an answer. "Or is he going out with his buddies, for some fun time? Huh? You brother officers? What are you doing, months away from home, what are you doing for fun, for sex?"

Tom said, "It's not an easy question to answer. Everyone has to live by his own considerations."

"Oh, don't give me this highfalutin' crap, Tom! Don't tell me you guys don't know how to get around those considerations! I don't want to know what you do. I really don't, because I don't care. I know what it's like, when you are in the prime of life, and the juices are flowing. And I don't mean just hormones. There is this aching desire to be with someone, to care, to caress, and not to be alone all the time. You must know what I mean, Tom. You are all alone now, and I am alone, temporarily, and I can't see what's so terribly wrong for the two of us comforting each other." Her last words came out in a half-choked cry. Tom went to her and turned her around. There were tears rimming her eyes. She put her head on his shoulder, and as he was patting her bare back he did not, this time, withdraw his hand.

He whispered into her hair, "Tell you what. Let's take the steaks out of the oven, put the salad into the fridge, and let's you and I go somewhere where we can comfort each other. What do you say?"

She took her time to reply. Not more than a minute, an endless minute until he felt her nod on his shoulder. She kicked off her shoes, took his hand and led him down the hall, bypassing what was obviously her (and Winston's) bedroom, to a guestroom. She did not switch on a light, but since the window looked out on the well-lit common park area below, it did not matter; the main furnishings were plainly visible, a double bed, a pair of nightstands, a mirrored dresser. In one quick swoop she tore the cover off the bed. To Tom she said, "Please put your uniform in the closet. I don't want to see it around for the rest of the evening. I'll be back in a minute." When he stood, mute, she puckered a kiss on his cheek. "Don't worry. We'll go with the flow."

It was much more than a minute before she came back. Tom was just bending down to pull off his socks when he sensed her entering the room. As he turned, still somewhat doubtful about this adventure, he saw her standing there in the dim light, her arms akimbo. The trees outside rustling in the wind were casting flickering shadows over her naked body. At that moment he was smitten. He stepped forward, cupped her breasts and kissed her. They embraced, and as in a ritual dance they approached the bed, and still caressing sank down on it, their congress interrupted only by the need to put on some protection. That was cause for some brief merriment when it became clear that both Phyllis and Tom had provided for it. But it did nothing to impede their ardor. Very soon after, sighing, they fell back and curled up against each other. Sleep overcame them intermittantly, as did their desire, although now their lovemaking was less frantic and more husband-and-wifeish. By midnight they rose, showered together and clad in robe and bath towel, went back to the kitchen. It was a meal of dried-up steak, hard potatoes and limp salad that they dug into, but they wolfed it down hungrily. Lingering over some espresso, loathe to let the magic end yet only too aware that it had burst, like a soap bubble, Phyllis said, "I am driving up to New Jersey tomorrow. No, wait! It's Saturday already, isn't it? Today! I am going up there in a few hours to pick up Margie, coming back Sunday night. Margie has to be back in school on Monday. The little ones have to rehearse, her class is putting on a Halloween Pageant, as the school calls it. Imagine! When I was three I was still playing in a sandlot." She slurped some of the hot liquid. "How about your little one, how is he coming along?"

"Bertie? Fine, very well in fact. Oh, I'll probably be leaving next week, Phyl. I'm not doing any real work anymore, and what with accumulated holidays due me, plus unused leave and stuff, it's time to call it quits."

"Oh."

"That's just as well, isn't it? Considering?"

"Yes." She straightened up. "Just as well."

He took her hand, "I want to say something."

But she withdrew it, "No, don't."

Unperturbed he continued, "You have done us both a great, kind, important favor. You have saved us from self-pity. We should be grateful."

She rose so abruptly that her chair fell over. "I'm going to bed now." Her face was red and she tried not to look into his eyes. "Can you let yourself out? And don't forget your parcel."

"Phyllis," but she was down the hallway already. He heard her bedroom door open and close.

He sat for a little while longer, wondering, for the first time even considering, the possibility of a new love. He wondered if he should pursue her in earnest; there was no question she had engaged his heart. By the same token, had her heart been engaged for him? He wasn't sure. All he was sure of was that a whole mess of complications would arise if he pushed things. With a sigh, he got up and picked up her chair. Best to let it be. To let it be. Just like that. Pick up his marbles and go.

He suddenly felt utterly callous. He'd had his fun, got his rocks off, time to go home, huh? Is that the way the game is played? Was it a game?

Barefoot, he tapped his way through the dark hall to the bedroom. He knocked lightly on the door. "Phyllis? I want to talk to you. May I come in, or do you want to come out? Just for a moment?"

He heard a muffled sound, but no footsteps. He opened the door. In the half-dark room he saw her stretched out on the bed, still in her bathrobe, clutching a pillow. As he approached her, she did not tell him to go away.

"Phyl," he took her hands in his, "I'm sorry about the asinine remark I made out there. It was stupid. I just couldn't find the right words."

She nodded, not saying anything. Her cheeks were moist, glistening in the reflected outside light that came from the window.

"What I meant to say, Phyllis—and please bear with me if I still don't get it right—I haven't much practice at this sort of relationship. Anyway," he leaned over and kissed her hands, "I want you to know that you touched me, my heart has been opened by you. I don't know what happened to me, with Nettie's death and all, and I haven't the vaguest idea yet where I am going from here. But I can tell you this much, meeting you, and being with you has been a wonderful, heartwarming moment in my life. That's what I meant to say, out there in the kitchen, when I said grateful. Damn inadequate word, I know."

Phyllis said nothing, but he felt her clutching his hands. Then he saw her nod, and releasing his hands she half rose and put her arms around his neck. He embraced her. They swayed back and forth, hugging. In the end she kissed him on both cheeks and released him.

He stood up. "I must go now, Phyllis."

"Yes," she whispered. With her fingers she wiped the sides of her eyes.

"And, Phyllis, I will not write to you. Okay? You understand?"

Again she whispered. "Yes."

He said, "Yes," nodding to her, and without looking back left the room.

He dressed quickly, his tunic open and shoes in hand. He tiptoed through the apartment, picked up the parcel and quietly let himself out.

He knew that he would not be able to sleep. After he got out of his uniform and put on his old sneakers, he returned to his kitchen and took a bottle of water from the fridge. Sipping it, he eyed the parcel.

It was a regular blue-and-red express box, sealed tightly in clear plastic and with a regular label attached outside in a stick-on envelope. On the sender's side of the label, even though it came from a medical publisher in Germany, it showed it was mailed from New York, with a street address he recognized as being in lower Manhattan. On the recipient's side, he was correctly identified as Dr. Thomas V. Campe at his home address including apartment number. He was quite sure that he had not ordered any books from Germany. His curiosity aroused, he took a kitchen knife and slit open the plastic sheeting, peeled it away and pried open the lid of the box. That proved cumbersome, as the box seemed tightly sealed all around. When it finally yielded, he pulled out a pair of large and heavy books, again sealed in plastic. Handbuch der Mikrobiologie, 3. Auflage, edited by a consortium of scientists at the Maximilian University in Munich. He was becoming a little annoyed; these books were—never mind how authoritative—expensive tomes that he had not ordered, and he would have to send them back before breaking their plastic seal. Where was the invoice? He looked into the box. Nothing. He took the shipping label out of its envelope on the box and studied it. It had been an economy two-day shipment, weight given as ten pounds and the value as $100, both figures being the upper allowable limit for this kind of express delivery, as he read from the small print on the label.

That struck him as odd. The weight seemed about right—he hefted the books in his hands—but the even one hundred dollars could only mean that the actual value was somewhat higher; he knew about the price of medical books. No way was he inclined to pay for this. So, where was the invoice?

Impatiently he cut a clean line across the plastic covering and worked it off the books. Taking volume one into his hand and opening it, he found he could not move the pages, they seemed glued together on three sides back to the binding. But most of the rest of the book, underneath the whole of the title page, felt soft to his touch. Probing carefully with his knife, its sharp point cut right through only to meet firm resistance again.

He stopped. A red light went up in his mind. Caution! Think, These books are fake, they are hollowed out. Why, and what do they contain? His heartbeat picking up speed, he stared at the books on the kitchen counter. Let reason prevail. List the possible, the likely contents.

A bomb?

He dismissed that idea when he considered that for such a device to work it would have to have a timer, and some kind of electrical trigger even if plastique was involved. As well, he could not imagine himself the target of a bomb plot; nobody stood to gain by the notoriety of such an assassination, and whoever the senders were they would invite immediate, official scrutiny.

What else, then: Drugs? Cocain? Heroin?

Possibly, but several kilos of either would, he guessed, have a street value of a million dollars or more. And even so, what could he be expected to do with it but immediately turn it over to the authorities?

So then—cui bono? Who benefits?

There had to be something else inside those books and now was the time to take a chance and find out what.

He strode back to his bedroom and pulled his medical bag out from underneath a pile of gym clothes in his closet. Made of expensive tooled leather—a graduation gift from his mother—he had never actually used it but he knew it contained a set of surgical instruments and sterile packages of gown, face mask and gloves which he proceeded to put on. The whole of which, he realized, would not save him from a violent discharge if such should occur but would serve well enough to keep chemical or other contaminants off his person. And so prepared, he approached his mystery shipment again.

He decided at first to give it an outer inspection. From his laboratory work he could guess dimensions and diameters fairly accurately. The textbooks' size—German ones especially—would have to be eight by twelve inches, with a thickness of three inches or better. He put his nose down to smell it, sniffing vigorously. No detectable odor, not even that of freshly printed paper. He lifted up both books and shook first one, then the other near his ears; he could hear nothing moving inside, no metallic clicking.

All right. He pulled the cap down over his forehead, and the mask up to the rim of his glasses, took from his instrument case a scalpel and a pincette and slowly, meticulously worked the cover page off its glued edges. He had it done in a few minutes. With thumb and forefinger of both hands he lifted the page and folded it over.

He was staring at three same-sized packages wrapped tightly, in the kind of opaque white plastic used for ice cream in grocery bags. The packages were kept together and in place by cello-tape.

Very quickly, and less carefully he went to work on volume two, and when he peeled back that page he saw an identical packaging arrangement inside. Returning now to volume one and then to two, he swiftly cut the tape all around the edges, lifted out the packets and cut them loose from each other.

He was staring at six identical little bricks, lined up on his kitchen counter. Same size, same weight, same compact feel.

His mind was still on drugs. Little packages of cocaine? He would open one, a random choice, he picked number five.

Again using his scalpel, he gingerly loosened the tape around the tight little something and unfolded the covering. It was an ordinary ice cream bag. He stuck his hand inside until his fingers clasped a bundle of sorts. He pulled it out and stared at it.

It was a bundle all right—he couldn't believe it—a bundle of money! Dollar bills, tightly wrapped in a sleeve. The kind of fat bundle he had seen only at race tracks, where cigar-chomping men would stuff them into their pants pockets after they had placed their bets. Moola.

Quickly he went to the next packet, number two, and came up a winner again. He had the same results four more times.

Six bundles of U.S. currency, used bills by the looks of it. It was only then that he noticed the denomination—one hundred dollars! Each and every one of them, as he flipped them through his fingers.

A lot of money. How much? He had to count at least one bundle. He did so, with trembling hands. Fifty . . . sixty—he wasn't even halfway through—one hundred . . . one ten . . . one twenty . . . one fifty . . . one sixty six.

One hundred sixty-six hundred dollars bills! Which makes sixteen thousand six hundred dollars. Times six bundles, comes to ninety-nine thousand six hundred dollars. He didn't need to count the rest of them to know that four of the bundles would have a hundred dollars extra to make an even hundred thousand.

Who would send him that kind of money? In cash? And anonymously?

He began sweating, so he pulled down his mask and took the cap off his head.

There had to be a clue somewhere. He examined the wrapping again, studied the shipping label, shook the shells of books but nothing fell out. On the bottom of volume two, as he was about to put it down, he saw a stick-on label that said "Open Here" with an arrow pointing into the upper right corner. That corner was unglued and when he pulled on it the whole bottom page gave way. A note was revealed lying loose underneath. He took it out. Typewritten, or rather done on a computer and printed out in bold capital letters it said:

WE BELIEVE IN THE SANCTITY OF ALL LIFE
WE ABHOR THE WILLFUL WASTING OF A LIFE
PLEASE ACCEPT OUR CONDOLENCES
AND OUR INADEQUATE INDEMNIFICATION

Stunned, he stood unmoving as if rooted to the floor, reading and rereading the note until his hands began to shake. Realizing that he would have to keep his emotions in check, that he would have to reexamine this parcel and its meaning when the element of surprise had worn off, he decided that he would defer everything until morning. In the meantime, he would put all the bundles back into the bags, and the bags into the books, and the books into the box. As he did so he was glad that he was still wearing rubber gloves; the money did not have his fingerprints on it. Perhaps owing to his fatigue, which he now was beginning to feel, he thought that significant. He had not accepted the money.

Carefully he restored the wrapping around the box and carried it to the bedroom, pushing it under his bed for the night. With a sigh he sank down on his mattress, and pulled the blanket over him. He was sorely in need of some shuteye.

The phone rang, once, twice, three times. He grabbed the receiver. "Hello," he had to say it twice to get the frog out of his throat.

"Tom dear, oh I'm so sorry, did I wake you? I thought I'd call this number first, in case you hadn't gone out to California this weekend. Tom?"

"Yes, mother. It's all right." He looked at his wristwatch, "It's time I got up, anyway." It was a quarter past eight.

"Well, I'm sorry. If I had known I would have called a little later. Can we talk? Are you alone?"

"Of course I'm alone, mother. In an empty apartment, too." He shook his head, and noticed that he was still wearing the green surgical gown.

"It's about Fos. I would want your advice, I think."

"What about Fos? Has something happened to him?" His stepfather's deteriorating health was a source of constant worry; he expected her to say, in her well-bred, understated way, that something dreadful had happened to her husband. But it turned out to be not quite as bad; Fos had been diagnosed with cataracts on both eyes, and corneal replacement of the worse of the two was to take place the following Tuesday. His mother was wondering what advice he could give. She had never given up thinking of her son as a doctor, no matter how many times he had protested to her that he was a researcher. She wanted to know what she should do in the way of after-care, considering that Fos was also getting chemotherapy for his prostate cancer.

Tom reassured her, told her to follow the ophthalmologist's instructions exactly. And that there was no obvious connection between the one ailment and the other. Then a sudden thought struck him, "If you like, mother, I could come up to New York next week. I have leave due me, and in any case I would like to store a few personal belongings in your place instead of shlepping it all the way out to California. When's the operation, Tuesday? I'll see if I can be there Monday night."

"That would be wonderful, Tom. Really. I'd be so glad if you could. You have such a positive influence on Fos. He admires you, you know."

"I admire him, too. You, too, mom. Love yah." They hung up with Tom's promise to call her back when he knew more.

It was a true wake-up call. Under the shower Tom decided what he would do, He would drive to the institute, talk to Colonel Snyder who would surely be there as he was nearly every Saturday, and ask for compassionate leave. He had no doubt he would get it. He would take the weekend to put the final touch to his packing and discarding, and by Sunday afternoon he would be on the road, staying overnight somewhere. And he'd leave a note for Phyllis to sell or give away what was left in his apartment.

Phyllis! My god—Phyllis. What a woman. He was annoyed when the thought of her made his prick itch. Damn. Time to get out of here, for more reasons than one.

Returning to his bedroom he spotted the parcel under his bed. Another problem that had to be dealt with. When he was dressed he stuffed the parcel into an old rucksack, piled all his dirty laundry on top of it and shoved it back into the closet.

Snyder was predictably irascible at Tom's request for immediate leave, and grumpily understanding in the end.

"All right, major, go. Vaja con dios. We have said our good-byes, all of us around here, haven't we? And lately, you have been about as useful as a tit on a football. So I'll have papers drawn up for you and I'll sign them before I get out of here. You can pick them up at the office downstairs later." And before Tom could salute and say thank-you, the colonel bounced out of his chair and came around, put a hand on Tom's shoulder as he escorted him to the door. "Good luck to you, Tom. It's been a rough time for you, but things do change. Just look after yourself so you can look after that kid of yours."

"Thank you. I intend to, Bill."

"There you go. Keep in touch. Maybe we can bend an elbow together one day when we are both in our civvies, huh?"

There was absolutely nothing for Tom to do except to sign off on instrument use, return his keys and parking space, and wait for the office to call him that his papers were ready. Saturday was a slack day with half the normal duty roster. There was nobody around with whom he could shoot the breeze.

As he was packing what was left of his personal things into his briefcase he came upon the little cardboard box from Study Group Computing that contained the dozen diskettes of software Nettie had ordered and that he had scooped up from her desk in their house in Goleta. He had gone through them before, running each disk one at a time through his office computer, using that one rather than his own powerbook because it had a larger screen and a faster scroll. With time to kill, he examined the diskettes again. They all dealt with scientific material of the more basic kind, educational and entertaining, includings fonts, utilities, programs and even games. He dawdled over disk number three, an AIDS primer and questionnaire. When he brought up the file and opened it, he saw among the half dozen documents one that now struck him as odd. Instead of the usual command Open Me First that meant to provide the user with an overview and which he had learned to ignore to save time, he read the heading as Open Me Now! Puzzled, he clicked it up onto the screen.

> This is a report on a possible case of willful infection with a virus.
> My name is Natalie Goldsmith Campe. I am a doctor of veterinary medicine working at the Goleta Research Laboratories in

Santa Barbara, California. The lab is a wholly owned subsidiary of White Cross Veterinary Products which in turn is owned by New Brunswick Pharmaceutical of New Jersey.

This is Tuesday, June 29, 1993. I am writing this at home, after work. My son Bertie has been picked up by my mother who lives nearby. My husband, Major Thomas V. Campe MD, USAMC, is stationed at the US Army Institute for Infectious Diseases in Fredericksburg, Maryland. When he leaves the Army he will also move to California. We have a happy marriage (harmonious). This 4th July weekend we will sail in the Santa Barbara Channel with our new boat. Our son will stay with my mother.

Nobody knows what I am writing about here. I will try to keep it as brief and as scientific as possible.

In our work at the lab, we maintain a large pool of animal subjects for use in research and for the production of vaccines. As a veterinarian it is my job (our job; there are five of us DVMs) to see to the good health and proper care of the lab animals. In addition, I work in the lab, Level III, on the preparation of kidney cultures derived from monkeys. We are the groundfloor, Dubuque/Iowa and Raritan/New Jersey are the end manufacturers of the vaccines. Our monkeys (macaques, and african green monkeys) are imported with Govt. License from the Philippines. They must be healthy when exported and healthy when received here. Stringent supervisory measures assure the health of our stock, and it is unusual for the animals to become ill while here.

It was a great shock, therefore, to discover that several of the monkeys fell ill with a fever that began to spread because of the throwing of feces by the infected animals. But quick measures of isolation, disinfection, and the removal of infected animals brought it under control.

We are now investigating the nature of the illness (a hemorrhagic fever) and how it occurred. The virus must have been introduced here since the monkeys arrived, as the short incubation period would have caused an outbreak during the 2-week transport by ship. The infection could have been caused only by accidental contamination, or by sabotage. Management has decided it was accidental.

I do not believe that that is so. I suspect that a coworker, a temporary research fellow from the Tropen Institute in Hamburg/Germany, by name of Olaf Runge Ph.D., has willfully introduced a viral agent into our monkey population.

Some weeks ago I saw him put a vial into the incubator that was not part of our strictly-adhered-to routine. When I asked him about it he denied doing so, and when I checked the incubator after the timer was off (next day) the vial was gone.

Also I came across a letter (when I went to answer the phone on his desk) that addressed him as a member of A. L. A. R. M., an animal rights group. He snatched it away when he saw me glance at it.

Olaf is an unpleasant man, small and pudgy, fond of sweets, odd, vain in the way he dresses (he calls it non-conformist) and with wispy beard. He pretends to be a lecher (I had to put him in his place on more than one occasion).

Last Friday was his last day at the lab. He made one last attempt to get to me by pushing me against the work bench trying to grab my behind. I felt a dull pain on my left buttock before I could push him away.

Yesterday, Monday, I woke up feeling ill. I thought it was PMS or the flu. But I am not getting better, just worse. Today I will draw some blood and do a culture; I should know in 24 hours. Meantime, in case I carry a virus, I have brought Bertie to my mother's place.

Wednesday, June 30th. This morning I talked with Tom, who is in Atlanta/GA attending a conference. I know I sounded cranky but I am feeling so lousy.

Wed. night, at the lab they identified the virus that killed our monkeys. A filovirus, of the same kind that broke out in Africa back in the '70s. It kills all it infects. It is not airborne but transmitted by body fluids/excreta. If that's what he injected me with I am doomed!

I can not believe it yet. What should I do? I can't think straight. I don't want to call anybody until I know for sure. So tomorrow I will go down to the boat and load it up for our sailing. I was going to do that Friday but by then it may be too late. Or I may feel better by Friday! Either way, I must be cautious. The boat is the best isolation ward I know.

Tom will come on Saturday! Then we will both know.

Bertie is safe.

I don't know what to do. I pray God help us.

Tom sat motionless, uncomprehending at what he was staring at on the monitor screen. He quickly read it through again, a dreadful certainty slowly settling down on him. This was Nettie speaking, his wife, his love, already at death's door when she spoke to him on this disk. Doomed, as she had feared. He buried his face in his hands. When they became wet, and when he felt watery snot seeping out of his nostrils he took his hands away. He grabbed a paper towel, cleaned himself up and blew his nose. But the ache in his heart stayed.

He looked around. There was nobody nearby. The last portion of Nettie's message was still on the screen. He quickly quit the file and ejected the disk. He looked for and found a small flat container of sterile gauze which he nearly emptied, put the diskette inside and placed some layers of gauze back on top of it. Then he hid it under papers in his briefcase. The box with the rest of the disks he put into his raincoat pocket; he would have to go through each of the diskettes later to see if there were any other messages hidden somewhere. He doubted it, but he had to make sure there weren't.

Suddenly feeling restless, he went downstairs and inquired about the status of his papers. The tall rangy PFC, a kid from Minnesota with a name tag of A. C. BRETT but known to all and sundry not as "Ace" but "Brains," said, "All ready, major. I was just about to call you."

"Thank you, Brains. I'm in a bit of a hurry."

"Yessir." He handed Tom an envelope. "Not easy, huh, major?" He scrutinized Tom with his steely blue eyes. "Leaving the Army?"

"No, it's not easy. Maybe you'll feel the same when you've been in as long as I have."

"I won't be staying in, as long I mean, sir. I'm letting the Army retire me, what with all the downsizing that's going on, and go to college on the money they'll pay me." He grinned. "The new G.I. Bill."

"Right. Good luck to you, Brains."

"And to you, sir." He saluted smartly. Tom returned the salute, and that turned out to be the last time he would have occasion to do so.

Cab Blumenfeld

As Tom drove north on Sunday afternoon, his mind a jumble of thoughts and emotions, there came to him one name, with such stentorian force that he banged his fist on the steering wheel. Charles Auguste Benet Blumenfeld.

"Cab!" he shouted. "Why didn't I think of him before!"

Why, indeed.

Cab—not Charlie, never Chuck—Blumenfeld was his oldest friend. They had met when Tom, a gangly ten-year-old and shy after his father's death, had been enrolled at University Grammar school and was assigned, perhaps with some malicious intent in view of his German surname, to the only Jewish boy in the class, Charles Blumenfeld. The program, pretentiously called alter ego amicus, was meant to allow a new boy to become more quickly assimilated to the ways and rules of the school by seconding a seasoned classmate to the neophyte. It could not have been a more felicitous choice. Both boys liked each other instantly, the lithe, sinewy Charles with the tightly curled dark hair and gray-green eyes that more often than not sparkled in mischief—mischief just committed or just contemplated—and the tall, blue-eyed Thomas with the serious mien, who found it hard to laugh spontaneously. They complemented each other perfectly. It was intuitive, instinctive at first.

"Y'know what they mean by alter ego?" There was a taunt in his voice when Charles said that. "It means like being a brother! You want to be my brother?"

"Yes," Thomas nodded earnestly, and offered his hand.

As if taken aback Charles hesitated a moment, then took his hand and shook it up and down. "All right! All right!"

And brothers they had become, inseparable at school, at sports, at home, to the consternation and, gradually, amusement of their families, for their backgrounds could not have been more diverse.

Where Tom's father had been an officer in Hitler's Wehrmacht and later a diplomat for the fledgling German Federal Republic, Charles' father had barely escaped from Berlin in 1939 and reached Shanghai, the only port in the world that would accept Jews without visas. Wolfgang

Blumenfeld profited from the experience, and when he came to the United States he had learned two valuable lessons: to look out for himself, and how to make money. He applied both of these successfully, eventually rising to the head of the corporation that employed him, an oil equipment leasing company.

Their mothers, too, would not have crossed paths without their boys' frequent visits. Eleanor Whitney came from about as blue a blood as runs in American veins, with relations like spider webs across the Yankee aristocracy. Yvette Benet, on the other hand, was a Haitian Creole, a ravishing beauty who was a student at the Sorbonne when Wolf Blumenfeld met her in a box next to his at the Paris opera. It was a whirlwind romance, the pale dark-eyed former convent girl marrying the worldly, older businessman at the Free Scottish Presbyterian church in Chantilly, both having given up their faiths for love. Charles, named Auguste Benet after his maternal grandfather, was born the same year as Thomas, and both boys remained their parents' only children. Their friendship grew with each year they shared at school, so that when it came to choosing a college, it was only natural that they would attend the same one, applying to all of the Ivy League schools in hopes of getting accepted by at least one. Princeton drew the lucky number, as most Whitneys had gone there before; as for Charles, his test scores were enhanced by his double affirmative action status, qualifying both as a Jew and a black.

College had a curious effect on the boys. Tom with a pre-med major hitting the books hard, with little time for fun and frolic, whereas Charles, "Cab" by then, had discovered the lure of women and money. Kept on a short leash by his father he fast acquired the power of the self-made man, by selling life insurance part-time not to college students—they had no money of their own—but to local businessmen whom he impressed with his smartness and expertise. The women followed naturally, as he tooled around town in his red Porsche and charmed them with his masculine good looks.

It was at graduation time that "the boys," as they were still known to their families, went their separate ways, Tom to the medical school of the University of California at Los Angeles—once again, the only school that accepted him, perhaps partly because he had contracted with the Army to become a medical officer. Cab, who simply moved back to New York and easily enrolled at Columbia law school, was furious at Tom's decision.

"Why are you doing this, Tom? El-Ay, plastic lotusland, and the Army? Why are you punishing yourself? What's going on here?"

"Money," Tom answered simply. They had not been seeing much of each other throughout their senior year, Cab breezing through it and frequently being absent, seldom without a blonde or a brunette on his arm. Tom, on the other hand, saw his father's small legacy dwindling away, and despite Foster Watson's repeated offers of financial help Tom was determined to make it on his own. It was a matter not of pride so much as of conviction that in order to be fulfilled in his chosen profession he would have to get there by himself. He eventually had his mother side with him, when she realized that her son did not bear the slightest resentment against his stepfather, rather that it was a matter of principle, a trait he undoubtedly had inherited from her.

"Money!?" Cab was incredulous. "You let money stop you? I'll give it to you, a loan of course, put you through med school, set you up in a practice on Park Avenue. It's a business proposition, Tom! We'll both profit!"

Tom smiled and declined the offer. Thereafter, they were three thousand miles apart, and even though they did see each other occasionally—Cab was best man at Tom and Nettie's wedding—their meetings grew sparser and less urgent as time went by. Still, there was no doubt in Tom's mind, and he was sure in Cab's as well, that they were the same old friends. A natural, easy reposing in each other's confidence. That had always been the hallmark of their friendship; they could tell each other anything, if they chose to do so.

With that disturbing tape of Nettie's inside his windbreaker pocket, and with those mysterious bundles of hundred dollar bills in his rucksack, Tom was in need of a friend's calmly considered opinion. Yes, Cab would be the man to see, his judgment invaluable.

He gnashed his teeth that he hadn't called him from the apartment; what if Cab was out of town? During the week Nettie died Cab was in Europe somewhere, his own mother was unable to tell Tom's mother just where Cab could be reached. Well, no matter. Chances were Cab would be in New York City; he had a business to run, a very exclusive, very profitable agency for insurance and estate planning. And the summer holidays were over.

Among the calls Tom did make from his apartment before he left was one to Santa Monica, explaining to Laura that he was going up to New York with the rest of his portable belongings which he would store with his mother, and to please bear with him a little while longer until he'd return to California. A thought occurred to him as he spoke with Laura, "Laur, I've been meaning to ask—what do you hear from Carla?"

"Nothing, actually, Tom. At least, she hasn't sued us yet!"

"But she lives nearby in that Brentwood condo? Where'd she get the money, a hundred thou or so, wasn't it?"

"I don't know. Al thinks she's always had some dough stashed away. I'm not so sure about that, my mother has always been hard up for cash, that was one of her problems making her such a bitch. I don't know, Tom. Maybe she got a loan, in anticipation of suing us for custody." She chuckled.

"Well," Tom decided to drop the subject, "I just thought I'd ask." Then he talked to Bertie, told him that he loved him and would see him soon.

The other call was to his mother, he said he was coming to the City for a few days and asked if he could bring some of his stuff to store with her temporarily. And did she think Max the doorman would find a buyer for his car?

Yes of course, was the answer to both questions, and a warm "glad you could find the time, Tom."

He made a final call to Phyllis's answering machine saying he had to leave for New York, family problems et cetera, and he'd be taking his clothes and valuables with him in his car. Would Phyllis please dispose of the rest of his things as she saw fit, for which he was leaving under her door an envelope with a blank check to defray expenses, and at the very least to buy a gorgeous, long-lasting plant as a token of his sincerest gratitude for all she had done for him. "I won't forget you, Phyllis. All the best to you."

The Sunday afternoon drive on the ninety-five was so smooth and easy Tom arrived on East Sixty-fourth Street by dinner time. Max volunteered to help schlep his belongings from the car to the deliveries elevator, and with a wink said that he might be able to get rid of the T-Bird "for a price". Tom winked back and told him to get the best price possible, "There's a twenty-five percent cut in it for you, Max."

"No problem," Max beamed.

Eleanor Watson nee Whitley, still known half kiddingly among her closest friends as "the baroness" from her marriage to Tom's father, seldom allowed her emotions to upset her composure, at least not at the drop of a hat, but when she opened the kitchen door to the back stairway where Tom's elevator had arrived she was instantly at his neck. "Oh dear Thomas," she whispered, hugging him hard, giving him barely a chance to drop the bags he had just picked up. "Dearest." She stroked his cheek. "I'm so glad you're here."

"Mother!" Tom was alarmed. "Has something happened? Is Fos . . . ?"

"No, no. Fos is all right, or rather unchanged. It's just that I had the most terrible dream, such forebodings." She shook herself as if to rid her body of demons. "I suppose I'm being very silly. We have been under a lot of strain, and so have you, and it all gets mixed up in my mind." She tried a wan smile. "Now you are here, I feel better already. Come, let me help you."

Later they sat down to a supper of salad and bread. Tom had been the good son visiting first with his ailing stepfather in the library; the old man's favorite place had become a sick room, with a hospital bed, infusion rack and a metal medicine cabinet arrayed incongruously amidst the dark wood-paneled shelves and leather club chairs. Foster's illness had taken a cruel toll, the former Princeton linebacker's erect and muscular body now skeletal, slumped against the raised back of the bed. His one remaining passion, to read when he was awake and alert, was being threatened by cataracts, his right eye worse than the left. It was the right one that would be dealt with by a famed eye surgeon on Tuesday. Tom pressed his stepfather's hand and reassured him, all would go well, and he, Tom, would talk to the ophthalmologist tomorrow to get the technical "low-down." Not to worry; the man's reputation was such that being accepted by him for surgery was a sure sign of a successful outcome.

He talked about that with his mother. "It's not the cataract I'd be worried about, Mom, it's Foster's general condition. We must be realistic. It may take years yet, but the metastases will progress eventually." He held her hand, "It is equally important that you take care of yourself. Are you doing that? Promise?"

"I am, Tom, really. I am not foolish. A nurse comes in during the day, and during the night Fos is so sedated. I put up the infusion before I go to bed, you'll see—he sleeps right through. Mrs. Wilkins has to wake him up to bathe him, nearly every morning."

"Private nurse, doctor bills, prescriptions, now eye surgery. How do you manage? Is the insurance taking care of that?"

"Well, not all of it, private nursing isn't covered, for instance. And there are deductibles and so on. But we are grateful that Fos' company still has him on their plan."

"What do you mean 'still'? Isn't that a right that is due him?"

Eleanor Watson's eyes began to wander, her hands fretting the napkin. "There has been talk that benefits would have to be curtailed, after those billion dollar settlements come in for breast implant failures." Her voice sounded almost apologetic.

"Breast implants? But Foster's company makes glass and crystal. Oh, I see! Silica. Silicone." He shook his head. "But that's ridiculous. Billions of dollars in damages, did you say?"

"That's the estimated total for the companies involved. And Foster's company has other problems, no more defense contracts and so on. So, we don't know what it'll do to his stock." Then she put her napkin back into her lap and said with forced cheerfulness, "But we are all right. We manage."

Tom sensed it otherwise. "Mother, you must tell me how you are doing. I know you bought this place with what you got out of the Palm Beach house. And you still have the Vermont summer cottage on Kashi lake?"

"No, we sold that earlier this year. One of the neighbors there made us an offer and we took it. We don't really need it anymore."

One of Tom's fondest childhood memories was of Kashi lake summers, swimming out to the floe and diving from it, canoeing, fishing, evening barbecues. He had thought of taking Bertie there after next Memorial Day, perhaps for a month or two. To get bonded, father-son, laying a foundation for the future. He said, "No, of course you don't. Better to conserve your capital. How are you doing, overall, d'you mind talking about it?"

"I don't mind. In fact I think you should know. But it's a bit technical for the two of us to get into it, here at the dinner table. Perhaps you would like to talk to our investment advisor where we have our money?"

"Mom, I don't want to snoop, but if you think it would help for me to be better informed. Please set up the appointment. Not tomorrow, I want to go see Cab, and Tuesday is the cataract operation. Wednesday is fine."

"Cab!" His mother smiled. "You mean Charles, don't you? Do you still call him Cab?"

"I do indeed, and he calls me Tom, and all is right with the world. You know us. The same old Katzenjammer kids. As his father called us."

"Katzenyummer, as I remember Mr. Blumenfeld's pronunciation."

There were only a few dishes to put away after their supper, and when Tom volunteered his help his mother shook her head and told him to pick up the phone and talk to Bertie, instead. This he did, for fifteen or twenty very satisfactory minutes, and then Eleanor took the phone and talked some more. Tom watched his still attractive mother—tall and slim, elegant even in her house dress, with hair that was carefully arranged and tinted just to avoid the drabness of gray—and wished she would not have this burden of her husband's illness to carry into her advancing age. She was only a year away from seventy, and it struck him that his father, had he lived would now be seventy already. How the time had flown by; Tom's memory of his father was frozen at the point he had last seen him twenty-five years ago. A vigorous, energetic man not much older than Tom was now. What would he be like today—a physical wreck like Foster Watson? Or, more likely, a match to his wife's liveliness? A feeling of pity for his mother overcame him. If only he could help, in some small way.

Cab! Cab would have some ideas. Another reason to talk to him. He only had Cab's office number, and there was no answer there on this Sunday night. Fortunately, Eleanor Watson still had the private number of the senior Blumenfelds, fellow members of support groups for the Metropolitan, the Philharmonic and the Guggenheim. Daringly—it was by now nine in the evening—Tom rang. And surprisingly the phone was picked up by a gravelly male voice. When Tom had identified himself Mr. Blumenfeld went on for several minutes, in the manner of those hard of hearing, asking him questions and answering them himself, "Where are you calling from, New York? With your mother, yes? She is well? Good, give her my regards. Your father, too, is well? Not so well? Say hello to him for me. You are in the Army, right? A colonel, by now? No? Lieutenant colonel? Major? Major. Of course, you are still young. How's the family?" It was at that point that Tom could say that his wife had died in an accident. Silence—then a torrent of condolent words, and apologies that he hadn't known. Did Charles know?

Another break for Tom. "Yes, sir, he does. And, Mr. Blumenfeld, do you have Charles' home number? I would like to talk to him."

Mr. Blumenfeld replied that yes, indeed, of course he had the number for Charles' place in North Greenwich, in Connecticut, and a grandiose place it seemed to be from the description Mr. Blumenfeld gave of it. And yes, the phone number was unlisted of course but Charles certainly would want Tom to have it. And here it was.

Relieved, Tom scribbled down the number given and repeated with emphasis which required Tom to recite it back; it was like a swearing-in ceremony.

"Whew!" said Tom when he finally hung up, and immediately dialed the Connecticut number. It took several rings but when the phone was answered Tom knew it was his friend.

"Cab—it's Tom."

"Tom! Hey Tommy, how're you doing?"

"Coming along, Cab, thank you. Listen, your dad gave me your number just now. I hope I'm not intruding?" There was some soft music going on in the background.

"You, intrude? Never. What's up?"

"I'm calling from New York, Cab, my mother's place. She's all right—before you ask—my stepfather is not so well, but that's not why I'm calling. I need to see you, Cab. It's sort of a two-ball golf club game."

"Ah," Cab's surprise was audible. "I hear you. How urgent is it?"

"Not tonight, but I'd like to see you tomorrow if I can."

"Of course you can. I'll be back in the city early. You have my office address, don't you? ICA Tower rotunda, third level. Suite 313."

"I'll be there at, say, half past nine? Okay. And, Cab? Thanks."

"Sure thing. See you tomorrow."

Cab and Tom did not join fraternities at Princeton, not so much because they had something against the "Greeks" as that they felt it was all rather juvenile, and having just escaped boarding school where same-age boy clanishness had pervaded their daily existence, often stupidly oppressive and overly competitive, they saw no reason to give up their new freedom at university. Instead, in their junior year—and this was Cab's idea who had acquired several insurance clients who were Freemasons—they asked for and were accepted into the mysteries of the Ancient Rites. It was right down Cab's alley, doing the degree work and declaiming in a mellifluous voice in open lodge. Tom was less captured by it, but he was intrigued by the long history and the "geometry" of the craft. They were, in that lodge and during that year, the only students so involved. They prudently kept their Masonic activities to themselves; the winds of change that were blowing then did not deal kindly with such "conservatism." Later, when he received his Army commission Tom asked for and received his demit; but kept alive between him and his friend were the moral imperatives of freemasonry. They sometimes referred to it in private talk. It gave them the assurance of absolute confidence and trust. Tom had just invoked that aspect in his telephone conversation with Cab.

The office of "Charles A. B. Blumenfeld, CLU, Insurance" looked innocuous enough from the outside. It had a highly polished brass plate bearing the name, and in the door frame a bell button with a small sign "Please ring." Tom put his finger to it, a buzz was heard and a tiny green light went on over the button. He tried the door and let himself in.

He was in an anteroom furnished with comfortable chairs and a magazine rack. Indirect ceiling light bathed the room in muted brightness, illuminating discreetly the wall that displayed Cab's diplomas: the BA from Princeton, summa cum laude; the JD from Harvard; the CLU from the American College. Framed also were his memberships in the New York city and state bars, and his licenses for insurance, real estate and securities. Very impressive for any prospective client kept waiting if even for a minute. On a small table sat a telephone, of the kind that was hardly in use anymore in that it cradled the receiver across its base; it also had no dial. Before Tom could do anything with it the door in the back of the room opened and there stood Cab, smiling broadly, his steel-gray eyes lively with intelligence.

"Tom!" He threw his arm around Tom's shoulder and drew him in to the office. Boxing him on the arm with his other hand, he said, "You are lookin' good, pal. Good to see you. Come on in." Locker-room-like banter.

"Cab!" Tom boxed him back. "Thanks for seeing me on such short notice."

"Hey, Tom, no problem. You'd do the same for me, wouldn't you?"

Tom nodded. He wondered about the tone in his friend's voice, his palsy-walsyness. This was not the intense, serious-minded fellow he remembered. Well, it had been a couple of years. And the way Cab was turned out, like a model from GQ, in suit and tie all right but so loose and light it was more Hollywood than Manhattan, brown tie on salt-and-pepper shirt under gray-green jacket, unpadded. Cab himself looked deliberately fit, his curly brown hair trimmed close to the skull, no beard on his pale face, his skin neither ruddy-pink like his father's nor alabaster as his mother's, his six-foot frame a straight line from chest to groin without a hint of a pot.

"You are looking good yourself, Cab," Tom said, and meant it. His own figure was beginning to get soft in the belly, and his hair needed cutting. And the tan wool suit he was wearing, with a white button-down shirt and the old Princeton tie was no match to Cab's formless fashion statement. He knew it would take a while to become a civilian but he wondered if he would ever gain the apparent ease of informality that Cab exuded.

Cab said, "Let me introduce you to my associate, Warren Watanabe. Whenever you see papers coming from my office initialed WW you can bank on them. Warren, this is Thomas Vonder Campe, my best and oldest friend." He made a grimace and rolled his eyes. "A Jap and a German. And here I am, a Jew."

"When he hired me he said he was black," Warren smiled, shaking Tom's hands. Warren was thin and hairy, with dark-rimmed glasses.

"That was before black became African-American," Cab said.

Warren said, "Ha-ha," and went back to punch the computer keyboard.

"Nice meeting you, Warren," Tom said.

"Same here." Warren waved with one hand while staring at the monitor.

Cab swept his arm around. "This is the operations center of my business. Warren and computers." He opened another door, "And this is my private office, where I do the deals. Come on in. What are you carrying in that canvas bag, guns?"

"Medical books," Tom replied.

"You never know, here in New York," Cab said as he closed the door.

The room had no outside window, was dominated by a large conference table with half a dozen armchairs around it, and had side boards with a phone and fax machine, a computer with printer, and a copier. It all looked very efficient. Cab motioned for Tom to sit down, and pulled up a chair next to him.

"So, speak to me." Gone was the tone of jocularity.

Tom asked, "Are we private here?" and pointed to the walls, the ceiling, the door.

"Totally. This is the inner sanctum. The East."

Tom nodded. He plunked the sack onto the table, shook it and let the two hefty volumes slide out. "I want you to see what I got in the mail the other day. By express delivery, from New York."

Cab looked at the half rewrapped parcel but did not touch it. "Books?"

"Medical textbooks, in German, on microbiology. I had not ordered them, and I became suspicious. I unwrapped them surgically, by that I mean with gloves and instruments. I thought they might contain acids."

"I won't asked why, yet. Go on."

"The books are hollow, all right. But no acids. What's inside them is money. A hundred thousand U.S. dollars, in bundles of hundreds."

"Now I am going to ask. Why?"

"A note came with it, from an anonymous organization. Expressing their belief in the sanctity of all life, and their condolences for my loss, and offering indemnification. Their words. Their money, too."

"Life insurance proceeds? On whose life?"

"Nettie's. She was deliberately put to death. I have evidence to that effect, on this diskette." Tom reached into his jacket pocket and put an envelope on the table.

"Wait a minute." Cab leaned forward, his gaze directly on Tom. "Just a minute, here. Before you go on, let me remind you I am not practicing law, I do insurance and investments. I cannot be your counsel, Tom."

"I don't want a lawyer. I have one. My brother-in-law in Santa Monica has very ably gotten me off the hook as a suspect in a murder investigation."

"Holy cow, Tom." Cab was shaking his head.

"What I want is your input, your counsel in terms of opinion and judgment. I need someone I can trust absolutely, to be what you were when we first met as little boys, my alter ego. Remember?"

Cab's gaze was unflinching. "You have that. Tell me the whole story. Leave nothing out. I will not interrupt but I may question you later." He got up and went to the phone. "Warren, I'm not in, until I tell you. Okay? And no calls, from anyone. Thanks." He came back with two cans of Coke from a small refrigerator. "Okay, Tom. Shoot."

It was for the first time the whole story that Tom told, cohesively and unmarred by the raw pain of Nettie's death. Where before he had declared that her death was an accident, and his own escape near miraculous, he could now unload the truth as he had experienced it, with the added insight of what had transpired later. It was revelatory, a cleansing experience that once or twice left him shaking with emotion. But he got through it, pushing himself from point to point until he had told his closest friend all that he knew.

Cab remained silent for a moment, playing with his empty Coke can. Then he moved his chair closer to Tom and put his arm around his shoulder. He spoke in a low voice, "You came to the right place, Tom. I am your alter ego, your other self. I am moved by your story, and I believe it. That is a given and will not need to be repeated. But, just to lend you a sympathetic ear is not what you have come to ask, is it." Cab shook Tom's shoulder.

"No, Cab. It is not. I need your advice. I am confused, off my moorings. I don't know where I go from here, what to do next. Nettie was murdered. An anonymous organization sends me a lot of cash money, and probably did the same for Nettie's mother, as I told you. For what reason? And what do I do with it? Do I go to the FBI? Do I tell my attorney, who with his wife is looking after my kid? Do we go to the Santa Barbara district attorney? Or what?"

Cab moved his chair back, and stretching out in it, one leg crossed over the other, said, "I will give you my considered opinion when I have had time to think about it. But right off the top of my head I can tell you this: you have to proceed very cautiously because you have already committed several unlawful acts for which you can and probably would be charged. Number one, you made a false statement to the authorities investigating your wife's death. Number two, you compounded that by lying under oath in your deposition. Number three, you withheld material evidence, to wit, Nettie's computer disk." He held up his hand. "I know, I know—you did not learn of the existence of that disk until very recently; but that'll be very hard to prove. Number four—by insisting that your wife died accidentally, you acquired additional life insurance proceeds—there probably was an accidental death rider on her group insurance, at least—fraudulently. And that's just for starters. I have no idea what kind of book the Uniform Code of Military Justice will throw at you." He paused, watching Tom groan and cover his face with his hands. He continued, "Even though I am a member of the bar, you have not come to me for counsel as your attorney. I am under no obligation, therefore, to treat your disclosures to me as anything other than personal and private. Would you agree?"

Tom nodded, of course he would. He rubbed his eyes with the balls of his hands, as if to dispel a bad dream.

"Under those circumstances, my advice to you is as that of a friend, an old friend, a trusted friend. And shall remain in the realm of total and complete confidence. Do we also agree on that?"

Lowering his hands Tom looked at his friend. "That's why I came to you, Cab. I need you, but not if it gets you into trouble as an officer of the court, as you lawyers call it. Now is the time to say so and cut loose."

"Don't be an ass. You have a tendency to be too straight, too literal. Of course I am with you, Tom. But being with you will be limited to referring you to the best criminal attorney I know if you want to throw yourself at the mercy of the Feds. You stand a reasonable chance of cutting a deal with the government that will allow you to escape with only minor damages except to your pocketbook and maybe your pride. You may also incur the wrath of the animal rights world that may dog you, if you'll pardon the pun, for many years to come. This, then, is your option number one."

Tom said quietly, "The way you have explained it, I am already tainted by unlawful behavior. I have lied and perjured myself. Right? That would preclude taking a chance on option number one."

"Not at all!" Cab gave a cackling laugh. "Lying and perjuring is part of our justice system. Prosecutors do it, defense lawyers even more, and judges expect it. Why shouldn't a hapless defendant, such as you, do it? You already got away with it, and you could twist it around and do it again. And win."

"That's a very cynical view you are espousing, Cab."

"I am not espousing it! I'm telling it like it is."

"Anyway, what's done is done. It's my own personal choice and my own private business, how I reacted to my wife's horrible death. I believe I acted in concurrence with her wishes. Under no circumstances am I going to reopen my case and in the process perhaps injure Nettie's reputation. So, option number one is out. Tell me about number two."

Cab spoke very deliberately. "Before I do, spell out for me, from your heart of hearts, what it is that you want to do. Don't spare my feelings, and certainly not your own. Tell me what you feel, at gut level."

Tom smiled, and his smile became a snarl. "Heart of hearts? Gut level? Okay, I'll tell you. I want to kill the bastard who killed Nettie. That's all. Then I'll think about what I will do next, where Bertie and I will live, and what I'm going to do for a living."

Cab sat up and slapped Tom's shoulder. He was elated. "Now you are talking! Now we've got a case, you and I." He crushed the aluminum can with his fist. "Okay. We're a team. Let me mull things over for a couple of days, do some checking, and lest we forget—immerse your money here into the finance stream, if the bills turn out to be genuine. Do you mind leaving the dough with me? Of course you'll be fully credited."

"No, I don't mind. I want it to go to my mother in the end, she is having a bit of a hard time, private nursing for my stepfather runs at about a hundred fifty bucks a day."

"I see. Sorry to hear about old Fos. How bad is it?"

"Prostatic CA, metastases, and tomorrow he has cataract surgery."

"How long do you think he'll last? Your professional guess."

Tom shrugged. "A year, could be two. Not much longer than that."

"I'll take that into account. What do you say we meet again on Wednesday for lunch? I know a real 'in' place on Lexington at Fifty-fifth. Great food. Bistro style. You'll like it."

"Sure." They rose. The meeting was over. Tom said, "What about this disk? Don't you want to make a copy?"

"I'll keep that, too. With your permission, I will put it on my secret hard disk, and this particular disk will go into my personal safe. All right?"

"Yes." They were at the door when Tom asked, "A personal question, Cab, if you don't mind. Is there a woman in your life?"

Cab grinned. "A woman? Always. All the time. I got that neat house in North Greenwich, where you called me at yesterday? It's my Shangri-La, my paradise. And there is always a woman."

Tom smiled and shook his head. Same old Cab. Still playing the field. He wondered, with a brief stabbing reminiscence of Phyllis, if that's what was in store for him, too, from now on. Maybe he could learn from Cab.

Close Calls

Even before she opened her eyes Emily knew that she had a headache coming on. There was no actual pain yet but she felt as if a vice were clamped around her temples. She lay still, the curtains drawn, the late sunrise of an October day a blessing. She also knew that this semi-darkness would only give her a brief surcease before the sun would pound against her drawn shades and come in around the edges; and then—oh gawd—the headaches would begin their drumbeat under her skull. It had been this way for a couple of months now, not every day but in each instance just before she would have her period. PMS, no doubt. The scourge of young womanhood, as her gynecologist had told her, smiling through his gray beard and scribbling a prescription for her.

She moaned and crawled out of bed, tapping her way to the bathroom where a single night-light was fading slowly against the milky whiteness of the narrow window. She opened the medicine cabinet and found immediately what she wanted—a flat box of suppositories. Foil wrapped, they looked like so many bullets. She took one out, hunkered down and pulling down her silk panties, inserted one. She rose up and leaned on the rim of the sink, looking at her mirror image. In the uncertain light, her eyes now beginning to focus, she did not like what she saw. Her hair was wild and tussled, standing off in all directions like a ragdoll's. Her eyes were bleary, with swollen lids. Yech.

She would have to wash her hair. More moaning. Might as well do it in the shower even if the conditioner would not hold. There was no time for two procedures, hair wash and dry and set, and bath. She had to be in the office by nine, come hell or high water. Important meeting. Plus, clients to see. Moan.

High water did come—she had put the plug down in the bathtub, unthinking as if she were drawing a bath, and the water had risen perilously close to the rim as she stood under the shower. This was an old apartment she was renting in the Century Club, aptly named, and no provisions had been made to drain an overflow. A piece of Park Avenue, still unchanged. Ladies only, too.

Hell, such as it was, came in the form of a phone call. Damn. She traipsed into the kitchen, trailing water, her hair in a towel.

"Emily? Emily—are you there?" She recognized the voice. High, with peculiar vowels, like the Queen of England's. Doreen, the English counterpart whom she was training to take her job before her own transfer to London. "You've got to turn on the TV, quick. CNN. There have bean some owf'l wildfires in California, burning up houses all the way down to the beach. Didn't you say your mother lives right on the beach?"

"Yes, yes. Where are they saying the fires are?" (The headache was coming on. Actual aches.) "Laguna Beach? Two hundred miles south from where my mother lives, Doreen, but thank you for calling. See you at the office." Groan.

She turned on the TV set, clicked on CNN. The fires hadn't just "bean," they were still going strong, worse than ever. Firestorms raging over the hills with a fury that came through even on her small desk set. The so-called Santa Anas, an annual Southern California phenomenon that—sad but true—one became concerned about only when it threatened one's own neighborhood. Still, it was a spectacular drama with high winds, dry air, a spark or two and—whoosh! The furies were unleashed. A day or two later the winds would turn, moisture would blow in from the sea and an eerie calm would settle over blackened chimneys and charred palm trees where the fires had cut their swath. Emily squinted at the map the TV displayed. Orange county. No connection to Santa Barbara county. Besides, her mother's house was miles away from the nearest brushland. She turned the set off. Doreen, with her English naiveté about American distances; Southern California could swallow up all of England, probably.

A sudden urge drove her back into the bathroom. Shit—the supp's fallen out. Insert a fresh one, Em, and lie down with your cheeks clamped shut for a while! And put a couple bullets into your purse, just in case. Now drink your coffee, and you might as well double your dose of vitamins, especially vitamin C. C, they say, helps in almost everything. E, too. Take an extra E. You gotta get through the day, go home early—well, by five, for sure—and rest up. On Friday she'd be taking the noon flight to L.A., on Saturday she'd get her period. She grimaced. Yeah. Great. Trade my headache for my cramps. Nick will be disappointed. Why don't men get a period, just once, so they'll know?

She made it to the meeting on time. She had dressed carefully in a black pinstriped suit over a salmon pink long-sleeved silk blouse that she closed at the neck with her favorite cameo brooch, one she got from her mother who claimed it was from her mother who in turn, and so on. It purported to bear the likeness of one Yvonne Brunner, Angelique's great-grandmother. Emily liked the name Yvonne and had secretly added it to her own as her middle name. She toyed with the idea of making it legal. Or at least use it privately.

Venturing out into the street to hail a taxi, she clutched an umbrella. Low-hanging clouds had begun to gather in the sky. She welcomed that and put on her sun glasses. No glare. She could have walked to the office, six blocks down and three blocks over, but that would have meant changing into and out of running shoes. The taxi driver cursed at her in his native tongue for the short fare. She cared not a whit and closed her eyes. She'd be closing her eyes a lot in the privacy of her office. On the phone, for instance.

By nine o'clock she entered the conference room, with a cheerful smile.

Mercifully, it was a brief meeting, a routine end-of-the-month recap and review. Emily hid behind her coffee mug and mumbled her assent to everything she was asked about. Vern Studley, the senior VP chairing the meeting, gave her a curious look once or twice but left her alone. He was close to retirement, and he had been around women associates long enough now to know what was good for him. And them. In a little over a year he'd be fly-fishing in Wyoming.

Back in her office Emily tilted the blinds to shut out the worst of the day's brightness. Fortunately, her desk was facing the interior of the room, something she had decided on when she moved in here so as not to be distracted by the spectacular Manhattan skyline. Then she put on her sunglasses. Aah—relief. Yes, she would make it through the day.

The phone buzzed. She pressed a button.

"Your ten o'clock appointment is here, Miz Dessauer." Her secretary's name was Liz, and after work the two of them were "Miz" and "Liz". Liz was from Jamaica and had a wonderful, whimsical sense of humor. "Your meeting was running late, and I was just about to reschedule the gentleman." Liz knew what ailed her boss, and she was unquestioningly supportive.

"What gentleman?" Emily asked, dully.

"Mrs. Watson's son. I have the Watson file here on my desk." Pause. "Ah, did you say we need to reschedule?"

"No," Emily croaked. "Show him in, Liz. Thank you." Get it over with.

She just had time to take off her shades and put them at the side of her desk when the door was opened by Liz who said, "Mr. Watson," and walked around him to put the file in front of Emily. When she closed the door going out she gave Emily an encouraging smile and a thumbs-up.

Despite her difficulty to focus Emily did take in who stood in front of her desk. A tall man in a tweed jacket and a wool tie who wore thin-rimmed glasses, had his hair combed straight back and who had a friendly, open face.

"Good of you to take the time to see me, Ms. Dessauer," he said.

"Oh, it's a pleasure. Do take a chair, won't you." She held out her hand. "How do you do?"

"Very well, thank you." His hand in hers was long-fingered, his grip firm but not a squeeze. Emily had a thing about hands, undoubtedly from her pianist days. They needed to be beautiful and harmonious with the whole, not bony, not stubby, and certainly not moist and fleshy. The hand she just shook met her criteria flawlessly. Perhaps this fellow was not a nuisance . . .

"You are Mrs. Eleanor Watson's son?" She opened the file and turned up the light on her desk lamp. "We have not met before, have we?" There was a need for her shades. She groped for them and put them on.

"Uh, no, we have not met before. I regret to say." When there was no reply forthcoming, he continued. "I've been in the Army until now. Away from New York."

"Have you. How far away?" Not really a question; she was making small talk. Anything to stretch the time.

"Not very far, except for the Gulf War. The Washington, DC area."

"The Pentagon?"

"No, an Army research institute. I am a research scientist."

"Really. How interesting. What do I call you? Captain? Colonel?"

"You can call me Thomas." He smiled at her. "In case you report back to my mother that we have talked. Tell her Thomas was here."

"I can't do that. Call you Thomas, I mean. I have a problem with today's easy familiarity. You must have a doctor degree. Can I call you doctor?"

His smile brightened even more. "Oh, sure you may. In which case I suggest that you take a couple of aspirin and let me call back in the morning, if you'll pardon my saying so." He stopped smiling and said sympathetically, "You seem a bit unwell, Ms. Dessauer."

"Well, I . . . " Her phone rang and she picked it up.

"Emmy," a male voice was heard before she switched off the intercom.

"Nick, you are calling at an inappropriate time . . . I know, Nick, but still . . . "

Thomas got up quietly and mouthed something, gesturing and pointing to the door. When he had let himself out and was at the secretary's station he asked, "Could you direct me to the washroom, please?" She pointed him down the hall and said to turn left.

In the washroom he went to the urinal for a moment and then came to the basin to wash his hands. Staring at himself in the mirror he murmured, "That's the woman you haven't been able to get off your mind, Tom. Since you stared at her in the flight lounge in Los Angeles back in July. Remember? Well, you can forget about her. She's an executive, she's probably married, and she's a bit weird. So, forget her. That's an order."

Back at the secretary's desk he said, "I think you were right," he looked at her name shield, "Miss Blair. Perhaps we should reschedule."

"Oh no, please. Miz Dessauer is sorry for the interruption." She got up and opened the door for him. "Please?" He shrugged and walked through.

"Dr. Watson, I am sorry for the inconvenience." Emily had her glasses off and had turned down the wattage of her lamp. "I do not take personal calls during client meetings. Liz thought, in her judgment, I should take this one."

"I understand. No problem. If I may, let me tell you why I am here. My mother is experiencing some cash flow problems, no doubt due to the low rates of interest her deposits are paying now. I was wondering if you could suggest an alternative that would yield her a higher return."

"I certainly can, yes. I know Mrs. Watson's situation. She needs a higher yield. We have made suggestions to that effect on more than one occasion. But the point seems to be that Mrs. Watson is dead set against putting capital at risk let alone drawing from it. In our considered opinion there would be nothing wrong to commit some of her funds to a no-load tax-free munibond fund for instance, that would double her income for the capital so freed."

"And she has said no to that? Your suggestion makes sense to me."

Emily nodded but stopped abruptly, holding her head by her cheekbones. A moment later she said, "Your mother is of another generation. So is mine. It is difficult to understand them sometimes. But that does not make them wrong."

He smiled. She liked to see his smile, it was so guileless, and his voice was a cultured sort of baritone, a match to his pleasant mien. There was a time, when she was still in puberty and her only male acquaintances were her roughly patronizing half brothers or pale and pimply piano students, that she would make up her "dreamboy" as she called it, a tall and good-looking fellow, handsome in manner and superior in behavior—kind, courteous, intelligent, sensitive. And more—dared she think it? Sexy! Instead, what she observed were the louts of summer camp, the fags of art and music, and the lechers of high school gyms. It took her years to realize that men were people, and had to be taken as such. They were good people, uninteresting people, bad people.

This guy, here, was good people.

Em, you do have a headache! Get him out of here.

"Are you all right?" Showing concern he leaned forward a bit as if ready to catch her if she were fainting.

"Ah, yes. Just a headache. A beastly headache. It'll pass."

"Have you had these headaches before?"

"A couple of months."

"Continuously?"

"No. Just before my period." What are we telling him here, Em?

"But prior to that, your periods were without headaches?"

"I guess so."

"What happened, between the prior and the now periods, that is different? That is the question you should put to your doctor, Ms. Dessauer." He leaned back, and half apologized. "I'm sorry. I'm out of line. Forgive me if I upset you. It, I mean, it just seemed so obvious, your distress, and I have an inquisitive mind." His smile returned. "A professional hazard. Often a pain in the neck."

She gave a weak smile back. "At this point I'd gladly trade my headache for a nice little pain in the neck, Doctor Watson. Thank you for caring, I know I am a mess today. Why don't you discuss our general suggestion with your mother, and if she is open to it, we could get into specifics next week?"

"Excellent. Will do. I'll ask Miss Blair to give me a new appointment."

Emily got up from her chair and came around her desk. He rose, too, and she walked him to the door. Reaching it, she said, "Thank you for coming in, Dr. Watson, and for your forbearance. Do give my best to your mother?"

"I will." He stopped at the door, hesitating. He said, "Don't fool with this," he pointed to her head. "Call your doctor." Then he smiled, "You see? I can't help it. All the same it was nice meeting you, Ms. Dessauer." And he was out the door.

Emily, walking back to her desk, was nodding to herself. The man was right. She'd call Dr. Fallon—not her own gray-bearded Park Avenue denizen, but a man her own age whom she had met at one of Nick's pool parties. Nice guy, with a certain panache about him, good talker, too. He said he had recently opened his own office in Malibu, in ob-gyn. She would be in Los Angeles this weekend, and Fallon could use new patients. Call him, Em, now! Through information she got his number and dialed it right away.

A very astonished Brian Fallon, still at home—she had been given his home number, and it was 7:30 A.M. in California—heard her complaint. It was a torrent of words, ending with a sob. When she told him that she would be in Los Angeles over the weekend he immediately agreed to see her Monday morning—would eleven be all right? —at his Malibu office.

She hung up, already feeling relieved. She knew now that she would get through the day; tomorrow was Thursday, she ought to feel a little better, and by Friday she'd be in Los Angeles. Lots of things happening that weekend—her birthday falling on Halloween as it always did and it was her thirtieth, too! At the new Sutters Beach Hotel, Sunday the whole mob would move on to her new place in Malibu, for a housewarming brunch even though the place was still not fully furnished. When Monday came around she should be herself again, and be able to work with Dr. Fallon on fixing this jinx in her head. And Tuesday night the red-eye back to New York. It would all work out great. Except, of course, for no sex with Nick. She felt oddly relieved about that. To her sex was not just sex but something deeper, a saying yes to someone. And for reasons she couldn't quite fathom, such a commitment to Nick did not come easy . . . even though Nick was such a nice guy.

Her mind jumped. She had to thank this Thomas fellow for pushing her into the Fallon appointment. She'd tell him that next week.

When she was a school girl Emily had developed a passion for puzzles, big, colorful pictures of paintings of the masters, none with nude bodies in them—well, not entirely nude; veiled breasts here and there as in a Botticelli or a Watteau were the most that could be gleaned—and none that were too dark like a Rembrandt or a Holbein. Her preferred puzzles were bright and naturalistic every square inch of the picture, by Dutch and English masters mainly, that almost teased her along to completion. Oh how she despaired, deliciously, when she had emptied the box and flattened out the pile of small pieces. How to begin? Which should be the first piece fitted to the second? And how she exulted when, in the end, it was inevitable that the whole picture would fall into place. Of course she knew where she was going; the puzzle box made it no secret. It was the getting there that proved a challenge, and get there she would, in the end. Emily had learned a vital lesson. She always knew where she was headed, she had a clear picture of her goal in her mind's eye. And she never failed to get there if she would, patiently and intelligently, apply herself to the task. In her business life the early lesson had paid off.

Yes, that's how she would have to deal with Nick. Patiently, putting the pieces together, until it all fit perfectly. So it was without any qualms that she immersed herself in her California weekend. Everything should go like a stage play, with Nick the producer and she the female lead in one act and the director in another.

What she had not counted on, real life not following a script, was the denouement in the third act.

Nick picked her up from the airport. On the drive into Santa Monica she thought it best to tell him that she was "naturally indisposed for the next several days," sorry about that.

"Are you, really?" Nick did not take his eyes off the road.

"Of course, I am! It's my body I am talking about, Nick!"

"I meant us, you and me. Are you really sorry, from that point of view?"

"Nick, don't be daft. It's my period! And I have had one hell of a headache these past couple of days. Do you think I planned that?"

Nick said nothing, just patted her thigh lightly, bringing his hand back to the steering wheel immediately.

At the hotel he walked up to the room with her, and tipped the bellboy. When the door had closed and they were alone, he said, "I know you are having dinner with your mother tonight. She was kind enough to invite me, too, but I declined. I hope you don't mind?"

Emily put her shoulder bag on the bed. "I don't mind, if that's what you want, Nick. We are just going to talk shop, about furnishing my house and so on. But tell me why. Is there a problem with you and her? How is her project going, are you having disagreements?"

He smiled, "Of course we are having disagreements. Angelique is a hard-headed businesswoman. Her project is coming along, not as fast as we would have wished, all of us, but that's the economy for you. Everything is a little harder and takes a little longer these days. No, that's not why I declined to join you for dinner. When we have dinner together, you and I, I want it to be just for you and me. We need to talk." He stopped and held her by her shoulders. "Unless you allow me to make an announcement tomorrow at your birthday party, Em."

"An announcement?"

"That we are engaged to be married. You won't recognize the ring you sent back to me the last time. I have had the stone reset, with little extra ones around it. Quite handsome, actually. I'm sure you'll like it."

She took his face in her hands and kissed him. "I am sure I will, Nick. That was sweet of you. But tomorrow is the wrong time, the wrong place."

"So what are you telling me—put the little gem back in its place?"

She laughed. "Your choice of words, Nick! I'm never sure if you are joking. But yes, let's wait for the right moment." She kissed him again and dropped her hands, gently freeing herself from his grip.

"I'm not a smart as you are, Em, you've got to help me here—how do I know it's the right moment? Divine the innards of chickens?"

Emily walked to the window and opened the blinds. The late afternoon sun of a hot, dry day was blazing against the glass. She quickly tilted the shutters up again. With her back to him she said,

"I am the chicken, Nick, and it's my innards." She turned around. "Do you remember you introduced me to Brian Fallon? Well, I have an appointment with him on Monday. I haven't been feeling right lately."

"Fallon? Doctor Fallon? What do you mean, in what way haven't you been feeling right?"

He sounded so alarmed that Emily raised her hand. "Nick, please—don't make something of this, okay? And don't tell my mother. Let me sort this out by myself. It's probably quite trivial."

Nick sat down on the edge of the bed. "My God, Emily, now you really got me going. Do you want me to cancel the party tomorrow night?"

"How many have you invited?"

"Oh, only about two dozen of your closest friends. I'm joking, Em. Six couples, plus your mother and myself, your obedient servant. All we are going to have is a nice dinner on the ocean terrace, and there is a jazz combo in the lounge that we could dance to. If you are up to it." He shook his head.

"Sounds lovely, Nick. And of course I am up to it. I am not an invalid! Whatever it is that's not right with me has to do with my internal chemistry. I thought I had to tell you. And only you."

"All right." He got up. "Thank you for your confidence. I appreciate it. I would have butted my head against an invisible wall. When is your appointment on Monday?"

"Eleven A.M., at his Malibu office."

"I'll drive you."

"No, thanks. My mother's surprise birthday gift for me is a new car. I am driving her back in it to Santa Barbara on Sunday, after the brunch at my new house. I am coming straight down from there to Fallon's Malibu office."

"Okay, then." He made ready to leave. "Em—Brian happens to be ob-gyn, and from what I hear a very good one. But Brian and I are not friends, we were fraternity brothers. You should not feel obligated to be nice to him, for my sake." He had the doorknob in his hands, and turned around once more, "Get some rest, Em? You do look a bit frazzled. Call you in the morning."

She blew him a kiss.

Dr. Fallon's office was with the Carillo Medical Group, in the new red-tiled, adobe colored shopping center. The medics had put themselves smack-dab between a very "in" restaurant and a fashionable food market, no doubt all vying for the same clientele. The Malibu "movie colony" was not far away.

Emily parked her car and walked towards the building. She was feeling a bit foolish, her headaches were gone, her period normal, her sleep had been restful and the parties wonderful. On her birthday Nick had been a perfect gentleman, dancing with her—he had bribed the band to play "nice to-dance-to stuff," and the pianist had Cole-Portered like a veritable Bobby Short. Nick had been unobtrusively attentive. She was almost sorry about being "out of action"—his words—when he whispered to her it didn't matter.

The Sunday brunch at her high-on-the-cliffs Malibu place was a rustic affair with pancakes and waffles and eggs and bacon and sausages, and fruit and cheeses—almost too much but since it was catered (her mother's treat) nothing went to waste, people took their time munching, hunkering down on the floor. The sun was blazing hot and the winds blew dry. Far to the south the sky still hung dirty from the Laguna Hills fires. Emily tried out her beloved old piano, a little Schubert, a little Chopin. Against the wood-pegged floor and the raftered ceiling the music resounded warmly, as on a much-beloved cello. Emily almost—almost—felt sorry Nick hadn't brought the ring; she would have cried and said yes, for heaven's sake.

Dr. Fallon was a man she would not have recognized as the one in her memory of two years ago. Where he had down to the neck and over the ears hair then, he was now short-shorn, his reddish-brown hair evenly cut down to about a half inch, continuing on into a beard that went all around his face. Then he had been clean-shaven. Where there had been wide-lens glasses there were now none. Had he gotten contact lenses? And had he always been blue-eyed?

Fallon gave her an amused look, "You hardly recognize me, is that what you are thinking, Miss Dessauer? Don't be embarrassed. I hear that all the time. The fact is, now that I am on my own, time is often short. Not having to shampoo and shave cuts fifteen, twenty minutes off my morning routine. And contacts are easier on me when I wear surgical garb. But I am still the same old Brian. Which is what you should call me. If I may call you Emily?"

Emily said quickly, "Yes, of course." But she regretted it immediately. Why hadn't she said no?

"All right then. Tell me what brings you in. You sounded desperate on the phone last week." He sat down behind his desk and looked at her.

"Well, I do feel better now," Emily began talking, slowly at first before she found the right words. They poured out of her when she was reliving the pain and strain that beset her during the past few days. Fallon took some notes but did not interrupt her.

When she had apparently finished he said, "I learn more from what my patients tell me than from the presumptions I make about what ails them. Let me escort you to an examining room where Nurse Kramer—her name is Joyce—will take your history and draw some blood. It is very helpful to have a complete blood picture at the beginning. Urinalysis we'll skip for you this time. After Nurse is through with you we will meet here again." He opened the door for her and inclined his head almost like a bow. When she had passed through he preceded her with nimble steps.

Nurse Kramer was a middle-aged woman in a white coat, her graying hair gathered in a bun with a tiny white cap on top. She came into the room soon after Fallon had brought Emily in. The very efficient-looking office was equipped with the latest gadgets and gizmos, including a computer with keyboard and monitor on a movable stand. The only thing familiar to Emily was the examining table with stirrups and the surgical lamp that hung from the ceiling like an inverted wok pot. Nurse Kramer—"call me Joyce"—went to the computer and punched up Emily's name on the screen. The information Emily had scribbled onto the registration pad in the waiting room was already on line. The interview itself was done efficiently and quickly, the nurse clicking the keyboard after every answer. There was a physical examination, also done by the nurse, that included everything Emily was accustomed to having performed by a doctor, but she was secretly glad that it was the nurse that did the palpation of her breasts. The drawing of blood was a full sterile procedure including rubber gloves and face mask. Emily found that technical wizardry odd but in a reassuring sort of way. Dr. Fallon was running a very clean shop, obviously.

Back in his office Fallon brought up Emily's file on the screen as she sat waiting, hands primly in her lap, in the chair across his desk.

"I see nothing here that indicates any obvious pathology," he said, tapping his pen against the screen. "You are an apparently healthy young woman. I expect your blood values and chemistry to be in the range of normal, too. If you could come back tomorrow morning I will have them ready for you. If you like I'll fax the results to your New York doctor, or you can have him contact me if you prefer that."

Emily nodded. "I'd prefer that he contact you, Dr. Fallon."

A brief smile by Fallon. "All right. Now, you are still waiting for me to tell you what's wrong with you. Of course I don't know that, at this point; we'd have to do some cytology and exam in mid-cycle. What I can tell you is that you check out well physically, including reflexes, although, to be on the safe side you may want to consult a neurologist about your headaches. But I do have a theory." He tapped on the screen again. "You answered yes to taking birth control pills."

Emily nodded.

"Did you bring the compact?"

"No,"

"Tell me what the pills look like, and how many?"

"Sort of pink, and twenty-one of them. I skip seven days."

"Starting again—when, on Sundays?"

"On the fifth day from onset of my period."

Fallon was satisfied. "All right. That tells me what kind and strength. Now, you know that these pills work by suppressing ovulation, and by changes in the cervix and the uterus, essentially making it damn hard for sperm to get through, and if an egg did escape, to prevent fertilization and nesting. Almost one hundred percent foolproof. But—that is quite a bit of mucking about in a person's hormonal system, and since everything in our body sort of hangs together it is not uncommon for other systems to become involved. We call that side effects, and the list of those is quite large with birth control pills. One of the side effects is a migraine-like headache, which I suspect is what happens to you each time before your period. The cure for that is to get off birth control pills, in fact I would advise it even if your headaches are not migraine. You should discuss that with your own doctor."

Emily said, after a moment, "It's that simple? It's the pill?"

"In my opinion, yes. But you should definitely have it counter checked." Fallon said, smiling again, "You are engaged to Nicholas Grady, aren't you? My old fraternity buddy? There is something I need to tell you. Unlike Nicholas, I am a homosexual. Not a fag, not gay—I hate those words and the bathhouse culture it stems from, but to put it another way, it's not women I lust after. Ideal for my business for my patients are safe from me, in more ways than one. I am HIV negative—you need to know that—and we go to great lengths in my practice to avoid even the possibility of being exposed to body fluids." He looked at Emily, who sat immobile, staring at him. Fallon continued calmly, "At the first meeting many patients do not even get to shake hands with me. Also, as I do now, I make full disclosure. Then it's up to them if they wish to consult me again or not." He smiled at her.

"My God," Emily stammered, "I had no idea. Of course, I don't mind And by the way, Nick and I are not engaged. We were once, and we may again. I don't know." She knew she was blushing.

"Well," the consultation over, Fallon switched off the computer, "I am running behind. Sorry. Please come back tomorrow at eleven and pick up your blood test results. There'll be a copy for you at the office desk in case I'm not here. Please take it to your New York doctor. When are you flying back?"

"Tomorrow night."

"Okay." Halfway out, he poked his head back in. "It was nice meeting you again, Emily. I remember you quite well from the first time. You are a very nice person. Nick is a lucky fella." He winked and left.

On the drive down to her place Emily tried to sort things out in her mind. She agreed with Fallon. It had to be the birth control pill that gave her migraines. She would not go back on the pill, and she would not go to a neurologist until her next period had passed. She wondered about withdrawal problems, but would discuss that with her doctor in New York.

Fallon was a nice enough guy, but a homo? It gave her a queasy feeling. It was not that she had anything against homosexuals. Heaven knows there were plenty of them in New York, of both genders, in her own circle of acquaintances. She had always viewed them with detached amusement but would never have entertained the thought of getting close to them. And Fallon? Brian Fallon was an obstetrician; no exchange of body fluids was a joke there, wasn't it? He'd be up to his elbows in her juices if he were her OB man, and he'd be the one cutting her baby's umbilical cord. One false snip into his fingers, and snap! His blood would be commingling with her baby's. She knew she was being ridiculous, and obviously unfair to a nice gay. Not gay! Guy, I mean guy! Geez! Emily zipped right past her left-turn lane and had to go to the next stoplight to turn back. Forget about Fallon. He was a one-shot deal. Time for lunch.

Emily was all alone in her new home, and she loved it. She liked everything about her little house, and right now at high noon, the early November sun slanting into her living room and outside the azure-blue sky over the dark-blue ocean holding her eyes again and again, she felt that this is where she would want to live. If Nick played his cards right he would have an easy time making her say yes. Yes—with nary a thought to New York, and to MetroBank, and to international banking . . . well, hold it there. After her tour of duty, as she called it, in London; then, maybe in a year's time, she would settle down to marriage and babies.

Two, she would have two. No, not two marriages; two babies! By her mid-thirties she would have taken care of that, her next major goal. She was thirty now. One more year of freedom—no, freedom was the wrong word. She'd be just as free being a mother, perhaps more so. Just in a different way. She'd probably love it, would even do some work out of her house, from right here, using the coming "information highway." Wow. Amazing.

She went to the kitchen to whip up an omelet. She had not eaten in the morning, thinking that would be best prior to a doctor visit. She now felt ravenously hungry, and instead of an omelet she made french toast while she nibbled some of the left-over canapés, sipping from a carton of milk. After lunch she'd go plant some of the azaleas and mums people had brought her as gifts. There was a plateau halfway down the slope where the previous owners had let a rose garden go to weed. She'd make a flowering paradise out of that.

And at four her mother's interior decorator would come to discuss "style" and "decor." Actually, all she needed was some nice furniture, and not too much of it. She liked open spaces, and this was just a little house.

Predictably, Dr. Fallon was not in when she came to his office the next morning to pick up her laboratory report. Nurse Kramer explained to Emily that her RBC count was a bit low, "Of course, you're having your period, dear. Do take your vitamins and minerals, though, won't you?" And her triglycerides were a bit high, "Two hundred is ten percent more than we like to see. We should run another test when you have had a normal day and have been fasting."

Emily said thank you, took her report, paid her bill at the front desk and left. Walking to her car in the parking lot she chanced to look up to the mountains. A milk-white plume was rising from the distant ridge, like a stratocumulus cloud that had lost its way. A wind, hot and dry on her face and bare arms, was coming at her in a steady stream. By the time she reached her car the white cloud had visibly grown and spread its reach higher into the pale-blue sky. She saw a lick or two of red at the bottom of the cloud.

Fire! That was a wildfire coming up over the mountains!

And now there was more white smoke rising to the right of the cloud!

Emily stood agape, her car keys still in her hand.

"Looks bad!" she heard a raspy voice say. She turned her head. An elderly man, in a blue polo shirt and a white golf cap, spindly legs under tan shorts, was looking at her. "Hope they can stop it before it gets here."

"Here? Gets here?" Emily asked dumbly.

He nodded. "Sure. Back in September of '70 I lost my house over there." He pointed in the other direction, towards the ocean, "Right on the beach. Burning timbers crashed into the surf. Fire jumped the highway, you know." He grinned with yellow teeth, "That was a quarter century ago, almost, we are due for another one, wouldn't surprise me. Well, you take care." He got into his car and waved at her as he drove off.

"Silly old goat!" Emily hissed under clenched teeth. "What're you trying to do, scare me?" But she was not so sure that that's what the old man was trying to do. Other people in the parking lot were running to their cars, getting in and driving off, and Emily quickly did the same.

What would normally be a matter of less than a minute to drive out of the parking lot and onto the Pacific Coast Highway took four or five times as long, there were so many cars pushing to the exit lane. Emily sat in her new Jeep watching through the windshield as the white cloud was billowing higher, with angry flames now licking the rim of the mountains. The powerful engine of her four-wheel drive vehicle was throbbing, the wind rushing past her open window was making an incredible noise. Emily turned on the radio and found a station that was reporting on brush fires in the Calabasas and the Thousand Oaks areas. It was obvious to her that the station had not caught on to the real news; those locations were in the San Fernando Valley some twenty miles away. It scared her. If the fires had traveled that fast from that far away to reach Malibu by now, then this was not just a brush fire, this could be a major firestorm! The winds were certainly gusting up strongly.

She suddenly had only one desire. She had to get away from Malibu, drive south to her house and wait and see. Malibu Canyon was like a trough that the winds used as the path of least resistance, and it opened like a gaping mouth onto the beach, as the old man had said. Topanga Canyon was another such trough that had also seen fires in the past. Her house was about five miles south of Malibu and two miles north of Topanga. She would be safe there, the fires would burn themselves out when they had reached the open sea.

Traffic was crawling, though, both lanes spurting forward a few yards and then stopping again. The wail of fire engines could be heard from both directions, police cars and highway patrol motorcycles, sirens howling, were coming into view. When Emily looked at her arm stuck half out the open window she noticed thin white flakes on her elbow. Ash! Quickly she rolled up the window and let the air conditioner take over. The noise level dropped dramatically, but the radio blared reporting the fire approaching Malibu. The bright noon sky darkened as if rain clouds were gathering. She was not yet out of the fire area, she realized, and fear began to crawl up her chest. Finally she had some smoother passage; with hardly any traffic coming from the opposite direction cars began to weave out and speed along, Emily doing the same, a few hundred yards at a time. In this fashion she reached her property driveway, making a quick unhindered left turn up the steep incline.

It was with unspeakable relief that she saw the tranquillity of her home as she brought the car to a stop. She jumped out and ran towards the hillside, her property extended all the way up to the firebreak road at the crest of the hill. She had to see where the fire was headed, or should she say fires, as there were those puffy white clouds rising to the right of her as well as to the left!

She found it tough going climbing through the chaparral and the tufts of dried grasses. She lost her footing a couple of times and once even stepped on the hem of her dress, nearly ripping it. Her breath was short and labored as she reached the dirt road where she could walk upright again. It annoyed her, she prided herself on being fit. It was the air, so dry and hot it made her tongue stick to the roof of her mouth.

A few paces along the road she could see over the side of her hill. What she beheld was a panoramic view of the mountains and canyons to the north, towards Malibu, and it frightened her. Thick gray smoke was rolling like a malevolent tidal wave down hill and dale, enveloping everything in its path. Red flames crept along at the bottom, exploding like giant firecrackers from the tops of trees. The wind had picked up speed, Emily could feel the hot air on her face, and in her lungs when she took a breath. Alarmed, she turned and ran back, half sliding down the hill until she reached the even ground where her car was parked. She got in—the door was still ajar—and started the motor. That made the radio come on. She listened as she wheeled the car back and forth on her parking space to make it point in the direction of the coast highway. The fire was big news now, every station she changed to was carrying reports from helicopters and forward fire fighting units, one more dramatic than the other. But one fact stood out. Her part of the greater Malibu area, the southern end of it, was not involved, not as yet. Was she too timid? Was there something sensible that she could do?

She decided that she should change clothes, for one thing. And make some phone calls, and turn on the television set. And get some bottles of spring water left over from Sunday's party. That would make sense.

Emily rushed inside the house to her bedroom and shed her skirt, her blouse, her loafers. She grabbed a cotton shirt and dungarees, socks and outdoor shoes and put them on. From her purse she removed her wallet and stuffed it into her pants pocket. Anxious for news, quickly taking the remote control she flicked at the TV set in the heavy oak cabinet, pressing the "on" button several times as she tied her shoelaces. When she looked up there was no picture. She went to the set and turned it on manually, but the screen remained dark. She tried the lamp switch—no light. Concerned, she walked to the kitchen and opened the fridge. No light came on inside. Her kitchen had a door and window to the back of the house, opening onto the back patio. Twenty yards across was a stand of Washingtonia palms that separated the area from the chaparral beyond. The palm fronds were bending in the wind, making rasping noises as they swayed against each other. The bright sunshine was gone, it was as if dusk was settling early. She could not see up the hill from where her window was, and she was half glad that she couldn't; and as she thought that she saw a deer running in queer jumps across the tiles of her patio, head stretched forward, ears back, eyes wild.

"Oh my God," Emily whispered. "Oh God, don't . . . please . . . help us . . . "

She remained motionless for only a few seconds, then she picked up the phone right next to her. It did not surprise her that it was dead. She now wished she had brought her cellular phone from New York, but that resided safely in her briefcase in her rooms at the Century Club on Park Avenue, a world away.

Taking a plastic bottle of water from the refrigerator she walked out of the kitchen, down the hall, and opened the front door. An enormous cacophonic sound rushed at her, a gale force wind was wresting the doorknob from her hand until she caught it again. With all her might she pressed the door shut and ran back to the kitchen. It was dark outside now, and the window panes seemed to be bulging. Thoroughly frightened, Emily ripped a kitchen towel from the stand, turned on the faucet and with the trickle of water that came out soaked it as well as she could. Pressing the wet towel to her face she ran to the backdoor at the other end of her house and found it opened easily. She was outside, but it was as if she had stepped into a furnace. She dared not look back though she did, for a brief glance. The inferno had begun to roll from atop the hill towards her house. To run away from it meant running down the lower side of the incline, through more chaparral and towards the chain link fence that marked the end of her property halfway down.

Unsure, she looked about her and saw, a hundred yards away and twenty feet below, her nearest neighbor's house, with a man on its roof clad only in shorts and loafers and with a straw boater on his head who sprayed a feeble stream of water from a garden hose onto the flat roof. She knew him by the name of Josh, a retired optometrist who had come to her party and bored anyone who cared to listen with tales of past and present real estate values.

"Hi, Josh!" she shouted. She found the mere sight of him hugely reassuring. And, look! The sun still shone on his house!

He waved back at her, gesturing her to come over. And so she did, climbing over the low picket fence that separated their properties.

Maybe the situation was not as bad as it looked.

She was probably just too scared, too taken by surprise.

From his office on the thirtieth floor of the General Electric building on Spring Street in downtown Los Angeles Nicholas Grady was casting a glance out the window when he had finished his intense if tiring perusal of a new statute, the heavy book resting on his lap. It always gave him ease and pleasure to let his eyes wander all the way to the west, over distant Beverly Hills and farther, the office towers of West Los Angeles, until the horizon was met. On clear days the Santa Monica Mountains would come in, edged darkly against the blue sky. Today was such a clear day. In the far distance, a pretty white cloud was wriggling upwards, like an Indian smoke signal. Smoke! On an exceptionally clear day with hot Santa Ana winds!

Nicholas Grady was a true Angeleno, not easily fooled by anything and alert to only two dangers: fires and earthquakes. During his lifetime of just over three decades he had taken his measure of both and had learned to take both very seriously.

This was a fire he was looking at, far in the distance. No doubt about it. So, where was the fire, exactly?

He switched on the television set built into the right-hand drawer of his big desk. The local stations were all on the story with the afternoon news: Firestorms of suspicious origin were blowing from Thousand Oaks and Calabasas across the Santa Monica Mountains towards Malibu. Fire engines could be seen racing up the Pacific Coast Highway, fire fighting crews were being trucked in, water bombers were coming on the scene unloading reddish tons of liquid that contained "not just water but fire-retardant chemicals and grass seeds." Now there were scenes shot from a helicopter hovering over grassy and brushy knolls that exploded into fireballs even as the reporter spoke. Studio anchors were predicting "another outbreak of deadly fires like the ones in Laguna Beach a week ago" and hoped they were wrong.

Nicholas had seen enough. He grabbed his suit jacket from the back of the visitor's chair by his desk and ran out, yelling to his secretary to cancel all appointments, and that he'd call in when he could.

He gunned his car, a vintage Porsche, out of the parking slot in the underground garage. Tires squealing he shot up three turns until he reached street level. In another minute he was on the Harbor Freeway, turning west onto an increasingly crowded Santa Monica Freeway. "Emmy, here I come!" he shouted. "Hang in there, kiddo!"

His expectations of reaching the coast before disaster news would bring out more vehicles were soon dashed. By the time he reached West Los Angeles it became clear that more people were doing what he was about to—rushing to help or evacuate loved ones. And just as predictably, the authorities were putting a stop to that by clearing the main roadways for emergency vehicles only, blocking off the major thoroughfares.

Nicholas was not fazed by that. He got off the freeway past Beverly Hills and proceeded almost without hindrance, on "surface streets" in the jargon of the traffic reporters, winding his way by skillful turns and twists into Santa Monica. All along he kept tuned to the radio. The news got worse by the minute. Malibu was now directly threatened. The sky that he could see through his windshield had taken on the color of opaque milk glass. He knew all too well what that meant; those were white ashes that would descend on everything like gentle snowflakes. Getting white ashes so soon in the game meant fires of enormous heat and proportions.

"Emily, smarty-pants, I hope you got the hell out of there!" he growled as he sped down San Vicente Boulevard, that broad avenue with a median strip of blood-red coral trees. Farther down, just a few blocks from the bluffs that tower above the coast highway and the beach, the Grady family owned an apartment house taken in lieu of payment from mobster Mickey Cohen back in the 50s who had hired Grady senior, successfully, as his tax attorney. The building, a half-timbered pseudo-English with palm trees and swimming pool had once been a haven for visiting film stars of British provenance doing movies for Samuel Goldwin and Cecil B. De Mille. Douglas Fairbanks, Ray Milland, and Errol Flynn had slept there, and often not alone. The place had lost much of its sheen in recent times, what with modern movie stars moving to secluded mansions but more to the point, because rent control had made its upkeep uneconomical. Now, young attorneys and MBAs of both genders, with their BMWs and Volvos, had taken up residence there at below-market rents, and pool-side barbecues had acquired a certain up-scale glitter, French vintage wine bottles filling the trash bins. Nicholas Grady had an apartment there, too, the best of the lot with a balcony that had a view of the ocean and the mountains. It beat his hi-tech downtown condo that was his weekly abode, and he loved to steal away to "Vicente Manor" on weekends.

It was past 3:00 P.M. when Nicholas pulled into his parking space in the back of the building. He raced upstairs and looked at the fire scene from his balcony. The situation had become worse, much worse than he had feared. Thick dark towering clouds were reaching high into a disappearing sky and stretched far out over the ocean. The afternoon sun was a mere pink spot in the billowing conflagration.

Nicholas picked up the phone in his kitchen and called his office. He instructed his secretary, "If or when Emily Dessauer calls tell her I am on my way now to try to make it to Malibu—yes, it's a mess out here, a full-blown disaster—but I'll be on my mountain bike, so don't try me on the car phone, Judy, call me on the cellular one. If you hear from Emily, tell her two rendezvous points: the entrance to the Getty museum, or if the fire has gotten there, too, the Bel Air Bay Beach Club. Okay? Thanks, Judy, I appreciate it."

Methodically Nicholas went about to ready himself, changing into light clothing and sturdy boots, filling the water bottle clamped on his bike and taping an additional one to the frame. He put on his helmet and his goggles, grabbed a pair of work gloves, slipped a hunting knife into the tool kit that was fastened to the saddle. His phone and his wallet went into his pockets, and a radio was clipped to his belt, with the earphones at the ready around his neck. He couldn't think of anything else he might need, so he clambered down the stairs with his bike held aloft, got on it and pedaled away.

It was clear to him that all the roads leading to the fire area would be cordoned off to civilian traffic by now. Pedestrian traffic through the residential area of the Pacific Palisades would, he gathered, be unaffected; he would, therefore, ride on sidewalks until he could do so no more. At that point he hoped to be at or near where the Palisades meet the Pacific Coast Highway. From there he would see; Emily's property was only a few miles down the highway.

Of course, eventually, if he succeeded that far, he would be in the thick of it. Stalled cars, fire engines, rescue vehicles, the Highway Patrol, County Sheriffs—all would crowd onto the one lifeline that snaked along the ocean's rim—the Pacific Coast Highway. As a lawyer he knew that under emergency circumstances police powers were absolute, that he had no legitimate reason to be where he was going. He would be an impediment, endangering his own life. That's what they would tell him if they stopped him.

The idea was not to get caught, though, but to push forward through the melee until he had found Emily. He had complete confidence that he would be able to do that. It was not for nothing that he was a Marine.

Semper Fi, Emmy. I'm gonna come and get you . . .

"Josh, yoo-hoo!" Emily shouted, and waved at the spindly figure on the roof who was shaking the garden hose with both hands as if that would help to increase the water pressure. Gusts of wind sprayed drops of precious water back at him. "Josh? Come down here, please! We've got to get out of here!"

Josh leaned over the edge, "See if the faucet is turned up all the way, will ya, honey? Right by the house, there!" He pointed to it.

Emily went over and checked. It was turned up as far as it could be.

"Josh, let's go, come on, there is no time to lose!"

The old man shook his head. "Nah. The wind is going the other way. See?"

Just as he was saying that there was a dull thud and an angry red flame shot up into the air, on the other side of Emily's house.

Emily ducked instinctively, then screamed, "Josh! Come down here, now!"

"That was a car going up. Wheeeh!" He gave a cackling laugh. "Embers falling on it. Was it yours, hon? That's a stupid thing to do, bringing a car up into the fire area. Leave it on the highway is what you do."

Emily looked back. It must have been her car. Imagine if she were still in it, if this had happened just a few minutes earlier when she was turning it around! She shuddered. Now the red-hot gasoline fire was wind-driven against the palms trees, the flames running up the trunks like so many angry squirrels. From there to the back porch of her house it was just a few yards.

She had to get away from here. "Josh, I am leaving!" she shouted. "Are you coming?" His answer for her was a shake of his head. She let him be.

It was to her great surprise, as she was running down the driveway from Josh's house, to see a fire engine rumbling up, gears whining in low, helmeted men clinging to bars on the side and in the back. One of them shouted at her, "Get down there, Miss, right now," as he pointed to the coast highway.

"Save my house, please! It's the one up there!" she screamed back, but nobody seemed to hear her. She wondered for a brief moment if she should wait and see, then realized that there was no point in that at all. She trudged down the hill, the hot wind behind her back, the dark cloud of ash and soot now catching up with her.

The Pacific Coast Highway was a mess of cars, those that were stationary pushed to either side of the road, with a narrow center lane kept open for fire trucks and emergency vehicles. There were police everywhere, sheriffs, highway patrol, motorcycle cops, and a lot of people running around carrying babies, pets, suitcases, bird cages. They were all directed south towards the distant stoplight that kept changing from green to red in regular intervals. From there police cars and buses would take them out of the fire area. And those were the orders.

Emily kept standing by the edge of the highway, the surf braking against the rocks below. The wind was so strong that it blew plumes of spray back over the waves. She wanted to wait and see if the fire engine had reached her house even though the dark smoke had begun to obliterate any clear view.

Someone tapped her on the shoulder. A young man in a colorful surfer's wetsuit, she saw when she turned around.

"D'you want to go out by boat?" he asked. He was a kid, a teenager.

"By boat?" she asked. "What boat?"

The boy pointed to a zodiac pulled up on shore. "That one. And see the cabin cruiser out there? It's my dad's. Another guy and I brought him out here, he has a lot of stuff in his beach house right up there that he needs to get out, before it burns, okay? We are goin' back now, we are not allowed to stay, okay? But you can come if you like." He shrugged as if it was all the same to him.

"Why me?" asked Emily.

"You are by yourself, right? You got no kid, no cat or dog, no luggage. So, you qualify, okay?" He grinned a perfect white-tooth smile.

"Okay," Emily said quickly. The boy turned and walked down the pebbly strip of beach to his zodiac. He wore dirty-white deck shoes. Emily followed, half pushed by the wind. Her hair flew wildly ahead of her.

It was a very bouncy ride over choppy waves to the boat that hove no more than a hundred feet out on the sea. Emily sat on the bottom slats of the inflatable, hanging on to the straps on either side. The boy very skillfully steered with the tiny outboard motor until they had reached the back ladder of the cabin cruiser. A young man aboard helped her up, then he and the boy fastened the zodiac flat to the side. Directly after, the heavy diesel motor began to throb as the young man who had helped her aboard threw the controls into forward.

Emily followed him into the cockpit. "That's very nice of you to pick me up," she shouted over the engine noise. "My name is Emily."

"Zach brought you, huh? That's just like him. Zach's my little brother. Maybe you know him. He's starring in that TV show, Hollywood and Vine?"

Emily had only the vaguest notion of what was going on in the TV sitcom or drama field. She shook her head. "Sorry."

"I'm Stew." He shook her hand briefly. "Zach's the one who's the star. My dad and I work for Zach. Dad writes and produces, I'm the gofer."

Zach came up to them. "It's a mess out there over Malibu. Jesus! Just look, it's getting worse! You got family out there, Miss?"

"It's Emily. And you are Zach?" She left it open as to how she knew his name. "No, no family. Just a house."

"Just a house, huh. That can be replaced." He looked at her intently. "Do I know you? Are you in the business?"

"I work for a bank."

"Zach means show biz," Stew said. "You look like a film star. Isn't that what you mean, Zach?"

"That's very flattering, both of you," Emily said. "Could I have a cold drink, please, if you have it aboard?"

"Hey, sure! You bet. Zach, take the wheel for a moment, will yah?" Stew stepped away as his brother took over. He led Emily down a few steps into the galley where there was a small refrigerator next to the sink.

Just then the boat began to heave and slap back down hard onto the water, once, twice, three times. "Whoa!" Stew held on to the railings of the galley counter with one arm and with the other caught Emily by the waist until she could steady herself by catching a wooden grip on the cabin wall. Stew's arms were muscular and sinewy, his hand on the railing all knuckles and veins. "Gust of wind will do that to yah, from the shore, whipping up the waves against each other, comin' and goin'. Won't last long." He cast an inquiring glance at her. "You all right, Emily?" They were about the same height and for a moment they were face to face. His breath had a faint trace of garlic.

She was going to say yes but she was seized by a nausea so sudden it was all she could do to bend over the sink and vomit. A violent retching convulsed her whole body. Stew was steadying her by the waist repeating, "Now, now, easy now," until she had no more to give up.

"Aughhh," she breathed with a throaty moan. Cold sweat pearled on her forehead and snot was dripping from her nose. "Oh God," she moaned again.

"You're okay now." Stew gave her a paper towel. "Take it easy. You lie down here, come on, I'll show you."

"I'm sorry about the mess," Emily snuffled, straightening up.

"No problem. I'll take care of it." Stew led her down another step where the cabin was lined with cushioned benches on either side. He helped her down and put a pillow under her head. Then he disappeared and Emily could hear him at the sink, flushing her vomit down.

"Oh God," she sighed and put an arm over her eyes. The slapping noise from the bottom of the boat had lessened, and the rhythmic up and down movement was beginning to make her drowsy. She felt as if in a cradle, back in her childhood. She had seen photographs of herself as a baby, in an elaborately carved crib with a canopy all tulle and voile, a crib that could be rocked gently and probably came from the Old Country. She had last seen the crib in the attic of her parents' house. Had Angelique saved it? Emily couldn't imagine she would have given it to the boys. Emily thought, and a smile played over her lips, I will want it for my baby. I'll love that baby so much.

She awakened slowly when she became aware that the noise of the boat had changed to an even, steady thump-thump-thump. The cabin was dark but light fell in from the oblong windows. Emily raised herself on her elbow and looked out. It was dusk, with illumination from light standards on both sides of the channel the boat was putt-putting through. She rose and somewhat unsteadily made her way up to the deck.

"Hi," she was smiling bravely. Stew was at the controls, Zach could be seen crouching at the bow.

"Hi there," Stew smiled back. "Feelin' better?"

"Much," Emily lied. "Thanks for your help."

"Hey, nada. Glad you're okay. You've been through a lot. Just look at the sky. It's not even five o'clock yet and it's dark. Thick black clouds! The whole of Malibu is burning. Unbelievable!"

The whole of Malibu? Her house. "Where are we?"

"The Marina. We'll dock in a few minutes and then we'll go up to my place, see that round tower up ahead? I have a condo there."

Emily said, "Stew, maybe you should just drop me off dockside. I'll get a taxi."

"Sure. Whatever you wish. Maybe you'll want to make some phone calls, tell your folks you're okay? They must be worried about you."

"Oh God, yes."

"You can do that from my place. Clean up a little, you know."

Emily looked down at herself, at her hands, her shirt, and felt the peltish tongue in her mouth. She must look a fright. "I shouldn't presume on your kindness any longer, Stew. You have been enormously helpful, you and Zach both. I owe you a lot."

"Naw. We were going to Malibu, anyway. My Dad has his beach house there, not far from where we picked you up. All his scripts and stuff are there, and his laptop. He can't function without them."

"Wasn't that pretty dangerous for him to go into the fire zone?"

Stew shrugged. "I don't think so. He didn't think so. Anyway, he said it's hard getting in because the police block you off, but easy to get out, just follow the crowd. He figured he'd be out in less than an hour."

Emily remembered how fast the fire was moving and thought an hour was taking a lot of chances. "I'd be worried," she said.

"Zach is," Stew nodded in the direction of his brother.

"I'll go talk to him." Emily climbed up onto the deck and walked over to where Zach was sitting at the spit of the bow, his legs dangling down, his arms outstretched holding the wires of the railing. He reacted with a start when Emily touched his shoulder.

"Hi," he said. "Feeling better?"

Emily nodded. "Much." She squatted down beside him. "I want to thank you, Zach, for rescuing me. That was a great, wonderful thing to do." She put an arm around his shoulder.

"It's okay."

"It's more than okay, Zach." She gave him a sisterly kiss on his right cheek. "As I said to Stew, I owe you guys."

Zach gave her a sideways glance. "You kiss him, too?"

"No as a matter of fact, I did not. You are the one who rescued me. Stew helped, too, of course, but it was different."

"How different?"

"Stew—well, let's just say I don't go around kissing people at random. Not that Stew hasn't been very kind."

"So, why'd you kiss me?" He didn't wait for her answer. He said with some vehemence, "Because you think I'm just a kid, right? Too immature?"

Emily looked at him, stroked some of his long blond hair back behind his ear. "You have heard about this legend where the person whose life is saved by another makes them bound to each other forever? That's why you are different." She smiled. "Besides, I don't think you are a kid anymore."

Zach sighed and threw the gum he had been chewing into the water. After a while he said, "I'm glad I did what I did when I saw you scrambling down to the beach. You looked scared, like a deer. I liked you immediately, Emily," he said that almost shyly. "Can I call you Emily?"

"Of course." She held out her hand, "Friends forever, Zach?"

He shook her hand but said, "Like how—friends?"

"Like, you come to my wedding, I come to yours. Something like that. And we can tell each other things." She shrugged. "You know, real easy."

He nodded earnestly and looked into the far distance. Emily wondered what it must be like to be a TV star while still a teenager, and was reminded of her almost career as a pianist. She had been able to bail out in time; Zach seemed already caught up in the show biz whirl. She felt sorry for him. Rising, she said, "I know your dad will be all right, Zach."

He got up, too. He was a good head taller than her and had to bend down to put a quick kiss on the corner of her mouth. Then he busied himself picking up a coiled rope and made ready to jump onto the dock. They had arrived.

It turned out to be a crazy night. Emily took Stew's advice and made calls from his condo apartment. First to her mother, who was almost hysterical in her relief to hear her daughter's voice, hale and hearty. She had seen the TV reports, knew only too well where the Dessauer property was and that it had to have been involved in the firestorm. "You must come up to Santa Barbara, darling, now! Immediately! Charter a private plane!"

"Mother, I'm all right. I'm staying here until tomorrow, then I'll rent a car and drive up. Don't worry, please?"

Her next call was to Nick's office, which was closed except for the night service; she left her name and the number of Stew's apartment. She did the same with Nick's Santa Monica answering machine. Then she took advantage of Stew's offer to shower and wash her hair; everything on and about her reeked of acrid smoke and she couldn't wait to get rid of it. Zach volunteered to throw her jeans and shirt into the washer-dryer, and Stew, surprisingly, came carrying over his arm a couple of dresses the origins of which he did not reveal except to flip his eyebrows up and down. She luxuriated in a long hot shower with lots of soap and shampoo. After she had dried off and toweled her hair she found that the pile of dresses

Stew had delivered also contained—more surprise—panties and bras. She selected a beige housedress and half hoped that Stew, who was evidently well prepared for female company, would also have stashed away somewhere a box of tampons. Eureka! There was a pack in the medicine cabinet.

So restored and refreshed she stepped back into the living room. The furniture Stew favored was big, wide and comfortable, from the leather sofa and chairs to the rustic glass-top-on-tree-trunk coffee table. The ceiling lights were dimmed, to better reveal the drama that was on display both outside in nature and inside on the large TV screen against the wall. The windows looked northwest towards Santa Monica Bay, framing the eerie spectacle of rings of dark-red fires that burned fiercely on the distant mountains, with thick black clouds stretching far out to sea. The TV screen, with a smaller inset from another station, showed reports from the ground and the air, people fleeing their homes, firefighters trying to hold the line against the disaster, and airplanes and helicopters making water-dropping sorties over and over again. It was like reports from a war zone.

Yet, here they were, snug and clean and warm and safe, just a few miles and a couple of hours removed from the inferno.

"Bourbon or Scotch?" Stew asked from the kitchen.

"Oh, bourbon please, with ice and soda? Thank you." Emily sat down next to Zach, who was sipping a beer. He had changed into slacks and a T-shirt.

"Dad called," he said softly to Emily, "he's back home. No sweat." He smiled at her, "You smell good, Emily."

"Thanks, Zach. About your dad? I'm glad he's safe."

Stew came over and handed her a drink. "A guy called for you, Brady or something. I told him you're safe. He said for you to call him back."

Emily took an eager swallow from the honey-colored liquid. She almost gagged on it. "Oh wow, what is this?" she said and coughed.

"One hundred one proof," Stew grinned. "It'll get you there."

It went down her gullet like the fire outside. "Geez," Emily rolled her eyes and took another, more careful sip. Wherever the "there" was, she needed to get to it. "So, Grady—not Brady, it had to be Nick Grady, my boyfriend, Stew. He called? What'd he say?"

"I couldn't hear him too well, there was a lot of background noise. I gave him this address. I think he said he'd come and pick you up when he was out. Words to that effect."

"Out? Out of the office?"

Stew shrugged and went to pick up his own tumbler from the kitchen.

Zach said, "I ordered pizza, one triple cheese, one pepperoni. Hope you like pizza, Emily."

"I sure do. Right now I could eat a horse."

Stew came back with a tray of tortilla chips and salsa. He put it on the glass table, right over the tree trunk, and sat down in the chair opposite the sofa. The soft leather nearly swallowed him up, as it did Emily and Zach, who were deeply cushioned on their chaise lounge, Emily's legs resting on the edge, making her calves flatten out.

"Here's to you guys," she raised her glass. "Many thanks. My gratitude is boundless." She was beginning to feel all warm and comfy inside.

They all said "Cheers!" and drank some more.

The doorbell rang. "I'll get it," Stew rose and scooped up some bills from the kitchen counter. "It's the pizza man."

But it wasn't the pizza man. It was a disheveled Nick, in shorts and polo shirt and cleated boots who cast a wild glance at the scene.

"Nick!" cried Emily and jumped up. "Come in, come in! These are my friends, Stew at the door, and Zach here. They saved my life. Come in, Nick, for God's sake, don't just stand there!" She rushed up to pull him over the sill. She gave him a kiss. "Gosh, Nicky, where have you been? You smell funny!" To the brothers she said, "Stew, Zach—this is Nicholas Grady. If you ever need a good lawyer, he is it." She jabbed a pointed finger at him.

Before they could all say hello, the pizza man also showed up, and Stew was busy paying him off and taking the cartons to the kitchen. When the door was closed the men shook hands. Nick was asked if he would like a drink and said, "Whatever she is having." He kept looking at Emily and shaking his head.

There wasn't much talk at first but plenty of pizza, and tortilla chips and a couple of drink refills. Nick had been offered one of the easy chairs, where he gradually sank in. He kept shaking his head as Emily, her voice a bit thick but her talk unimpeded, told him what had happened to her. "Zach, here, picked me up off the beach," she took Zach's hand and held it with both of hers, "and Stew piloted us safely to the Marina. This is Stew's apartment. Stew and Zach are in show biz, Zach's in Hollywood and Vine, the TV sitcom. Stew and Zach are brothers, in case you are wondering." Emily gave a significant nod with her head.

"Why should I be wondering?" Nick said through a full mouth.

"Real brothers, you know? Not frat brothers like you are with Brian Fallon."

"What, Em, what's Brian got to do with it?" He chewed on a pizza crust.

"Brian Fallon is a flamin' homo, Nick! That's what!" To Zach she explained, "Brian is a frat brother of Nick's, and a gynecologist. A gay gyno! Ha-ha! I went to him, and Nick here, he didn't say peep!"

"I think I may be gay, too," Zach said softly.

"Oh come on, Zach!" Stew sounded angry.

"Oh geez," Emily moaned. "Don't kid me about that!"

"No, really, I think I may be gay. Most women don't interest me, and many men do. Not that I've had sex with them or anything."

"Zach, stop it! You've hardly ever had sex with a woman, either!" Stew was really angry now.

"It takes one to know one," Nick grumbled, and nodded sagely.

"Okay!" Emily spread out her arms. "That settles it, Zach. You and I are going to have sex, and then I'm going to tell you if you are gay or not. No, no, I mean it, it's the least I can do for my life saver, I mean, the saver of my life. Nick, I'm sorry, you stay out of it. You hear me?" She leaned over to Zach and gave him a kiss. "We can't do it tonight, I'm still having my period. But next time I'm in town, we do it. First thing. Okay?" Turning to Nick again she said, "I'm sorry, Nick, but you can see my point, can't you."

"Absolutely," Nick replied but the noise from the TV set, reporters babbling and copters whirring, half drowned him out.

"Nick! Nicky!" Emily went over and sat on the round edge of his chair. "You are not going to be mad at me or anything, are you?" She turned his face to her as she scrutinized him. "Gee, Nick, you smell awful! Where have you been?"

"In jail," Nick said matter-of-factly.

"Jail! You've been in jail? Whatever for?"

"For trying to rescue you, Emily. Except I wasn't as lucky."

"Nick! Don't joke with me, okay? This is hard enough for me as it is." There were "shish" sounds in her speech. "Tell me the truth, Nicky."

"The truth. You want to know the truth? I'll tell you the truth. I saw the fire, I rushed home to Santa Monica, I got my bike because cars couldn't get through, and I pedaled like crazy through the Palisades and made it all the way to Topanga Canyon on the Coast Highway." He pulled her down onto his lap. "You want to know why? The truth? Because I was worried about you. You are the stubborn type, who would throw buckets of water at a firestorm. I had to get you out of there, fast. The fire was getting pretty bad. I managed to sneak past the police lines, and there is this butt-faced CHP officer who roared up on his motorbike and told me to stop, but I ignored him, see? Then the bastard drew his gun at me, yeah, his gun, point-blank, but I'm a Marine, and I told him so, and he said you're a fuckin' nuisance and you're under arrest, and he handcuffed me! Then he hands me over to an LAPD woman officer and she puts me in a van with a couple of real scruffy characters and off we go, to the West L.A. police station. So I'm in a holding tank for a couple of hours. Then the usual song and dance about charges—crossing police lines, resisting arrest, obstructing rescue efforts, and a couple more—and finally they accepted my check for bail and let me go, and you know why? Because the booking sergeant was a Marine reservist, like myself. I called my office, got your message, called here. Took a taxi straight from there."

"O God, Nicky. I'm sorry for all the trouble I caused you." Emily, tears coming on, screwed up her face. "Lost my house, too, I bet."

"It wasn't your fault, Emily. This is one thing you just can't take responsibility for. Shit happens."

Stew and Zach had been watching the scene wordlessly. Now Stew got up and said, "This calls for a drink. I like happy endings."

"No more, thank you." Nick pointed to Emily who had her face buried in her hands. "She's had enough, and I didn't come here to party. Thanks, just the same. Some other time, for sure. I'll call you. You guys have been great."

A taxi was called, and when it arrived Nick carried Emily down who had fallen asleep. She awoke from that, and as he put her in the back seat she asked, "Where're we going?" rubbing her eyes.

"Home, sweetheart. You're going to my Santa Monica apartment."

"Oh Nick," she started to cry again. "I don't want your apartment. I want my house, my cute little house."

"It's just temporary, Em. Just for the interim. Trust me."

Greenwich Weekend

Tom looked at his watch when he came out of the MetroBank building. It was about a half hour until his lunch meeting with Cab. The weather seemed to be holding, the clouds were breaking up. He decided to walk the few blocks to the Bonne Raison Bistro; Cab had said it was one of his favorite lunch places "where it's so noisy and so busy you can talk confidentially without being overheard." Along the way he did some window shopping on Fifth Avenue, a couple of blocks up and down again, and he enjoyed the experience. He was a New Yorker born and bred, and despite the fact that in all probability he would not live there anymore he had a proprietary feeling about his old stomping grounds. In quiet moments he would admit to actually liking the place, at least as he remembered it. Past history, most likely. Bertie would grow up a Californian, certainly not a New Yorker, so far as he could see.

Bertie. He had talked to him again last night. The boy had said, quite audibly, "When are you coming home, Daddy?" Coached by Laura no doubt, but still, he had said it. "In a couple of days, Bertie," he had replied and meant it. As soon as the tedious business with Cab was settled, he'd fly out to the Coast. He and Cab could just as easily be dealing via telephone and fax.

The restaurant was easy to find, getting a table was another matter. It appeared that there was no reservation under the name of Blumenfeld. Sorry. Tom craned his neck to look around the already filling-up dining area, but no Cab. A moment later someone slapped him on the shoulder. Cab. "Hey, buddy, I see you beat me to it," he grinned. To the maitre d' he said: "A quiet table, if you will, Pierre," and Pierre—who looked like a Renoir character, mustache, white apron and all—swept up two menus and said, "This way, Mr. Charles."

Tom smiled when they were seated, "Mr. Charles, huh?"

"That's one of the many lessons you learn in this town. Rarely, if ever, use your last name in public—it can be overheard by others." Cab did a pantomime of looking right and left and over his shoulder. "The same goes for leaving things at the cleaners, ordering takeout, or telephoning in public, and so on. It's in the same category as not making eye contact in the subway—if you must use the subway at all—or keeping your real wallet in your back pocket.

It's a crazy burg, the Big Apple."

"Really." Was it, real that is? Or just another one of Cab's cynicisms? Tom wondered. "Funny, about real last names. The account executive I saw on my mother's behalf at the bank this morning called me Watson."

"There you go! The guy did you a favor. Doctor Watson! I like it."

"No guy. A woman."

"A woman, huh? Young, old?"

"Young."

"Pretty?"

Tom smiled. "And very likely married."

Cab scrutinized his face. Then he nodded. "She got to you."

"What do you mean?"

"I can tell, the way your eyes go. She's still on your mind."

"Oh come on, Cab," Tom protested. "That's ridiculous."

"Is it? What's her name?"

"Cab, give up!" Tom leaned back and laughed.

"Tell me her name."

"Emily Dessauer."

"You remember the name."

"Of course I do! I can read name plates! Besides, I only left her office less than an hour ago!"

"Yeah? You remember the names of people you have met only once? At a party, in a store? What's my assistant's name? Come on, zap-zap!" He snapped his fingers.

"Uh . . . Walter . . . Watanabe . . . "

"Warren Watanabe. I rest my case." He smiled at Tom, and winked.

They ordered the special. Cab said he always ordered the special, it was never a mistake and besides it saved time. Tom allowed himself a scotch, Cab ordered a Virgin Mary explaining, as if he had to, that he didn't drink during business hours.

"Speaking of business," Tom asked, "how is it going?"

"Yours or mine?"

"Let's start with yours. How are you doing in these times of economic constriction?"

Cab replied wryly, "It's becoming tougher, which is fine with me. It gets rid of the small guy, the nuisance competitor and the marginal client. That leaves the field to the rest of us big producers, and the really important prospects. So in answer to your question, I am doing well. Quite well."

"And where do you live, Cab? I only have your business address."

"In Connecticut. In Greenwich. I segued from esquire to country squire in one not so easy lesson."

"The lesson being?"

"It literally doesn't pay to live in Manhattan. The Apple is rotten at the core. When I'm in town I stay at the Waldorf. The manager there is an old client of mine, we made a deal where I get any prepaid but non-claimed room for half the going rate. We both come out ahead; it would cost me more to pay for a crummy walk-up apartment, not counting clogged sinks and dirty linen. By Friday I leave town for Greenwich. My housekeeper picks me up, or leaves my car at the station. You must come out and visit. How about this weekend? I'm giving a sort of Halloween party."

"Thanks. Can I afford it? How is my business going?"

"Two parts to that. One, your money is good. I tried it, had a couple of random samples checked at the hotel and my bank, and I am pleased to tell you they are the genuine article. I have some ideas as to what you should do now."

"Such as?"

"Set up a private annuity, disbursed through my office, to send your mother a monthly check sufficient to cover the home nursing expenses. The old gentleman is not likely to outlive it. For yourself, I suggest a life insurance policy with your son as the beneficiary. I'll give it to you at cost, which means money will flow back into the pot once the policy is issued, which we apply towards the second year premium. After the second year, we'll see. That still leaves a margin of about fifteen thou, for you to use as you see fit. We may have to draw from it for expenses we may incur, which brings me to point two. To ferret out information relating to point two, as to the who and why and where. That may take a while."

"Any ideas?"

Cab nodded, "This is not the place to discuss that. Come out to the country this weekend and we'll talk." The waiter was bringing their food, which turned out to be meatloaf with a side of cole slaw and crisp French bread. Tom wondered how his friend could stay fit and trim with this kind of caloric intake, and asked the question.

"I work out," Cab said. He grinned, "Besides, there is an old French saying whispered into my ear by my Creole grandmother when I reached puberty. Roughly translated it means a good barnyard rooster never gets fat."

"Ah," Tom said when it sank in. "And are you? A good rooster?"

Cab laughed. "What is it you Army guys say? Be all you can be? A good rule, even for us civilians." He winked at Tom.

A little later Cab pulled out a bill from his wallet and waved it, "What do you say we try one of your Franklins here, for a case in point? Philippe!" He summoned the elderly waiter to his side and spoke to him in a low voice, discreetly pointing in the direction of the opposite banquette. The waiter bowed and palmed the money. Tom raised his eyebrows questioningly, but Cab wagged a finger, "Not yet."

Tom kept his eye on the waiter, who came back carrying a silver ice bucket with a white napkin over the top, the gold neck of a champagne bottle sticking out. He took it to the table of three young women who had come in earlier and were still examining the menu. Much surprise when the waiter set up three flutes and pointed in the direction of Cab as he began uncorking the bottle. A little shriek of recognition, and another. Two of the women, both blondes, one with wavy hair down to her shoulder, the other's straight and cut short, recognized Cab now, laughing and raising their hands. The third woman who sat with her back to the room just smiled and shook her head; she had dark hair, not long but long enough to flow freely with the movement of her head. Tom noticed that she could see what was going on by looking into the mirror that stretched along the banquette top.

"Come on," Cab said. "Let's go say hello."

Tom declined. "You go, Cab. Friends of yours?"

"Get up, Tom. We are going to go over there and act like gentlemen." He smiled. "Remember cotillion class? Same thing. I always had to drag you."

Tom followed, somewhat reluctantly. He had never been very good at this sort of thing, not then—"too straight, too serious" in the opinion of Madame Van Buren who strove mightily to make little gentlemen out of gangly boys—and not now, certainly not now.

The two blondes each had their arms out for Cab, hugging him as he bent down. Tom stood back until Cab introduced him as "Major Vonder Campe."

"Is Major your first name?" the short-haired blonde wanted to know.

Cab didn't let him answer. "Major, as in U.S. Army Medical Corps. Tom's his name. Great guy. We went to school together."

Introductions did get made, with much laughing. Beth, Margie and Tookie. Tookie was the dark-haired one who didn't say much. Margie invited Cab and Tom to sit down and share the bottle, and thanked him for the champagne. But Cab, with much natural gusto, declined, telling the women to go ahead and enjoy but that he and Tom had to run. Business.

"Are you buying a policy from this man?" The Beth woman asked.

"I think Cab is selling me one," Tom smiled.

"Touché," Cab said and shook hands. To the dark-haired one he said, "I am sorry, I didn't catch your name?"

"Theodora Kephalides. 'Tookie' is what my friends call me." Tom liked her smile; it lit up her pale, classic face. Greek, obviously.

"Tookie is an orthodontist. Too late for you, Cab!" Margie said. "Your teeth are beyond help."

"Don't I know it." To Tookie he said, "Let's trade cards, d'you mind?"

Apparently she didn't, for she rummaged in her handbag and came up with a silver case out of which she extracted a card to give to Cab. She smiled at Tom but made no move to give him one, too, nor did Tom ask her for it.

When they were back at their table Cab said, "Let's go. No point in lingering." And they left. It appeared that Cab had an account at the restaurant which he settled once a month. It was another one of his conveniences—no waiting for the check and automatic gratuities.

On the street Cab said, "Old girlfriends. We still like each other."

"I could tell."

"What'd you think of the dark one—Tookie? D'you like her?"

Tom shrugged. "She's all right. Why? Does it matter?"

"I'm going to give her a call." They were walking against a sudden gust of wind. It obviated a further discussion, somewhat to Tom's relief. He wouldn't put it beyond Cab to finagle a date for him with one of his old girlfriends. There was no way Tom could do that. In any case, both blondes wore wedding rings.

They were seated in Cab's conference room again, with Cab spreading out some papers over the wide expanse of the table. He spoke, eyeing Tom steadily. "Let's be clear about something. You have come to me for advice, and I shall give it to you, selflessly. Pro bono our old friendship. Yes? Okay. It means that in technical matters relating as to how we proceed from here, I expect you to go along if you agree with what I am proposing. No cute shilly-shallying, once you understand the process. Agreed?"

"Agreed."

"Good. That'll cut eighty percent of the crap I have to shovel out of the way with my regular clients before we can get down to brass tacks. Now, I'm proposing a face amount, not of a hundred thousand—that's too little—and not of a million—that's too conspicuous in your present circumstances. Five hundred thou is what we should apply for. I know I can get you that much even though you are a former armed forces member who is not expected to be familiar with large sums of money. You are smiling, but the underwriters will look at every facet of your life, how much you want to insure your life for, and why. That's point two of this exercise. In the process of underwriting we will uncover exactly what you look like under scrutiny, your personal background, your financial means, your health. Speaking of health—this will require a medical examination and a blood and urine test. Any problems there?"

"None," Tom smiled.

"How about HIV? There is a separate form for that."

"Negative. At the Institute they ran HIV tests on us every three months."

"Excellent. I run one every six months, myself. The way I live, I can't be too careful."

Tom was still smiling, but he did not say anything.

"Okay." Cab shuffled some more papers. "I am proposing an interest-sensitive whole life policy. No term—term is too cheap and the underwriters will question your motives, especially when they find out about your wife's accident and the criminal investigation you went through. They want to see a commitment on your part. Six thousand bucks kind of commitment. Money talks. By the way, it'll be a good deal for you in the long run. You can stop paying premiums in ten years, or at age sixty-five get two dollars back for every dollar you put in, a nice little retirement nest egg. Meantime, if you croak early, Bertie gets the whole slew." He smiled. "Any questions?"

"Where do I sign?" Tom smiled back.

"See what I mean?" Cab sighed. "It's easy. Beats being a lawyer. I do this a couple of times a week, every week of every year, most cases bigger than yours, by the way, and bingo presto, I'm in the money, as the song goes." He sighed again. "You wonder sometimes, what the hell for, know what I mean? There's only so much you can do for yourself, and then it becomes boring. So here you come along, with a little challenge, and I go for it."

"How little is that challenge, finding out about the guy who killed Nettie?"

"I've got a plan. I'll tell you about it over the weekend, I have begun to put the word out, some of it may trickle back to me by then. We must have patience." He leaned over and boxed Tom on the shoulder. "We'll get there."

Tom spent the rest of the afternoon filling out forms and signing them. He was told to come back the next morning for an examination to be done by a paramedical organization that would also take blood and urine samples from him. Cab advised him to set up a new checking account in New York City, for which he would give him a cashier's check in an odd amount of just over nine thousand dollars that would not invite bank reports, besides which in any case he suggested Tom use the bank in Cab's building, for convenience of future transactions.

All of that, plus attending to Fos Watson whose eye bandage would be coming off that same day—the operation had gone well, and was fascinating for Tom to watch—kept Tom busy. He took his mother out to dinner on Friday, down the street to the new French hotel whose restaurant was giving Lutece some competition. They had a warm, wonderful time together. Tom broke the news of an impending annuity payment to her, which she could hardly fathom.

"Thomas, where on earth is that money coming from?" There were reddish spots on her cheeks, her skin was as translucent as old parchment.

"Actually, mother, it is part of a cash settlement following Nettie's death," he said, not untruthfully. "I have just bought a new life insurance policy from Cab with some of that money, and the rest is being annuitized, as Cab would say. A small amount of it will be taxable to you, I am told."

"Goodness, Thomas, shouldn't you be using the money for yourself? You are out of a job now, and need to look for a house, and what not."

Tom assured her that it was all right, the money was "extra" and in any case wouldn't last more than two years based on the current costs of in-home nursing care. He eventually succeeded in quieting his mother's concerns. It touched him to see how the relatively small sum of money affected her, as if her burden had suddenly become lighter. What a difference that was, to the golden days of Palm Beach, and the wedding she and Fos hosted for Tom and Nettie! That was just over five years ago. Had times really changed that much?

On Saturday afternoon he set out for Greenwich, Cab's directions pasted to the dashboard of his car. Max had not been able to sell his T-Bird, not yet, his many assurances and prognostications to the contrary. It was a lovely day of late-late Indian summer, the leaves were falling but what foliage was still on the trees was in glorious color. Once he was off the Merritt Parkway he rolled down his car window and took in the warm breeze, redolent with the rich odor of forest and mulch. He was on a winding country road near Round Hill; what Cab had neglected to mention was that his property was quite a bit to the north of Greenwich proper, in a secluded, woodsy section of quietly elegant country estates, near the New York state border. Wherever Tom looked, whatever he could espy from the road beyond the gated entry ways, these were the homes of people of substance. He was, without envy, glad for Cab; he had made it.

Cab's property was in the hollow between two gently sloping hills, and Tom almost missed it, so hidden was it by greenery. There was no iron gate, just a paved driveway. Tom had slowed down because he had been watching the house numbers and knew that Cab's was just about there.

He made a sharp right-hand turn and the house revealed itself. It seemed disappointing at first sight. No palace this one, just a low-slung one-story affair of the kind described in real estate brochures as "ranch style" with a long roof line. The only windows were to the left, the entrance was in the middle, and the garage was on the right. Its smallness was accentuated by the many trees that were towering over and around it, beech, fir, ash and elder. Tom circled the paved forecourt and came to a stop on the side, facing the road again. He got out, took his overnight bag from the trunk and went to the door. There was no doorbell, just a rapper in the form of a horse head. He let it fall back with two brief knocks.

Presently the door was answered by a maid, in apron over a housedress and dark hair swept up under a head scarf but so young and so surprisingly foreign-looking, in a voluptuous Mediterranean sort of way that Tom wondered if perhaps he had come to the wrong house. Surely this could not be Cab's oft-mentioned housekeeper.

"Uh, is this the Blumenfeld residence? I am Tom," he said.

"Yes." She nodded, earnestly, and opened the door wide for him. "Please to follow me." She closed the door after he stepped inside, then walked ahead, motioning him to follow along a hallway to the left and down a flight of stairs to the lower level of the house. She opened another door. "Mr. Charles says this is the room for you."

It was a book-lined study with a desk and a couch. "Thank you," Tom said. "Where is Mr. Charles?"

"I will tell him you are here," the maid said, turned and walked away. Tom, peering at her as she climbed the stairs, noticed well-shaped legs that even her clog shoes could not despoil, and a nice round behind. "Cab," he shook his head. "She's his housekeeper?"

He threw his bag onto the couch and went to the window. There was a curtain to be pulled and blinds to be raised. Sunlight flooded in. What he saw was a park-like garden, with a terrace to the right, and in the distance at left, the shimmering corner of a swimming pool. Tom realized that he had misjudged the house. The lower portion of it opened up to the grounds hidden from the street, taking advantage of the slope of the hill against which it was nestled. This was quite a spread Cab had given himself here.

"Well, how d'you like it?" Cab's voice came from the back. Tom turned around. A smiling Cab, in swim trunks and a towel around his neck, leaned against the doorway.

"Very impressive," Tom said. "Congratulations."

"You ain't seen nothin' yet. Come on, I'll give you a tour."

Tom went after Cab who was already at the stairs. "We'll start with the top, and then work our way down."

It was not a large house, although, now that he had become aware that there were two stories Tom realized it was certainly not as small as it seemed from the road; but it gave the impression of a most comfortable habitat, one obviously suited for a man of cosmopolitan tastes who, in escaping to the country, favors a rustic look without eschewing his big-city cultural roots. They walked past a formal dining room seating eight around an oval table, stepped down into an equally formal living room that led to the right into a den-library, which in turn opened onto a deck outside shaded by a stand of pine trees. And everywhere one looked was a tasteful selection of furniture, paintings, mirrors and chandeliers.

"Very nice," Tom said. "I suppose you had an interior decorator?" He knew not much of such things as what furniture to put where, or what goes well with which, on walls, or floors, on shelves, nor how to "treat" windows or doorways; his sophistication lay elsewhere. He did know, however, that he was either pleased or offended by the impression a well-cared for home gave off. This one instantly pleased the eye.

Cab grinned, "Would you believe I bought this place lock-stock-and-barrel, from an owner who had gone bankrupt before he could move in? A lawyer client of mine put me on to it, and we got it for a song. Comparatively."

"Yes," Tom nodded, "that sounds more like you. A good deal."

"You bet." Cab slapped him on the shoulder. "You'll get there too, one day. Now, let's go to the kitchen." Cab pushed open a door. The young woman—the maid, the housekeeper?—was busy at a counter, doing something. "You must have met, when you arrived? Shoya, this is Tom, my oldest and my best friend. Tom, this is Shoya. She is from Iran. She was a little girl when the Ayatollah killed her father and kicked out her mother and her. Shoya, you can trust Tom as you can trust me. Shoya keeps my house for me, Tom, quite well as you can see. During the week, when I am in the city, she looks after this place. She also attends classes at UC Stamford." Shoya smiled, her full red lips baring perfect white teeth, and shook Tom's hand. Tom said hello. Then he looked around, taking in the kitchen layout, avoiding Shoya's limpid green eyes. This was a very beautiful girl Cab had under his roof. Some roof . . . some girl . . .

Now Cab hastily ushered him out of the kitchen; Cinderella had been met. They were in the hallway leading to the bedroom wing when Cab stopped, saying under his breath, "You must be wondering about Shoya. Let me tell you."

"No need, please," Tom interrupted. "None of my business."

"Right. Nevertheless, I'm telling you. Her father did business with my father, during the Shah's time. After the revolution, her mother, near destitute and with little Shoya, came to him for help. My father did what he could, he sponsored her for immigration, and eventually my temple took them on as one of our special cases, because by then Shoya's mother had become quite ill, mentally ill. It is one of my modest charitable acts to provide Shoya with a roof over her head, a job and enough wages for her to pay for her own tuition. She has no one else. I am a big brother to her, and she is sort of the little sister I never had. I thought you deserved a brief explanation, such as it is."

"Okay. My respects."

"I just don't want you to get the wrong idea. A lot of people do. Not surprisingly, considering my sybaritic lifestyle. But Shoya is off limits, hands off, completely."

"I appreciate the confidence. I have no designs on her, Cab."

"It's going to be a potentially fractious weekend, as you will see. The people here may have their own ideas of fun. Also, I have invited a young woman for you who came out, I must tell you, just for you."

"Thanks, pal. But hey, I thought we were going to talk business!"

"We may do that, too, although there isn't much new to report as yet. I like to get in a little bit of living between the daily grinds. That's what we try to do here. You in particular can do with a bit of cheering up."

"And your idea of cheering up," Tom haw-hawed, "is shacking up? With a blind date, yet? Am I getting that right?"

"Let's not get off on the wrong foot here. The young lady's interest in you may not be romantic. But you handle it your way, Tom. I'm not worried."

They were now traipsing down the staircase to the lower level. There was a changing room, with benches and locker-like cabinets, and shower stalls next to a work-out area full of exercise machines, all gleamingly new.

"The gym was my idea," Cab explained. "This used to be a storage area." He led Tom to a door that had a window in it. "See there?" He pointed to the pool outside with flagstone decking all around and a water slide at the end. "That's where we are at the moment, taking advantage of the mild sunny day. Now, here is where the swim trunks and towels are." Stepping up to a cabinet he pulled open a drawer. "These are mine. They are clean when they are back in the drawer. If you wish, you may select a pair and come join us at the pool?" With a slap on Tom's back, Cab smiled and went out through the door.

Tom peered out the door-window after him. He saw some chaise lounges poolside, and padded chairs around an umbrella table. Further down on the flagstone decking, two of the chaise lounges were occupied by women, one reading a book, her face shaded by a straw hat, the other lying prone, sunbathing, her right arm dangling over the side of the chaise, petting the head of a dog that was lying curled up underneath. At the table sat a couple, long drinks by their side, playing what appeared to be Scrabble. Cab was now approaching them. Everyone, Tom noticed, was in bathing suits, so he decided to change. He didn't bring swim trunks for the simple reason that he hadn't any in New York; all his summer stuff was in California. After selecting a pair of shorts from the drawer, he went back to the study to get out of his city clothes; he was in blazer and slacks. He stripped, and taking the shorts into the bathroom he found that this was one to be shared with the next adjoining room. He peeked into the adjoining bedroom which contained twin beds sharing a wide night stand. There were women things lying and hanging about, on the bed, from the open closet door, and an open suitcase on the dresser. He quickly pulled back; this shared bathroom business was not for him. Better to use the gym shower and toilet. He put on the swim trunks and slipped on a pair of moccasins from his bag, grabbing the sunglasses he kept in his coat pocket. Before he left the house he cast a quick glance at himself in the mirror he was passing in the changing room. The boxer-like trunks were hiding the incipient bulge but nothing could hide the pristine whiteness of his skin. He hadn't been out of doors much, lately.

"There you are!" Cab got up from the table and walked towards him. The dog, alerted, came slinking along. It was a German shepherd. When Cab stopped, the dog stopped, half crouched as if ready to leap. Cab touched the dog on the head and said, "Easy!" Then he shook Tom's hand and, speaking to the dog, said "Good friend, Zeke, good friend!" For emphasis he took Tom's hand and made him touch the dog. "Speak to him," he said to Tom, and Tom did, stroking the animal's head and neck until its tail began to wag. He liked dogs; they had been part of his childhood, cocker spaniels, a weimaraner, nothing lately but Nettie had talked about getting a golden retriever.

"Now that you have met the boss," Cab said, laughing, "come meet the rest of the gang. Everyone, this is Tom Vander Campe." He took him to the table. The couple there were Evelyn and Duncan Reinecke who said hello, looked up and shook hands but did not interrupt their game. Next Cab led him to the two chaise lounges. Tom saw that the young woman who had been sunbathing was turning around and affixing the top of her skimpy bikini. She was a brunette with long hair, long lashes and long legs. When she smiled hello it was with a wide mouth. Her name was Freddie, which Cab explained was short for Frederica. Tom thought that that was the only thing short about her. "Hello Freddie," he said and struck by her beauty, once again thought that Cab was one lucky fellow.

"And this is someone you have met before," Cab said as they moved on, "albeit just once." The woman with the sun hat and the book, the book now on her thighs, she looked up at Tom, a slow smile playing her lips. Taking off her large sunglasses revealed a fine straight nose and clear intelligent eyes.

Cab snapped his fingers. "Quick, tell me her name, Tom."

"Theodora Kephalides," Tom shot back. "One of the winsome threesome at the bistro. Right? Known as Tookie to her friends?" He was pleasantly surprised. She was an intelligent woman. "Nice to see you again."

"Didn't I tell you?" Cab was delighted. "Didn't I tell you he'd remember? It's not for nothing this guy is a scientist. Phenomenal memory."

"So it seems. Unless of course, his memory was primed?" She appeared amused. "Hello, Tom. I am flattered you'd remember me."

"Primed—hell!" Cab protested. "Tom had no idea you'd be here. So, Tom, some refreshment?" Everybody was having daiquiris, he was told, and Cab went off to get him one. Tom pulled over a chair and placed it next to the chaise. "May I?" he asked. "Tookie?"

"Sure. But please—no more Tookie. It's my Holyoke sorority nickname. Away from the sisters, I am Thea." She pulled herself up in a sitting position. Her bathing suit was a relatively modest affair, circling her thighs properly and being of one piece, the top of the suit nicely tucked up.

"Thea," Tom said approvingly. "Much better; and quite uncommon."

Cab reappeared, carrying a small tray with two small glasses and a bowl of peanuts. "I freshened up yours, Tookie, just in case," he said.

Tom smiled and looked at her. She gave a little laugh, "I've just been letting Tom in on ex-Tookie, and that I am now Thea. I'm sorry that I never got around to telling you that, Charles, but you were doing most of the talking, most of the time."

"Thea, huh? Okay." He was unperturbed. To Tom he said, "I had to do a lot of talking."

"He fast-talked me by phone into coming here," Thea interjected. "He eventually persuaded me into believing I'd be doing everyone a big favor, myself included, but you especially, Tom. Isn't that right, Charles?"

Cab said, "Certainly. Freddie drove her up. Didn't you, sweets?" He half turned to the other chaise. "Tell us what you gals were talking about."

"Not nearly as much about you guys as you may flatter yourself to think, Chaz." She chuckled. "Also, neither of us knew beans about you, Tom, and to my great relief Thea and I found lots of other interesting topics."

Thea asked Tom, "Did you really not know I was coming?"

"No, I am sorry to say, Cab did not clue me in. I'm here because Cab invited me, and I hadn't seen his place. Of course, I'm delighted to be here."

"Well, as for me," Freddie said, rising languidly from her chair, "I came up because I have been here before, and as I told Thea, if we play our cards right we'll be having a hell of a good time." Everyone watched as she strode to the edge of the pool and dove in, gracefully as a dolphin.

"Actually," Thea said, "we did talk about you, Charles, or Cab, or Chaz, whichever you prefer."

"Cab, is fine. You girls put me through the wringer?"

"More like, I grilled Freddie about you, Charles, asking what kind of a fellow you are, and so on. I think you should know that."

"No problem. I suppose you're not going to rat on what Freddie said about me."

"You are right." Thea smiled mischievously. "She can tell you herself."

"You bet she will," Cab said and took a running start to jump into the pool. The dog, who had followed the exchange with perked-up ears, ran alongside him and plunged fearlessly into the water with his master.

"A happy family," Tom said. He noticed the Scrabble couple getting up and walking to the pool, she testing the water at the shallow end before sinking down and parting the water with her arms, he taking a dive and crossing the width of the pool under water. Shouting and much splashing ensued.

"I guess now it's our turn," Tom looked at Thea.

"Frankly, I prefer to take a little walk." Thea rose. Her body was fine-boned and gracile, as a Degas dancer's.

"Well, so would I. If I may join you?"

"Certainly," Thea said. They went towards the house, along the pool.

"We are going for a walk!" Tom shouted to the wet heads.

"Dinner's at eight, cocktails at seven!" Cab shouted back.

The room assignments were as Tom had suspected. He had Thea as his immediate neighbor. Nor was Thea surprised. "I'll be ready in about five minutes," she said as she firmly closed the door.

They met in front of the house, both turned out in jogging suits, hers a froggish green and his a military olive. "Good match, we are," Tom said, holding his sleeve against hers.

Thea smiled, "Wouldn't you know it!"

The unintended double meaning of the exchange silenced them for the moment. Thea set a brisk pace up the winding country road for about a half mile, then turned onto a footpath that led towards a stand of trees. It was so narrow they had to walk single file. Tom asked if she knew where they were headed and she replied, not really except that the map she had studied in the car indicated that there was a lake close by.

Thea was right. They came upon a small inlet within minutes. The water was a brackish green, and there were granite rocks lining the shore. The footpath itself ended right there. There was much forest detritus about, rotting leaves, dead branches, a fallen tree trunk or two. Tom produced an army knife from his pocket. "I always carry one," he explained when Thea looked surprised—and cut himself a sturdy stick, swinging it a couple of times like a baseball bat.

"Cut me one, too?" Thea asked. "A smaller one, more like a walking stick?"

"With pleasure," Tom said and went about selecting one for her that would have a little knobby end, like a handle. "There," he said when he was done. "That should do it." Thea, pleased, thanked him. It fit well in her hand, and she thanked him again.

There was nothing more to do. Tom picked up a stone, threw it up in the air and whacked his stick against it. It made a nice arch and hit the water with a dark plop.

Thea said, "Can we talk?"

Tom, who was scraping leaves away with his foot to find another stone, stopped doing so and said, "Sure!"

She hesitated, searching for the right words, then threw back her head and looked up at him. "I just think it's important that you understand why I am here."

Tom nodded, "Right."

"I mean—it's not—I'm not like Freddie. I didn't come up here on a date, so to speak, on a sex kind of weekend. Now, don't misunderstand, I have nothing against Freddie. She is an extremely intelligent girl, not just a pretty face and a to-die-for body. In fact—you probably know this, but Charles rescued her from modeling and made her enroll at Columbia School of Journalism, and she is getting all As. And nothing against sex, either, given the right person and the right time. I mean—gosh, this is coming out all wrong, this has nothing to do with you, Tom, nothing personal, okay?"

"I understand," he smiled.

"Well, maybe you do. I just didn't want you to get the wrong idea, what with adjoining rooms and all." She smiled back, "Now, let's get back to the point about why I am here."

"All right. Why are you here, Thea?"

"Because Charles asked me to sort of get to know you."

"Really? To square the equation, boy-girl, boy-girl, boy-needs-girl?"

"That would hardly have enticed me out of New York, I assure you, although I must admit that turns out to be a convenient plus. No. Charles made a strong case for my presence here when he found out who I am and what I do." She paused, shaking her head as if despairing of her ability to make herself understood. Tom said nothing, and she continued. "You see, I am a forensic expert, specializing in medical and dental cases. Most of my work is done for personal injury and homicide cases, for which I am retained by attorneys. My actual specialty of orthodontics is fast receding into the background, although I am still a member of a group practice in Queens. Charles found all that out about me, and said he wants to retain my services, provided his client would agree. Apparently, you are the client?" It was a question.

Tom said, "What else did Cab tell you?"

"About you? That you are a nice guy, which you are; and you're single, but why are you wearing a ring? Never mind, it doesn't matter; and that you're a doctor. Charles thought that would clinch it, but actually, Charles is very persuasive of and by himself. So, I'll ask again. Are you the client?"

"If I were, what would be your services?"

She sighed, "The old Socratian trick of answering a question with a question, huh? Look, you are talking to a Greek, we invented it. Tell you what, we'll leave it hanging for the time being. No rush. Meantime, you know who I am and why I am here."

"I appreciate it," Tom said.

"You are welcome."

Tom laughed, "I mean, thank you. Very much."

She looked at him out of the corner of her eye, nose crinkled, and turned back onto the footpath, swinging her stick.

Tom followed. So in Cab's scheme of things there was a reason for him to be invited up there this weekend, other than pure hedonism.

Dinner was informal, if you ignored the fine china, the heavy crystal and the modern silverware, all of which glittered and glimmered in the reflection of the flickering tapers in the two three-armed candlesticks. The country ambiance suggested casual attire, but the men all wore ties and the women gems or pearls, in the case of Freddie, both. They had cocktails, from the finest brands, in the living room, dispensed skillfully from a bar by Cab. The chatter was inconsequential and voluble, good feeling permeating all around stoked by the firewater. Nobody smoked, but tantalizing odors wafted in from the nearby kitchen. Everybody was affable, becoming more so by the second round.

It was bound not to last, not the whole evening. Tom, at least, was hoping it wouldn't. Deep down he felt out of place, never having been much of a partygoer, and the wound of the loss of Nettie as raw as ever. Would that ever change, he wondered as he joined the hearty laughter following a witty remark made by Evelyn Reinecke. Haw-haw-haw. Soon it would be his turn to say something funny, the jokes had gone the round except for him and Freddie. For the life of him he couldn't think of a single funny line.

And now here was Freddie, with a limerick about "a country lasse, who had a magnificent asse, not round and all pink, as you probably think,"—she wagged a playful finger at Cab—"but gray, with long ears, that eats grasse."

Howling laughter. "Ogden Nash!" shrieked Evelyn.

Saved by the bell, the delicate Limoges dinner bell sounding from the dining room. "We had better not keep Shoya waiting," Cab said. "Let's go in, shall we?"

The seating, as he suggested it, was simplicity itself. He and Freddie presided at the opposite ends of the table, and he had the ladies to either side and Freddie the gentlemen. The only mixing possible was to put Tom next to Evelyn and Thea with Duncan Reinecke, but Thea obviated that by quickly grabbing the chair next to Tom's.

The dinner centered around leg of lamb, following a clear broth that had a searing but pleasant aftertaste. There were mounds of rice and vegetable on the table, and the idea was that Cab would carve and they would all be on their own with what would go on their plates. Shoya poured the first of several bottles of fine wine that Cab had standing on the sideboard, and withdrew. Cab raised his glass, "Two of us are not familiar with the rest of us around this table, I discover to my chagrin, so please allow me to make amends and identifications. Charming Thea," he lifted her hand to his lips, "is a practitioner in the art of dental beautification, commonly called orthodontics which I trust you will bear in mind as you smile at her. And her table companion is my old friend Tom, a doctor whom you would consult in vain at a dinner party about your aches and pains, for his esoteric specialty is the little things that bug us."

"A shrink!" Evelyn cried tipsily. "I knew it! Just look at his eyes!"

"Ev, my dear," Cab kissed her fingers also, "your perspicacity has never failed you. It was time, therefore, that it did, just to keep you humble. Tom is a researcher, a hunter of microbes, of viruses and staphs and streps and coccusses and things."

"I know, I know—and whether pigs have wings, you old walrus you!" She leaned over and put a smack of a kiss on Cab's cheek.

He said, "Thank you, I think," and then turned to address Thea and Tom. "Evelyn and Duncan and I are chicken neighbors. You know, as in 'why does the chicken cross the road?' We live across the road from each other. In real life Duncan is a lawyer, in fact we were law school classmates, and he has ambitions to become a lawmaker. There is a good chance he may run for Congress next year. Dear Evelyn here, as you may have guessed is a journalist."

"Why?" Evelyn interjected. "Why would they have guessed that?"

"Because of your penchant for asking questions, for which I am personally very grateful. If you hadn't found out this place was up for grabs, Evy, and if you hadn't asked me if I was interested I wouldn't have bought it."

"In other words, you are calling me a nosy bitch!" She growled and made a gesture of strangling him which he laughingly warded off.

Now Freddie raised her glass, "As the nominal hostess of this love-in, may I say welcome, all around, and especially to Tom and Thea." She had a lovely glow on her prominent cheeks, and her hair hung loose but artfully cut around her face. She wore a pastel pantsuit so fluid it revealed as much of her figure as it concealed. She looked truly beautiful.

Tom, who sat to her right, said, "Thank you. I'm glad to be here."

"So am I," said Thea. "And, people, let's stop being witty, please? And talk about something interesting?"

"That's a challenge," Duncan intoned, with his deep bass voice, "at any gathering. But I'm with you, Thea. Once I have eaten. I'm famished."

So, it seemed, was everybody. Cab did the carving, and the dishes were passed around. There were also colorful bowls filled with what Cab called Shoya's Persian chutney, "sweet, sour, spicy" and they helped themselves to that. Bottles of white Bordeaux made the round. The chatter did not stop, and little cries of "excellent" and "superb" could be heard now and again.

In the course of the dinner Freddie paid more attention to Tom, who ate quietly, than to Duncan, whose attention to her was becoming more than casual. Tom couldn't blame him; the young woman's mere presence, with the subtle but beguiling perfume that emanated from her body, was intensely erotic. He would have wished that she concentrate on Duncan more—even under normal circumstances he would not have wanted to pursue her; she was much too young for him or rather, he would not have been able to muster the kind of ongoing infatuation for young-maidenly charms that was Cab's apparent indulgence; nevertheless, he was flattered that she spoke to him again and again, that she wanted to know what kind of work he was doing, whether he was married—which he artfully dodged with "not at the moment" wondering what if anything Cab had told her about him—and, clever she, if that meant he had been married, whether he had any children. "A son," he said, adding, to forestall further probing, "he lives in California, where I am headed next week." She wanted to know how old he was. "Three," Tom smiled, and when she touched his hand, saying "how nice!" a jolt went through him. Maybe Cab wasn't all that wrong, searching for that fountain of youth.

Later, Freddie got up and went to the kitchen, to return in three trips with heaping platters of cheeses and fruits, and a tray with a coffee urn surrounded by paper-thin mocha cups. Cab used the occasion to suggest that everyone bring their plates to the kitchen, saying, unnecessarily, "Shoya is not a maid; she retires at ten o'clock" as if her absence had not been noted already. In the ensuing commotion the places they had around the table got mixed up, Cab sitting down next to Freddie now, where Duncan had been, who, dislodged plunked himself down next to Thea where Tom had been sitting. When Tom came back from the kitchen the place left for him was where Cab had been. Fine with him; the conversational center of gravity would be at the other end of the table. He didn't much covet that attention for himself.

However, he hadn't reckoned with Evelyn. Peering at him with heavy-lidded eyes, and speaking while chewing pieces of cheese and apple, she said with a thick voice, "So, you're not a shrink, Tom. I apologize."

"That's okay," he smiled.

"No, it's not okay by me. I pride myself in knowing about people. I have to, in my job, if I want to get anything out of them. Know what I mean? I'm a reporter. Ain't no free lunch in my business, baby."

"Probably not in anybody's business, so far as I know."

"Yeah. You pay for what you get. Trite but true." She picked up a grape and squished it between her front teeth. A drop if juice dribbled down her chin and disappeared in the void below the table. "So you are—what? What do you call that what you do, your specialty?"

"Epidemiology."

"The science of epidemics, correct? Now we are getting somewhere."

Tom wished they weren't. At the other end of the table Duncan seemed to be telling a fascinating story, no doubt to impress Freddie who was cradled in Cab's arm.

Evelyn continued, "That means you're not in private practice, right? I go a lot to doctors, and I have never seen a sign that says, 'Joe Shmo, MD, Epidemiologist.' People would think he'd be a foot doctor or a derm, huh? So, do you work for some institution, a university, or the government?" She was trying hard to catch Tom's eye.

Tom, who was peeling an apple, said, "Right. The U.S. government. The Army, more specifically."

"The Army! You guys are keeping tabs on what creeps and crawls out there so that our boys and girls in uniform are safe from bugs, any bugs, anytime, anywhere. You're nodding yes, no? Wait, let me finish. By extension, that means what keeps the Army clean will also keep the rest of us clean. Right?"

"I couldn't have put it better myself," Tom said. Thea was now paying attention. With Evelyn's strident tone, that was unavoidable. Even Duncan had caught the drift and was looking over. Evelyn had the floor.

"You gotta understand something about me, Tom, I'm just your average news hen working for a small provincial paper, up in Binghampton where we live when we're not here. I don't have the same access to sources as Big Mother Times, but I figure my readers have the same right to be well informed as the Park Avenue crowd."

"What are you getting at, Ev?" Cab called over in a friendly voice.

"I tell you what I am getting at. Duncan knows, don't you Dunc? Tonight by pure coincidence I am sitting next to a source, an epidemiologist source no less, even though I won't use that big word in my report. Infectious diseases, is what I'll use. AIDS is an infectious disease, isn't it? So then, what's the straight poop on AIDS, doctor? Are we going to have more of it, or less? What about the fudging up of figures that come out of the Centers for Disease Control. What am I going to tell my readers? Our government lies to them?"

Duncan, suddenly alarmed, shouted, "Ev, please! This is not the time or the place!"

"Aw shut up, Dunc. You and your conservative pals have been grumbling about it for months. Here we are, a bunch of taxpayers, and I'm asking a member of our government to come across with some answers. How about it, Tom?"

"Well, first of all, you do me too much honor calling me a member of the government. An employee, is more like it." Tom grinned and glanced around the table. He thought he caught a raised eyebrow from Cab. "Secondly, in direct answer to your question, Evelyn, I must inform you that at this moment I am still a member of the United States Army, and as such I am expressly prohibited to speak for the Army in any way without prior authorization."

Evelyn burst into a cackling laugh. "Sure. 'What's up, doc?' is not a question you can answer to. Okay, all right. I'll get back to you when you are out of the Army. No sweat. When will that be, Tom?"

With a look that he hoped was disarming, Tom replied, "Soon, I hope. I am on discharge leave. All I can say now is that you may be on the right track."

Evelyn said, "And you may be wondering why I bother. Well, it so happens my family owns a pharmaceutical business which by the way pays nice dividends, witness a certain Connecticut country home and a budding political career. If you've ever wondered about genetically engineered artificial blood, come see me. We may be able to interest each other."

"And with that, dear people," Duncan rose from his chair, "it's time for us to go home and hit the hay. Thanks for a great dinner, Charles, we had a real great time." He bowed to Freddie, then looked at his wife, "Evelyn?"

"All right, I hear you." She pushed her chair back, and said to Tom, "Know what I am allergic to, doctor? Bullshit. And I get a lot of it these days. You can't imagine."

Tom, getting up to help with her chair back, said, "I can. Believe me."

"You can?" A bit unsteady on her feet, she stood focusing her glance on him. She nodded, "Maybe you can. You give me a call, honey, and we'll talk."

Cab said, "We'll walk you across. Won't we, Freddie? Do us good."

"Not me, but you go, and take the dog," Freddie laughed. "I'll clear the table and start the dishwasher."

"I'll help," Thea said. Tom said he was good at KP and that he would do the rinsing and stuff and the three of them moved to the kitchen.

Later that night, Tom awoke from an uneasy sleep. He had plunked himself down on the sofa in the downstairs study without bothering to pull out the bedding from underneath it, just covering himself with a blanket. He switched on a lamp and looked at his watch. It was only about one in the morning. He cursed. The way he had slept he thought it was closer to getting-up time. Now he had to contend with five or more hours of tossing and turning.

He thought he might as well use the bathroom, but halfway there turned on his heels and decided to use the one in the gym. No point in waking up Thea with his splish-splash and flushing.

As he opened the door to the gym he was instantly transfixed by what he saw. In the shower stall that was all Plexiglas and indirect lighting stood a couple under multiple jets of water, their bodies glistening with foaming soap, the woman's long hair streaked with wetness. The woman was working a big sponge over the man's back, and now he was turning around to do the same to her, she turning with him, her lovely buttocks—all round and pink—moving to his loins.

It was Cab and Freddie, unaware of his presence.

Tom knew that he should withdraw instantly. Still, for the moment, he could not. It was too lovely a sight, beautiful Freddie—could there be a more perfect body?—being cradled by lean and hairy Cab, who had now dropped the sponge, caressing her with his hands in slow motion, from her pubis to her breasts and back, up and down, his hands gently parting her thighs, then gliding up again to cup her nipples, Freddie's arms bringing down his head to hers, kissing him.

In true panic of discovery, Tom stepped back into the dark of the corridor and closed the door quietly. On tiptoes he stole back to his room, crawled back under his blanket and tried to quiet his racing heart. Sadness engulfed him. Would there ever again be a time in his life when he could love a woman, when the innocence of romance and mutual desire would favor him?

There was a knock, from the door of the connecting bathroom. A voice, "Tom?" It was Thea's. "I saw your light. Can't sleep either, huh?"

He got up and opened the door. "Thea!" He remembered now that he was in his underwear. "Something wrong?" He would have to put on his pants. He said, "Let me put on some pants," and left the door open as he went back to do so.

"Look," she said, "I hope I am not disturbing you?" She was in a housecoat over a long nightgown.

Freddie's image still on his mind, he said to himself, "Disturbing, is not the word for you, Thea, no offense." But his excitement was abating. The real world was returning. "Not at all, come in," he said from where he was picking up his slacks. "Just give me a sec." Army practice indeed made him slip into and zip up his pants in seconds.

"If you don't mind." Thea moved forward, leaving the door ajar. The bright light of the bathroom framed her shadowy figure like a halo. "I just thought, if we both can't sleep, we should talk. The mocha was very strong."

"Sure." Tom pulled up a big leather chair for her. "I think there's a wet bar in this cabinet here." He went over to open its doors and found a sink over a small refrigerator, drink bottles and glasses on pull-out racks at the sides. He asked her what she wanted. She told him "anything, no hard stuff." He poured her a soft drink. For himself he made a scotch and water. Then he sat down on the sofa.

"We've got to get something squared away, Tom," Thea took a sip, "and it might as well be now. I mean—about what it is that Cab and you want me to do for you."

Tom drank and said, "I don't know if it's that easy to explain."

"Let's start from what makes people tick, from the bottom up. Sex, money and power and all derivatives thereof. Now, we can rule out sex. I can't imagine I was brought up here to be seduced by either one of you guys. Don't answer that. It's a given. Money? Not in the cards, from what I can see. Power—which is where crime fits in. Cherchez le crime, as we say. Hey, I'm a forensic expert. So, Tom, are we talking crime here?"

Tom rattled the ice cubes in his glass. "It's very difficult for me to answer that question because I don't know how or even if I should."

"Take it easy. Two things are coming out. Your friend is concerned, you are involved, and the question is, was there a crime?"

Tom spoke more resolutely now, "Yes, there was a crime. Cab had nothing to do with it, except that he is acting as my sole confidant. That's why I am not sure that I should involve another person."

"Okay, I can see that. Can you answer this—what is the crime?"

"Murder."

"Of whom?"

"My wife. Look, this is a very complicated matter, and everything I say will sound suspiciously self-serving. Let me put is this way. Officially, my wife died in a boating accident which I survived. For a while, I was suspected of having done her in, but there was no evidence to support that, and no charges have been brought. Only I know for sure that my wife was murdered and that I didn't do it. I know it, and the person who murdered her knows it."

Thea's eyes narrowed. "Assuming that you speak the truth, how do I verify that?"

"You could check with Cab, if I were to ask you to. He has direct evidence that is known only to him and to me."

"If the evidence were to be made available to me, how in your opinion would I be able to help your case?"

"I suppose, because it has medical origins, and you are an expert, as you say, in a medical-related forensic field. On that basis, I would give you permission to check this out with Cab."

Thea sat motionless for a long moment, looking at him. Then she said, "Before I do that, answer me one question, and no equivocation, please, just a straight answer, or no answer at all."

Tom nodded. "Go ahead."

"There are, as you say, three people who know what really happened: you, Cab, and the murderer. Now, listen carefully. What do you intend to do when you find the murderer?"

Tom, elbows on his knees, stared into his whisky glass. Then he drained it in one gulp, slamming the empty glass onto the lamp table with such force that it made the light flicker. His cheeks were flushed and there was a quiver when he opened his mouth, making him cough. When he had cleared his throat and calmed himself he said in almost a whisper, "Nettie, my wife, and I had a happy marriage, I assure you, and it produced a child, a three-year old boy who will never know his mother. Nettie died a horrible death, just unspeakable, the details of which I will spare you unless it becomes necessary for you to become involved." Again his voice broke, and he was searching for a tissue.

Thea jumped up and ran to the bathroom, bringing back the box. She sat next to him, "Here, use it, and don't be a hero. My Dad cried rivers when my mother died, and he's a tough NYPD detective."

Tom blew his nose, twice. "Thank you. It always gets to me when I picture what they did to Nettie."

"They? There was more than one?"

"One perpetrator, with an organization behind him that may or may not have put him up to it."

"Now, can you answer my question? What do you intend to do when—not if, but when—you find him?"

Quietly, he answered her, "Do away with him. Kill him, probably."

She seemed to have expected that, for she nodded and said, "You, personally? You, a doctor, are capable of taking a human life?"

"I can see no other way." Tom had found his composure. "I know what you are getting at. Hippocratic Oath, turning the other cheek, and so on, it doesn't apply here. This is basic, Old Testament stuff. An eye for an eye."

"Interesting." Thea moved to the other corner of the sofa. "You have no idea how interesting. I have a story to tell you, my story, which is equally as confidential as yours, Tom. Keep that in mind as you hear it. Five years ago last Labor Day, my mother disappeared from a Greek-American picnic on the north shore of Long Island. The picnic is an annual affair, and usually Dad attends it with her except that year he was assigned to the security detail for one of the political candidates in New York City. So Mom goes alone, there are oodles of friends she is with, and it's supposed to be a fun afternoon. When the picnic was over, Mom was gone. Disappeared. No trace." Thea pulled a tissue out of the box. "This gets to me, too, Tom. Okay? All right. To cut a long story short . . . "

"No, please, tell me. Take your time. I want to know."

"Some of the details I won't tell you. That stays in my family. Anyway, I was doing my residency in orthodontics at the time. My older brother is an assistant D.A. in Syracuse. Dad's a homicide detective. Now, total disaster—Mom's missing. Okay, the first assumption is that my mother fell from the stone jetty and was carried off in the current. There are two things wrong with that assumption: Mom would be no stone-clambering fool, and she was a former champion swimmer. Usually, bodies get carried out to sea, but some don't make it into the outer currents and eventually wash up ashore. When that happens, you can tell forensically when death occurred, and more. Sure enough, Mom's body was found beached a mile away five days later. Now, here is where I come in. I glommed myself onto the coroner—Dad's influence helped—and find out all there is to know about my mother's last day on earth. Next, Dad, who never for a moment believed it was an accident gets going on his own theory that Mom was murdered. Rob—my brother, my equivalent of your pal Cab—also joins in. Alas, the official verdict is accidental death by drowning. Case closed. But not for us; between the three of us we have access to the FBI main frame, the New York State police, and more. We bury mother, Greek Orthodox rites, Dad takes compassionate leave from his job and starts sleuthing on his own. You see, we know our mother. Someone would have had to hurt her, then push her to drown her. But push her, from what? A boat? Start from there, then ask: how did they get her on the boat, lure her away from the picnic grounds?" Thea was becoming agitated, fidgeting with the tassels of her housecoat.

Tom reached over and put a hand on her shoulder. "Easy," he said.

"There's no easy in this, Tom. Get that straight." She shrugged off his hand, took a tissue and twisted it around a finger, making a knot with it.

"Thea, please. Maybe we should leave this to another time."

"No. I'm all right, to the extent that I'll ever be all right again." She gave a short, sarcastic laugh. "Okay. It took us a while, but questioning all picnickers my Dad found that there were state park security guards on duty, who all knew each other, except one. So there was one more guard who was not known to any of the others. Dad concentrated on that one, got a description—well, one of the park police even seemed to remember that that guy was talking to a woman, a woman with dark hair, in shorts and a big bosom—my Mom. Mom's big boobs the subject of conversation one more time. Sorry, no disrespect but this whole thing makes you so damn cynical."

Tom looked at her. In the light from the table lamp, the shadows around her were more pronounced, the fine features of her face that he remembered from the restaurant meeting were sharply lined. Now she was wiping her nose with the back of her hand in a small-girl gesture that was quite endearing. He wondered what pain was hidden behind those eyes as she brought her fingers up to them to brush tears away across her cheekbones. He wondered if he should insist that they stop now; it was clear that her story was deeply troubling.

But Thea continued, "I'm gonna skip all the detective work that my Dad did, painstakingly assembling known facts and making reasonable assumptions. For myself, it was an agonizing tour de force across criminal pathology. If it hadn't been that Dad was so well known and respected, and that one of the coroners was of Armenian descent, which my mother was, too, so that he let me hang around the lab and bring in more and more of Dad's 'crazy' hypotheses to check out, we wouldn't have gotten very far. Anyway, we found out, with reasonable certainty that my mother was abducted, drugged, raped, and thrown overboard."

"Good God!"

She nodded. "It gets worse. Lung tissue examination indicated that she died of asphyxiation. She did not drown."

Tom again leaned forward and touched her hand. "I am so sorry."

Thea shook off his hand; this was no time for sentimentality. "Listen! What questions would you, a rational person, ask next?"

"Who did it?"

"Number one." She nodded assent. "And what else?"

"Why?"

"Exactly! I see you are on the same wavelength. The question is not how and where, those follow from the others. The important ones in this case are who did it and why? That's what we concentrated on. Now, two things were clear from the beginning. One, my mother had no enemies who could do that to her," she spat out the that like venom from a snakebite, "and two, she would never go with a stranger. We're from New York, Tom! We watch our every step! The only reason she may have done it is if the stranger was a fellow officer, like her husband."

"The phony park policeman?"

"Right. Now the second question—why? Assuming my mother was a random choice, was that the murderer's m.o., in other words, had he done this before, not necessarily in the same disguise?"

"A serial killer?"

"My father thought so from the beginning. An instinct based on his own professional memory bank, a hunch which he has played before, at times with success. Tom, I don't want to get into the technical stuff with you, but it took several months of day-by-day work, most of it on the quiet because Mom was dead and buried as an accident victim, and the department had no case on her. So, let me zoom in to the close. The most likely suspect turned out to be a man who plied the inland waterways up and down from Rhode Island to the Florida Keys in a motor yacht. There were five unsolved disappearances in Hatteras, Beaufort, Cocoa Beach, Key Largo and years earlier, the accidental drowning of a wealthy matron in Newport, Rhode Island whose only son inherited the family loot including the cabin cruiser from which she fell overboard, the same one on which he now lived most of the year, and wintering in Sarasota, Florida. He was our guy, all right, all the pieces of the hypothesis fit together. We caught up with him around New Year's. My Dad and Rob went down there to check him out, and I insisted on going along although I had to promise to stay back. One morning at the crack of dawn we stepped onto his boat, Dad and Rob flashing badges and whatnot, totally without authority in the State of Florida but what the hell, we were after a confession, right?"

"Did you get it, the confession?"

Thea nodded vigorously. "You bet; that was part of our plan. I kept out of the cabin, and put something into his refrigerator in that cozy little kitchen he had on board. So I didn't hear what he said to Rob and Dad, but he certainly confessed, and he seemed half relieved at the opportunity." She paused, hesitated, then said, "Dad and Rob looked pale and ill when they got off the boat, and they weren't going to tell me what they had heard, but I insisted. And then I started screaming, and they had to hustle me off the dock."

Tom feared the worst—cannibalism? "You don't have to tell me," he said. He really didn't want to know, but Thea ignored that.

She continued, "The guy was a snuffer. In case you haven't heard the term, those are the weirdoes who get their rocks off when the woman they rape is in her death throes from suffocation."

"Oh my God!" Tom exclaimed, truly horrified. "My God, Thea!"

She nodded, "That was the one item we hadn't figured on, this added bit of perversion. It tipped the balance in favor of proceeding the way we had sworn ourselves to act." Thea got up and walked to the bar, pouring herself a brandy. Tom got up, too, and refreshed his own drink. They were standing side by side in the semi-darkness, leaning against the bookshelves.

Tom said, "Your story is not quite finished, is it? If you can go on, I'd like to know how it ended."

Thea tilted her head back against the row of books behind her. Her eyes were closed. After a while she spoke. "I presume that you are not as familiar as we are in our family, with the justice system. People are mostly ignorant as to how it works, or I should say, how it can be perverted if there is enough at stake. By enough, I mean money. Here is this society playboy type who turns out to be a sexual deviant serial murderer. Let's say he is brought to trial. A famous shyster lawyer is hired by his wealthy family, for multi-million dollar fees. The deviant is cleaned up, put into nice clothes, and rehearsed as to what he has to say. He is sane now, but he was mentally ill, some psychobabble disease got hold of him and made him do these things that he now regrets. A whole army of experts is trotted out, the jury is bombarded with pseudo-facts, and they are confused. They have been selected in the first place under special scrutiny by a juror-profile system that has become very sophisticated. There'll be a few naives who can be counted on to vote not guilty, so the jury is hung. New trial? Nah. Plea bargaining. The deviant belongs in a hospital, where an army of psychiatrists can go to work on him, making him a better person. The deviant lives. And everybody comes out ahead, the shysters anyway, but also the experts who have gained not only fees but reams of material for publishing, the shrinks have another interesting guinea pig, and even the sucker jurors can claim to have done their civic duty. And not to forget the media. Check your local listing for the TV movie."

Tom said quietly, "Poor Thea."

"Poor Thea? Let me tell you what 'poor Thea' could have meant. Today, the victim is the suspect, the ultimate culprit. Do you know what they would have done to our family? First, all of this would have been splashed all over the papers and pulps and TV documentaries. My mother's memory would have been dragged through the mud. My father would have been suspected of perhaps having 'engineered' her abduction and murder, and every effort would have been expended to show that he and my mother had fought. We are not your average WASP family, Tom. We are verbose and volatile in our behavior sometimes. They'd have tried to say that he had a honey on the side, and that my mother was a big-boobed hussy, and before you could refute all that the trial would have started and you'd have to do it in court. Gotcha. Even if nothing is proven, they say sorry but we had to do that to be sure. But some of the dirt sticks in the mind of the jurors, adding to their precious reasonable doubt."

"I daren't ask," Tom said. "There was no trial, was there?"

Thea shook her head. "The deviant took off. Dad and Rob had told him that they'd be back with a warrant for his arrest. We saw him pull away from his dock a half hour after we had left him."

"So, what did you do then?"

"We went home. A week later his boat was found drifting in the Gulf, and he was found dead in his cabin. The coroner's report cited salmonella poisoning as the cause of death. Case closed. As was ours."

They stood silent, sipping their drinks, slowly, to the last drop. As they were putting the glasses back into the sink, Tom took Thea into his arms. She felt small and fragile against his chest, and she let him hold her, making small noises and rocking back and forth. When it came time to let go, he gently brought her back to the sofa, put her down and covered her with the blanket. "Sleep, Thea," he whispered into her ear. Then for himself, he pushed the two leather chairs together, alongside the couch. He went back to close the bathroom door and turned off the light in the study. Climbing into the chairs, he said, "Thank you, Thea. We are on the same wavelength, as you say. We shall talk more tomorrow. For now, let's try to get some shuteye."

From the depth of the pillows that Tom had put under her head came a sigh and Thea's good-night wish. Then, silence, and blessedly, sleep.

They awoke early, just as soon as the first light of dawn began to brighten the window shutters. Matter-of-factly, as if they had discussed it before, they decided to return to the City immediately. Tom left a note to Cab and propped it up against the hall mirror upstairs. In it, he thanked Cab for his hospitality, adding that he would call him later. "And give lovely Freddie a brotherly kiss from me." Thea scribbled her own thank you line below, saying that she had asked Tom to take her back to New York and that she hoped to see them again soon. The dog was attentively watching them from the entrance of the bedroom hallway, and when they opened the front door he came skulking along. They barely had a chance to get out and close the door on him.

"That animal gives me the creeps sometimes," Thea said.

"Who, good old Zeke? Nah." Tom laughed.

"You know how his name is spelled, don't you?"

"Z-E-K-E, I would think."

"Uh-uh. I thought you were missing it when Cab explained it at the cocktail hour, you were so busy ogling 'lovely Freddie'."

"I was?"

"Charles was saying that when he had bought the puppy, his father, who hated everything German, greeted the dog with 'Sieg Heil', and Charles said something like, 'Good idea for a name, Dad,' and called it 'Sieg'."

"Seems to me I haven't missed much," Tom laughed. When they had seated themselves in the car and were pulling away out of the driveway, Tom said:

"'Lovely Freddie'—I know I called her that—is Cab's girl and I would not for a moment presume it to be otherwise. And even if it were, or could be otherwise, I doubt that I could work up enough emotional steam to woo her, so to speak. I just thought I should mention that."

"Methinks thou doth protest too much," Thea laughed. "What brought this on? Did I say anything?"

"No, no, no. Just a clarification. Sorry."

"She is on your mind, isn't she? Freddie is lovely, gorgeous even. Most men would covet her. But not you?"

They were driving down the winding country road, there was no traffic that early in the morning but Tom kept his eyes peeled. Presently he said, "I don't know how to say this. I feel sometimes that I am out of the loop, the ordinary pleasures of my contemporaries appear trivial to me, far removed from my reality." He shook his head. "I don't know."

Thea touched his arm. "I know. The trauma is still too fresh." Then she said, "Let's stop somewhere for breakfast, would you mind?"

They went down across the parkway and the interstate and found a nice little inn by the water that was just opening its dining room for the day. A table near the window, with a pleasant view of sailboats bobbing at anchor in the bay, was theirs for the asking. They opted for the breakfast buffet, went back for this and that—mostly fruit and sweet rolls—several times and otherwise continued talking.

Tom raised the point that he wasn't clear on what exactly it was that Thea could do in his case. "You see, there is not and never was an autopsy. My wife's body was burned, cremated you might say, in the fire that destroyed our boat. Nor was her identity ever in question."

"I gathered as much, from what little information Charles was willing to give me. Standard forensics I don't think is the issue here, anyway. So, let's start from where we left off last night. Was there anything in my story that struck a familiar chord?"

"Oh yes." Tom nodded. "What happened to your mother equals in monstrosity what happened to my wife. I have a couple of questions for you, personal ones for which I ask forbearance." He looked at her questioningly.

Thea did not avoid his eyes but seemed to qualify her answer. "I'll try to be as truthful as I can," she said.

"Fair enough. What did you call him—the deviant? May I deduce that the deviant's death from food poisoning was not accidental?"

"You may well draw that conclusion," she replied evenly.

The answer was purposely ambiguous, Tom knew. "That leads me to my next question. How does one live with that reality?"

Thea tried a little joke. "The same as one lives with an eight-hundred pound gorilla, very carefully." But her eyes clouded over. "It is a very serious problem that is almost open-ended in a sense that one carries it to the grave. Are you a religious person, Tom?"

"In a moral sense, I hope I am."

"Then you have to observe two imperatives. Do not act out of vengeance but from justice. Vengeance is the Lord's, as you know."

"How can I be sure that I know the difference?"

"Except by faith, you can't. We sinners may well become the instrument of the Lord's vengeance." She poked around in her already empty grapefruit.

"What is the second imperative?"

Her reply came quickly. "Penance. You must do penance. My sitting here with you, telling you my story last night, is an act of penance. That, too, is almost open-ended, although my faith tells me that there is, ultimately, the forgiveness of sins."

Tom sat silent for a while, until he asked another question. "How moral is it, in your opinion, to pursue the wrong-doer yourself? Or is one supposed to resign oneself to the inevitable?"

"How moral? If society, the human institution that sets up and enforces human behavior, is breaking down, for whatever reason, then individual humans of high enough moral character have the duty to reset the stakes. Those too apathetic will give in to what they would call the inevitable."

"I find that a very dicey proposition, frankly, Thea. Smacks to me of justification for a Jihad, a Holy War, a Holocaust."

"As well as of saints, and reformers, and visionaries! Look, Tom, we are getting away from what we are discussing. We are no philosophers. We are practical people living in the here and now. You told me your wife was murdered, by a person or persons unknown as yet. What are you going to do? It is never too late to go to the police, you know."

"I am past that point, I'm afraid. But I am very grateful to you, Thea. Your penance is working. May I draw on it some more?"

"Yes. And it's pro bono, in case you wonder. Part of the penance." She smiled at him. "Although at this point I don't know what more there is I can do for you."

"I'll let Cab decide that. May he give you a call?"

She nodded. "Of course. So may you, for that matter. Wait, I don't want this to be misunderstood. I'm not asking for a date here!" She laughed.

Tom said, smiling, "I see. I don't come across as date material?"

"Oh you do!" she smiled back. "But, someone else does more. No offense?"

"None taken. I'd be a terrible bore, anyway."

"Putting ourselves down, are we?" She searched his eyes. "You know, I believe you are unaware of how attractive you are to women! You are manly yet gentle, you bring out the best in our instincts. You are dynamite! You'll be breaking hearts again before long, trust me!"

"On that high note," Tom laughed, "I do believe it's time I took you home, to that special someone," and he called for the check.

On the drive into Manhattan, as they were crossing the Triborough Bridge Tom said, "Thea, I don't want you to get the wrong impression about me. I'm afraid it is vengeance that drives me; I want to kill the bastard who put my wife to such a horrible death. I felt that way from the moment I realized what had happened to her, and more so since I found the computer disk in which she recorded her own feelings! Getting the police involved, even if it had been possible—which it wasn't—I had already dismissed out of hand. I knew it would be fruitless and would just add to the agony all round. No, Thea, I'm not good, I'm not you. I feel I have a job to do, and I am going to do it. You should know this, whatever your involvement in my case might be."

Tom phoned Cab later that day and told him that he was flying out to California on Monday. He asked that Cab keep in touch, and Cab said he would, of course. There was great joy in Tom's heart at the prospect of seeing the one person again whom he still loved—his son, Bertie.

Thea's Work

It is one thing to fly into Los Angeles as a visitor, the return ticket safely tucked in the back pocket, and quite another to arrive there knowing that this is home. Tom had read a satirical comment once, by a San Francisco columnist who compared the experience to hearing about Hell in Sunday school, versus actually being condemned to it. Laughingly, he had quoted it to Nettie, just at the time when her new job had been confirmed and with it their move to Southern California. Nettie was not amused; heatedly she said, "You went to med school there, Tom, and from all I have heard you brag about surfing in the morning and skiing in the afternoon, you'd think you'd be pleased to get back there! At least give us a chance!" He had quickly consoled her, taking her in his arms and assuring her that she was right. But deep down, uncomfortable even to himself there lurked the condescending prejudice of the Yankee, and worse yet in his case, of the hidden part of him that was the European aristocrat. Thereafter he was careful never to make a derogatory remark about Los Angeles—or "El-Ay"—again, not even in jest.

But he had to admit to himself that he was not happy "to be back" now that he was ensconced in the guest house—a converted garage, actually—of the Beckers, Al and Laura. Little Bertie made him happy, though, very much so. How the boy had grown! And how he could talk, no more the baby but the child! Tom was quickly acquainted with all his progress, the little two-wheeler he could race up and down the sidewalk, his remarkable skill in working the remote control for VCR and TV, and his astonishing enthusiasm for Beethoven which, Tom would learn soon enough, had nothing to do with music but with a movie about a big dog. None of this ever had come to the forefront during his quick weekend visits in the past. Laura said that Bertie was a very bright child, and they should be thinking about enrolling him in pre-kindergarten early next year.

Laura had done a wonderful job with his son, Tom realized, and he told her so more than once. Each time Laura blushed and whispered "I love him!" Her deep attachment to the child was obvious. Bertie, too, had taken to her as if to a new mother. Tom found this worrisome; he knew he needed to do something to bond his son to himself, although what exactly that something would be he knew not.

As is frequently the case in a fast-moving age, outside events came to intrude into private musings, playing havoc with personal plans and hopes.

The day after Tom arrived, wildfires exploded into a dry and cloudless sky with such ferocity that by mid-afternoon the sun had disappeared behind billowing mountains of smoke, plunging Santa Monica into an early, gloomy dusk. By night, the top of the hills were aglow with red lining, tongues of it licking into the darkness. The Beckers' house was not threatened. Santa Monica the city was too far away from the mountains named after it, but the onslaught of the fires was a thoroughly frightening spectacle just the same.

The Beckers, and Tom carrying Bertie, walked the short distance to the canyon to view the spectacle, the little boy clinging to his father. There they stood, the ocean invisible, the sun a red pinprick in a thick black cloud, people crowding to the edge of the fence, pointing, exclaiming, taking pictures. A gust of hot wind blew soot and ash their way. Bertie started crying. Laura, hovering nearby, took him from Tom's arm and soothed him, cradling him to her breast. It had the desired effect. Bertie recovered quickly, but he stayed with Laura, both his arms around her neck.

It was this little gesture, this picture of his son being more comfortable with Laura than with him, that made Tom realize how far down the road they were towards a possible estrangement from son to father. He said nothing, but he resolved to work quietly to change this, for Bertie was his son, and he was Bertie's father, simple as that.

Professionally, things weren't looking up, either. The jobs that, less than a year ago he and Nettie thought he could get easily had been filled, dried up or were nonexistent. The economy was to blame more than anything else but there was the added problem of Tom's licensing. While admitted to practice in California since his medical school graduation days, he was wholly lacking in continued education credits, and except for research, he was without a clearly defined specialty. It became painfully clear that he was unemployable unless he undertook a complete new residency program in say, family practice, or went up and down the state applying for a research position. In the end, a small community hospital in the Antelope Valley offered him a position as assistant pathologist, at a laughably low salary, but by then it was close to Thanksgiving and Tom had a new set of problems to tackle.

His mother called, obviously distraught. Fos had suffered a stroke, not massive enough to kill him but quite disabling, nonetheless. He was hospitalized, paralyzed on his right side with loss of vision in his recently done cataract eye, rendering him de facto blind. Fos' condition was such that a return home was out of the question for him; he would spend the rest of his days in a nursing facility.

Tom knew that new financial problems would arise from that for his mother. He mentioned it in one of his many telephone conversations with Cab.

"Leave it to me," Cab said. And the Monday after Thanksgiving he called to say, "I found a solution, such as it is, Tom. It's financial only, but it may help some. Bottom line—the nursing home care will be paid for by Fos' old company."

"Paid for? How is that possible?" Tom was incredulous.

"Essentially, what we did—we, that is I talked to the chairman of the executive committee—we did a little refiguring. Your stepdad's pension is set up on a full-and-two-thirds annuity basis, that means when he dies your mother will get two-thirds of his pension for the rest of her life. Now, actuarially speaking Fos will probably croak before he has used up his assumptions and since the pension is funded internally his company has it at their discretion to use the reserve they have set aside for their former CEO, based on his normal life expectancy, in a different way. They bring his one-third pension portion forward to fund his monthly nursing home costs. D'you follow?"

"No," said Tom.

"It doesn't matter. It's a win-win situation. Your mother will get a letter explaining that soon. And even I come out ahead. The chairman has asked me to review the company's pension scheme. Big potential bucks."

"I don't know how to thank you, Cab."

"Nice of you to say that, Tom, but it is I who has to thank you. It was a terrific lead. Change of subject. When are you coming back to New York? I got some juicy bit of info from Tookie."

They had agreed that in their telephone conversations they would refer to Thea by her nickname. Thea had been very busy, practically since their return from Greenwich, following up every lead, every query that Cab had given her. This was after she had seen the disk Nettie had left behind, and after Cab had filled her in on all that had happened since that fateful Fourth of July. In one of his calls to Tom, Cab had asked, "What'd you do to that woman? She's all hepped up about you. Did you sleep with her?"

"In a manner of speaking," Tom replied, and declined to say more.

When Cab said now, "Come back to New York," Tom was quite ready to agree. There was nothing he could accomplish in California, and besides, far dearer to his heart, this would be his chance to regain his son. For without a question Bertie would move to New York with him. Tom had advised his mother of their coming and his mother was overjoyed. She promised to clean up the apartment of all traces of sickroom paraphernalia and to redo the guest room as a little boy's room. "I am so glad, Thomas," she whispered into the phone. "Bertram is my only grandchild, you know, and I was half despairing I should not see him again."

"Mother!" Tom made himself sound cheerful. "Of course you would have, whether I had stayed in California or not. As it happens, we are coming back East. I am glad you are glad, though. It'll be good for the boy to spend some time with his other grandmother. You'll be doing all of us a huge favor!"

The reference to the "other grandmother" was not without cause. Al had cautioned Tom that Carla was burrowing away at her attempts to gain full custody of Bertie, looking for proof that Tom was an unfit parent, a charge that she could not make stick. "Not so far, anyway," Al said. "You've barely gotten out of the Army and returned to your son promptly, right? But we don't want to give her any cause; I mean, don't go traipsing off for any length of time, leaving your child behind. Carla's lawyer would pounce on it."

Tom told Al that that was good advice, and wherever Tom's job would be that's where he and Bertie would settle down. And then he asked how Laura would take it if the job were "out of town."

"Funny you should ask," Al gave a sly grin. "Since we have Bertie, Laura has never been more passionate, I mean, like, wow!" He rolled his eyes. "If we don't click now we'll never click. But I think it's already cluck." He nudged Tom confidentially. "This past month, no more 'not-now-honey-I'm-unwell'. Know what I mean?"

Tom patted him on the shoulder; and wished them good luck. And at the Thanksgiving dinner, which they had with the Smedley's and their children, Laura excused herself twice from the table, ate a lot of cranberry sauce and dipped her dark meat in mustard. Al winked at Tom.

By the end of the second week of December, Tom and Bertie, with some ten pieces of checked luggage including a small bicycle, flew to New York. Cab had rented a limo and met them at the airport. It took them over an hour in the evening traffic to make it to the East Sixties. A light snow was falling, an experience for Bertie who kept his nose pressed to the window when he wasn't fiddling with the small TV set in the passenger console. Tom and Cab were having a drink.

"I need to see you as soon as you have the time," Cab said.

"Not this weekend," Tom said. "We need to settle in a bit."

Cab nodded. "We're making progress, Thea has been fantastic. With your permission, I'll set something up for Tuesday. Okay?"

"Okay. Oh, and I am much indebted to you for what you have done for my mother. She'll probably ask you over for Sunday brunch."

"I'll be in Greenwich for the weekend," Cab smiled. "This limo will take me there, after I have dropped you off."

"And after you have picked up a certain beautiful lady?"

"You like Freddie, don't you? She likes you, too." Cab was still smiling.

Tom laughed. "Give Freddie my regards, and tell her no way."

"No way, José," Bertie piped up.

"You see? Us Campe men mince no words." Tom grabbed his son and wrestled him, making the boy squeal and giggle. "Say it again to Uncle Charles, Bertie!"

"No way, José! No way, José!"

Cab laughed, too. "Famous last words. I'll tell her she's being rejected by both of you. Maybe I'll rephrase that a little."

"You'd better!" Tom said. "Besides, aren't you going to marry her?"

"Me? A totally inbred guy? Freddie deserves better."

"Inbred! What the hell are you talking about?"

"Genetics. On my father's side all the Ashkenazim have intermarried, and on my mother's side all the Creoles have, too. I'm a genetic time bomb, ready to produce a monster."

"You are kidding! Aren't you? Cab, with all due respect to your great legal mind and business acumen, you are as wet as a noodle there. I'll give you a crash course in genetics one day."

"Sure. Anyway, I won't marry Freddie."

"I won't, either. But don't tell her that!" They were laughing again.

"No way, José!" Bertie had the last word.

The meeting with Thea took place in Cab's office on Tuesday afternoon. Just prior, Cab had taken Tom to lunch at the Bush 'n Bull.

"I always take my clients to lunch when it is policy delivery time," Cab had said when Tom insisted it was his turn to be the host. "Your policy is here, issued without any restrictions. You came through the underwriting with flying colors. No speck of dirt anywhere on your record, including the military. And of course, no HIV red flag."

"That was as we expected it, wasn't it?" Tom asked. "Or should I be surprised?"

Cab shook his head. "Maybe a little grateful. In my business, you never know how it goes until you got it. Anyway, you're okay. Congratulations."

Thea was already waiting for them when they returned from lunch. She got up from the waiting room chair and gave Tom a slight peck on the cheek. Tom returned it, and they both said they were glad to see each other again.

In the conference room, doors closed and Warren on "no interruptions" notice, Thea unzipped her briefcase. As she laid out, fan-like, three, four, five pieces of paper in clear plastic envelopes, she looked at Cab, and when he gave his nodded assent she started to speak.

She began by giving a brief overview of her methodology which she defined as taking elements of Tom's case and checking it back against known parameters and if the preponderance of the data proved confirmable she would then move the elements from conjecture to probability.

"Hold it!" Tom interrupted. "Thea, please. I can see you have done very good work here, and I'm all for rational, scientific approaches to complex questions. But one thing I have learned in my Army job is, that if you can't put it in simple words the question probably hasn't been answered yet. Just tell me what it is you have found."

"Bottom line?" Thea looked hurt.

"No. That's just a currently popular cliché. Sorry to be so stubborn, but if you could tell me where you went, and what you got?"

"I think you should listen to Thea, Tom, and see if that isn't exactly what she is doing," Cab advised.

"Well, actually, I can understand his feelings," Thea said. "Tom has been waiting several months now to unravel the mystery of his wife's death. But that's where you are on wobbly ground, Tom, if you let your feelings be your motivation. Facts are what you need, and we've got some here for you."

"Okay," Tom grinned. "Touché."

"No sweat," Cab said. "Teamwork."

Thea smiled, "Exactly; we are all on the same team, Tom, and perhaps I am too wrapped up in the technical stuff. My work in forensics happens to be rather technical, just as you are in your own work. Anyway, I have access to certain sources." She picked up one of the envelopes and showed it around.

Her sources were the FBI Academy, as was evident from a letter in which someone wrote to "Dear Theodora" and the National Center for the Analysis of Terrorist Acts, a non-profit organization funded by a number of philanthropic foundations, who had sent a fax in reply to her inquiry. Thea explained, "I started from the premise that the person who perpetrated that heinous act on your wife, Tom, was either a psychopath on the order of the kind that are or become serial killers, or a cold-blooded terrorist. The FBI behavioral scientists have developed a model for the former. It was oddly comforting for me to learn that our own private assumptions had been instinctively correct." Thea looked at Tom when she made this remark, and Tom nodded his understanding. He wasn't sure if Cab was in on Thea's own sad story. Cab said nothing.

Thea went on, "The person we are trying to identify, psychopath that he or she may be, falls into the latter category. I must tell you though, Tom, that I did entertain the possibility that you yourself could be the murderer. I cannot blame the authorities for having looked at that angle. It would take a high level of intelligence to bring off a homicide of the kind that occurred on that boat of yours, and you have that. What dissuaded me from it was the explosion and fire. You could have gotten killed by it yourself."

Tom readily agreed that everybody was suspecting him at first, and that there was no defense against it except for his own word. "That's where it still stands, essentially—that I could have killed my wife. I wonder if I will ever be relieved of that burden of suspicion. But then comes the question about the explosion. Why would Nettie risk killing me in the process, making our child an orphan?"

"I thought about that also," Cab said. "There may be a simple answer. Your wife, Tom, underestimated the explosive might of that propane gas she unleashed. You said the cabin windows had been pulled shut, right? The police did find a cigarette lighter in the debris? It would have taken only a flick from the flint to spark the explosion. Nettie forgot about the gasoline cans in the forward hold. Instead of a contained incineration she achieved a full-blown immolation that she had not foreseen. Yes, you could have been killed, too, if you had been any closer to the cabin. Then Nettie's sacrifice would have been in vain."

Thea quickly took over again. "My line of inquiry centered around the question why your wife was the victim of such a ghastly assault. Charles let me read the disk Nettie made. A very moving testament but I must tell you both, it would not stand up in court as evidence. Anybody could have tapped that out on the computer, you included, Tom, long after the fact, particularly since it was not shown to the authorities at the very beginning."

"I didn't come across it until just recently," Tom said quietly.

Thea nodded. "I believe you. Maybe even a jury would believe you. But a good defense attorney would tear you to shreds."

"That's why we are here," Charles said. "To obviate a trial."

Thea went back to her notes. "What interested me especially was the company your wife worked for, Tom. Goleta Research Laboratories, subsidiary of White Cross Veterinary Products which in turn is owned by New Brunswick, or NB Pharmaceutical. Giant in its field, stock traded on NYSE—you know all that. Now think. Does a company like NB Pharm have enemies, make enemies—and I don't mean just competitors. I asked myself, in today's political climate, what with national health insurance and all, what do drug companies have to fear most? Adverse publicity ranks high on the list there. So I did a little research along those lines. I wrote to NB Pharm on my forensic letterhead stationery and asked them to tell me what if any animal experiments they still do in their research labs. Here is their reply." She handed Cab and Tom another set of her plastic envelopes. The press office of the company's Research Foundation made some interesting statements. That the total number of animals used in research had been reduced in a ten year period from 620,000 annually to a current level of 125,000; that the vast majority of animals used were rats and mice; that only 347 dogs were currently being kept all of which were specially bred for their genetic blueprints, that no cats were currently being used—the previous year had still seen seven cats employed for tests—and that all animals benefited from rigorously humane standards approved by the relevant animal protection agencies. The letter closed by stating that "the results of our research experiments have an applicability-to-humans rate of 80-85%, which fully justifies the continued if limited use of laboratory animals for the battle against disease." Thea looked at them, "Now tell me, what comes to mind when you read this letter?"

"They come across as defensive," Cab said. "Apologetic, almost."

Tom shook his head, "No mention is made of monkeys! Nettie's lab supplied monkeys to NB Pharm."

"Right!" Thea was triumphant. "Exactly, Tom. Monkeys have a special role in medical research because they are primates. They are just a step away from the apes and us humans in the development chain. Moreover, certain peoples in Africa and Asia attribute mystic qualities to those humanoid creatures. I asked myself if there could be a connection between the importation of monkeys to Goleta Research and your wife's death. After all, she makes special mention on her disk of monkeys falling ill and whatnot. Why did they fall ill in the lab and not on the weeks-long sea voyage? Did somebody make them ill? Your wife makes a very strong insinuation to that effect. Did she not say that she found that out, and also accuses a German coworker of introducing the virus into the lab?"

"She more than insinuates," Tom said. "Nettie flat-out states that the virus was willfully introduced, and that that fat, repugnant Olaf fellow injected her with it! Killed her, in effect!" Tom was breathing hard.

"Impossible to prove," Cab sighed. He added quickly, "Not that I doubt her, mind you."

"Well, I got in touch with the Terrorist people in Washington, to see if and what they have on NB Pharm with regard to animal rights activists." Thea pulled out another envelope. "They got plenty. NB had a lot of trouble, to the point where some of their labs were invaded, vandalized, their people threatened. In each case, NB settled for sums of money, out of court." Thea smiled sarcastically. "I guess they don't trust the court system, either. Anyway, the method of blackmailing the government or a company for money is straight out of the terrorists' bag of tricks. They have all done it, the IRA, the PLO, the Baader-Meinhof Gang; it is their preferred way of raising funds. And they get it because, up to a certain threshold, the companies or governments will pay off rather than get involved in a public dispute, especially not with those animal rights nuts. All it takes is to show how those cute little animals are gassed and tortured, plus the Beautiful People in Hollywood getting in on the act of pointing accusing fingers at the drug industry, and the companies don't stand a chance. Look what happened to the fur wearers."

"Where does that lead us, here in our specific case?" Tom asked.

"When I agreed to work for you," Thea replied, "I did so under the presumption that I have your carte-blanche permission, Tom, to extract all the information from Charles that he has received from you." Tom nodded his agreement. Thea continued, "Somewhat reluctantly, Charles told me about the shipment of books that you received not long ago, and what it contained. Now this is pure conjecture on my part, but in the light of what we know, this gratuitous act has all the earmarks of a payoff. By whom, you ask? Listen, assuming that large corporations keep their security arrangements as secret as possible, for obvious reasons, and furthermore assuming that such work is often contracted out to professional security firms, I played a hunch that NB Pharm of New Brunswick, New Jersey, if they had gone that route would hire a contractor in New York City. Your parcel was mailed from New York City, wasn't it, Tom? Now, I don't know about the laws elsewhere but here in the Big Apple security firms have to be specially licensed as some of their operators may be carrying concealed weapons and so on. So I asked my dad to check and see which major firms would likely be providing security for pharmaceutical companies. It came down to two. I called them both, trying to bluff them into admitting they worked for NB Pharm. Never mind how I presented myself on the phone; of course I did not do so under my wonderful Greek name. Well, what do you know but at one of them, a woman clerk who I sincerely hope will not get fired for revealing this information, did say that NB Pharmaceutical Corporation is on their client list. I thanked her, told her I'd get back to her and hung up. Slim and inconclusive as this lead is, it makes some sense to me."

"To me, too," said Tom.

Cab said, "Why would they go to all that trouble to make it look as if the animal rights nuts were behind it, including even a note of condolence?"

"From a genuine sense of regret at something having run tragically afoul? And to induce me to feel right about keeping the money," Tom guessed. "I also think now that the man who came to my hotel door in Santa Barbara after Nettie's memorial service may have been one of their guys." What occurred to Tom as he said that was that Carla's sudden wealth could have sprung from the same source.

"Either way," Thea said, "the real donor would under no circumstances want his or their identity revealed. After all, they were the people who had hired that fat German creep to work in their Goleta subsidiary. Which brings us to my final handout." It was a letter from the U.S. Immigration and Naturalization Service regarding one Runge, Olaf, H., Ph.D., who had a temporary work permit to conduct research at the Goleta facility of White Cross Veterinary Products. It showed Dr. Runge to have crossed into the United States at Blaine, Washington on May 1, 1993, and to have left the country via the same border station on July 2, 1993, well ahead of his visa's six-months expiration date.

"The INS has no other data on him except that his visa was issued on a specialist hiring request from White Cross," Thea said. "I would suggest that you fellows follow up on the creep's Canadian whereabouts and his German antecedents. Also, regarding the animal rights organization your wife mentioned, Tom? ALARM, an acronym for Animal Liberation and Rehabilitation Movement. You will be surprised how much information is available on this and other animal rights organizations in the New York

Public Library. I didn't even try to delve into it deeply, but I did make a copy of what was listed under the ALARM banner." She rummaged in her briefcase and came up with a single sheet. "Well, gentlemen, that is it. End of lecture."

"Great work, Thea," Cab said.

"Fabulous. Thank you, Thea." Tom came over and hugged her. "I'm in your debt."

"Not in mine," Thea whispered. "It's all yours, Tom." Aloud, she said, "I shall leave now, fellows. I'm out of here, not just physically but mentally as well. The stuff I gave you, I hope you treat with the utmost confidence. If not, I shall deny ever having been here. We do understand each other?"

"We do and we thank you." Cab rose and went to shake her hand. "Won't you reconsider sending us a bill?"

"No. Tom and I have an understanding and that's where it shall remain."

"At least let me call you a taxi," Cab said.

"I'll walk you to the street," Tom said.

"No, thank you, Charles, thank you, Tom. I'm out, okay? Good-bye."

True to her word, Thea walked through the doors that Cab opened for her and was gone, without looking back.

"Great gal," Cab said when he came back into the conference room.

"She truly is," Tom agreed.

"You two?" He wiggled his hand. "Serious about each other?"

"Not in the sense that you mean, Cab," Tom mimicked the gesture. "No bells are ringing. But we understand and respect each other very well."

Cab took some cans of soft drink from a wall fridge and handed one to Tom. "You gotta think along those lines one of these days, Tom. I mean no disrespect to Nettie's memory, you know that. But you do have a son and you have to become a family again."

Tom nodded. "Don't think I'm not aware of that, Cab. First things first, though. It'll take a little while to digest the information Thea has given us but one thing is clear already. The ALARM people and NB Pharm are two giants locked in combat, and my wife got ruthlessly killed in the process. Frankly, I don't care about the giants but I will not rest until I get the creep who gave her the death shot."

"The creep—let's call him that from now on, shall we? Cover name, sort of? He's disappeared into Canada, according to this." Cab pointed to the INS sheet. "One of my major insurers I'm dealing with is a Canadian company. I'm going to make some inquiries in Toronto, see what they can dig up for me."

"And I'm going to spend some time in the New York Public Library, researching the animal rights movement in general and the ALARM people in particular. We may not be able to get to the Creep except through them."

"Don't do anything hasty," Cab warned. "Let's meet periodically and put our heads together, shall we?"

"Not to worry. It'll be Christmas soon, Santa Claus time for Bertie. Be prepared to come for Christmas dinner at my mother's house. Bring Freddie."

"Sorry, pal," Cab grinned. "It'll be sailing time in the Bahamas for us. Among other things."

"Happy sailing," Tom said, and slapped his friend on the shoulder.

Scents and Rumblings

As it happened, Tom did not see Cab again until after the first of the year. They telephoned a couple of times without saying much of consequence, and then Cab flew off with Freddie to join their sailing buddies in the Turks and Caicos.

Tom spent a great deal of time with his son, whom he grew to understand more and more, forming an ever deeper bond. No longer the baby, little Bertram had developed into a bright and sensitive child. How sensitive, Tom would learn one day when he had taken him to Rockefeller Center to view the Christmas tree and enjoy the carol singers. Not unintentionally, Tom led him to the lower plaza towards the ice skaters who seemed to fascinate Bertie. They stopped and watched, the boy pointing excitedly at a couple of small children, wobbly on their skates, who were given their first experience on the ice by their mother, a lively young woman with pink cheeks and blond hair.

Tom asked Bertie if he would like to try something like that; yes-yes, Bertie nodded vigorously. Tom said, incautiously perhaps, that when he was that small his mother, Bertie's grandmama, had taken him here to this very place and taught him his first steps on the ice.

The boy let that information sink in, his eyes still on the squealing kids and their laughing mother. Then he turned to his father and, with a solemn expression that was beyond his years, he asked quietly, "Mom is not coming back, is she, Dad?"

It was as if a red-hot dagger had pierced Tom's heart. Pain welling up, he embraced his son and clutched him close to his chest. He held him, rocking him gently, kissing him on his cheek. Then he sat him on the balustrade and holding him at arm's length, locked eyes with his son and said, "No, Bertie, Mummie is not coming back. She has gone up ahead to heaven. There she prays for us, every day, as we pray for her here. And she wants us to be together, you and me, and to be good, and for you to grow up strong."

The boy nodded. No tears were in his eyes, Tom noticed as he fought back his own. They hugged once more, then Tom took his son down and made him stand on the bench.

"Now, pardner," he gave him a faint box on the chin, "what do you say we go see Santa Claus and ask him to bring us skates for Christmas, huh?"

It would be a joyful Christmas, all signs pointed to that. Tom had never seen his mother so animated, so bustling with red-cheeked energy, not since his growing-up years. She and Corinna, her long-time "daily" scoured the back of the hall closet for boxes of ornaments and tinsel, giving off little cries of surprise when they found yet another one. Tom made himself useful by going out and buying strings of colored lights of the new kind that had none of the little fragile bulbs that could break. He also ordered a six-foot northern pine, from a service that promised to deliver and set up the tree in your own home. For Christmas dinner Eleanor Watson conceded reluctantly that she should not be spending precious time in the kitchen and let her son take care of it. So Tom and Bertie set out for a deli in the Village that was advertising "full-course dinners of your choice, cooked and ready on Christmas Eve." Instead of turkey, ham or roast beef, Tom chose roast goose complete with apple stuffing, mashed potatoes and red cabbage. The proprietor, a rotund bearded man with a thick accent, was delighted when Tom also bought stollen and marzipan and promised to have all of it at their home, "piping hot, sir," by late afternoon Christmas Eve.

Another reminder of his youth was the long rosewood table in the hall where his mother would display the Christmas cards that were coming in; Tom, home from school, would read them all and wonder who the senders were, and how there could be so many of them, over a hundred or more. There were not that many this year. Perusing them at his leisure one morning—Bertie watching a TV show about a plump dinosaur called Barney—he came upon one glossy card with a group picture of the account executives of the Preferred Customer Service department of MetroBank, seven of them, men and women, black and white and oriental, a wondrous mix in all considering the smallness of their number.

One of the women looked familiar, a tall brunette perched on the arm of a chair, in a dark conservative suit but with a skirt short enough to display knees and legs, one foot hooked around the ankle of the other. Of course he knew who she was. His mother's account executive whom he had met back in October; a.k.a. the "dream girl" that he had ogled from afar in the LAX flight lounge back in July. What was her name? Emily Dessauer, yes.

He turned the card around because he noticed a plastic clip on the top edge of it holding a note, "From the desk of Emily Dessauer, Assistant Vice President" and handwritten underneath was "Dear Mrs. Watson, I haven't heard back from you since my meeting with your son Dr. Watson a little while ago. Please call if you have any questions? We're here to help, as always. Merry Christmas! Emily." Her signature was a curvaceous E flowing into an archy M, followed by a wave that ended in a downstroke. Very interesting signature, Tom thought. A bit on the flamboyant side. No, not flamboyant, more like impetuous, willful, with a dash of girlish charm, very much as he remembered her.

He pulled himself out of his reverie. Miss Dessauer deserved an answer. Tom took the card into the den where, to his amusement, he saw Bertie singing along with the kids on the screen who were dancing with that big fluffy dinosaur. He had no idea his son could sing, keeping the tune perfectly well. The card had been dated December 13th. This was now a week later, just a few days before Christmas. Hmm, Miss Dessauer might not be in, the way bankers keep hours. He was not surprised when that was indeed the case and he got her voice mail. He identified himself, leaving his name and number and saying that her efforts were very much appreciated, and that Mrs. Watson would get back to her after the holidays. The word holidays was a quick afterthought because just then it occurred to him that Dessauer might be a Jewish name and that that was the reason she was not in the office, the seven days of Chanukah not being over yet, or were they? Then he realized that he had left his last name of Campe on the tape, which could only confuse her; so he called back, amended his message by stating that he had inexplicably failed to correct her at their meeting when she assumed his last name was Watson, but he was his mother's son from her first marriage. He apologized and wished her happy holidays.

The Barney dinosaur show was over; Tom was dressing Bertie in boots and snow suit because they were going to visit the Central Park Zoo, again, when he heard his mother call his name asking him to please pick up the extension in the library. He told Bertie to hang on a minute and went to the phone.

"Dr. Campe, is it? Hi. Thanks for letting me know, about your name. Am I pronouncing it right?"

A woman's voice. Cheery sounding. Instantly simpatico, as the Frogs say. Or the Wogs, or whoever. Tom felt giddy. He knew who was calling. "Yes, you are, Miss Dessauer. Thanks for returning my call."

"Well, I just picked up my voice mail. What's the weather like outside?"

Tom looked out the window. "Light snow, some sun. Nice, actually." She must be in an inside room not to know that yet he remembered her office had bright big windows. Shaded, at the time he met her because of the migraine she had.

"It's going to be a nice and beautiful day here. Sun's just coming through," she reported.

Oh yeah? Perhaps she was calling from one of the top floors of the MetroBank Tower, above the clouds? "Really? That's good to know."

"Dr. Campe, I'm glad you called. I sort of feel like I owe you an apology, from when you were in my office and I was so totally dysfunctional."

"Not at all. I understand. No apology necessary."

"I was bombed, like a massive hangover. I shouldn't have come to work, except I had a meeting to attend, and appointments. You know how it is, you think you're indispensable. And gosh, telling you about my period and all!" An audible groan accompanied that statement.

"Really, Miss Dessauer, there's no need."

"I mean, here you are, a total stranger, and I unload all my troubles on you! I took your advice, though. I went to see a doctor, and sure enough, you were exactly right. It was my birth control pills. Apparently, I fall into the small percentage of women who get those side effects."

"Yes, that happens." Tom made a shushing noise to his son who had come into the room trailing his mitts behind him. The boy was querulant, "Da-ad?"

"I'm sorry, Dr. Campe, I'm taking you away from something."

"Oh no. My son just came into the room. We are about to leave for the park. No problem. I'm glad you called."

"Your son? What's his name? How old is he?"

"Here, I'll let you ask him that yourself." Tom held the receiver to the boy's ear. "Say hello to the lady, Bertie."

"Hello." A low-voiced response. Then a vigorous nodding. "Bertam," in a half whisper. "Uh-huh," nodding again. A hand going up with four pudgy fingers.

Tom laughed and took the phone away from him: "He's trying to tell you he is four, but he isn't quite yet. Some months short of four."

"He sounds darling! What's his name, Bertam?"

"Bertram, he can't manage the R yet. We call him Bertie."

"I bet he is very bright!"

"Too bright, sometimes." Tom felt bright and daring himself, all of a sudden. "Would you like to meet him? I invite you to have lunch with us at the Tavern on the Green!"

A warm, very womanly laugh that Tom found instantly endearing, "Fixing me up for a date with your son, huh? I'd love to, but I can't. Impossible."

"I understand."

"I don't think you do. I'm calling you from California."

"California? Where, exactly?"

"Los Angeles. Santa Monica, exactly."

Tom was dumbfounded. "Santa Monica? We've just come from there, a couple of weeks ago! My wife's sister lives there, and her husband! They live on Georgina Avenue."

"Oh, I know Georgina. I'm on San Vicente, just a block over."

"I know the neighborhood! Good Lord, I had no idea."

"I had mentioned it to your mother when I spoke with her. I thought—I guess I should have said where I am calling from."

"So, what are you doing in California? A new job, a promotion?"

"Yes, but not to California. I am here on vacation, which will culminate with my getting engaged on New Year's Eve." A slight chuckle.

Tom felt as if he had been hit with something. "Why?" he stammered.

"Why New Year's Eve?" she laughed. "Because everybody is out partying on that day anyhow, so if it doesn't work out it's still a New Year's Eve Party!"

"Why shouldn't it work out?" His inner voice nagged him. Don't be daft, Tom. Say congratulations to her!

"Well, of course, except it's the second time around for both of us. We've been engaged to each other before." A little laugh. "Once burned."

Twice shy?, his inner voice thought. To her, "I'm sure it will work out, Miss Dessauer. May I offer my congratulations."

"Thank you." A pause. "Well, Dr. Campe, it was nice talking with you. I wish you and your family a very Merry Christmas."

"Thank you, and the same to you. Thank you for calling, Miss Dessauer."

Click. End of conversation.

Very reluctantly, Tom pushed the antenna back into the phone. His mind was still talking to that woman called Emily, forming questions that would not be asked and never be answered. He cursed through clenched teeth. Why? Why was he doing this? There was not a chance of a snowball in hell that he would ever meet her again, and besides she was going to be married. And worse yet, she probably assumed that he was married, too. Not a chance? No way? He must have been saying that out loud, for Bertie, in rhythm, was pointing with both forefingers, "No way, José. No way, José!"

"Okay, wiseguy!" Tom scooped him up. "Let's go to the park!"

Christmas came and went, a long weekend suspended in time as if cut off from regular life at either end. There were visits to the hospital of course where Fos lay breathing shallowly; to St. Aldan's (where Eleanor's family had worshipped since her grandfather's days) for Christmas Eve Vespers which was deeply impressive for a solemnly round-eyed Bertram, and also visits to neighbors and friends.

Max the doorman had succeeded in selling Tom's car, for considerably less than expected, but what the heck; it was Christmas and who wants to haggle. A goodly portion of the proceeds went to the co-op staff, Max happily included, for their annual holiday bonuses. Tom had insisted that he pay them this year.

Santa Claus had not forgotten about the skates for father and son. So insistent was the boy to try them out that Tom sprayed the rather large back balcony with water after having removed all furniture and having plugged the drainage holes, hoping for an overnight freeze. And voilá, a mini ice rink for Bertie. Bertie got his first feel of skating, much of it on his butt. Then he caught on and made careful push-steps at the hand of his father, eventually gliding triumphantly in small concentric circles. A promise was extracted to take the show to Rockefeller Center, soon.

Bettina called from London, her annual Christmas Day exhortation not unlike the Queen's. Tom hadn't talked to her since a few weeks after Nettie's memorial service, when his sister phoned distraught at not having been present. Bettina always used the Christmas phone to impart and receive all the news that was fit to be exchanged, long voluble Englishy gushings that were her way of keeping in touch, in lieu of writing letters. Tom could just see her, comfortably ensconced in that big armchair by the fireplace in her Belgravia flat, stroking a purring cat, her spaniel curled up on the sofa nearby. Bettina couldn't live without her animals. Out in the Chilterns where she had her country house there were more cats, more and bigger dogs, and of course horses, a whole stable full of those. Dear Bettina. He loved her. Bertie, too, was able to get in a word or two, to her delight.

Return to reality came on Monday night, with a phone call from Al Becker in Santa Monica. It was only three o'clock there. He apologized for intruding at dinner time but Tom said that was all right, they hadn't sat down yet.

"Got a letter here from Washington, the F.B.I. Remember the agent who interviewed you, Thad Montgomery? Yeah, that's the one. He's asking me as your attorney, to ask you, my client, to make yourself available for some follow-up questions, by calling his number da-da-da-da. I'll fax you the letter."

Tom told him that his mother had no fax machine in her house, and asked him why he could not just give him the number now and put the letter in the mail. "Couldn't be all that urgent, Al, could it?"

"Hey, I don't know. I do know you don't futz with the FBI. Tell you what, though. I'll write him a letter back, making me a good boy, and tell him you have temporarily moved to New York where you can be reached at such-and-such a number and address, and then I'll copy the letter to you and send you the whole shmeer to New York. Nobody works between Christmas and New Year's, anyway, especially not in Washington. Okay?"

So it was. Tom got the letter, read it and did nothing. It could wait until Cab returned to the city, he decided. He wanted to get Cab's opinion first.

In the middle of the first week of January there was a call before nine in the morning. Eleanor Watson, ever mindful of her husband's condition, took it on the first ring from her bedside phone. Alas, it was for Tom.

Tom, who was giving Bertie his bath, shouted to please take the number and he'd call back.

When he did, his son sitting spanking clean and combed at the kitchen table spooning his cereal, he found that he was talking to some bureaucracy in Washington that took his name and number, connected him twice and then told him that he should hang up and stand by for a return call. Which came promptly. It was made by Agent Thad Montgomery, who reminded him that they had met in the fall, at the Army's Camp Frederick in Maryland. "Do you remember, Tom?"

"Yes," Tom did. "What can I do for you, Agent Montgomery?"

"Major, do you mind my calling you that? After all, you are still in the inactive reserve, and I'm a Marine reservist, myself. I am calling to see if you could spare me a few minutes of your time."

"For what?" Tom asked.

"Some follow-up questions having to do with your late wife's employer. You wouldn't mind, would you?"

"Go ahead," Tom said.

"Well, I tell you, since you are in New York City, it'd be a hell of a lot easier for us both if we could do it in person instead of going into a long rigmarole over the phone. It so happens I'm on detail up your way in New York on Martin Luther King Day. If you could come on the Tuesday after to the Federal Office Building downtown. You know where it is, don't you, near the Civic Center?"

"Agent Montgomery, I'm in New York for two reasons, to be with my mother whose husband is critically ill, and also to go job-hunting. Yes, I could met you there but things could come up between now and then. Making an appointment two weeks ahead of time could be dicey."

"I understand, major. Let's make it for 10:00 A.M., and I'll call you that Tuesday morning to see if you are free or if we need to reschedule. When you are in the building, identify yourself to the guard, I'll have you pre-cleared and somebody will take you to my office."

There wasn't much Tom could say except to agree. When he called Cab to discuss it the following weekend, Cab had just returned that Saturday. Cab said, "Let's talk about it. I might also have some stuff back from Canada about the fat creep." They agreed to meet on Wednesday in order to give Cab a couple of days to clear his desk after the holidays.

When Wednesday rolled around Cab phoned in the morning and asked if they could meet somewhere pleasant, where he could get some fresh air, but as it was snowing to beat hell they settled for the convenience of the facilities of Temple Emanu-El when Cab suggested that Tom should consider enrolling Bertie in the preschool program. "They have an excellent preschool program, and it is just a couple of blocks from your mother's house. Tom, you should start thinking along those lines for him. I have the clout to get your kid in, too." That was a point hard to refute.

So when Bertie was taken off their hands by a very kind young woman with skin the color of sandalwood—"Ethiopian," Cab remarked under his breath to Tom—and the boy went willingly, the two men repaired to the basement cafeteria for a cup of coffee.

"You know," Cab said, "I've been thinking about why the FBI wants to talk to you further. I don't think it has to do with you, personally."

"I sure hope not," Tom said. "I have nothing more to add to my previous statements."

"It may be about the Creep. If we are on to him, maybe the FBI is too. Therefore, the question we have to ask ourselves is, what are you going to say if it's about the Creep?"

"Play ignorant?"

"Ignorant so far as the stuff on Nettie's disk is concerned—yes. But it would not be unusual for you to know of the Creep's existence, when after all he was your wife's coworker."

"So what do I say?"

"Play it by ear, hear him out, give cautious answers. Remember, these FBI guys aren't fooled, they can see through it, so don't overplay it."

"I won't. Have you heard anything from your sources in Canada?"

"Not a word. Of course, they are not the RCMP. No official search is available to us."

"I've been thinking." Tom hesitated, then continued, "The Creep may suspect somebody could come looking for him, and disguise himself. If you or I would disguise ourselves we would think of false beards, wigs, and glasses or contact lenses, and that'd be about it. Right?"

"Go on," Cab nodded.

"I saw this movie a couple of months ago, about a very sexy girl who was actually a man."

"Are you saying the Creep is a transvestite?" Cab smiled.

"Let's consider it. It's not easy for a man to pass for a woman, given most men's physique. But if you are round and pudgy to begin with, you could without too much difficulty make yourself look like a round and pudgy woman."

"Ah yes! And have a different set of identity papers waiting for you in Canada. A Miss Creep may have flown the coop from the first airport!"

"Exactly. Now, my extensive reading in the public library on the subject of animal rights organizations—not the usual humane society kind, mind you—point to international interconnections. German, Dutch, and British. Mostly British, in fact. Much royalty involved, as patrons, many show biz people, in the U.S. especially. And all of them very well financed. There is a cross contamination with certain political movements, the Greens, for instance. And there may well be a hidden agenda—a sort of post-Marxist nostalgia."

"The possibilities are endless, Tom, if you put it that way!"

"Right. We cannot afford to get distracted from our goal—to get the Creep. Sorry, I mean my goal. You have already done enough, Cab."

Cab shook his head vigorously, "I'm in this with you, to the end." Then, changing the subject, he said, "Before I forget, I had a message from Evelyn Reinecke. Remember her?"

"How could I forget?" Tom smiled.

"She asked if I knew when you'd be out of the Army. She wants to meet with you."

"Meet with me? What for?"

Cab shrugged. "I checked with Duncan, just in case, from pal to pal. He thinks she may want to offer you a job. She is a Gooderham, you know. Big bucks, trust funds, moolah."

"A job? In journalism?"

"Remember she mentioned a pharmaceutical company? That may be it."

"Well, no harm in talking with her, I guess. Why don't you set something up, I am unemployed, I can use some leads."

"Will do," Cab said. "Of course, if you click, I get ten percent of your first year's salary."

"You are worth more than that," Tom smiled.

Agent Montgomery called the week before the proposed meeting, to see if they were still on schedule. They were, Tom assured him. Nothing had come up, Fos Watson was holding his own, and Tom's meeting with Evelyn Reinecke, was interesting if inconclusive in terms of job prospects.

He met her briefly for lunch at the Plaza Athenee, where Evelyn seemed to stay when she was in town. She made it clear that she wanted "the true poop" about AIDS statistics from him; clearly, feisty little Evelyn had an agenda. Assuming that Tom would come through she would recommend him to the head of a newly created biotech lab—a subsidiary of her family's pharmaceutical house—in Elizabeth, New Jersey, where they were engaged in research for the creation of artificial blood. In her opinion, Tom seemed ideally suited to that kind of work.

Tom was cautiously interested in her job proposal, but wondered what she needed the AIDS data for. For a scoop, she told him frankly. Her small paper was trying to come up with the sling of David to slay the New York Goliath—The Times. Tom's data could be the stone that would deliver the shot. It sounded too obviously political, but he didn't say that expressly. What he did say was that he didn't think that what he had was anything other than what was already in the public domain. Evelyn gave him a sly look, said they would talk again, and lunch was over. Tom left, puzzled and annoyed by the whole thing.

In reporting the matter to Cab at a luncheon the next day, Cab had some news about Evelyn Reinecke, part of which had been unknown to Cab himself.

"I've plugged her into an assets data base under her family name of Gooderham. Now, I must tell you that I don't routinely do that with friends; I respect their privacy. It's essentially a business service I subscribe to."

"Of course. No peeping, Tom or otherwise. I remember at Princeton when you bought that magnificent scope that could be trained at the night sky, but occasionally caught the back room windows of the Nassau Inn."

Cab grinned. "Memory like an elephant, huh? Anyway, guess what's on record about the Gooderham clan. They are the majority stockholders of, among other enterprises, New Brunswick Pharmaceutical Corporation. Our Evelyn's share is rather small, via a trust set up by her paternal grandmother, but her mother's is far more substantial, and Evelyn and her sister are the only presumptive heirs, as their father died a few years ago."

Tom shrugged. "What are you trying to say?"

"I'm not saying anything. I'm musing, speculating. Evelyn didn't know you when you came out to my place that weekend, but she might have checked up on you since, for her own reasons. Your late wife's employment with her family's company could have caught her eye. In hinting at a job offer, she might want to buy your loyalty to prevent a potential ruffling of the feathers of her golden egg laying goose. Hushing things up. Remember, that's what that whole security crap is about with NB Pharm, your money shipment and so on."

Tom shook his head. "This checking up on people, is that commonplace?"

"You bet. It's only the beginning; wait until the world of digital wonders opens up for us. This is our new culture, and like all cultures it has its benefits and drawbacks. Why do you think we sit and talk here in a place I chose only this morning, or why we talked in the cafeteria of my temple the other day? Electronically safe venues, that's why."

"That's sounds crazy, Cab. By your logic, Thea's visit to your office was already compromised, as was mine."

"Not at all. I am a businessman, who receives clients at his place of business. It's a normal routine. Now, having you come over again and again might arouse suspicion. Speaking of suspicion, you can bet that the FBI knows more about you than you imagine. Be on the alert, and remember they almost certainly have their own reasons for questioning you again."

"Thanks a lot, pal. I can hardly wait till next Tuesday."

Cab put a hand on his shoulder. "It cuts both ways, Tom. You may also glean some information from them. Just play it straight. Essentially you have nothing to fear. You are not the criminal, you are the victim. Remember that."

"Yeah. Sure." Tom sighed. "How did I get into this complicated mess?"

Cab squeezed his arm. "You were done wrong, kid. Nettie was done even more wrong. We live in crazy times. Maybe it all works itself out towards a better future in the next century."

"I like to believe that," Tom said. "Sometimes I feel the U.S. is in the midst of another revolution, just like two hundred years ago. Except I don't see the Washingtons and Adamses and Jeffersons."

"The prophets. You are missing the prophets. They'll come, when the god of the world wants them to come." Cab grinned, "Maybe they'll be computers."

"Some god, that'd be," Tom mumbled and downed the rest of his beer.

Monday was a holiday, Martin Luther King Day. Cup of coffee in hand, Tom went into the den to watch one of the morning news shows, while Bertie was having his cereal with his grandmama in her sitting room.

It was 8:00 A.M., news time. As the picture came up, there was a lot of exciting talk on the screen. Something must have happened, something unusual.

An earthquake in Los Angeles? Los Angeles! An earthquake? Tom sat stunned, eyes riveted to the TV. More news. A major earthquake, in the Los Angeles suburb of Northridge? Buildings collapsed? Freeways down? No power? Then a crude map of Los Angeles was thrown up on the screen, with the epicenter like a gun target marked over the west-end portion of it. No seismic data yet, but first estimates ran "in the magnitude of six-plus on the Richter scale . . . " Tom jumped up and grabbed the phone, dialing Al and Laura's home number.

Predictably, he got a busy signal. He looked at his watch. It was now about half past five in the morning out on the West Coast. Al and Laura would probably be up, jolted out of their sleep even though the quake occurred some fifteen miles to the north of them. Somehow, he felt uneasy, driven by an urge to make contact with them. Try the house again, he told himself, and then try Al's office number, leave a message on the tape there.

Dashing to his room to fetch his wallet where he kept the numbers, he passed his mother's room. "There's been a major earthquake in Los Angeles," he yelled as he raced by. "Turn on your TV, mother!"

Back in the den he made his calls. Both numbers were busy. There was one more number he could try, Al's car phone, although it was idiotic to think that Al would be on his way to the office already.

To Tom's surprise, the phone rang, and was picked up immediately.

"Hello," a hoarse male voice.

"Al?" Tom asked

"Whozziz?"

"This is Tom! Al, is that you? Al?"

"Tom!" The voice grew more distant when it went on. "It's Tom!" as if speaking to someone within earshot. Then, "Tom, where are you?"

"In New York! Al, it says here on the TV you had an earthquake, in the Valley somewhere."

"In the Valley, my ass!" A manic cackle followed. "Tom heard the earthquake was in the Valley! Heh-heh-heh?"

"Al, is that Laura with you? Are you all right? Where are you going in your car at this hour? Al? Can you hear me?"

After a moment, Al answered, in a more sober tone, "We are sitting here in our car in front of our house. It's still totally dark outside, no lights anywhere. Sirens you can hear all over the place, car alarms are going off with every new aftershock, and all we are waiting for is the next transformer explosion. Sure we're all right, Tom."

"Good Lord, Al, was it that bad?"

"That bad? I'll tell you how bad, and no past tense, either, we're goin' on and on with it. Oh-oh, hold on, honey!" The phone went silent for some seconds. All Tom could hear was static noise. Al again, "So, we just had another little rumble. You still there, Tom?"

"I'm here, Al. You were going to tell me how bad it was."

"Yeah. How bad was it, let me see. We were in bed, Laura and I. There was this immense creaking noise, and it shook so hard we couldn't get up, so we grabbed each other and pulled the pillows over our heads. The painting over our bed came crashing down on us, but it didn't matter, it hit our butts. I tell you, we had ourselves a real roller coaster ride." That mad chuckle again.

"But you and Laura are okay?"

"Sure, we're okay. We're breathin', eatin' a granola bar, drinkin' beer. The car radio says it's been in Northridge, but they haven't gotten around to Santa Monica yet."

"Well, thank God you're okay. Did the house get damaged?"

"Did the house get damaged, he wants to know! Yeah, it got damaged. It rocked and rolled, man! The chimney fell onto the patio and took half the wall with it. Everything inside fell out or off shelves, glass, dishes, lamps, books, clothes, you name it. Remember the big armoire with the TV set in our bed-sitting room? It came down, kaplooie, onto the floor. That's the room Bertie was sleeping in, Tom!"

Tom had a sudden horror vision of what-if. "I'm stunned, Al."

"Yeah. So are we. All the neighbors are out on the street, one guy has been passing out beer from his garage cooler, we're all gettin' soused and waitin' for daylight."

"The main thing is you and Laurie are okay." It was a lame remark, and Tom knew it. He was going to say if there is anything I can do, but found that totally inane. "Al, I'm thinking of you. Tell Laurie. Give her my love."

"I know you are, Tom. Thanks. I'll call you, in a couple of days."

After Tom had hung up, the thought that Bertie could have been in that disaster and possibly have been hurt or worse was unthinkable! It gave him goose pimples. What if he had not taken the boy with him to New York! Was it providence? Luck? It certainly was not foresight, and the temptation of leaving him with Laura in her caring arms had been there, strongly so. Yet he had felt even more strongly that he should take his son with him, that they should be together from now on. Was there a lesson in this? Or was it all just chance?

On Tuesday Tom, in a sour mood, went to his meeting with Montgomery. The news from Los Angeles had gone from bad to worse, all the networks were on it, all reporting from the same locations in the San Fernando Valley, with Santa Monica appearing only in the name of a freeway overpass that had collapsed in Los Angeles. No word yet from Al since their early morning talk.

His mood was not enhanced by the elaborate security measures he had to undergo, including the temporary confiscation of his pocket knife, until he reached the office of Montgomery on the fourth floor.

Montgomery himself was cordial, to the extent that his hard lined facial expressions allowed cordiality to shine through. He bade Tom sit down in front of his desk, gave him his knife back, and poured him a cup of coffee from a percolator nearby. The office was an inside one, with no windows, but brightly lit by fluorescent lamps recessed in the ceiling. Montgomery asked Tom to bear with him until the end of the presentation he would give, after which he would be glad to have the major's opinion. Tom thought of asking if the session was being taped but felt that would make no difference; he nodded. The lights were dimmed, and Montgomery started up a projector that threw images on the opposite wall. The subject matter of the slide show was revealed immediately, with one word: terrorism. In successive slides the theme was developed that there were either state-supported or state-directed terrorist groups, or non-state-involved ones. Montgomery, clicking quickly through the former categories then came to the latter, resting on a pyramid that showed the basic organization of such a terrorist group. At the very top, Montgomery explained, using a pointer, was the leadership cadre, made up of men and women of high intelligence and motivation. The aspirations of the cadre were aimed almost always at superior goals, goals that superseded those of society as a whole. Ordinary people were thought of in the abstract, as in "improving their lot" but were held in disdain individually for being too dull to see the point. Their only usefulness lay in two simple, albeit necessary functions. To serve as "the public" for media publicity, without which no terrorist group could achieve its aims, and as a recruiting pool for the functionaries that made up the next layer of the pyramid.

That was the activist faction, the foot soldiers of the movement, the people designated to do the dirty work; and dirty indeed it was, more often than not. Montgomery dwelt at some length on the necessity of the movement to resort to violence, not just to achieve its ends but also for the pure shock value and the attendant notoriety it would generate. The activist-terrorist generally had no direct link to the top of the cadre, for reasons of security. Instead, "cells" and "cut-outs" were used in directing the dirty work.

The broadest and lowest layers of the pyramid were populated by so-called "supporters" subdivided into the active and the passive kind. They were the ones who held fund-raisers for the cause, wrote letters to the editors of large newspapers, and when they were journalists or academics, authored columns and articles. As active supporters, members of royalty (in Europe) or celebrities (mostly in America) were avidly sought. The great masses of the "unwashed" passive supporters were ordinary people gulled by slogans and led by their desire to do good. They provided the backdrop of popular support, the quasi-legitimacy indispensable for the movement.

Montgomery put down the pointer and turned up the light. He remarked to Tom, "You may remember when we had our first meeting at the Army Institute, I asked you specifically if you were aware of any tension between the company your wife worked for and certain animal rights groups."

"I do," Tom replied.

"And that I gave you my card, in case you remembered anything in that regard." When Tom nodded, he continued. "I ask you again. Do you?"

"Do I remember anything?" Tom took his time to formulate his answer. "Not anything specific that would have prompted me to call you, Mr. Montgomery. You have to understand, my wife's death, and the manner of her death was and is a profound shock to me. It occupies much of my daily thought processes. I mull things over, agonize about what I could have done, and so on."

Montgomery nodded. "Certainly you do."

"Sometimes, scenes pop up in my mind, of our time together, unrelated to the disaster. Of what we did, or said, or laughed about, or worried about. You know, married couple stuff."

"Yes. Go on."

Tom hesitated, and not for show; he wondered if he should begin, ever so carefully of course, to reveal the true circumstances of Nettie's death. Or whether it would be smarter to concede small portions of the truth and see where it got him. He quickly opted for that. "One of the things we worried about was job security. Much of what we were planning for the future hinged on my wife's ability to hold a well-paying job. In that regard, there was a worry. A small worry, to be sure, and that's why it did not crop up again. It had to do with how some people viewed the nature of her work of husbanding and treating laboratory animals, especially monkeys that would eventually be used for testing purposes, although not at her facility. In other words, she and the other vets would work very conscientiously to try to keep all the animals healthy and thriving, to preserve them for a higher good."

"Were they successful in that?"

"Yes, of course. It's a job that has seen many humane improvements over the years. We at the Army Institute have the same problems and goals."

"But some people did not see it that way, is that what you are saying?"

Tom nodded. "Exactly. I remember her mentioning once that a certain organization called by the acronym A-L-A-R-M, ALARM, that seemed to be a pain in the neck."

"In what way?"

Tom shrugged. "A nuisance. A bother."

"Did she mention any names, of people involved?"

Tom shook is head. "She was too new to really know who's who and what's what. You know how it is when you start a new job, in a new town yet."

Montgomery went to his briefcase that lay open on a chair next to him. He picked up a file from it and put it on his desk, opened it and took out a page of paper on which a photograph was pasted on the top half. He folded it over, removing the lower half of the page from sight, and handed it to Tom.

"Does this person look familiar to you? Take your time."

Tom took the page and looked at it. The black-and-white photograph was of a round-faced man, with thick curly hair, heavy dark-rimmed glasses and a trim full beard, a neck that went into softly sloping shoulders, making his coat and tie fit awkwardly around it. He studied the picture intently, trying to memorize all its features. He knew he was looking at the Creep. In a controlled voice he said, "I have never seen him before," handing the page back.

"Did your wife ever mention a coworker named Runge? First name Olaf." Montgomery spelled the names.

"Olaf, Olaf?" Tom pondered how to proceed. The name was etched in his memory. Montgomery was an experienced questioner who would know if he lied. "It's an odd name, Swedish I believe. She might have mentioned him as one of her coworkers. The only odd one in a bunch of Toms, Dicks and Harrys." He affected a smile.

"Actually, the man is German. A staff member of the respected Institute for Tropical Diseases in Hamburg. His I.D. on which he was issued a temporary work permit was flawless." Montgomery, stretching his long legs, looked at Tom out of the corners of his eyes.

"Was it?" Tom deadpanned.

Montgomery picked up the pointer and slapped it into the flat of his hand. "I thought you might be interested in knowing that the name, and everything else about the man, is totally phony."

Tom said, "Why are you telling me this?"

"For the same reason that I showed you the slides," Montgomery replied, still playing with the pointer, slap-slap-slap. "The pyramid you saw? It's a model we developed for training purposes. The ALARM group fits it perfectly."

Tom nodded. "I gathered as much. Is that why I am here, for you to brief me on this terrorist group?"

"Essentially, yes." Montgomery sat up and slammed the stick on his desk. "Major, I still believe your wife was murdered. Not by you, either directly or by connivance. I've ruled that out almost from the beginning. No, I smell homicide here, by terrorism, which happens to be my specialty. It's my job to make sure that people who commit such acts, don't get away with it."

"Well," Tom was taken aback. What should he say? "I appreciate that."

"Bullshit! Somewhere along the line, you must have suspected this yourself. You have a science-trained mind, and your wife was no dummy, either. Two intelligent people, and they get blown up by a propane gas stove? Come on! It must have occurred to you that some kind of foul play was involved here." He looked at Tom intently.

Tom held his gaze. "You are right. It did occur to me. It changes nothing of the fact that my wife, whom I loved dearly and who loved me and our son, was taken away from us under the most cruel of circumstances. Now, I am going to tell you something, Agent Montgomery. If you have any specific evidence, if you have any leads that you can impart to me, clue me in."

Montgomery leaned back, "I'm afraid I can't do that, beyond what I have told you already. Regulations, rules, procedures. I don't make them, I just live by them." With a thin smile he added, "Imagine, if you can, where my ass would be if by some convoluted craziness the evidence would ultimately lead back to you. Here I was, feeding you the stuff up front!"

"Thanks a lot," Tom grunted.

Montgomery leaned forward again. "But you can be useful in searching your memory. Something may come up, not today or tomorrow but next week maybe, or next month, or whenever. Get in touch with me. Let's work on this together. If need be, we have trained experts to help you recover memory loss."

"Sure." Tom shook his head in disbelief. "With what you have so far, why don't you go in and subpoena the ALARM people? Squeeze them a little?"

"No can do. They are headquartered in England. One of the Royal Dukes is a patron. They do good. They are well respected. They sit in a nice old mansion in Oxford, plotting to save the animal kingdom from humanity. Squeeze them—squeeze the Queen. See what I mean?"

Tom gave a short laugh. "These days, squeezing the Queen is an English sport. But yes, I do see what you mean. If there is anything that I think I can do to help, I promise to call you."

"Good." Montgomery rose. The interview was over. He saw Tom out the door, then walked with him to the elevators. As they waited for a down car, he said casually, "You have a sister in England, don't you?"

Tom was taken completely by surprise. "A half-sister."

"Yes." Montgomery said. "From your father's first marriage." It was not a question, but a statement. "She's the editor of Horse and Hound, isn't she. I bet she'd have a tale to tell about the animal rights nuts in England."

The red down arrow pinged and an elevator door opened. Montgomery stepped in, and hesitantly, so did Tom.

"Why are you telling me this?" Tom asked. He could feel his heart beat.

Montgomery shrugged. "No particular reason. You people are an open book, as in Who is Who, and the Almanach de Gotha, not to mention the Justice Department's immigration files." He gave Tom a reassuring smile. "Maybe it's because I care, as a fellow citizen. And maybe because I want to tell you to watch your backside." They had arrived on the ground floor. Montgomery held the door open for Tom to step out, then went to his shirt pocket and pulled out his card, stuffing it in Tom's suit pocket.

"Take care, major." He let go of the elevator button and raised his hand in a quasi-military salute. Before Tom could return it he saw Montgomery's thin-lipped smile, like the Cheshire cat's, disappear as the doors closed.

Cab had said he wanted to hear about what went on in the FBI interview and had asked Tom to call him right after. "Let's meet for lunch," Cab had said. Tom, however, was so preoccupied with what he had heard from Montgomery that he began marching north along Broadway, not even thinking of hailing a taxi. The image of the phony Ph.D., the fat Creep of Nettie's demise, was burned on his mind. He cursed himself for not asking for a copy of the photograph, wondered if Montgomery would have given him one and decided that he probably would not. What to do?

Walking briskly across Washington Square and on towards Fifth Avenue, he spotted an arts supply store near NYU. Instantly he had an idea. He stepped inside and purchased a sketch pad with a faint undergrid of graduated markings on each page, a beginners book on portraiture, soft pencils, an eraser, and a box of pastel crayons. More purposeful now, he made for the Public Library. There he searched for a vacant place in one of the study cubicles and settled down. He had decided that he would draw, from memory that would never be as fresh again as it was now, the portrait of the Creep.

It was not easy going. In science and anatomy classes he had done a lot of drawing, mostly of cells, nerves, blood vessels and the like, but that was ten years in the past. His hand now was not as sure as he applied himself to render as accurately as possible the visage he had gazed at so intently less than a couple of hours ago.

Gradually, after several failed attempts a picture emerged that satisfied him. He could now concentrate on the finer points, starting from the top. The hair: curly, in a wavy, rather natural way. Forehead: wide but not high, in keeping with the squareness of the whole face. The eyebrows were thick and bushy, unusually so. The eyes—wait a minute, Tom whistled under his breath, we got something here. Big eyes, slightly drooping lids, one eyeball a bit askew—exophthalmus, ptosis, strabismus! No way that could be disguised, on this point alone one could recognize the man. And then the nose, and lips—both fleshy, sensuous, and that hint of a dimple in the chin. Tom was amazed what he could force onto the page from his mental imprint. The picture that had emerged stared at him. "I'll get you, bastard!" he swore as he closed the sketch pad.

From a pay phone he called Cab's office number.

"Hi, buddy, how'd it go?" Cab asked. "I've been waiting for your call!"

"Lunch—how about meeting you at the clock in the lobby?" Tom didn't have to explain; there was only one such lobby clock for them, in the Waldorf Astoria.

"Okay! See you there! Half an hour?"

"Right," Tom said and hung up.

They went from the lobby straight into the bar. Tom picked a table in a corner that had lamps on both sides, providing reasonable brightness. They ordered bourbon and hamburgers and asked the waitress to leave them alone.

While they were eating, Tom recounted, as verbatim as he could, his conversation with Montgomery. Cab listened, asking him a couple of times to repeat himself. When Tom was finished, Cab declared himself satisfied. "Now we've got something to work with."

"There's more," Tom said and from the arts store shopping bag that he had placed by his chair pulled out the sketch pad. He opened it to the last page he had completed at the library. "Voilá—the Creep!" He gave it to Cab.

Cab whistled. "Wowie! You did this from the FBI man's photo?"

"It's not perfect," Tom said. "It needs the artist's touch."

Cab agreed. "I know someone who is a police artist by day and a serious painter by night. I bought a couple of his watercolors, the ones that hang in the upstairs hall in my house; you saw them?"

Tom nodded, he couldn't remember. He said, pointing to the sketch, "Can you get him to do this better? With me present, to correct him if need be?"

"Sure, I can. He works this stuff on his computer, you know. Any input you give him, zip-zap, it's on the screen."

"When can we do it?"

"As soon as I find out when he is free. Any particular hurry?"

"Yes, a fading memory. The sooner the better. Also, I may want to go to England, to the source. Somebody there must know the Creep and where he is now. Then I go after him."

"We gotta talk about this some more," Cab said and waved the waitress over for a refill of their drinks.

"You're not going to talk me out of going to England," Tom said.

"No intention to. The idea is fine, if—if, mind you—we want to go on from here. There is always the possibility of letting Montgomery do it. Your tax dollars at work."

"No way. Montgomery and I have different motivations. Besides, I may still be vulnerable, you know. The Creep is mine. Swift justice."

"All right, then let's do it rationally. England. You have every reason to go there. Your sister invites you. Betts will, won't she?"

Tom smiled. "She already has, in a general way, in her Christmas message. Bertie is invited, too."

"I like that. Nobody is going to read anything into it. A family visit."

"Exactly."

"She has good connections to the upper crust, doesn't she? Someone she can wheedle the Creep's current address from?"

"It's worth a try," Tom said and sipped from his drink.

"More than that. It's the only chance we got."

"You keep saying 'we,' Cab. I want you out of it. You have done enough."

"Like hell I have. We are in this together. Besides, you'll need me."

"I don't know, Cab." Tom was playing with the plastic swizzle stick. "I haven't quite thought it through yet, exactly what I'll do."

"That's why you need me. A sounding board. A co-planner. A back-up man."

Cab took his drink and leaned back. "Your sister, Bettina. Last time I saw her was at your wedding. Attractive woman, in her own way, a bit like the young Katharine Hepburn."

Tom laughed, "Not your type, huh?"

Cab smiled back, "Too intimidating. I mean, total aristocrat, on your father's and her mother's side. English-German blue blood. They don't come any better. Is she married yet? She wasn't then."

"No. I don't know that she ever will be. She shares a flat in London with Pat McDougall, that solicitor friend of hers. They have known each other for a long time. Since Cambridge, in fact."

"And they haven't tied the knot? What's going on?"

Tom smiled, "You should ask! Betts and Pat get on well with each other. That's all that matters, really. Pat stands for Patricia, by the way."

After a long moment's silence, during which Cab scrutinized his friend's mien, he said, "You are saying to me your only sister is a lesbian?"

"As my only friend is a Jew. Or maybe a Black. Or both?" Tom shrugged. "I thought you knew."

"I did not. But you're right, it doesn't matter. Especially being lesbian. It's not like being gay. That I really couldn't stand."

"Knock it off, Cab. It's none of your business. Nor mine, either, or anybody's. Besides, I may be wrong. I have never asked Betts about it. To me, she is a wonderful sister, I love her very much. Always have, always will."

"Sure," Cab dropped the subject and finished his drink. "Let's go. I want to see if I can reach Andy Malek. He's the artist. We've got work to do."

They met with Andy Malek, at his studio which was a walk-up apartment in an old red-brick building in the West Eighties, on Friday afternoon, a time picked by Cab who would go on to his Connecticut house from there.

Andy was a spare, tall man in his thirties, with long red hair that was thinning over the top of his head, for which he made up by combing it straight back and gathering it into a wispy pony tail. Tom thought he looked like a 60s hippie, what with his wire-rim granny-glasses and stubblebeard face. In making small talk, he discovered that Andy was from the Los Angeles area, Westwood, and had gone to UCLA. So did he, Tom said, go to UCLA that is. Hey Bruins! High five. Andy's watery blue eyes shone approvingly.

"Man, I tell you," Andy said, "it's a mess out in L.A.. The quake really hit the Westside. UCLA Royce Hall? Closed. St. John's Hospital? Closed. And I mean really closed, condemned, evacuated. Finito. Also St. Monica's, where I was baptized and confirmed. Lots of businesses—closed. Apartment houses—condemned." Andy shook his head. "It's the pits out there, I tell you."

Tom knew; he had just talked that morning with Al and Laura who were beginning to clean up. They had told him the same litany of what got hit, and how bad. One of the apartment buildings on San Vicente Boulevard—"just a block over from our house, Tom!"—had already been bulldozed down and razed to the ground.

"Can we get to the point, fellows, please?" Cab said and consulted his watch. "Tom, do you want to engage Andy, or not?"

"You kidding? A Bruin?" Tom laughed.

"I take that as the affirmative. Okay. Andy, Tom is your customer, not I. He will pay you, all cash, and he gets all of the finished product. No residues remain with you, and that includes what's on your computer. Agreed?"

Andy was happy to oblige. He went to work, starting with Tom's sketch.

It was amazing how quickly a likeness would emerge, as Andy was transposing Tom's drawing to the screen. Now there was a chance to do what Tom's clumsy pencil could not—to alter the length of the nose, the width of the chin, the closeness of the eyes, and the computer performed that wizardry at the click-clack of the keyboard. Within the hour, the image most congruent with that on Tom's memory was logged onto the floppy disk Andy had inserted.

"Olaf Runge, Ph.D.," Tom said, and nodded to Cab. They had their man.

"Now, Andy, if you will, make this man look different. Cut his hair, thin his eyebrows, shave his beard. Can you do that?"

"Sure can," Andy huffed, "ain't nothin' this little gem can't do." He grimaced and sing-songed but sounded annoyed that Tom would think it couldn't.

In due course, a quite different likeness appeared, a fleshy face with pouty lips and bedroom eyes. "He knows why he is growing a beard," Andy said. "The only manly feature on his face."

"Suppose," Cab ventured to ask, "you made him look like a woman. What would he be like?"

Andy nodded, and his fingers flew over the keyboard. "Like so," he said. Curly hair over the ears, wayward strands falling over the left forehead, the lips drawn dark and sensual, a mocking smile playing the corners of the mouth, the brows now thin arches, the glasses stylishly large. "We can do contact lenses instead, if you like," Andy offered.

"Do both," Tom agreed quickly. "Incredible. Good work, Andy."

Andy was pleased, too. "Want to see the full figure?"

"You bet!" Tom said.

"Naked?" Cab asked.

"Either way, or both," Andy grinned.

"Do both, Andy, while you are at it."

"Okay. Now, from the sketch here I can deduce that the person is on the plump side, a couch potato. I can't tell his height but on average, such men tend to be under six feet." He was already producing an outline of a body, undefined as yet. "They generally have smallish feet, and being unathletic their lower legs tend to be without pronounced calf muscles, like so. Ditto their lower arms. Hands on the delicate side, like a piano player's." Several contours were overlapping on the screen until Andy found the one that fit his presumptions. "Now, the breasts wouldn't be pert 'n pointy, more like flat and wide. And the hips—man, it's cellulite-ville. Liposuction, here we come." Andy hooted, and looked up. "Like it?"

"Much," Tom smiled. Cab groaned, rolling his eyes.

The next commands Andy issued to his computer was to do "the woman" in clothes, dress and high heels in one, jeans and sneakers in the other. Tom asked him to put "the man" in similar modes of dress and undress; again, the results were startling. Different persons, different personalities appeared in each image. When Andy was done with it all, Cab asked if the disk would print out, and Andy said yes, provided you had the appropriate software on the printer. Pointing to his, he said he could provide color printouts of the whole or part of the saved images. He was encouraged to go ahead and do so. It was done in no more time than it took for them to pour themselves cups of coffee and sit around drinking, making small talk. Andy was a Dodger fan, albeit a disappointed one last year. "Can only go up from here," he said, and Tom and Cab agreed in unison.

When they left Andy's apartment, cash having changed hands, disk and pictures in a simple brown envelope, Cab made a suggestion. "Leave them with me, Tom," he said. "I want to make copies and put them and the diskette in your file in my safe. Also, I'm going to a lab I'm using and have them do photographs of some of the printouts plus some retouching perhaps, of the facial lines where the computer model was not too discerning. That way, we can use actual photos when we go around asking people if they've seen this man."

"Or woman!" Tom laughed, and agreed to Cab's proposal.

By the end of the month it became apparent that there was nothing more for Tom to do in New York, nor were there any immediate job prospects. Evelyn Reinecke had not called back, and in any case Tom was not too keen on a job in Elizabeth, New Jersey. Much more enticing was what Bettina suggested on the phone, in reply to a letter he had sent her. Would she mind if they—he and Bertie—came to England for a visit, in about a couple of weeks? The way Tom phrased it he had made it sound inconsequential, a casual visit long overdue. It had given him pangs of conscience to put it that way, for clearly that was not the reason for his visit at this time. The thought of deceiving his sister, however benignly, made him uncomfortable. But then, he told himself, perhaps there would be a way to take her into his confidence, at least partially, and make up for it.

Bettina's phoned response was immediate and enthusiastic. "Yes, do come, straight-away. To London. There's lots of room in our flat. And such a grand idea to bring Bertie! We are so looking forward to it!"

They, Tom wondered but didn't need to ask, for Bettina explained in the same breath, "Pat has wanted to meet you, Tom. She knows you only from pictures. She'll be so pleased! She's on the Continent presently,

Belgium, then France I think, some conference of sorts. Be back the first week of February."

Tom promised to call as soon as travel arrangements had been made, and Bertie had been to the doctor for a checkup and some shots. Ta-ta, and an audible smack-kiss from Bettina.

One other thing young Bertram needed was a passport of his own. For which it was necessary to dress him up and take him to a photographer. Which required a haircut and the purchase, at Saks Fifth Avenue, of a blazer and tie that would not only make him look better but also serve to make him appear somewhat older than his age, an important consideration if he was to use the passport for the next few years. The pictures turned out to be so good that his grandmama ordered an enlargement and a silver frame from which, on her writing desk, the adorable tyke smiled at her cherubically. Wallet-size versions of the photograph were given to Cab and sent to Laura and Al.

Al called Tom shortly after, "So you're going to travel, huh?"

"Yes," Tom said quickly. "Just a couple of weeks, to England. My sister lives there, and she hasn't seen Bertie at all yet. While I'm still here on the east coast, and while I'm still at loose ends, I thought we should do it."

"Does that mean you're planning to come back to the west coast?"

"Eventually." Tom hastened to change the subject. "How are you doing, getting back on your feet?"

Al gave a short dry laugh, "We got six thousands bucks from FEMA, for the loss of our chimney."

"From whom?"

"The Federal Emergency people. Doesn't even cover the half of it."

"How is Laura doing?"

"All right. Hey, you're the doctor. When a woman has missed her period, and then has a heavy period two weeks later, does that mean she's been pregnant?"

"It could, but not necessarily. What's her doctor say?"

"She hasn't been to him, yet. Too busy. It gives me hope, though. If she caught on once, maybe we can do it again. Know what I mean?"

Tom laughed. "Keep on truckin', brother. Give her my love, and Bertie's."

When young Bertram Vonder Campe's passport arrived in the mail two weeks later, there was a phone call one morning.

"Major! Thad Montgomery here. How are you you?"

Tom did not hide his surprise. "Montgomery! I'm fine, thanks."

"I see your son is going to England. With you, I believe?"

How did he know that? Tom wondered. Dumb question. He must have realized from the passport application. Tom aloud added testily, "Yes, we are. To visit my sister for a couple of weeks. That okay with you, Montgomery!"

"Oh sure. No problem. Look, Tom—may I call you Tom? And I'm Thad, okay? I have a suggestion for you. You still got my card, right? You can get in touch with me from there, too. Just go to the U.S. Embassy in London, ask for Security and show my card. They'll put you right through."

Tom said okay, forcing himself to add "Thad" as they hung up. It left a feeling of unease, though. Was he under scrutiny? He'd have to shake that.

The Cumberland Clue

They almost didn't make it to the airport in time for their London flight; a heavy snowfall that wouldn't quit clogged the streets, bringing traffic to a halt in a madly sporadic way—here, there, seemingly everywhere. If it hadn't been for Cab and his resourceful limo driver, Tom and Bertram would not have taken off that day. But Fernand, the light-skinned Haitian who drove for "Mistah Blue-mong-feld" with total devotion—Cab had deftly financed the purchase of his vehicle—knew the byways and detours of the Five Boroughs like a native. Fernand delivered them to JFK in time for check-in and boarding.

"Got the pictures of the Creep with you?" Cab asked. Andy's work had been enhanced by a photographer's tricks of trade, showing actual photographs of the Creep—full beard on one, clean-shaven on another, and also a woman's head and shoulders—that could easily be taken for the real thing. A bit too soft on the brushstrokes perhaps, but the pictures' lack of sharpness was more than made up by their apparent veracity. Tom had been pleased.

"I sure do," he said, patting his flight bag.

Cab nodded. "Good. Now, don't forget about the computer."

Tom smiled. "I won't. For Bertie's sake, as well. I'll introduce him to a little interactive magic. I don't want him to get bored over there, what with yet another relative to get used to."

"When you are set up, log on to Aurelius immediately. Got his handle?"

"Yes, in my wallet. Don't worry, Cab. In a couple of weeks we'll be on the Trans-Net. Although I may not have much to tell you at that point."

Cab and Tom had decided to communicate via e-mail, not only for speed and convenience but also for privacy reasons. They had briefly considered an encrypting service, but rejected the idea as counterproductive; in Tom's opinion, the very act of encryption would be like waving a red cape at a bull, the bull in this case being their friendly monitor at the FBI. Much rather, Tom said and Cab agreed at once, they should segue in quietly onto the digital highways, drawing no attention to themselves. Cab, not surprisingly, came up with an additional fillip. He had a "cut-out" he said, for some of his confidential e-mail, a guy he knew only under the name Aurelius who was located in Vaduz, Liechtenstein. Aurelius, whose handle denoted elements of his name and place, was absolutely reliable in remailing messages back and forth, after removing the header. He charged a fee for his services which subscribers—only a few, Cab among them—remitted to a numbered Swiss bank account. Unlike most other users of remailing services, Cab and Tom were not anonymous to each other. It was the transport per se and the finished product at either end that they wished to protect as much as possible. They also agreed to some key phrases that would have a true meaning different from the apparent one, a bit of "mini-encryption" as Tom put it. They laughed, touching fists, and felt once again like the schoolboys they had been, plotting a prank, or later, when they were studying in total privacy for their degrees in Masonry.

On the night flight to England, sitting in the darkened cabin with his eyes closed, his son curled up in deep sleep on the seat beside him, Tom could not find the repose he knew he needed to be refreshed upon landing. For some reason there were dark clouds in his heart that he could not command away, with waves of anxiety lapping at his mind's edge. What he was embarking on was not just a long-postponed reunion with his sister, although he had told everybody that that was the simple purpose of the visit. He was going over there to hunt somebody down, to find the murderer of his wife, to mete out retribution. To take justice in his own hands. He forced himself to say it—to kill! Tom instantly gnarled at himself not to be a weakling. The Creep had been a cold-blooded killer under circumstances that had put him out of society's reach of justice. That did not mean, however, that no other form of justice would apply. Since time immemorial, men had taken it upon themselves when all else failed, to right wrongs that would otherwise go unpunished. Tom recalled a question he had put to his father when he was a small schoolboy, just beginning to read history. He had asked his father what had been the most important event for him during the Second World War. Expecting to hear repeated such classroom topics as Pearl Harbor, or D-Day, his father had instead slowly shaken his head before answering deliberately, "The 20th of July 1944, when the best of us tried to kill the worst of us and failed." His father had patted him on the head, and had left him, bewildered, in his room. It was years later that Tom understood the meaning of his father's words. Tyrannicide. The attempt, the failed attempt, to kill Hitler. Tom's subsequent readings on the events filled him with awe and dread, more so when he learned that his father's older brother, the uncle he never knew, was one of the officers strung up on meathooks by the Nazis. Even now, Tom shivered at the thought of the noble righteousness of the plotters and the cruel price of failure. Had the daring been worth the sacrifice, and in the cold light of reality, would it have made any difference if they had succeeded? Each time he had answered yes to both. Now as the aircraft was hurtling across the ocean, Tom fretted that his own daring was but a fraction of that which the plotters had to muster, and that the miscreant he sought was no tyrant but a pathetic, aberrant creature not worth the effort, best to be left to his own miserable life, to be forgotten. But he had killed Nettie! Was Nettie's suffering to be forgotten, too? Tom groaned and hit the armrest with his fist. No! Not now, not ever!

Bettina was at the airport, and even though she was almost hidden in the crowd, and was wearing an unfamiliar ankle-length coat, her brown hair tucked under a fur-brimmed hat, Tom espied her immediately as he and Bertram emerged from customs. He waved at her and called her name. She saw them, a big smile parting her lips, and waved back gesturing to a place away from the crowd where they could meet. When they did, Bettina had a hug and kiss for Tom and a kneeling-down version of the same for a shy Bertram, who stood looking at his shoes. "It's good to see you, Betts." Tom felt this well-worn phrase had never been more true.

She looked up, giving him a radiant smile, and said, "Welcome, Thomas," her slim hand stroked his cheek, "and Master Bertram." Bettina picked up the boy and held him close. "You must be awfully tired after such a long journey. Let's go home, have some hot milk and biscuits." She hustled them away, toward the exit, motioning the man with the baggage trolley to follow. There was a car waiting outside, a Jaguar with a woman at the wheel who got out of the car when she saw them coming.

Introductions, made by Bettina, were superfluous. Although they had not met before, Tom knew the big blonde with the stylishly short skirt that revealed nearly all her legs as she climbed out of the seat had to be Pat McDougall, Betts' friend. As such, Pat had seen enough photos of Tom and his son to recognize them instantly. She pumped Tom's hand with large up-and-down motions. For Bertie, she had a hug and a kiss and a nice round lollipop.

Tom saw to it that the baggage was stowed in the "boot" and the man paid off. The front seat was his when he got into the car. The Jag was of the kind that had a stick shift. Inching forward and weaving into and out of Heathrow traffic required a lot of shifting. A nice round left knee was constantly in Tom's view as he leaned half back to converse with his sister and his son. The fact that he noticed the knee irritated him. So, for that matter, did the occasional glance from Pat as she smiled or nodded to what was being said. He had the impression that he was being patronized, in the friendliest, kindest way that could not possibly cause offense, but patronized just the same. He quietly resolved to be on guard, also in the friendliest, kindest way, for Bettina, he remembered, did possess a domineering streak that was quite all right for when she was ten and he was five. But that was then and this was now.

Bettina's house—or rather, Pat's and Bettina's house, for he learned later that they had purchased it together—was on Cavendish Lane, far enough removed from busy city traffic to feel quiet and secluded, with the back windows looking towards the trees and greenery of Chelsea Gardens, where on occasions when the wind was right one would catch a whiff of the dark, broad waters of the nearby Thames or hear the tooting of ships' horns. It was a pleasing spot to be, the room Tom was given being one of three that looked out that way. Bertie was to share it with him, on a cot next to Tom's bed. There was a huge cavernous bathroom next door, and beyond it a sewing room that had been given over to the dogs, an enormous black Newfoundlander—Pat's darling—and Bettina's brown and white springer spaniel. Across the hall, the layout was identical, the two women's rooms being separated by a bathroom.

While the upstairs accommodations were not out of the ordinary, the downstairs floor of the house was quite a different matter. There, walls had been removed to create a large area of elegant comfort that encompassed sections for dining, lounging, reading and music-making while at the same time, not unlike an intimate hotel's lobby, providing the ambiance of a salon for entertaining. "Good Lord!" Tom exclaimed when first shown around the premises. "What do you do with all this space, have the neighbors in for a bash?"

Pat smiled happily, and Bettina nodded, "We both have rather large circles of friends, colleagues and clients. As you will see."

And yet there seemed to be no inside help, no butler, cook or maids. It was explained that such impedimenta were a thing of the past. One hired a weekly cleaning crew, and cooks and servers when there was a party. One did one's own laundry in the basement, and changed one's own sheets and towels. As for meals, breakfast and quiet suppers were taken in the kitchen or, weather permitting, on the garden terrace. At any rate, by eight in the morning both women were off to their places of work, Bettina to the editorial office of Horse and Hound and Pat to the chambers of Sullivan and Mack, Q.C.s, where she specialized in liability law. As Tom would learn, it would often be twelve hours before Pat and Betts would drag themselves back in, the rumble of the garage door opening underneath the house signaling their return. Theirs was a busy life; he began to have a quiet admiration for their pluck and style.

The first days passed quickly for Tom and Bertie. Father and son did much exploring of the sights of London, sitting close together on buses or in taxis with Tom pointing here and there, Bertram nodding earnestly, holding on to his daddy's arm and occasionally piping up when he needed "to go" or wanted a snack. It was still quite cold out, and when there were gusts of wind Tom would carry the boy to the nearest warm oasis. In this fashion they lunched at Fortnums and Masons, shopped at Harrods for new, more English-looking boys' clothing and had tea and ice cream at the finest spots. In between, Tom kept his eyes open for the computer setup he wanted; eventually when he found one, he made arrangements for it to be brought to the house and to be connected.

Evenings, after drinks before the telly and microwave dinners in the kitchen, the women would take over all of Bertie's time, spoiling him by seeing to his every wish and exclaiming admiringly at the utterance of yet another new word, cuddling him and, at long last, carrying him upstairs to tuck him in. Tom, although largely ignored, didn't mind for two reasons. One, because the child was taking to it like duck to water, and two, it gave him the time once he had the computer installed, to establish his connection with Cab. He heard back from him instantly when he downloaded his e-mail the first time the next morning. Cab had nothing new to report, but was hoping soon to be able to latch on to an important lead. "Way to go!" Tom mailed back.

That "soon" turned out to be several days down the pike, and it was as tentative as it was tantalizing. In Cab's words, the "shadow government" behind the ALARM organization was the top echelon of the former World Animal Rescue Board that at one time was headed by the Prince Consorts of certain Royal Houses of Europe. The princes had doddered into ignominy at last, one or two of them tainted by financial scandal, and a new leadership had emerged, drawn again from the ranks of high aristocracy but, so Cab ventured to guess, bolstered by a number of political and business interest groups this time around, making the aristocrats mere figureheads. Cab had found out the current "Chairman of the Leaders Group" was right there in London: the Duke of Cumberland, with an office somewhere in the city. Tom could almost hear Cab's guffaw, "Loads of stuff on the Cumberlands in the Britannica, so remember, ol' buddy, when you meet H.R.H., the American boy does not scrape and bow!"

Naturally, the first thing Tom did was to go downstairs into the library and pull out volume six of the Encyclopedia Britannica. Cab was right. There were lots of entries under "Cumberland, Earls and Dukes of." The title went back to the times of the Tudors, died with this or that esteemed holder (or not so esteemed, for one of the Dukes was known as "Butcher Cumberland"), until it was revived by the Hanoverians. The fifth son of George III of Revolutionary fame, was made Duke of Cumberland upon the death of his brother King William IV and sent off packing to the original Hanoverian fiefdom of the British Royals. As King of Hannover, he soon made a name for himself by his autocratic methods, such as in suppressing the Göttingen Seven of whom the Brothers Grimm were two. His son was deposed by Bismarck in 1866, and on it went, to the present Dukes of Brunswick, one daughter of the tribe marrying the King of the Hellenes and becoming the Queen-mother of the deposed King of Greece and of the present Queen of Spain. La-di-da, Tom drummed his fingers on the tome of knowledge. He was bored with all that European inbred royalty stuff, being decidedly republican himself. But what of the present Duke of Cumberland? The Encyclopedia Brittanica, vintage 1972, was silent on that.

Betts would know. She surely would, as she dwelt in a blue-blood world, both personally and as an editor of a magazine for the horsy set. He popped the question at dinner that night, asking nonchalantly if anyone knew the Duke of Cumberland.

The reaction he got astounded him. Both Bettina and Pat dropped their forks and passed looks at each other. Bettina tersely said, "Why d'you ask?"

"Oh, nothing, really. Doing some reading, on the Hanoverian succession and all that. Been part of our father's family haven't they? The Hanoverians?"

"Nonsense." Bettina's voice was resolute, as she had been with him when he was a small boy. "Our father's family is of Dutch origin, as you well know, or should know if you cared to look it up. So why the sudden interest in the Duke of Cumberland?"

"Is there a Duke of Cumberland, then?" Tom parried the question with a question.

Pat took over. "The Duke of Cumberland is a client of my firm. And as such is not a fit subject of discussion outside those environs."

Tom shrugged and busied himself cutting Bertie's meat into small pieces. "I obviously didn't know that. Sorry I asked." The subject was dropped, but Tom wasn't sorry at all for having asked.

Later, lying awake in bed, he replayed in his mind the curious conversation, and wondered what it might imply. There certainly was a Duke of Cumberland, neither of the women had denied that. And Cab had identified the Duke as the patron member of the Leaders Group that was behind the ALARM people. No question about it, the hunt was getting warm. Now, all he had to do was to wrangle an invitation to the Duke's presence, shove the Creep's picture in his face and say, do you know this man and where is he? Why? Because as it happens I have a bone to pick with him, Sire. Bow; scrape.

He sighed. Of course, this was not the way to go about it. Still, he had to wrangle a meeting with that Duke character. As luck would have it, Pat was the conveniently available avenue for that. He would ask Pat for a consultation as a client. She could hardly deny him an appointment, and once he was a client he, too, would be in that cocoon of confidentiality. Then they would see how far he would get.

Their dinner conversation had been on a Friday. The weekend was given over to preparations for the big party the women were planning for the following Saturday. Much running around ensued, to the butcher's, the baker's, the candlestick maker's. The cleaning crew was to come on Tuesday, the cooks were to move in on Friday. Tom volunteered minding the dogs along with Bertie, taking the bunch out to Henley to enjoy walks along the riverbank, feeding the ducks and simultaneously holding on to a water-loving spaniel.

On Monday morning, over a hurried cup of coffee in the kitchen, Tom asked Pat if she would take him on as a client, in a personal matter. Soon.

She agreed saying she'd check her calendar and let him know sometime that evening.

Tom shook his head telling her that in his mind "soon" meant tomorrow while Bertie was with Betts. Bettina had promised the boy a visit to her office, Tuesday being the cleaning crew's day.

After a pause, during which she scrutinized his face, Pat agreed to meet him at eleven o'clock the next day and gave him her business card.

Tom showed up on time at the solicitors' chambers, dressed almost like an English gentleman, except for brown shoes and too loud a tie.

Pat's office was very tastefully furnished, in much dark wood and green leathered chairs but with a touch of the feminine—a large bouquet of flowers on the coffee table and a full-size poster of Alma-Tadema's "Spring" on one of the walls. She rose from behind her desk and shook Tom's hand firmly, a bright and friendly smile on her face. Pat, normally eschewing jewelry during the day, was wearing gold earrings and a matching pin on the lapel of her blue suit. Tom also thought that she had applied a darker hue of lipstick, which seemed a bit out of place but contrasted nicely with her rows of healthy white teeth and the pink tip of her tongue.

Pat had tea brought in and they retired to the chairs at the coffee table. Pat poured, milk in first, and handed him his cup, smiling.

"Now then, Tom, here we are. Do make yourself comfortable."

Tom said thank you and put in two lumps, stirring his tea. He knew the opening line was his but he didn't know how to begin. Besides, there were her round knees again, this time pointing directly at him, albeit primly pressed together.

"Uh, Pat, I don't quite know how to say this, but the matter I wish to have your counsel on is not one of law at all but rather more personal. It is possible that I am wasting your time with it." He shook his head as if to berate himself for his obtuseness.

"As long as I don't know what the matter, as you call it, is all about, we can't pass judgment on that, can we?" Her large blue eyes were trained on him and her face was unsmiling.

"No. I mean, you are right." Tom put his cup down and straightened up.

"What I am after is information and an introduction. Simply put," he made a gesture with his hand, "a discreet favor."

"Do go on."

"Simple as that may be, it is also very personal, and for that reason, rather confidential. Strictly between the two of us, client and counsel, and I must have your assurance that it will remain so." He wanted to be a bit dramatic here to see how she would respond. Would she take him seriously, become curious and interested, or the opposite, disinclined to pursue this further?

Pat answered with a sigh and a stretch of her arms to fix the back of her hair. "Well," she said when she had brought her arms back down, "I must say, Tom, whenever I hear such advance disclaimers, I prepare myself to deal with something that in the end has very much to do with the law and very likely touching on either sex or money. Which is it in your case? Do speak up. You can trust me, you know."

"How perspicacious." Tom was smiling and was going to say more but Pat cut him off.

Putting her hand over his on the chair's armrest—a warm, fleshy hand—she said with some urgency, "Now, look here. There is absolutely no reason for either of us to be guarded in this conversation. We are both professionals and there may come a time when I shall be in need of your services, you know. We must treat each other with openness and respect. Nothing less shall do."

"You are quite right. I appreciate your saying that. So here goes, I should like you to introduce me to the Duke of Cumberland."

"Oh dear!" Pat did look taken aback. "What on earth for?"

"That's where the personal comes into the equation. I must speak to him under circumstances that will be congenial and friendly. Had you not said that he is a client of yours, I would not have come to you with this request."

"Oh dear." Pat repeated, "Dear, dear. He is not an easy fellow, that duke, not at all."

"Are you saying it's impossible to meet him?"

Pat shook her head. "It seems improbable that you should want to meet him. He is rather a different chap than you are."

"Different in what way?"

Pat sighed again. "How shall I put it? It brings us into the netherworld of upper class male depravity. The ghastliest kind of maleness—pederasty and transvestitism. How do you fit in there, Tom?"

"Ah!" It was Tom's turn to be surprised. "I do not, Pat, let me assure you, but the piece of the puzzle that I hold would fit indeed."

"What piece would that be?"

"Male depravity, as you put it. Homosexual, is it?"

"Yes, but I'd rather we did not use that word in this context. It gives it a homophobic ring. Quite undeservedly; painting all of us with a broad brush. Most homosexuals are not depraved."

Tom nodded. He asked, "When you say us, you mean that personally as well, don't you? As in you and Bettina?"

"Quite right. I am sure you knew that before you asked that question."

Tom nodded again. His facial expression was attentive and unsmiling.

"Yes. In the sense of having believed it to be so, although it was never denied or confirmed to me directly. May I presume you are confirming it?"

"You may." Pat adjusted her skirt, making her knees point the other way. She smiled. "I see you are taking it well."

Tom smiled back. "Why shouldn't I? It's none of my business, is it? My love for my sister is unchanged. And I'm growing rather fond of you, too."

"Are you?" Pat's cheeks reddened. "How nice of you to say that! Betts and I have talked a lot about you and your darling son, and how lucky we are to have you both with us. Really?" She blew her nose in a lace-bordered handkerchief she took from a pocket in her skirt.

"Well then," Tom said lightly, "let's get the show back on the road. This duke—what can you tell me about him? Is he really a Duke, capital D?"

"Oh yes! The title is hereditary, although it had lain fallow since the last King of Hannover. Until this bounder came along and claimed use of the title, being the direct descendant thereof. The Royal Genealogical Society had to issue him the patent, all the previous claimants having been tainted by taking part in two wars against Great Britain. Here this chap, too young to have been affected, comes to Britain as a legal immigrant, and is allowed to call himself Duke of Cumberland!" She shook her head in wonderment. "No Peer of the Realm, though. Prince in Hannover he may call himself, outside of Britain. Note the in, as opposed to of; there being no Kingdom of Hannover anymore, and no Prince as the German peer equivalent of Duke. All rather complicated and neither here nor there, except of course, in the circles where titles still matter." She made a grimace of disgust.

"Hmm. Complicated, but interesting to me. So, what does he put on his calling card, Duke, Prince, or what?"

"Neither. He's too clever for such an obvious ploy. Instead, he's a simple George E. August, Estate Agent. With offices on Halfmoon Street, near Piccadilly. Name of his company is very fittingly Mezzaluna Estates, Limited. I have his card. I'll copy it for you if you like."

"Please do, Pat, thanks. Now where does his depravity angle come in?"

"Ugh! I can't tell you any specifics, that falls under confidentiality for his lordship, but our barristers have bailed him out many a time when he was caught in questionable company. Sorry. That's all I can say."

"Quite all right. I needn't know the specifics, anyway. Could you arrange an introduction, do you suppose?"

"Under what pretext?"

"No pretext at all. Perhaps you can ask him to your office, saying that an American client of yours wishes to meet with him, about . . . uh . . . his favorite charity, the Animal Liberation and Rights Movement, ALARM for short."

"Good heavens, Tom, you are full of surprises! ALARM is on our client list through the Duke. I can't do that, either! You see, we are treading a very thin line here as Bettina's magazine has been the target of ALARM's criticism. For using hounds to hunt animals, and for tearing polo ponies to shreds, and for drugging race horses, and on and on. It's been dreadful. Poor Betts has to be ever so careful about what she allows into print. No, no, I don't think we can use that angle. Think of something else. Why do you want to meet him, anyway?"

"To get some information from him, some clarification. That's all. Not to worry, His Grace will come though the ordeal unscathed."

Pat sat back and gave him a searching look. "Does any of this," she began slowly, "have anything to do with that computer you have rigged up in your room, Tom? Getting and sending messages at odd hours? We've been wondering. Surely it's not just for the delectation of little Bertram, is it?"

Tom quickly agreed. "No, it's not just for Bertie. A friend of mine in the States is corresponding with me. I hope it's not too much of a bother?"

Pat became wary. "No, it's not. Unless you are up to something, what with the Duke and ALARM. I don't want any trouble for any of us!"

Tom took her hand that was fluttering when she said that, and held it. "Pat, I don't want Betts or you or any of us to get hurt. I'm sorry if I am causing anxiety, and of course you need not introduce me. What you have told me about him, and giving me his address, is more than I could have expected to learn otherwise. I am grateful. We can leave it at that."

"What are you going to do, then?"

Tom released her hand and said cheerfully. "I shall ring him up and make an appointment. Much easier and much better, all round."

"The name Von Der Campe will immediately bring Bettina to mind!"

"Right, again! I shall be, let me think, Major Nemo! How's that?"

"Nemo, as in nobody?" She smiled. "I'm a Scot, Tom. Our motto is well known, especially in these days of agitation away from Britain. Nemo me impune lacessit. 'Nobody attacks me with impunity.' Remembering his bloody ancestor, he'll think you are an avenging, secessionist Scot!"

"So much the better! Put a bit of fear into the bugger." Tom was not dissuaded. "That motto—nobody attacks me with impunity—it suits me! I may become a voluntary Scot. Won't take much, imbibing the highland dew as I have become accustomed in doing. Speaking of which, will you lunch with me? We will have to tell Betts something about our time together!"

"We shan't lie to Bettina!" Pat spoke in a serious tone. "We've had a professional consultation, that is what we shall tell her. Bettina will know better than to inquire further. And Tom, we certainly shall not mention the Duke of Cumberland and your desire to meet him. It's a mystery even to me!"

Tom weighed several strategies of ways to meet the Duke, all of them dependent on making an appointment, at which he would have to state his name and business. In the interval, until they were to meet, would the Duke not wonder who this "Major Nemo" is and become suspicious, perhaps even decide to cancel, by having his secretary call the number Tom would give? And what number would that be, Major Nemo? Bettina's? Or Pat's? Perish the thought!

On the other hand, a temporary domicile might do the trick. Checking into a hotel as a tourist, for whatever number of days it would take to make the connection, would create the illusion of normal business practice.

In the end, if all else failed, it would come down to the simple expedient of just walking in to his office on a given day, that day having to be one on which the Duke-fellow was actually in. Which would require some advance skulking around to see just when "George E. August, Esq." would arrive habitually at his office. Tom had a pretty good idea what the Duke looked like from descriptions that Pat reluctantly gave him, and from news photos he saw at the archives of The Times. He was a surprisingly tall and portly man, as seen in one of the photos where he was shown with his ponies at a polo match, and in another photo with an equally surprising appearance of baldness. The Duke's head looked as smooth and oval as an ostrich egg. Tom wondered why Pat had made no mention of such a shiny bald pate, until he realized that the man, vain as he seemed to be, was very likely the wearer of a toupee or, for that matter, of a wig, a woman's lovely hair when cross-dressing was the order of the day (or night).

At the house, the women's party preparations consumed most of the time otherwise given over to leisure and conversation, from evening to night. Tom found this to be an excellent opportunity to announce that he would be spending the weekend away for a change, a bit of pub-crawling perhaps, or night-clubbing, some R-and-R, so to speak, if he could leave Bertie in their capable and loving hands.

Bettina protested with raised eyebrows. "Must you do it this weekend, Thomas, when so many of our friends will be arriving! They should be wondering why you aren't here, after all I have told them about you! Really, why not pick another day!"

Pat, who seemed to understand that this was somehow connected to the Duke's business, warned archly, "Do be careful, won't you! London can be rather a horrid place!"

Bettina suspected that Tom would be on the prowl for female companionship, and Pat wondered secretly if the prowling would be in the seedy joints frequented by the Duke and his entourage; still, they could not make Tom change his mind. On Saturday morning, swinging a half-empty suitcase, he hailed a taxi and had himself deposited at the Grosvenor House Hotel. When he stepped up to the front desk, he proffered his real passport but insisted that he be registered as Major A. Nemo, USA, giving the clerk a significant look and inclining his head in the direction of the U.S. embassy. It worked, as it probably had numerous times before, particularly as he made a substantial cash deposit against his account. The room he was given was small, but it did have a partial view of Park Lane traffic.

Having the whole day ahead of him, Tom went out for a walk in the park, towards Marble Arch, turning left past Cumberland Gate and on along the Ring, strolling here and there, enjoying now the first signs of spring in lawn and leaves, looking out for birds, and for toddlers suddenly crossing his path, until he reached the Serpentine Restaurant where he stopped for lunch.

Afterwards, refreshed, he made his way over to Harrod's, where he moseyed around not knowing what he was doing there, until he gave way to some hidden impulses. He bought jodhpurs and ankle boots—in case he ever was invited to ride somewhere, at Bettina's country house for instance. He would bring Bertie here next and have him outfitted, too; hard hat, as well! Speaking of hats, what about one of those English caps he had always thought he'd look silly in? He bought one. Plus an umbrella, one of those tightly furled "brollies" one really should not be without in London weather. Sensible chaps, those Englishmen. Righto!

From a phone booth, he called his hotel and asked for Major Nemo. He was told the major was out and asked if he would care to leave a message. He replied, "Yes, please. Meet you for drinks at the Dorchester bar. George. Ta-ta."

He did go to the Dorchester, after a shower and a change of suit and shirt, and had himself a wonderful single-malt the name of which he had never heard before and which he asked the bartender to refill for him twice. They were serving steak and chips at one end of the bar, and he had that, falling into conversation with a mustachioed gentleman who was a major himself, as it turned out. "Knew you were a fellow officer at first sight, you know. Haven't ever been wrong on that score. You American, what? There you are. Chin-chin."

It was a late night that Tom sank into bed, heavy with malt and meat. And it was a genuine hangover he nursed when he returned to the house, where cleaning people were still busy mopping up after the party and he had to fight his way to the kitchen sink to get a glass of water. Plopping a fizzy tablet into it, he climbed the stairs, stopping twice to take a swallow.

He found his son in Bettina's bed, pink-cheeked and happy, sharing breakfast on a tray with his indulgent aunt.

"You are a bit wan around the gills," Bettina said with a smile. "Had a good time, Thomas, did you?"

"Very," Tom said and finished his medicine. "And you?" He went over to plant a kiss on both of them.

"Oh, we did splendidly. Didn't we, Bertram?" So they did, judging by the enthusiastic nodding of the boy who had been taught to know better than to speak with his mouth full.

"He was the life of the party, he was!" Pat came into the room, wrapped tightly in her bathrobe. Her short blond hair fell in strands over her eyes. "Introduced himself to everybody like a proper little gentleman. 'How do you do, I am Bertram Vonder Campe. What's your name?' So sweet. People thought he was Bettina's love child."

"You had him at the party?" Tom was incredulous.

"Quite right." Bettina looked amused. "By the by, one of the guests—not a friend of ours but escorted by Chatham Walsh, our accountant . . ."

"A notorious womanizer!" Pat hurrumphed.

"Pat, please! At any rate, she burst out laughing when Bertram came up to her and gave his spiel. She said, 'So you are the blind date I missed!' and then she explained to me that you had talked in New York, inviting her to lunch with Bertie! And of course, she thought I was your wife!"

Tom looked nonplused. His head was still dense. "Really?"

"Her name is Emily Dessauer. I have her card here somewhere if you want to call her. She explained that she was Eleanor's account executive at MetroBank, but now she is working out of the London office. Nice woman."

Emily Dessauer! What if he had been here last night, and they would have talked, really talked, and perhaps connected? God, what a mess. "Yeah, I remember her," Tom said. "Met her once, for mother's account." He shook his head. Great timing.

"And how did you do last night?" Pat asked, a bit too sharply.

Tom waved his hand vaguely. "Oh, walked around a lot, the parks and so on, bought some riding boots and pants, Betts, in case you ask us up to your Chinnor country home. Had a bite to eat and a drink at the Dorchester with a retired major from the Eleventh Hussars. Tried to drink each other under the table. Britain won. Now, if you don't mind, I'll go have a shower and take a nap. Or the other way around—take a shower and have a nap? Or nap first, and then shower? Anyway. It's awfully bright in here." He peered at the sunlit curtains and made his exit.

The women just looked at each other and shook their heads—men.

Tom did not return to the hotel until Monday morning. He had thought of taking Bertie along but dropped the idea; the bright little boy would blabber about his daddy's new room and raise unwanted questions. Instead, he asked Bettina to take him to the office once more. As for the future, "We should consider some sort of pre-school activity for him, Betts?"

"Yes, certainly. There are wonderful day schools for little tykes." She glanced at him quizzically. "How long are you planning to stay, Tom? Not that you are unwelcome, mind you. Quite the contrary. You must have some plans, for the future?"

"It's all a bit uncertain, as yet, Betts. I'll let you know, thanks."

Bettina nodded, and said slowly, "Are you—I don't know how to put it—engaged in some sort of scheme, for the government, perhaps? I feel silly to ask, but your computer sessions, and now this absence of yours."

Tom agonized over the answer. "Something like that," he said at last. "But it's no spy stuff, if that's what you are thinking. It's more along the lines of my research. I wish we could talk about it, Bettina, I truly wish we could. But I must say, there is a potential, however farfetched, of danger. Nothing specific but it's there, in the outer realm of possibility. That's why I feel very strongly that Bertie ought to be in a safe haven, with you, here, and not always visibly with me. I know he is safe with you and Pat."

"Thank you for saying that." Bettina straightened up, as she used to do when they were children and Tom had just confessed a mishap, like breaking someone's window, or stepping on her corgi. "It needed airing, the matter, don't you agree? Of course, we shall take very good care of darling Bertram."

From his hotel room Tom dialed the Duke's business number. He had decided that he would use the slight Maryland twang that he had almost acquired when he was living there. Not quite southern, it gave his English a hint of charm, of folksiness that he believed his regular speech did not have. In any case, it went with the persona he meant to adopt in his dealing with the Duke as being a squareshooter, an ordinary fellow who was courteous and respectful but not deferential to persons in high positions. A man who said what he meant, and meant what he said, if you got his drift.

As expected, the first person on the line was a secretary, a woman with a bored and nasal voice.

Tom said this was Major Nemo at the Grosvenor House Hotel, and could he speak to the Duke, please. His Highness, is that what he should say? She should forgive his ignorance, but he is unaccustomed to such titles.

Ignoring his question, she asked in what matter.

He replied, in an especially soft drawl, that it was personal. Quite personal, and no offense intended. Would she please put him through?

A pause, during which he was undoubtedly put on hold. Then a new voice came on the line,

"Who is speaking there, please?" The voice was a man's, and the accent distinctly German. His words were a direct translation of the German phrase, "Wer spricht da, bitte?"

Tom said, "This is Major Nemo, sir. Do I have the pleasure of addressing the Duke of Cumberland?"

"Yes."

"Do I call you Your Highness? As I told your secretary—that was your secretary, the charming lady I spoke with before, wasn't it?"

"Yes. And never mind the Highness, we are not at Court. So Sir will be sufficient. What is it you want?"

The tone of the man's voice was bothered, irritated, and the inflection clipped, of the North-German variety. Tom wondered, if the Duke made his living selling real estate, how could he be sure that Tom was not a prospective customer who should not be offended but rather welcomed? Poor business manners, unless business was not his prime concern. "Thank you, Sir. That'll be so much easier on me. I am calling to ask for an appointment to see you. Sir."

"To see me? What about?"

"Well, it's a delicate matter that I'll be glad to explain to you when I see you, Sir."

"I see no reason why you cannot tell me, here and now, what it is you want to talk to me about."

"Well now, I'll put it this way. Why would I have come all the way over here if I could have picked up the phone and called you? I don't particularly like getting jet lag, which I am only now gettin' out of. And that airline food is no home-cookin'. See what I mean, Sir?"

A slight hesitation on the other end—then, "I am a very busy man, Major Neemow, is it?"

"Yes sir. Major Nemo, United States Army, Reserve. I appreciate you're busy. It doesn't have to be today. Tomorrow will be fine."

"Are you here in an official capacity, Major Neemow?"

"No sir. Not at all. This is private."

A well-heaved sigh. "Well, in that case, we can fit you in for a half hour at eleven tomorrow. Punctually!"

"Eleven sharp, tomorrow. Thank you, sir! See you then." Tom hung up. He banged his fist on the hotel table, making the phone jump. Gotcha! Action!

And now, back to the computer to tell Cab and to plan the next step.

Game Plans

Tom's first message reached Cab's computer at the crack of dawn in New York; by early afternoon, Tom and Cab were busily engaged in a lively exchange of opinion and ideas. It finally crystallized itself down to a game plan that was both simple and practical: Tom would use every feasible means, from cajolery to threats, to coax the Creep's name and whereabouts out of the Duke. If the Duke would seem genuinely unable to supply that information, he would be asked to refer Tom to someone who could.

Once the location of the Creep had been ascertained, Tom would go after him, alone (Cab had grudgingly conceded that point). Such location was either in London, or elsewhere in the U.K. which would require Tom's traveling thereto. Technically, however, "Major Nemo" would continue to reside at the Hotel Grosvenor House, a role that would be taken over by Cab, who would fly in for that purpose as a tourist, with his separate hotel arrangements under his own name elsewhere. In the event that the Duke had lied to Tom about the Creep's location, Cab would exert new pressure on the Duke, "and he ain't gonna go gently into the night, you can bet on that, Tommy-boy!" Cab had tapped out.

They agreed that was about all they could do at the moment, Tom's meeting being the next day already.

Tuesday promised to be a busy day, indeed. Bertie was to report, so Bettina had arranged, at eight o'clock, at the Brompton Preparatory School for Girls and Boys from ages three to thirteen. Tom threw himself into his only good blue suit, fixed up his son in his best togs, the boy almost sparkling in freshness with his slicked-down blond hair and rosy cheeks, and off they went with Betts in her Jaguar. Both Tom and Bettina spoke reassuringly to the kid, in the car, and upon entering the red-brick portals of the school; but to their surprise and relief, Bertie overcame his initial shyness as soon as he saw other kids his age having fun in a large, bright schoolroom full of interesting things to play with. "Looks okay, huh?" Tom patted the boy's bottom as he shoved him through the door. "See you later, pal! Great kid, that," he marveled, turning to Bettina. "Let's sign him in?"

Bettina smiled, "A true Vonder Campe! We don't scare easily, do we?"

Tom didn't know what to make of the peculiar look his sister gave him. "We certainly don't!" he said lightly.

"Nor do we show our emotions much, hmm?" She ran her hands down his lapels and straightened his tie. "Nice suit! What are we up to, after this?"

Just like Bettina in the old days, Tom thought. "Oh, I don't know. I'll get a haircut, probably."

"Meeting someone?" Her eyes were still on his.

"Meeting someone?" He was taken aback. "Who?"

"Whom. Perhaps that young lady who was asking about you at the party? The MetroBank branch is on Park Lane in the Barklay's Bank building. You can't miss it."

"Really!"

"Really." Bettina stroked his cheek as she turned from him. "Let's go to the office, I'll do the signing up, you just leave your signature on the parental consent card."

"Would you do that, Betts? That's awfully nice of you. And perhaps just for today, could you pick Bertie up again?"

Bettina's smile was a little mischievous, "Off you go. Ta-ta."

Getting a haircut was not a bad idea, Tom thought. Come to think of it, if Cab was to look even vaguely like "Major Nemo," then it was time for the major to begin to look a bit like Cab. Off with the glasses, and in with the disposable contact lenses which he always carried with him in a little container attached to his key chain, just in case there was something wrong with his spectacles. And off, also, with the longish hair that had sprouted on his head since his arrival in England. And off, finally, with his seal ring bearing the family crest! He slipped it from his finger and knotted it securely into his handkerchief. Time he thought about things like that! The first impression the Duke had of him would be the one that would linger.

He got his haircut as the first customer at a fine shop on Knightsbridge that catered to "discerning gentlemen's grooming and shaving needs." As he sat in his wood-paneled cubicle attended by an elderly East Indian, and looked at himself in the mirror, he ordered his hair to be cut short, "and I mean short, as short as you can make it without it looking ridiculous!"

"Are you a military gentleman, sir?" Came the sing-song question.

"Yes. But the vacation is over, and I'm getting back to basics."

"Indeed, sir. I shall do a very good job for you, rest assured, sir."

"And I shall be appropriately grateful."

In the quiet of his cell, the clip-clip of the shears the only noise, Tom had to think of Bettina's remarks. What had Emily Dessauer told her? She was engaged, wasn't she? To that fellow in Los Angeles? What point would there be for him to walk in at the MetroBank office here, what would he say if he saw her? Congratulations on your engagement, and when's the wedding? Nuts.

True to his promise, the barber had done a very good job for him. Tom examined his new look in the mirror. Short all around with just a hint of a part. A Marine cut, almost. Tom was pleased and left a generous tip.

Still some time to kill until his eleven o'clock appointment. Tom walked to his hotel, went up to his room and put in his contact lenses. He was not a regular wearer of contacts. When he looked at himself in the bathroom mirror he found that he had brown eyes; it was a mistake when he had his prescription filled at the optician's. He had let it go at the time, thinking he would use up the half dozen lenses in the box and then go back to his regular blue ones. Now he grinned at himself. A guy with a brush cut and light-brown eyes grinned back at him. So be it! Major Nemo, sir! He saluted his image.

At quarter to eleven he picked up the phone and called the Duke's office, just to confirm the appointment, he told the secretary. She got back to him a moment later saying His Highness was on the phone, long distance. She asked if he could call Tom back? Of course, Tom said, and gave the hotel and room number. He'd be waiting.

The call came after eleven o'clock, His Highness himself on the line. Apologies for not being punctual but unavoidable business et cetera and so on. Then, "I'm wondering, Mister Neemow—would you be free for lunch, by any chance?"

Tom said yes, he was.

"Oh good. Let's say I'll fetch you at a quarter to twelve? Good. I'll call your room and wait for you at the lifts. I am likely to be the tallest man in the crowd; we can't miss each other."

The Duke's call came at close to noon; Tom had to smile at the one-up-manship implicit in the keeping-you-waiting game. He said he'd be right down.

The Duke was not only the tallest man in the crowd but the only one. A gaggle of oriental women chattering in high voices were tripping into the elevator even before Tom had made it out.

"Hello!" Tom said, hand outstretched. "Nice to meet you, sir."

"How do you do, Major." Tom's hand was clasped and double-clasped by two meaty paws that were warm and a bit moist. Tom almost recoiled at the touch.

"Sorry to keep you waiting. Now I am the one not being punctual, ja?" A thin smile was meant to be ingratiating.

Tom shrugged as he withdrew his hand, "No matter. I've made the time."

"Very good. In my business, my time is not always my own, you know." The smile was still there.

They turned and walked. The Duke looked around disdainfully. "Not a good place to eat. Too touristy. Don't you agree?"

Tom, shrugging, said, "We could go to the Anglo-American Club. I have privileges there. It's not far from the embassy." It was a total lie; he did not even know if there was such a club. He expected the Duke to counter.

The Duke did. "I have a table at Claridge's. If you don't mind?"

"Perfect," Tom agreed quickly. "I've never been there." True, this time.

The Duke had a Rolls Royce waiting outside, with a uniformed chauffeur who would have been well cast in a Hollywood movie. He was young, with long blond hair brimming around his cap, blue eyes, broad shoulders, narrow hips. He rushed, in small eager steps, to open doors, the Duke's first, then Tom's on the other side. He gave Tom a brilliant look.

Asshole, flashed through Tom's mind. He felt an intense instant dislike for the man, and at once chided himself for the prejudice. What if the man was a refugee, from Eastern Europe, say, with a wife and kids in Warsaw or Prague?

It was not much of a ride to Claridge's. "You can take the car back, Fred," the Duke said. "We can walk back, can't we, Major? Will do us good." The car had stopped.

"Certainly," Tom said, and opened his door to climb out.

"Jawohl, danke, Hoheit," Fred lifted his cap a little, then jumped out to open the Duke's door.

The maitre d' at the Causerie bowed and led them without delay to what had to be an important table, secluded yet visible. There was marble and crystal everywhere, and a lot of Edwardian pink, and the tablecloths and serviettes were highly starched. No menu was given out; His Highness would discuss the fare with Alphonse the headwaiter who would hover by his ear and take no notes, just nodding now and then, and with Clive the sommelier who sidled over as soon as the headwaiter had departed. Tom's consent was not solicited.

Score one for the Duke, Tom thought. Or two, maybe, counting the Rolls.

It was clear from the way the Duke devoted his full attention to the food as it was being served, that any substantive discussion was out of place, ausgeschlossen, at least until desert and coffee. Tom watched how the big oval face became enraptured, thick red lips now closing voluptuously over spoon or fork, now forming a perfect O for wine to pour in or for oysters to be slurped up, now smacking in delight, all the while big grinding jaws doing their masticating. With each new course the Duke flashed his eyes at Tom, eyebrows raised in renewed anticipation. Tom had no choice but nod and smile back, then quickly stare at his plates. Some fish en croute, venison larded with something and snared by white asparagus spears, pink-sleeved lamb chops surrounded by tiny pieces of lasagna, and at last chocolate dumplings with raspberry sorbet. All of this á la nouveau in wee portions on thin, probably ancient porcelain; and with suitable wines, of which Tom partook only cautiously.

The repast over, glory be, and the Duke wiping his lips and opening his leather cigar case, offering one to Tom who took it, and the smelling and cutting and moistening and lighting of the Cuban masterpieces behind them, it was now time, by Tom's reckoning, to turn the table, so to speak.

"That was a delicious lunch. Thanks, very much, Count."

"I am a count, also." A smile broadened his mouth, revealing upper teeth that were yellow and uneven. "Of Lauenburg-Bottorp. You knew?"

"No, I'm sorry. Highness? Or may I stick with Sir?" When he got a resigned nod, Tom quickly went on. "I really appreciated the meal, in these fancy surroundings, but maybe you shouldn't really have bothered, as I just wanted to ask you a couple of questions. Sir."

More nodding, impatient now. "I like company when I eat, Major. Besides, I am more peaceful when I am sated just in case your questions will upset me. Will your questions upset me?"

"I certainly hope not, Sir. So, with your permission," Tom fumbled for an envelope in his jacket pocket. "I've got some pictures here I want to show you." He brought out one photo of the Creep, heavy glasses, bearded, male. He held it up, "Do you know this man, Sir?"

The Duke examined it with narrowed eyes. "I don't think so."

"Or this one?" More Creep, but beardless with his hair cut short.

"I don't know. Should I know him? Who is he?"

Interesting, Tom thought. He remained in the singular, he must know it is the same person because at first sight, the pictures were quite dissimilar. "You are a member of the board of the animal protection organization, ALARM?"

"Of the Board of Patrons, yes."

"Board of Patrons, I stand corrected, thank you. A very prestigious organization, isn't it, one that derives that prestige, in no small measure, from its distinguished patrons, of which you are one, Sir."

The Duke grunted his assent.

"It would follow, then, that anything that besmears its escutcheon, if that's the word, would reflect badly on the patrons, if you know what I mean, Sir." Tom raised his voice to make it sound like a question.

"Of course! Is there a point in all this, Major?"

"Yes Sir, there is." He pointed to the photos. "This man, under the name of Dr. Olaf Runge, came to my country to engage in certain unlawful activities. He came recommended by your organization, Sir."

"That is preposterous! We do not condone unlawful activities!"

"I am sure you don't, Sir. The man in the picture came to the U.S. with a false passport and phony credentials. He has fled the United States. He is wanted for questioning. There is reason to believe that the ALARM organization has been sponsoring him. If you could supply his present whereabouts, it would be a great help."

"Questioning for what?"

"For a homicide and industrial sabotage."

"You mean he killed somebody? And sabotaged something?"

"He is wanted for questioning, Sir."

The Duke contemplated the photos. He snipped at them with manicured fingernails. "What concerns me only about this man—Dr. Runge, is it? Name sounds German. Is he German? Olaf is more Danish—is whether he has any connections to ALARM." He narrowed his eyes looking at Tom, "Who is your—what do you call it in English—Auftraggeber, principal? Is it the U.S. Government?"

"No, it is not."

"What, then?" He poked the wet end of his cigar in Tom's direction.

"A private source. I am not at liberty to divulge details."

"A private investigator? A detective, are you?" The sneer was audible. "Then why should I talk to you, Major or Mister Neemow?"

Tom shrugged. He went to his wallet and extracted the card of agent Montgomery. "You don't have to. You can talk to him, if you like." He handed the card over, the Duke holding it with the tips of his thumb and forefinger.

As he had hoped, Tom received the card back very quickly.

"No need to involve the authorities, I am sure. We do not fancy this kind of publicity, Major. Nor, I might add, do we condone criminality!"

"That's why I came to you privately, sir," Tom agreed earnestly. Bingo, he thought; I got you where I want you.

"All right. Tell you what I will do," the Duke said, blowing some smoke against the ceiling. "It'll be Easter next week. I always go home to Germany for the holidays. I will make some inquiries. May I keep these photographs? You will hear from me, one way or the other. I'll be back here after Easter Monday. Where can you be reached?"

Tom grinned. "I may be moving to cheaper digs. Why don't I call you?"

Not quite so amused, the Duke said sharply, "You call my secretary, not me. I will leave a message for you." He folded the photos and put them in his pocket. "This is a distasteful matter, Major. I want to be done with it."

"I agree, Sir, totally." Tom put down his cigar and pushed his chair back. "If you don't mind, I'll be leaving now. Great lunch. Thanks for having me. And for your help, Sir, one way or the other, as you say."

Tom made no attempt to shake hands. The Duke hardly looked up.

Crossing the lobby Tom thought he saw the figure of the Duke's chauffeur leaning against a marble pillar, broad-shouldered, blond, his cap tucked under his arm, reading a magazine. Had Fred not been sent home? If not, why not?

He decided to have a little fun. Pretending to be preoccupied, Tom brushed past him as he made for the swing doors. In the glass reflection he saw the young man straighten up; out on the street, he observed him emerge through the doors also.

All right, let's see if we are being followed. Tom ambled up towards Brooke Street, hung a left, and at Grosvenor Square crossed over past the Roosevelt Monument. On the park's circular footpath he increased his speed, now almost running. At each turn he cast a glance around as if checking traffic or scanning the skies to see if it would rain as it had in the morning. Each time, he caught a glimpse of old Fred some distance behind him, heading the same way. Coincidence? Hardly.

He went straight towards the entrance of the U.S. embassy, throwing a smart salute to the Marine guard and getting a salute in return. Inside the door he lingered a moment to check on Fred, but couldn't see him. If he were him, Tom would stay around the park keeping an eye on the whole building. Was Fred smart?

Making some inquiries—as he had wanted to do, anyway, about preschool activities for American kids—he spent about a half hour getting shuffled around from one desk to another, leaving at last with some brochures including one on several forthcoming Fourth of July bashes. The date sent a cold shiver down his spine making him even more determined to do what he was doing. He left, his head lowered against a gust of wind blowing across Grosvenor Square.

And there, rising from a bench, was tall, blond Fred. Tom had half a mind to confront him but decided on one more ruse. How about MetroBank on Park Lane? That'd be good for another round of heel-cooling by the lad!

Off he went, a man about his business. What would be more logical, if you are private dick in a foreign country, than going from the American embassy to an American bank? Besides, Tom chuckled to himself, he did want to see if he could catch that elusive Miss Dessauer!

Elusive she proved to be, once again. A very solicitous Brooks Brothers gentleman informed him that Emily Dessauer had left for her permanent posting at the bank's newly opened St. Petersburg branch. He asked Tom if there was a message?

"No," Tom said. "Just tell her Mrs. Watson's son called. And good luck."

He left the bank building with a feeling of disappointment so strong it bothered him to be aware of it. Why? Why was he disappointed, and anyway, hadn't he settled the point earlier, when he was getting his haircut? What could he have said to the lady if she had been in—except utter some banality that in the end would prove embarrassing? Nuts, and nuts again, Tom old boy!

It did look like rain now, and he wouldn't want his only good suit to get wet. He ran across the street towards Park Lane, heading for his hotel when he almost bumped into Fred who stood near the Dorchester entrance, cap on his head, coat collar up, a cigarette in the hollow of his hand.

"Hey, Fred!" Tom's anger had found an outlet. He grabbed the young man by the lapels. "I'm going to my hotel now, the Grosvenor House, next one up the street. No point in you tagging along. Got that?" He pushed his fist against the young giant's chest. "You tell His Highness if I see you following me again I'm going to have you arrested!" He released his grip and dropped his hand. There was no response from Fred, only an unblinking look from his ice-blue eyes that shone like steel.

Tom turned and walked away, around the corner. Those eyes had set off an alarm inside him that was beginning to drown out his anger and his disappointment. He resolved that in addition to his report on his meeting with the Duke he would add a description of Fred in his e-mail to Cab. Just for the record.

Easter, it was declared by Bettina, would be celebrated en famille at her country house in Oxfordshire, just the four of them with no guests. "I'm not keen on having the local gentry wondering if I am harboring an escaped Borstal Boy, Tom!" This was a reference to Tom's new look which had met with disapproval even though he had put his glasses back on by the time he returned to the house from the hotel. And so they went on Maundy Thursday, in the Jaguar. Pat was driving with Tom again in the left front seat, Bettina and Bertie in the back, and the two dogs crouching at their feet. Off on a much needed four day holiday.

It was total observance of Good Friday at Bettina's house. There was no food, no radio or TV, only liquid refreshment until supper time, and before that there would be attendance at the little Norman church in Chinnor for services.

Tom opted out of it. He said that the crucifixion of Christ was too daunting an experience for Bertie to absorb just yet. He asked if he could borrow the Jag and take the boy to Oxford instead. He got his wish, to the rolling of eyes heavenward by both women.

They had a fine old time, father and son wandering about after having parked the car, poking around this college and that and even entering unhindered the Sheldonian Theatre. The painting on the vaulted ceiling, allegorical of Truth as well as of Malice, seemed to Tom a reasonable substitute of the Holy Day for a young mind to absorb, even though Bertie pointed more to the cherubs. At lunch they repaired to the Randolph where they quietly dined on fish and chips and large glasses of milk.

Tom had a telephone brought to the table, and dialed Cab's office number in Manhattan where it would be about nine in the morning. As luck would have it, Cab was in, and mightily surprised to hear Tom's voice.

In a low tone, Tom explained where they were and that the call would be brief. He asked if there was any news?

"Yes. Glad you asked. Mr. and Mrs. Blumenfeld—you know? Charles and Freddie?—are planning a trip to Europe next week or so. Taking the cure, I think it's called, at Baden-Baden. Also, Major Neemow will want a room again at the Grosvenor, at the same time."

"Really?" What was Cab up to?

"I'll send you the details when I know more. B.B. is one, and M.N. the other. Keep that in mind."

"Sure. B.B.? M.N.?"

"Well, nice talking to you, sir. We got everything under control here for you. I'll mail you more info when I get it. Okay? Bye for now."

Click. Tom pushed the antenna back in. That was a call of less than a minute. Cab never loses a beat.

They were out riding horses the next day, Tom and Pat. Bettina was taking Bertie along with her to the market in Thame, to do some Easter shopping.

The gently rolling Chiltern hills had their first tint of bluebells and the birch trees were hung with gossamer green. The horses were trotting eagerly, snorting and pulling their heads against the reins, champing the bits. Tom's was a big bony gelding that Bettina had acquired cheaply from the Guards, and Pat's was a nice brown mare with a round belly. The sun was shining, dappling the path they were riding on the edge of the tree line. A glorious day. They rode without talking much, galloping now and again, until it was time to give the horses some slack.

"I say, Tom," Pat said, looking at him from underneath the visor of her black hat, "can we have a word?"

"Certainly." Pointing at the houses, "Shall we give them a little rest?" They were at the crest of an escarpment. Below them, fields were stretching towards a village beyond.

Pat nodded, and they dismounted and loosened the saddle straps.

"How did it go with the Duke of Cumberland? I never asked." Pat sat down on a log and Tom sat down beside her.

"Oh, very well, actually. Sorry, I should have mentioned it."

"Never mind. You did get what you wanted."

"Yes, in a way. It was useful."

"That's all that matters." Pat stared into the distance. She spoke again, "You recall, perhaps, that I mentioned the situation with your sister and me."

"Yes, I do." He leaned forward, trying to catch her eye. "That you are lovers, you mean?"

"God—I'm having such a hard time being direct in these matters! It's the system, you see. It forces one to be circumspect even when nothing but the most blunt expression of truth will do!"

"Right." Tom gently patted her hand that rested on her knee. "Speak to me, kiddo. You can count on a sympathetic ear."

"It's more than your ear I want." A faint smile as she turned to look at him. "You'll be shocked, I shouldn't wonder."

Tom smiled back. "I don't shock easily anymore. It's probably a character defect," he shrugged. "But there you are."

"Here I am, indeed, in a most extraordinary pickle."

"Say it. Put it into words."

Pat sighed. "It's—" she shook her head. "I've never talked about this before with a man."

"Maybe I can help. Is it a medical question?"

"Very much so. Yes. Totally." She nodded emphatically. "A medical question."

"Good! I am a medical man. Fire when ready, Gridley."

"Gridley? Oh, it's one of your American sayings, isn't it? Well, all right. I have to get it out somehow." She held on to the log with both arms. Another sigh, "I am thirty-two and I'll be thirty-three in September. Perfectly healthy, in good shape all round. Nothing wrong with me."

Tom smiled. "So far, so good. Take two aspirins and call me in the morning. Another American saying."

"Oh Tom, don't be an ass! It's perfectly obvious I am working up to something, don't you see? And it is rather serious, so please just listen, will you? Just listen."

Tom stopped smiling. "Sorry. I will."

"All right. Bettina and I, we are very fond of each other, in a permanent sort of way. We can't, either of us, see us going our separate ways ever again. We have discussed what kind of a future that would mean for us, and we believe it will be a good one."

Tom nodded. "Yes. I can see that, too."

"There! I know you mean it, Tom." She touched his shoulder, then quickly withdrew her hand. "The one point about which we are undecided, so to speak—and we have gone over it many times—is having a child. Adoption or artificial insemination is what it comes down to. D'you see?"

Tom said, "I am listening."

"Yes. Thank you for that. Since we have had your son here—Bertie is such a wonderful little chap—it's given us a new impetus. A new angle." Pat took a deep breath. "Well, here it is. You, Tom, could inseminate me and the child we would have would also carry some of Bettina's genes. It would be the most perfect answer to our prayers." She said that rapidly.

Tom managed a faint smile, "You weren't kidding when you said you wanted more than my ear."

"Right." Pat jumped up and went to fetch her horse that had wandered off a few yards. "I'm glad I got it out. Now you know. You needn't say anything just yet, Tom, in fact I'd rather you wouldn't."

Tom got up, too, and tightened the saddle straps of his horse. "Does Bettina know of this conversation we are having?" he asked.

"Not that we are having it this moment, no. But we have talked about it. It's something she thinks could be considered. One never knows what one gets from the sperm bank," she added with a grim smile.

Tom grinned. "No rush, though, is there?" he asked.

Pat had found her humor again. "In terms of the here and now—certainly not. What would the horses think? But generally, the sooner the better." She came over to him. "Dear Tom, do not say anything now, I beg you."

"Well, that's a relief." He patted her on her ample behind. "You are really something else, Pat."

"What do you mean—oh, another American saying?"

"You got that right," Tom grinned.

They returned to that theme on Sunday night. Sitting in the wood-paneled lounge of the eighteenth century former manse that Bettina had inherited from her grandmother, Pat had hinted to Tom to stay behind "for a brandy" when the boy was taken up to bed by Bettina. The promise of "just one more" from his Easter sweets and of Aunt Betts reading a story to him, resulted in quick good-night kisses and a scampering up the stairs by Bertie.

So here they were, on opposite ends of a deep cushiony sofa, eyeing each other over the rims of their crystal goblets. Tom had a hunch what was coming. Pat gave the cognac a good swirl before she spoke, "I say," she began, and stopped.

"Do," Tom smiled.

Pat exhaled a determined, "Yes. It's just so bloody awkward, isn't it? Not the easiest thing to put into words."

"Sex never is," Tom said. "Easy to put into words, I mean."

"Quite right. It wasn't meant to be a wordy sort of activity." Pat found her humor again. "You have recovered from the shock of my proposition?"

"Well, I have had time to put it into the proper perspective, at least the proper perspective from my point of view. The way I understand it, you are asking me to act as a sperm donor, for all the right reasons of lineage and breeding and so forth. Correct?"

"Yes," Pat replied, fidgeting in her seat.

"And perhaps, as a special concession, affording me the pleasure of your personal company in the transmission of same. Or did I get that wrong?"

"No. I mean, yes." Pat blushed deeply. "No, you did not get it wrong. And yes, regarding the mode of transmission."

"A very generous offer, from a man's point of view, I must say. One not to be taken lightly considering whence it comes. Surely you know you make an impression not just on women."

Pat stared at her glass, then raised it to her lips and drained it. "You are mocking me," she said, not looking up.

"Pat, no, not at all! I am sorry. I should explain myself better. First, yes, I have thought about it, and the one thing that sticks in my craw—two, actually, maybe even three, but let's take them in sequence. All right?"

"Yes." Pat's eyes met his. "Go on."

"Okay. Number one. Sperm meets egg. Fertilization, embryo, fetus, a normal delivery. A baby, a new human being! As such, it is entitled to parents, a mother and a father, and unless one or the other or both are removed by a stroke of fate, it is legally and morally entitled to their attention, their love and their care." Tom saw her nod, and continued, "My question number two that looms large in my mind is how would that work out in your case, with Bettina and you as mothers? Is that new little menschkin ever going to know who its father is? Because one day it will have to be explained to him or her, won't it, just how he or she came about?"

"We would grant you every access, every consideration that you might wish!" Pat replied heatedly. "It needn't be a problem, not amongst civilized people."

"Granted. There is an added point, though, that needs consideration. As a physician, I can tell you that about five percent of all obstetric cases encounter some deviation from the norm, some minor, some major. While that is only five cases out of a hundred, it is four dozen out of a thousand, and in a city the size of London, it may well approach the tens of thousands. The point being, what do we do if a miscarriage occurs or a stillbirth? Do we try, try again or am I to be absolved from further consideration? D'you see?"

Pat cradled the bottom of her brandy snifter in her hands, staring at the golden liquid. When she looked up she said, "I do see. Of course. We'd have to take it as it comes. Basically, it changes nothing. All I can tell you is, if a baby is born it will be as much yours as ours. And we would love it as your child as much as our own."

Tom got up and went over to her. Leaning down, he kissed her cheek. "I know you would. In fact, you already do love my child—Bertie." He straightened up. "Which brings me to question number three. Would you and Bettina take care of him if, as the quaint saying goes, something should happen to me?" Having said that, he bit his lip. What about Laura, to whom the boy was already bonded? He'd have to leave a letter for Cab, giving instructions . . . decide later . . .

Pat answered immediately. "Of course we would!" She glanced up at him, shocked. "What a question! Should we worry about you? Tom, is there something going on we don't know?"

He went over to the bar and refreshed his drink. "Nothing really to worry about. I may have to go out of town next week or so, for a couple of days. In everything we do, there is an element of risk, isn't there. In my situation, the risk is very, very low. But there's no denying it exists. The boy has already lost his mother. He can ill afford to lose his father as well. To think that you and Bettina would act in loco parentis would be enormously reassuring." He turned back to her. "That should also give you a measure of my trust in you. And perhaps, when all is settled, we can deal with the moral and ethical conundrum that attaches to your proposition. I am not a zealot, religious or otherwise, in fact I can see the merit of your case, up to a point. And then," he took a sip and began to smile, "there is the practical side that should be taken into account. Making a woman pregnant is not always a one-shot deal. It could take weeks, months even, before it clicks. How would we handle that, you and I? Saying to Bettina, again and again, 'Excuse us, we have some private business to take care of'?"

Pat put down her glass and came over to him. "I don't know. I only know that I want a child and of all the possibilities you represent the best, the most desirable one." She put her arms around him and leaned her head against his shoulder.

Tom didn't know what to say. He stroked her head. "Well," he murmured, and it disconcerted him that he felt a desire rising. "Let's table the motion, sine ira et studio, isn't that how you legal eagles put it?"

He felt her head nod. "As long as it is not sine die," she sniffled.

On Tuesday, towards noon, Tom phoned the Duke's office. The secretary had a message. "Dr. Ulli Ullmer, Biochemisches Institut, Heidelberg." Tom thanked her, and hung up. That evening, he transmitted the information to Cab.

Baden-Baden

The e-mail message from Cab, after a couple of days of silence and non-response to his queries, was as tantalizingly brief as it was puzzling. "B.B. Arrive United Heathrow Wed 4-13 0900 GMT Res Room M.N." Puzzling, because the meaning of the initials had slipped his mind, until he remembered that telephone conversation at lunch in Oxford. Then it became perfectly clear:

"B.B." stood for Mr. and Mrs. Blumenfeld—Charles and Freddie—and as well for the spa town of Baden-Baden in the south of Germany. "M.N." was, of course, Major Nemo. Translated further, it meant simply that Cab and his girlfriend Freddie were on their way to Baden-Baden, and would arrive at London-Heathrow on United Airlines on Wednesday April 13th at nine in the morning Greenwich Mean Time. Room reservations for Major Nemo were required.

Tom did some more puzzling out. The Creep was located in Heidelberg. Consulting a map, he found that Baden-Baden was an easy hour's drive from the old university town near the confluence of the Neckar River and the Rhine. It implied that Cab and Freddie, as Mr. and Mrs., would take up residence—"taking the cure," didn't he say?—in Baden-Baden, providing back-up and cover while Tom was going after his prey. To disguise his London whereabouts, the fictional Major Nemo would once again check into the Grosvenor House Hotel. That check-in would have to occur on the Tuesday before, and on Wednesday morning Tom would be at the airport, not only to welcome Mr. and Mrs. Blumenfeld but to go on to Germany with them, possibly on the same flight if a seat should prove available. If not, there were plenty of connections from Heathrow to Germany, at almost any hour.

An agonizing weekend was between the message and the Tuesday following.

Tom felt fidgety and nervous. He proposed that Bertie be given his first taste of riding by taking him to a stable Bettina recommended that was still doing business on Rotten Row in Hyde Park. There the boy could be eased into the feel of sitting on horseback and perhaps have some fun in the bargain. It worked out that way, Bertie being quite eager to get on, with his dad running alongside the pony holding him reasonably upright.

It passed the time. On Monday at dinner he mentioned casually that he would be out of town for a few days.

"Out of town?" Bettina raised her eyebrows. "Where to?"

"The north of England," Tom replied, making a vague gesture.

"Whatever for?"

"Some unfinished private business. I shouldn't be gone for long."

Bettina gave him one of her penetrating looks. "I don't suppose we are going to be told what that private business is about."

"It's rather a bore, I'm afraid. D'you mind looking after Bertie in the meantime?"

"Of course we don't mind," Pat said quickly. "You know that."

"Yes, I do know. You are marvelous, the two of you." He meant it. He resolved to have some flowers sent to the house, a big impressive bouquet. What would he do without these two women?

Bettina was not mollified, "There is no need to butter us up. Our little fellow will be well looked after. We shall have him ready to speak to you on the telephone, every time you call. Which I suggest, should be regularly."

"Yes, of course." And why not? How could they tell where he was calling from? "And when I am back, I shall try to make it up to you." Good Lord, Pat might misunderstand! "I shall send you off on a holiday, while Bertie and I look after your house and your dogs!" And never mind that bouquet, too tacky.

Finally, Bettina smiled, "We shall see about that."

On Wednesday morning he brought Bertie to school, using the same taxi to take him to Heathrow. He had packed an overnight bag with just a change of clothes and an extra pair of shoes. He was wearing his dark blue raincoat and a floppy hat; an additional amount of clothes and his shaving gear he had left at the Park Lane Hilton where he had checked in the day before, again as Major Nemo, except that he used the Duke's presumption and spelled it "Neimow."

The Blumenfelds emerged at last from customs, trundling a baggage cart. Tom recognized them instantly in the crowd of humanity that spilled endlessly from the bowels of the airport into the arrivals hall. They were wearing new matching Burberrys, Freddie with a silk scarf slung over half a shoulder, Cab with a New York Mets baseball hat and shaded-lens glasses. Tom hurried over.

"Hello, you two!"

The greetings were perfunctory, as Cab seemed anxious, somehow. He wondered why Tom was carrying a bag, and when Tom explained the Hilton Hotel setup Cab said, as they were pushing towards the exit, "Okay. Here's the deal. Freddie and I have a room at the airport Sheraton here, for the day. Our connecting flight is at 5:00 P.M. on Lufthansa. So, we check in, then take a taxi into town. Freddie wants to do some shopping. I will meet you at the Hilton, you go on ahead now and wait for me. The rest we'll discuss there."

Tom, who had thought he would be buying a ticket to Germany for himself at the airport, said okay, and went on ahead to the taxi station. As his car pulled out he saw, looking back, Cab and Freddie boarding the Sheraton shuttle bus. Tom had the feeling that Cab had been a bit brusque, or was it just nerves?

The answer came with Cab's knock on his hotel door a couple of hours later. "Hi, old buddy!" Cab said when the door was closed behind them. He was carrying a duty-free bag, from which he took a bottle. "Rare private label bourbon, fifty proof. Knock your socks off." Same old Cab. No problem.

Tom brought a couple of glasses in from the bathroom. Cab poured a two-finger shot. "Here's lookin' at you!" He held out his glass.

Tom touched it with his. "Cheers." They sipped. "Now, what's going on?"

"Glad you asked," Cab grinned. "I have it all up here," he pointed to his forehead, "and I want it to go straight there!" pointing to Tom's. "All verbal, just between us." He looked up. "This place bugged?"

"Hardly," Tom smiled. "Unless they bug all rooms. What do you think?"

"Fuck 'em." Cab walked over to the phone and picked up the receiver. He peered at the house numbers and dialed.

"What are you doing?" Tom asked.

"Ordering room service. A big lunch. We got work to do. Besides, it'll establish me as the Major, makes my face familiar to the help here. You stay out of sight when they knock."

"Why?"

"Because you, Tommy-old-trout, will be traveling to Germany, impersonating me. Dr. Thomas Vonder Campe, a.k.a. Major Nemo, will be here and never have left England. By the way, I like your haircut."

Tom grinned. "It takes one to know one."

"You betcha!" Cab boxed him on the arm. Then he plunked himself down in the armchair and kicked off his loafers. "Do I have a cover story for you!"

"A story of deception, no doubt."

"And perception. Story as old as mankind. Stuff operas are made of."

There was the story, and there was a drill, and a repeat drill until they had every detail down pat. They even uncovered a couple of necessary changes and made improvements as they went along.

Shortly before three o'clock Tom walked out of the hotel and entered a taxi. He wore everything Cab had been wearing: coat, cap, sunglasses, suit, shirt and tie, socks and loafers, fountain pen and wrist watch. The only item Tom did not part with was his gold wedding band. He ordered the driver to take him to the Sheraton Heathrow.

He had a key to the room on the fifth floor and let himself in. Freddie called from the bathroom, "Hi, is that you, darling?"

"It's me all right," Tom shouted back and sat on the edge of the bed. "Anytime you are ready! We still got to check in, you know."

Freddie poked her head out the door. She was fully dressed. "I'm just putting on makeup. Everything go all right?" She did not wink or otherwise let on that she knew he was not Cab.

"Perfect," Tom nodded approvingly. He meant it both ways.

They left the hotel together, Tom tipping the bellman, and took the shuttle over to the Lufthansa terminal. At the airline counter Freddie and her luggage went to the first-class section, and Tom, his coat now over his arm and his cap and glasses put away, lined up with the coach passengers. He only carried Cab's overnight case. The ticket for him had been bought by Cab in New York, however under his, Tom's, real name. It was the one concession they made to veracity; it would be foolish, they both agreed, to risk being tripped up by customs and passport control before the charade had even begun.

For the entire two-hour trip from boarding to disembarking at Stuttgart Tom did not speak to Freddie. He passed her first-class seat on his way to his own, but Freddie, deep into a magazine, did not look up, and then the curtain was drawn between the classes. At Stuttgart they still went their separate ways until Freddie showed up outside the terminal being trailed by a baggage porter, where Tom was waiting near a purring Mercedes. Tom wore Cab's coat again, and baseball cap. He was impossible to miss.

"Oh there you are, darling," Freddie said. "Is that our car?"

"Yes," Tom said and made it sound impatient. "Let's get the show on the road, shall we?" He had to smile at the aptness of the remark.

Freddie got it, too. "Yes, let's." She smiled back with perfect teeth.

It was about a hundred kilometers to Baden-Baden. Cab had arranged for a chauffeur to take them there and had already prepaid the fare. Mr. and Mrs. Blumenfeld only traveled first class.

That pertained to the hotel, too, the renowned Brenner's Park Hotel in the best section of the even more renowned spa town. The Empfangsdame—lady manager—made a show of welcoming them, there was no vulgar check-in procedure, inasmuch as a sizable deposit had already been entered on the ledger via Cab's Platinum American Express card. All Tom had to do was show it, and the passport, and that was the end of the formalities. The Dame, chatting amiably with Freddie in perfect English, led the way, followed by "Cab" and the bellman, up an elevator for a brief quiet ride, out along a red-carpeted corridor, around a corner leading to a foyer with settees under massive oil paintings. Doors to the apartments were recessed into the wall, each with a buzzer and a polished brass number. A key with an identical brass plate opened one of them, and the procession moved inside, first into a hallway where a master light switch was turned, then to the sitting room where the lady discreetly put the key atop the reception package onto the coffee table, which itself was half covered by a large bulbous vase brimming over with salmon-pink roses. A fruit basket was on the dresser, a cooler with a bottle of Sekt nearby, a stiff white napkin around the bottle's neck. The bellman hung up their coats in the hall closet, put their suitcases on built-in wall racks and withdrew.

The lady was still with them. Pushing the shutters aside and smiling, the dame explained, "The bedroom is up this step behind the shutters. It's a double bed but with two separate mattresses for better sleeping comfort; the bathroom is adjacent and the balcony can be accessed from either the bathroom or the sitting room. Press this button to close the drapes and this one to open the armoire for the TV/VCR. Call us if you have any wishes, any time at all. And have a restful night."

When they were alone, Tom stood there, uncertain what to do next or what to say to Freddie with whom he had hardly exchanged a word, not even on that car ride from Stuttgart when Freddie had leaned into a corner and closed her eyes. The champagne. "Shall we open the bottle, have a welcome drink?"

"Not just yet, Thomas, if you don't mind?" She rummaged in her purse until she had found a key. "This is for Charles' suitcase. It's the smaller of the two. You can start unpacking already. Leave me about two-thirds of the drawer space?" She smiled sweetly. As Tom took the key and turned away he saw out of the corner of his eyes how she shed her shoes, her dress, and God-knows what else.

He went into the hall, glad to be doing something normal. His apprehension was rising anew about how he would manage to live in such close proximity to beauteous Freddie, whose full name was Frederika Lindenstromberg, as he had learned from Cab during their meeting, and whom he knew as Cab's girl. Cab had laughed about it.

"Freddie is nobody's girl except her own. And very much so. You can't tell her what to do unless she wants to do it of her own free will."

"Look," Tom had said, "we are going to be cooped up in a hotel room for a couple of days."

"And nights!" Cab grinned, "Don't forget nights! Same bed, probably. Unless you act like a fool and sleep on the floor!"

"Geez, Cab, this isn't funny! My life is weird enough as it is and just looking at Freddie makes me dizzy. How do you expect this to go? Huh?"

"Naturally, my boy. Just naturally, easy, don't force anything."

"Of course I wouldn't force anything, you numskull, what do you think I am, a rapist? It's sleeping in the same bed with your girl I am talking about! Cohabitation! Or do you lawyers have another word for it?"

"Hey!" Cab had sat up and looked serious, "You don't get it, do you? I don't own Freddie. When she sleeps with me she does so on her own terms! And whether or not she'll want to sleep with you, she'll tell you. And get this, Freddie doesn't sleep around. From what I could ascertain, the number of men she's been intimate with you could count on the fingers of one hand, even if you are added. Above and beyond all that, she is a real mensch, warmhearted, kind, and honest. She has a vague idea why she is here with us and what we are up to. I say vague—she knows no details; but I had to tell her something to make her come along. So, please, trust her! Live with her! And if you are lucky . . . "

"Shut up, already!" Tom raised his hands. "I got the point. Okay?"

Now, unpacking Cab's clothing, Tom sighed. Getting the point wasn't enough. There was that sofa in the sitting room, he could move there, close the shutters to the bedroom.

"Thomas?" Freddie's voice. From the bathroom.

"Yes?" He poked his head around the corner.

"You can open the champagne now, if you like!"

"Yeah, sure." He would have to bring her a glass. And here's hoping she has used the hotel's bubble bath packet.

She had; it hadn't worked entirely, but it certainly smelled good.

"Thank you." Freddie smiled at him. "Fill your own glass, pull up that bench, and sit down? We have to talk."

"Yep." Tom did what he was told. He held out his glass to her, "Here's lookin' at you, kid." Dumb phrase. Ogling, more likely.

They drank. Tom drained his glass. It wasn't a big glass, anyway.

Freddie smiled again, a warm smile, her eyes directly on him. Big true-blue eyes, under unplucked blond eyebrows. "I know all about you, Thomas. Or almost all. From Charles, and from Thea. Remember Thea?"

"Of course! Wonderful woman. Great person, great personality."

Freddie nodded. "I know you must be nervous, being together here with me? I am not nervous about you, Thomas. And I don't want you to be nervous about me. All right?" Sweet smile, again. Red lips, white teeth, pink gums.

Tom tried to sound casual. "I'm not. Cab explained your relationship."

"I am his friend," she said quickly. "You are his friend. At this point, you and I are not friends, not yet. We have to be honest."

"Of course! I quite agree."

"We are thrown together by circumstance. That does not automatically confer intimacy." Sipping, she eyed him over the rim of her glass.

"Certainly not." Tom refilled his drink from the bottle he had brought in. Condensed water had made a puddle around it on the marble floor. "I will sleep on the sofa. No problem. Really."

"Sofa? No way. You'll sleep in the bed, on one side, I on the other. That's no problem. We are mature people, you and I and Charles, too." She put down her glass onto the floor by leaning over the tub. Pink nipples emerging. "Please, Thomas, rinse me off, would you?" She handed him the detachable shower head as she rose full length from the water.

Tom complied, he had no choice. The gentle spray dissolved the soap bubbles, from Freddie's round shoulders, down her back and over her pink round tush, her straight firm thighs. Then she turned around, and again he sprayed away the last vestiges of the concealing foam. Her breasts appeared, neat and firm, as he had seen them once before, albeit from a distance, in Cab's gym. His eyes had not been deceived. They were perfect. Now here she was at arm's length, in a close-up more real than he could have dreamed.

It was almost too much. He stepped back, knocking over the champagne.

"Thank you, Thomas," said Freddie and stepped out of the tub, wrapping herself into the hotel robe. "There is one more thing you should know about me. I am not a prude. I refuse to resort to false modesty in my private life. When it is natural that I be naked, I will be naked. You are a doctor, naked bodies are no problem for you, right?"

Tom managed a weak smile, "In my business, the naked bodies are no objects of—ah—admiration." He caught himself just in time. The word that had been on the tip of his tongue was lust.

Freddie shrugged her shoulders and began rubbing her hair with a towel.

Tom decided that his services were no longer needed; he certainly was not going to be a witness at the rest of her toilette. He picked up the bottle that had rolled, emptying itself, towards the floor drain, and withdrew.

One thing for sure about Freddie, she didn't beat around the bush and she was right about the impracticality of being prudes, although he wasn't sure that he would want to parade around her in the buff, horniness and all.

He needed a drink. There was the usual hotel refrigerator underneath the TV in the armoire, and the Scotch it carried was a cut above average. He soon poured himself a stiff one. He drank it neat, for the punitive burn it inflicted on his gullet, and ate little cheese-and-cracker bars with it, and salted peanuts. He was determined to achieve, and in the shortest possible time, what the fat Germans around here would call Bedschwere, bed heaviness, and with it oblivion until the dawn of a new day.

The bottle was half empty—or half full—when Freddie emerged from the bathroom. She was still in her robe. And probably nothing else.

Tom waved the bottle at her with a questioning look, but she shook her head, thank-you, it was getting late, it had been a long day since New York, she was turning in, but not to mind her.

Not to mind her! Tom watched as she shed the robe. Ah, he was right! Nothing else! She stepped up to the bedroom area. She switched on the lamp and slipped under the covers, choosing the bed stage right.

For a few minutes she flipped the pages of the hotel magazine, then yawned and said good-night.

Light off, covers up, silence.

Tom had a ways to go yet with the highland dew. He lingered over it, taking his time, brooding, getting increasingly angry at himself. What was he doing here with this woman? Why hadn't he told Cab no dice? The object was to get himself to Heidelberg and kill a man, not to dilly-dally with that blond Venus in a high-priced luxury hotel. To hell with Cab and his "security," and "cover," and what not. He could have flown straight to Frankfurt, gotten a car, done the deed in nearby Heidelberg, and flown right back. One day, two tops. Who'd have known?

And speaking of car, he didn't have a car. What was he going to use for transportation, if you please? Cab had said strictly he should avoid any evidence of his being in Germany, leave no receipts, pay cash for everything, merge into the crowds, and when he was done, fly back to London from Hamburg or Berlin. Then Cab would fly out and show up at the Park Hotel, being himself, having a holiday with his lovely bride, "taking the waters in the Kurhaus and getting massages, perfect cover, Tommy! Trust me!" Sure.

Tom finally achieved his heaviness, albeit more in his eyelids than his body. He went to the bathroom, took off his clothes down to his shorts, peed, brushed his teeth, removed his contacts, padded to the bedroom, taking up residence at the other side, stage left. He fell asleep almost at once but became dimly aware that he did not enjoy his rest, tossing and turning as he was.

Towards the morning, when the room was diffused with a half-light around the heavy curtains, he fought his returning consciousness as long as he could. He heard the toilet being flushed, and as he forced his eyes open, observed Freddie returning on tiptoe, breasts whipping in sync, to her side of the bed.

He let out a low moan.

"Thomas?" Freddie leaned over. "Are you awake?" she breathed.

"Aaoow," a muffled response. Tom rolled over on his back, eyes closed.

"Thomas?" She touched his shoulder. "Do you desire me, Thomas?"

He forced his eyes open. Her nose was practically on his cheek. With some effort, he croaked a nod and managed a silly grin.

"I desire you, too, Thomas."

Her lips were so close, her breath so sweet, it was impossible to ignore her. What the hell. With his hand he gently pushed her head down and sought her lips. A testosterone flash raced through his body when he kissed her. Reason sank into the abyss. You said she wasn't your girl, Cab, remember . . .

In their heated struggle to accommodate their bodies, their lips never apart, Tom shot his wad before he was inside, shuddering and groaning.

He entered her anyhow, became relaxed and flaccid, and very nearly fell asleep in her arms. Only when she began to disengage herself did his senses return.

He felt awful, and immediately said so. Terrible. Long abstinence, hair-trigger response and all that.

Freddie smiled and said that was all right. Sex was like any other physical activity, you need to exercise to be in peak form.

Tom was not so easily consoled. He remembered he hadn't used a rubber. Good Lord! Imagine if he hadn't come early!

Freddie sat up and lifted her left arm. Touch this, she said and guided his hand to the inside of her arm just above the elbow.

With his fingertips he could feel welts just under the skin, six match-like sticks spread out like a fan. He knew what it was; he and Nettie had talked about it for just after their second child would have arrived. Timed-release birth control implants. He nodded yes to Freddie. But what about the unspeakable, he was going to ask her, what about the ever-present goddamn AIDS scare.

She pressed his head against her breasts and whispered, her lips in his bristled hair. "You worry too much, Thomas. We must all seek some happiness. That is normal, even now. And we must take it where we find it. Because time, you cannot roll it back, like a video. What's gone is gone."

Her words, simple though they were, had a soothing effect on him. She was right. He worried too much. What's gone is gone. Wow. And this beautiful, young, smell-so-good woman whose body he now pressed to his, she was like a gift from heaven. They were friends now, weren't they, the way she was with Cab? Gratitude—or was it affection?—welled up in him. She deserved his attention, as she had given him hers, and yes, he desired her. He would make love to her the way he remembered it, slowly and gently and deeply.

They spent all morning in bed, until the buzzer sounded at the door, and Tom rushed into the bathroom as Freddie went to let in the maid who trundled in the breakfast cart to set up their table. As soon as she had left, Freddie joined Tom in the bathtub and they soaped and sprayed each other like kids, the water running rivers into the drain on the floor. She did her hair while he shaved. They grinned at each other like honeymooners.

At the breakfast table, each in their robes, Tom asked her what her plans were for the future. Marriage?

Not just yet; first she'd finish her master's at Columbia. Then she'd go to Europe, Sweden especially where her folks were from. If possible she'd marry a Swede.

"Not Cab?" Tom asked, casually, buttering his toast.

"Charles, you mean? I wish you wouldn't call him Cab, Thomas. Anyway, not him. He's, I don't know. He has such complexes, about race and all. No. I think if he marries, it will be Shoya."

"Shoya, the maid?" Tom was speechless.

She nodded. "Act surprised, if that should come to pass. Don't tell him I said that. I don't want his feelings hurt."

"No, of course not." It was on his mind to ask, just playfully, if she would marry him, but he bit his tongue. There was no way he could see a marriage to her working out in the long run; not with being a mother to Bertie, she was just too young for all that. But, by God she was fun in bed. He hadn't felt so good in a long time—revitalized, restored, and ready for more.

They discussed what their plans were; Freddie would go check out the gym facilities and the fabled baths at the Kurhaus. And Tom? Oh, she almost forgot. Charles had given her an envelope to give to him! She got up and went to her purse, came back and handed him a plain business envelope. It felt as if there were pages and pages inside. He flipped it onto his bed, to look at later. No point in getting egg yolk or jam on it.

When he did get around to opening it—Freddie had already left, dressed in a cute jogging suit—he had a surprise. Inside a plain piece of paper were twenty bills of one thousand Deutschmark each, and a yellow note, typewritten, that said "Call me at the hotel from the main post office." That was all.

Tom whistled, put on Cab's coat, sunglasses and hat and left the hotel by the back entrance that led directly into the park. It was warm out, a few clouds in an otherwise sunny sky. He took off the coat and put it over his arm. The main post office was on the Leopoldsplatz, less than ten minutes from the hotel. He had some smaller denominations of German money that he had bought in London. He exchanged some of it into coins and stepped into one of the telephone booths. It would be an hour back in London now; about 10:00 A.M.

He called the Hilton and asked for Major Neimow. Cab picked up the phone on the second ring. "Nemo here!"

"Yes. Ditto. You wanted me to call."

"Yeah. Give me the number. You're at a public phone, right? Okay. Shoot."

Tom recited the number he read off the phone. Cab told him to stay there he'd call him right back. Tom imagined that Cab would rush to a public phone himself, located outside the hotel. A few minutes later the phone buzzed.

"Hello, Kiddo" he said, picking it up. They had decided in their meeting to use generic nicknames over the phone lines. Crude, and puerile perhaps, but one more effort at obfuscation.

"Hiya, Bubba." Cab's voice. "How're you doin'? Gotten any nooky-nooky in Baden-Baden?"

Tom was annoyed. "Cut it out, will you? Come to the point."

"You got some nooky-nooky." A chuckle. "Okay. You have the envelope?"

"Yes."

"Good. It's for your car. Go to Auto-Hansli on Stauffenberg Strasse, near the cemetery. Got that?"

"Wait." Tom took his pen and jotted it down on the edge of the phone directory page. "Got it." He tore out the edge, put the piece of paper in his pocket. "Go on."

"I called the guy yesterday, his first name is Manfred, confirming our previous arrangements and my arrival at the hotel—your hotel—and that I'd be by this morning to see what he has to offer. It'll be a used car, and it'll be a lease option. You'll pay him half the envelope, and you'll say that you'll let him know within a month if you want to keep the car, in which case you'll pay him the other half."

"Got it."

"In the event that you 'don't like it' he gets to keep the money you paid him. It's a good deal for the guy, either way."

"I agree. How'd you get on to him? And does he speak English?"

"I worked on him from New York. He is a referral from one of my sources. Yes, to English, anyway I only spoke English with him and he knows I don't speak German. Now, here's an important point. The car will come fully papered, registration, insurance, the works. You know how picky the Germans are with Wagenpapiere. Still, you don't want to get stopped by the police if you can help it. And always park in a parkhaus, I mean, don't bring the car to the hotel or even let on that you have a car."

"I wouldn't, Kiddo. Trust me."

"Hey, where would we be if I didn't? Now, later in the day you should call the Creep at the institute. You still got the number I gave you?"

"Yes."

"Make an appointment. Insist on one. Then be there, day or night. In fact, you may want to be there a little early."

"We went over that, Kiddo, in our meeting. Remember? Nooky-nooky didn't burn out my brain cells."

A short laugh. "Glad you are having some fun. You, plural." A pause. "Okay, Bubba, that's it. Call me from the other place when you get there. Day or night, rain or shine. Me, I'll be watching TV a lot. You have no idea what they can show here, stuff that'd be X-rated at home. Any questions?"

"Nope. And Kiddo, I'll kiss her good-night for you."

"You do that, brother, you do that." Click.

Tom looked at his watch. It was getting on towards high noon. He'd have to hustle to catch the guy—Manfred, was it?—before he went on his mittagessen, noontime break, very important for Germans. Businesses shut down for it.

He made inquiries, practicing his German, before leaving the post office. To get to Stauffenberg Strasse you take the main road south to Hahnhof, then walk up left until Hahnhof Strasse becomes Stauffenberg

Strasse. A bus runs down that way every fifteen minutes, right from here. Danke Schøn.

Auto-Hansli was hard to miss. At the junction of the two streets Tom saw a huge sign rotating on a pole, with "Auto Hansli Porsche-Audi-VW" blazing on either side. The lot had used cars up front and new car showrooms indoors behind glass. Plastic flags in bright colors were fluttering all over the place in near-perfect imitation of U.S. dealership practices. Couldn't miss it. Tom walked right onto the lot and asked the nearest man for "Herr Manfred Hansli." He spoke in English and made the German name come out with a drawl in exaggerated American. The man gestured to follow him and took him to the main building, handing him over to a secretary there. That young lady spoke into the phone, and presently a door opened and a thin, dark-haired man not older than Tom, came towards him, hand outstretched.

"Mister Blumenfeld, hallo! How are you? You must be tired after your trip!" The greetings were rendered in passable if dialect-flavored English.

Tom shook his hand. And with that he was ushered into the office, the door closed. It seemed, after a brief preamble of courteous statements, that the car available for Mr. Blumenfeld was an Audi-100, near new with low kilometers. Four door, with—hand movements now—"what do you call it?"

"Stick shift?" said Tom.

"Yah, stick shift. I must remind me the word. You want to see it. Now." Herr Manfred Hansli held up a thick brown folder and a set of keys.

Not a question. Of course Mister Blumenfeld wanted to see it. Now.

Both men rose and went into the yard behind the building where several cars were parked on a separate lot. One of them, a dark blue one, was apparently for Tom. They went through the motions of inspecting everything, hood up and trunk open, starting the car, revving the engine, trying the wipers, the lights. Seemed to work fine. Tom said so.

They went back inside and resumed their discussion. Manfred—it was Manfred and Charles now, after mutual thank yous and a handshake—produced a form with pages of triplicates that was already filled in. Manfred held out his pen for a signature. Tom, glancing at the contract, said, "Wait a minute, Manfred. Wasn't the lease price supposed to be for ten thousand Deutschmark? It says here twelve thousand. Or am I reading this wrong?"

Manfred smiled ingratiatingly. "You are right. It is twelve thousand, the new lease rate. The twenty thousand for the purchase is the same. You see? Here?" He pointed to the page.

"What happened between when we set this up in New York and now?"

"You don't know?" Round eyes of astonishment.

"Apparently I don't."

"The strike!"

"What strike?"

"Herr Blumenfeld—uh, Charles!" More astonishment. "They do not print news about Germany in America?" Manfred was incredulous.

"Tell me the news, Manfred. And how that ties in with the lease price."

Manfred obliged. "The unions, you see. I am a union man myself but this strike was going too far. Everybody says so. The Public Service Employees are going out on strike, it is almost certain, by Monday, unless a last-minute settlement is reached, which nobody believes anymore. It is terrible."

"I still don't see how the lease . . ."

"You don't understand!" His hands implored the heavens. "You Americans have everything private, yah? Here in Germany, everything is public and the boss is Vater Staat. Yah? Trains, buses, streetcars, all that is moving. Yah? So what happens when they stop moving? The private sector!" He made it sound as if he had read that in the Frankfurter Allgemeine. "People still need to move! You have a car, you move. You have no car, you buy one or rent one. Yah? Every car I have I can sell or rent for fifty percent more. Minimum. For you I charge only twenty percent, because you did not know and I treat my customers from America especially fair." He shrugged his shoulders. "But as you wish. You can try Hertz, except they already have no cars left. I know that. Here I treat you fair. A deal is a deal, as you say, yah?"

The answer was Yah across the board, Tom knew he had no choice. Besides, what the hell, only two colorful sheets of paper more. He picked up the pen and signed. He asked, "All public transportation will be affected, is that it?"

"More! All Public Services! Garbage, post, hospitals, schools, everything! Everybody working for the State—pfft! Out." He swung his arm across his desk. "Yes. It is very bad. The Ossies, they want too much too soon, and where do we get the money? Can you tell me?"

Tom shook his head. The East Germans, "Ossies" as opposed to "Wessies," the latter being the good guys, were becoming increasingly restive in their economic disparity. He had read about that, even in the New York Times.

"It can't last very long. No industrialized country can afford to be without transportation."

"But we will not be without transportation! Everything will be private, cars, buses, trucks, everything. In my business, we will make a lot of money." Manfred mercifully refrained from rubbing his hands together.

Tom peeled out twelve notes from his wallet. "This deal includes a full tank of gas, I hope?" he asked. He would put the car into a parkhaus immediately, not use it until he went up to Heidelberg. On a full tank he could go up and back without refueling.

"Yah, naturlich! Full tank, and I will give you two extra canisters, full, to put in the baggage room. That will be one hundred kilometers more driving, if you cannot get to a service station. Good reserve, yah?"

Tom agreed that it would be a good reserve, and realized that "baggage room" was the literal translation of "trunk."

He took possession of the folder Manfred gave him containing the all important papers Cab had referred to and a copy of the lease contract. On the contract were entered the passport and international drivers license numbers of Blumenfeld, Charles A.B., New York, N.Y., USA. Manfred had sweated over the spelling and the numbers, and Tom had been helpful, holding it up for Manfred to read, his thumb on the face of the passport picture. The twelve thousand Deutschmark, cash, disappeared into Manfred's trouser pocket.

It was afternoon when Tom drove the Audi down the hill and back onto the main thoroughfare. There was a parkhaus on the Augusta Platz downtown, where he turned in and left the car. He walked over to the post office and again placed a call to the Hilton in London. Major Nemo, please.

"Sorry, there is no answer, sir," the hotel operator told him. "Would you like to leave a number and a message?"

"Yes, the message is 'please advise if there is a strike'. Signed, B."

"B, sir, as in the letter B, or if it is a name, would you spell it, please, sir?"

A lot of strange foreigners calling at the Hilton, apparently. He wanted the call to end, it had already taken too long. "B, as in Bubba, B-u-b-b-a. He has the number. Thank you."

Stepping out of the post office, he saw a branch of one of the major banks, right across the street. He needed to be more liquid, and thousand-mark denominations just wouldn't do. Exchange at least, say, two thousand into smaller bills. It came as a surprise to him when the clerk, accepting his money, wanted to see his passport before she counted out the hundreds, fifties and twenties. He handed the passport over wordlessly, and she hardly looked at it. But it illustrated to Tom two things worth bearing in mind. In Germany, identifications were frequently asked for and the more routine the event the less likely people would be to look at the picture.

Next, he bought a number of German papers and a couple of long, juicy hot dogs, with which he retired onto a nearby park bench to begin reading and munching.

There was no doubt about it. A strike of the nearly three million public sector employees was in the offing, and would occur at midnight Sunday if a last-minute settlement was not reached. Verkehrs-Chaos was predicted, a traffic chaos having such side effects as mile-long clogging of all autobahns, and inner-city traffic coming to a standstill. Even now, people were already making efforts to take to the streets on anything with wheels. But that was not all. Garbage would pile up, municipal hospitals would treat only emergencies, buses, trains, planes and even ferries would not run, and everybody would be very, very upset. Manfred had been right.

Tom pondered this for a while. Had he and Cab known this—damn, how could they have missed this in the papers? They would probably not have scheduled their coup at this time. But that was so much water under the bridge now. He was here, he had the car, and the Creep wasn't going anywhere, either, under the circumstances. So, on with the show. A little chaos might just work to his advantage, what with everybody being very preoccupied.

Oh, there was something else he could do now. He could take advantage of the pre-chaos days and lay in the stock of supplies he had wanted to buy when he was in Heidelberg. He needed to find a drugstore here, to buy some surgical tape, some kind of emergency kit that would also contain a basic set of instruments, injectible insulin if he could get it over the counter, bottles of alcohol, of ether, of iodine, and if they had it, a stethoscope and rubber gloves.

He did so, and got everything he wanted and more, a veritable travel clinic when he identified himself to the pharmacist as an American doctor who was on his honeymoon with his slightly diabetic wife and who knows what would happen during a strike if they had an emergency, and so on. Tom was obviously knowledgeable about medical matters. The sale came to several hundred marks. He walked out of the Adler-Apotheke with a large plastic shopping bag.

Shlepping them over to the parkhaus he also became aware of his need for some basic food stuffs, such as water, bread, cereal, fruit, candy. He stopped by a market and laid in a supply of that. All of it he stowed in the spacious "baggage room" of the Audi. He couldn't think of anything more to do, so he walked back to the hotel.

Freddie was sunning herself on the balcony. She was reading a paperback and hadn't heard him coming into the room. Tom stood at the door, gazing down at her. Freddie was in her self-described "private" mode—unclothed.

When she noticed his presence she looked up, blinking, holding her hand up against the slanted rays of the late afternoon sun. "Thomas! There you are! How was your day?"

"Oh," he gestured with his hand. "Busy, running around, making phone calls. Cab sends his love, by the way. And how was yours?"

"You mean Charles. Is that what you are doing, giving me his love? Don't answer that. And my day? It was wonderful. Terrific. I worked out at the gym, went over to the Trinkhalle to cool down with some really groovy Evian-type water, then at the Augustabad I had a Stahl-bad they call it. Like Stahl as in steel? Which is like getting jets of hot soda water sprayed at you from all sides? Then they gave me a massage and put me out to pasture on the quiet lawn where I slept like a baby. And here I am reading the latest bestseller while I am waiting for you." She smiled up at him. "Come over here, you friend of Charles." She patted the side of the patio chaise.

Tom, still in suit and tie and with the coat over his arm, said, "Let me get rid of this first, Freddie." He smiled, a bit embarrassed, and turned.

"Get rid of all of it!" She called after him, giggling. "Let's make this a level playing field, Thomas!"

He poked his head back in, "Out here? On the balcony? Tsk, tsk. What will people think?"

"What people? There's the awning above us. We're on the fifth floor, the top floor, Thomas! And these geraniums on the balcony rails are as high as an elephant's eye! Who's going to see us?"

"Fourth floor," Tom was going to say, but he shrugged. The ground floor did not count as number one in Germany, and besides, what did it matter? He went back in and got rid of his coat, jacket and tie, brushed his teeth and washed his hands. Looking at himself in the mirror, he had a flash worry about what was becoming of him. Would he engage in some more torrid sex with this alluring young woman out there and then blithely drive off tomorrow and go kill a man? It was unsettling, this juxtaposition of events about to happen.

He moved his face closer to the mirror and searched his eyes. Up until now, everything he had done had been justifiable, in one way or another, in the name of Nettie, revenging her death, closing a nasty chapter of their past in order to get on with his life again. But going out there buck-naked, embracing Frederika, that gorgeous Svenska Flicka, as if they were lovers, or on a honeymoon even, with not a care in the world—uh-uh!

He shook his head. He had already slept with her in a great outpouring of desire, wasn't that what she had said? "Do you desire me, Thomas?" Yes, he had desired her, and no regrets there. She was a woman, and he needed a woman. He was not for the monkish life and certainly not up for sainthood. But Freddie herself, how must she feel about all this? Was she guileless in giving herself to him, and in that sense, was he not taking unfair advantage of her?

Again shaking his head, he stepped away from the basin.

"What is it, Thomas?" Freddie was standing in the door to the balcony, a towel wrapped around her waist. "You are shaking your head, is something wrong?"

Tom saw her, strands of her blond hair coming loose from the comb that held it in place, her face serious, eyes round, lips half parted, her breasts free and easy. There would never be a girl that beautiful crossing his path again. What was he doing shaking off her signals!

"Well, yes. Or rather, I don't know, exactly. Maybe we should talk."

"Certainly." She came over and took his hand. "Let's sit down." She went ahead to the sitting room and took one chair, motioning him into the other. "Tell me what you are thinking, Thomas."

He noticed how she gathered her legs under her, then cupped her chin in her hand, her elbow resting on the arm of the chair. Irresistible.

Her thighs in nearly full view, her knees round, even her feet were perfectly formed. He said, swallowing, "It's just that I don't know, Freddie, if we are doing the right thing. Please don't misunderstand, but playing at Mr. and Mrs. Blumenfeld when neither of us are either, and then here in private you and I acting as if we are having a jolly good time, in fact having a jolly good time, when what brought us together is damn serious business, at least for me it is."

"Do you feel guilty, making love with me?" She looked at him calmly.

"Yes, in a way. You are so much younger than I. Am I contributing to your future unhappiness? What will you tell that Swedish hunk of yours when you meet him? And besides, what about feelings, yours and mine? Suppose we get used to each other, and I ask you to marry me. What would you say?"

Freddie smiled now. "One question at a time, Thomas! First, don't worry about contributing to my future unhappiness when you are contributing to my happiness now. I like making love, but very selectively, you know? For any other friend of Charles' I would not have gone along on this trip. I guess that takes care of the feelings part of the question. I feel happy with you, and maybe if along the way you asked me to marry you I would say yes, although I don't think that will happen."

"There is that Swedish hunk," Tom nodded.

She laughed. "It's not that so much, except that your life and my life are running on different tracks? I still want to do things, I can't settle down yet, whereas you need to have a wife right away and a mother for your son." She uncurled herself and came over to him, giving him a kiss. "Don't be sad, Thomas. Don't worry so much."

He cupped her breasts with his hands and ran his thumbs over her nipples. "I wish I knew what to do, Freddie," he whispered, "I wish I knew."

"I do," she said brightly and straightened up. "I am going to get dressed and then we'll go out for dinner to a nice little Schwarzwald Inn where they serve genuine home cookin'. I'm famished!"

It was well before midnight when they returned. They had found that nice little Weinstube just off the main promenade where they were given a table—it was still early—in a vine-covered booth that shielded them from the eyes of other patrons, an important point as curvaceous Freddie attracted oglers almost inevitably. They had a dry white Badenser that gave them a pleasant buzz as they talked. Tennis, Tom learned, was Freddie's game, as was skiing, the cross-country kind. They ordered venison with Spaetzle and fresh vegetables and dallied over it with a clean young Burgundy. More revelations. She was working on her master's thesis on social adaptability by analyzing the Icelandic community at Gimli in

Manitoba, Canada. Astonishing, as it seemed to involve a great deal of physical travail; Tom was impressed. When Freddie excused herself to go to the bathroom, Tom went to the front desk of the establishment where he had seen a showcase of semi-precious stones for which the region was famous. Waving one of his large bills, he made a quick deal on a well-cut aquamarine set in a gold pendant. When Freddie came back to he table, he sat with his closed fists planted on the checkered table cloth and told her to choose. Which one, right or left? Right, of course, she said merrily, and tapped his left hand. He opened it up. The stone was in there. Freddie was speechless, blushed, wanted to refuse it but couldn't, whispered thanks, and put the pendant onto the thin gold chain she was wearing perpetually. The stone fit perfectly, just above the valley where her breasts were parting. Freddie's lips quivered and her eyes were glittering wet in the candle light.

They walked back, close together, Tom's coat over her shoulders. Inside their room they did not even turn on the light. Wordlessly they undressed, embraced, and sank down on the bed. Their lovemaking was as quiet as it was intense, and then they crawled under the sheets. The pendant pressed tight between them, they fell asleep, still entwined.

A message was blinking on the telephone when Tom awakened at dawn. The operator read it to him, "Mr. Blumenfeld," over the phone. It was from London, 2015 hours and said, "Yes to your question. Call me from Creepsville. Pronto."

The operator laboriously spelled out "Creepsville." Tom thanked her and hung up. Freddie was sitting up in bed, still heavy with sleep. He went over to embrace her. "Sweetheart," he told her, "Charles called. I have to go."

The Neckar Drop

The traffic he encountered was heavy from the moment he had steered the Audi out of the parkhaus; Tom had expected it, but he did not think it would take him an hour to maneuver through the city and the ten-kilometer stretch of road leading to the No. 5 autobahn on-ramp. He put the car radio on. The news was grim. The state and federal governments issued statements appealing to the "spirit of service to community" they presumed to be still present in the minds and hearts of their "fellow civil servants." The unions of "Offentliche Dienste," a conglomeration of various and sundry civil service, transportation, post and communications, sanitation and whatnot unions countered with equally pious if more vehement proclamations of "the right to living wages." The spirit missing in all the charges and countercharges was that of compromise. There was no question but that the nerve center of the most powerful industrial nation in Europe would be paralyzed by 12:01 A.M. Monday morning.

Tom gave a Bronx cheer to all that. Cheer was the right word; he saw the calamity working in his favor, both in terms of what he had to do and in his disappearance after he had done it.

"It"—that was another matter. Did it stand for "Execution," or was it "Murder"? He dismissed the latter definition instantly. For too long he had in his mind wrestled with the ultimate definition of his mission; murder it was not, most definitely not. He knew that if he felt otherwise he could not go through with it. Although—a twinge of unease there, barely perceptible but there, just the same—the almost total relaxation with Freddie had had the effect of softening up his iron resolve just enough to entertain the possibility of chucking it all, perhaps even of running off with her.

Freddie had suggested as much when they embraced for the last time, saying good-bye, standing in the hallway.

"Tommy," she whispered in his ear, and he could feel the wetness of her eye on his cheek, "would you stay if I told you, yes, I will marry you?"

"Dear Frederica," he tried to make light of her question, "do not tempt me. You know how easily I succumb to you."

He heard her sniffle. Gently disengaging himself from her, he took her face in his hands. "This is the wrong time, the wrong situation to deal with such an important question. Maybe when we are all back in the States, under normal conditions, we should talk again. But not now. Not here. Trust me."

He kissed her. She kept her eyes closed and when he released her she turned, unspeaking, walking back into the room. The last glimpse he caught of her was of her figure silhouetted against the slanting beams of the morning sun. Such was the twinge he felt, as if touched by the sun himself, that he almost followed her. It was his disciplined, rational mind that made him turn in the opposite direction. When he pulled the outer door shut behind him, he knew that he had left something irretrievable behind.

It was a good thing that the traffic on the autobahn required all his attention. This main south-north artery he was on, from Basel to Hamburg, was full in both directions, the slow lane packed like a huge diesel-fuming snake with trucks, tankers and big rigs carrying goods from the four corners of the continent. It took constant vigilance for Tom not to lose his spot in the fast lane, although fast now meant a crawling pace. He switched over to the number six autobahn that, coming from northern Bavaria, crossed the number five and turned north on a parallel track. For a brief stretch he actually could drive the Audi at 125 kph, but then it was time for him to get off when he saw the sign "Schwetzingen-Heidelberg-West" looming ahead.

He had been to Schwetzingen before, during the fall build-up of troops later deployed in the Gulf War. His tour of duty at the Frankfurt U.S. Army Military Hospital had lasted six months, much of it a boring routine that he alleviated by taking drives into the countryside, one or two-day excursions where he would let his spur-of-the-moment curiosity be his guide. Schwetzingen had been one of his discoveries, along with Heidelberg, Mannheim, Speyer and much else of the historic Palatinate. He remembered a baroque castle and park that was right by the little town of Schwetzingen—or was the town right by the castle?—and how he had enjoyed his meal at the quietly distinguished dining room in the Hotel zur Post on the town square. He headed for that now.

In small towns in Germany, he had learned, you don't drive up through a porte-cochere to have your car parked by an attendant and your bags carried in by a bellman. You found parking somewhere and jolly well brought your stuff in through the main door yourself.

Tom didn't mind that in the least. He found a twenty-four hour parking garage a few blocks away and left the car there. As he had no bags—he had walked out of the Park Hotel carrying nothing—he decided now that he would buy some clothing that he might need anyhow, and stuff it all into a newly purchased suitcase. As he knew there would be, a Kaufhaus department store was right on the town square. He bought shaving material and underwear, running shoes and sweatshirts and shorts, a windbreaker, denim shirts, sunglasses and, when it caught his eye, a rather expensive sports watch with everything on it including a compass. He doubled back to the sports section and picked up a sleeping bag as well, in case he would have to spend a night outdoors. His final purchase was a leather suitcase, small enough to be comfortable to carry and large enough for all his purchases. He sequestered himself into a public toilet, threw all the items he had bought into the suitcase and all the wrapping into a rubbish bin.

Shortly after noon, a well-dressed Mr. Blumenfeld, a lawyer from New York according to his passport, checked into the Hotel zur Post and was given a very comfortable Einzelzimmer on the second floor with a view of the castle.

Minutes later he descended back into the lobby, asked the porter, who spoke English of course, to reserve a Mittagstisch for him for one o'clock and then stepped out to, as he said with a smile, catch some fresh air after a long journey.

There were stalls on the market square, of local farmers selling their fruits and vegetables. Tom pushed his way through the crowds until he saw what he wanted—a public telephone booth.

The first number he dialed was that of the Creep at the Biochemisches Institut in Heidelberg. He was put through to an extension, where the phone rang and rang until the operator came back on telling him that Dr. Ullmer must be on lunch break and asking if there was a message? "Yes, tell him it's Major Neimow." Tom spelled it for her. "And I'll call back around three."

His next call was to Cab's hotel in London. Much to his surprise the phone was picked up on the first ring after he had been connected.

"How're ya doin', Kiddo?" Tom said.

"Bubba! Geez, I've been sittin' here waitin' for your call since dawn! Gimme your number."

"Sure," Tom recited the area code and number of the public phone.

"Five minutes!" Cab said and hung up.

It took longer than that, with Tom fidgeting and play-acting phone use, until Cab was on the line again.

"Okay," he growled. "Some joker was hogging the phone box here on Park Lane. So, tell me where you are."

"Schwetzingen," Tom said and spelled it out.

"Where the hell is that?"

"About thirty kilometers west of Heidelberg." Tom peered out and read it off a sign, "It says here, the Asparagus Capital of the World. Also, there is a beautiful baroque castle here of which I have a view from my room."

"Room with a view, huh? A castle, yet. You bluebloods." Cab was still growling. "Okay, first give me the parameters."

Tom gave him the address and phone number of the hotel, and the make and license number of the Audi and where he had parked it. He told him that he had tried the Creep's number but that the Creep was out to lunch; he would call back later and in any case, intended to go to Heidelberg by streetcar which he remembered connected the two towns, and check out the institute.

"Speaking of streetcar," Cab said, "there is going to be one hell of a mess if the strike goes through. The last chance I have to fly into Germany, I am told, is on Sunday night, before the strike hits. So I bought a ticket from British Air, and a return ticket for you, both under my name. Now, here's the kicker. I'm not landing at Frankfurt but at Munich where there is a brand-new fully automated international airport, the point being that the strike is not likely to affect arrivals and departures there because supervisory personnel will press all the right buttons. Or so they tell me."

"Sunday!" Tom suddenly felt pressure. "Suppose I can't get to the Creep by Sunday?"

"You've got to try! Go to Heidelberg, hit him where it hurts, and leave town but not before calling me here. Okay? Bubba? You listening?"

"Yes. I'll be there, come rain or shine. Give me your flight number and arrival time." He noted it down when Cab did so.

"Are you all right?" Cab asked.

"Sure I'm all right. Why're you asking?"

"I dunno. It's okay for you to poop out on this deal if you don't feel like it, you know."

"Poop out? Now, after all we've gone through? How can you even think that?"

"Take it easy, Bubba. I just don't want you to go haywire on me. By the way, I sent a postcard from Newcastle-Upon-Tyne in your handwriting to your sister's house, addressed to the kid."

"Newcastle? Well, why not. How'd you fake my handwriting?"

"Printed the whole thing, as you would to a kid, Bubba. You can explain it all to them next week. And also, don't leave home without me. Keep in close touch. We need to coordinate everything to make this work. Got that?"

Tom said he got it. There wasn't really much else to say, and mercifully the subject of Freddie didn't come up. They made an arrangement to talk again early morning of Saturday, the next day, by Cab calling the same phone booth and Tom being there, in his jogging outfit, picking it up on the fourth ring. That would be at 7:10 A.M., Schwetzingen time; 6:10 A.M. in London. Cab groaned, "You owe me after this, Bubba, plenty!" and hung up.

Back at his hotel, there was a table ready for him in the dining room. It was not possible for Tom to be inconspicuous in this relatively small space that held not more than a dozen tables, each occupied by serious eaters. Light flooded through large windows. The loudest sound, above the rumble of low-voiced murmurs, was the click-clack of the silverware being pushed around on china plates. Even the waiters, with their ridiculous black bow ties and white aprons, spoke and bowed in the hushed manner that befitted the ancient tradition of the establishment. Tom knew he was being observed out of the corner of every eye and that if he did anything the least "outlandish" he would be remembered for weeks to come. He knew that he had better blend in and act the out-of-town German, not the obvious foreigner, American yet, bumbling his way through the menu with the waiter.

He grabbed the Frankfurter newspaper from the rack before he sat down, and told the waiter, in his near-perfect German, to bring him a Helles, a regular beer, on tap. The waiter went to place the order at the bar, and Tom studied the menu in the plastic stand on the table. He knew he had to have something with asparagus, although he did not care much for this odd pale-white vegetable that was edible only when it was cooked to death and smothered in butter and cream; and that the meat to go with it had to be veal, not his favorite, either. He declined the waiter's suggestion of a bouillon, instead opted for a cucumber and bean salad. That done, he buried his face in the paper, not so much to read the news as to avoid staring back at the people staring at him. No eye contact.

He wondered, as he rustled the paper, sipped at his beer, turned a page or two, if he was being overly sensitive. He hadn't done anything yet, nothing illegal or even immoral had occurred. Well, making love to Freddie was not immoral, certainly not. Not by her standards, not by his. Nor, if the idea he had discussed with Cab in London could be brought to fruition, could he be accused of murder in the ordinary kill-you-dead definition of that word. And that being the case, why would he be apprehensive now? Why would he care if anyone in this restaurant wondered who he was?

Because, when all was said and done, what he was up to was what it had been from the moment he fell to his knees on that stony island after Nettie's fiery death. He had vowed retribution, a vow of revenge as old and as hot as ever burned in the breast of man. That vow had to be fulfilled. In civilized society, the law was to step in for the individual. The law abhors vigilantism, even of the subtle, sophisticated kind that he and Cab were engaged in. In some instances the law is impotent, however, stifled by procedure, gagged by outside influences. Thus Tom had convinced himself from the beginning that not only would no justice accrue in this situation, but that a Pandora's box of unforeseeable consequences would be opened if he would meekly submit to normal procedure, the slow but sure grinding of the wheels of justice, as it was called. And "normal" was not the operative word here, Nettie's death had not been normal, her case if it had come to trial would not have been normal considering the forces arrayed against it, nor would a normal jury have been likely to find in his favor. On the contrary, it could well have ruined him professionally and financially and jeopardized his son's future. No, he had no qualms, he knew his mission. That had been Nettie's dying plea, to take care of Bertie; that was her testament on her computer disk, to indict the person who had given her the lethal injection. And that, lastly, was why he was sitting here, at this idiotic Mittagessen, far away from home and family, plotting his next and last move to carry out the dictates of his conscience.

The Biochemische Institut was located within the modern complex of medical research centers and clinics on the opposite side of the Neckar river. Tom boarded the streetcar in Schwetzingen and was told to transfer to the line that would take him across the bridge to the suburb of Neuenheim; his stop would be at the "Zoo" exit. Tom estimated the travel time, all stops included, at about a half hour, and he was right within minutes.

It was a sunny spring afternoon, there was a breeze in the air that somewhat lessened the humidity coming from the river. Tom was still in Cab's suit and tie, and was wearing Cab's light-sensitive sunglasses that he would keep on even inside the building. He was carrying nothing else, no kit, no briefcase. The idea was to see if he could speak to the Creep in person, and then set something up for the next day.

He checked in with the receptionist in the institute's lobby, speaking English. "Major Neimow," he produced one of the cards Cab had given him, "to see Doctor Ulli Ullmer, please."

The young woman took his card and dialed a connection. He heard her saying in German that an American major dressed in civvies, was here to see him.

"What about?" she was asked, and so repeated the question to Tom.

"Tell the doctor it has to do with his American research findings," Tom replied quickly.

She passed that on. "Doctor Ullmer is very busy," she came back to Tom. "Can you make an appointment for next week?"

"I'm sorry, that's not possible. I'm on my way through here, and what with the strike coming on, I don't want to get stuck here." He smiled at the young woman. "You can understand that, can't you? Please ask Doctor Ullmer to come out to the lobby for just a few minutes. All I want to do is confirm some of the findings."

She relayed the lengthy message without missing a beat in German. "He'll be out in a moment, sir," she said to Tom in the end.

"Thank you," he searched for her name tag, "Fraulein Ebling. You speak English very well!"

She blushed a little. "Thank you," and went back to her calls.

Tom retreated to a seat in the corner and picked up a magazine. There was a steady coming and going of people through the lobby, and he soon gave up guessing who of those coming out from inside could be the Creep.

When he did look up because somebody said "Hullo? I am Doktor Ullmer," he was momentarily stunned. This was the infamous Creep, this androgynous figure standing in front of him in black jeans, a white lab coat open over an egg-shaped torso, curly brown hair flowing over ears and down to the neck?

But the important, tell-tale stuff was all there: the bulging eyes, the drooping lids, the dimpled chin. A perfect match to the photographs . . .

Tom got up. He caught himself quickly. "Hello, Doctor Ullmer. Thank you for coming out to see me." He handed him the Major Neimow business card.

Ullmer put on reading glasses and studied it. He seemed to nod, but said nothing. Tom glanced at the institute name tag clipped to the pocket of his coat, "Dr. U. Ullmer" it read, underneath a photo that showed him with shorter hair.

"May I presume, doctor, that you are able to converse in English?" Tom asked.

Ullmer squinted at him over his glasses. "Yes," he nodded.

No questions—not what do you want, or who are you. Just a nod. This was not going to be easy. Tom decided to be as direct as possible. "I am here in connection with a laboratory incident that occurred at the Goleta Research Laboratory in Santa Barbara, California, in late June of last year. Are you familiar with a Doctor Runge, first name Olaf?"

Ullmer was stirred a bit. He fidgeted with the glasses he had taken off now. His voice was surprisingly high pitched, "Doktor Runge? Nein, leider . . ."

It seemed to Tom that he was about to turn on his heels and walk away. He spoke in a low voice but made it sound threatening, "Doktor Ullmer, I have your name and your address from the highest echelon of the organization called ALARM, of which you may yourself be a member or a contract employee. It is believed that you may be helpful in my inquiries."

"Ah," Ullmer dropped his arms. His opaque blue eyes showed signs of resigned wariness. Then came the question, "What is it you want to know, Mister . . . uh . . . Neimoff?" It was tentatively put, like an afterthought.

"A number of questions, all interrelated, that require clarifications. It will not take long but it may require some elaboration." Tom pointed to the lobby, "This is probably not the place in which to hold such a discussion. I wonder, could we meet in the privacy of your home, tonight perhaps, or tomorrow morning?" Tom affected a smile. "My time is limited. I want to be able to catch a plane out of Germany before the strike starts."

Ullmer was in full agreement. "Yes. Not here, this is not a good place, and of course I have work to do." His eyes narrowed. "Tomorrow," he nodded, "yes, that would be possible. But not at my home, I have only a small apartment, and on my day off I like to be out in the fresh air."

His voice, almost a falsetto, grated on Tom's ears. "Of course," he said. "Tomorrow is fine. Breakfast?"

"No. That is also indoors!" Ullmer gave Tom a look. Was he daft? "I like to walk. Along the river. We can meet at the Theodor-Heuss-Brucke. You know where that is?"

Tom said, "I would imagine the bridge is on my tourist map. I'll find it. Which side and what time?"

"This side. At noon." Ullmer turned now. "I have to go. Till then." He half offered a limp hand but when Tom seemed unaware of it he walked back towards the laboratory entrance. Tom watched him go. So this was Nettie's murderer, the lecher, the saboteur, this stoop-shouldered, effete Milquetoast slouching along on riffle-soled black running shoes? Tom felt an almost physical revulsion about having to meet with him again, perhaps even to touch him.

He left the building, and started walking. His insides began churning, he felt nauseous as after a bad meal, which he overcame when he forced himself to think of the Creep not as a person but as an object of rational inquiry. Still, he knew it would not be easy to come back here tomorrow.

He decided he'd go towards the Theodor-Heuss bridge to stake out a place where he'd be tomorrow in advance of the noon date. The bridge was not hard to find, it was the next one up the river. There were boat docks for little excursion steamers and for pleasure boats on both shorelines, and a sign advertising Bootsverleih, row boats and pedal crafts for rent. He stood on the bridge, breathing deeply of the warm, moldy smell that rose from the surface of the water. There were many people walking across the bridge, or riding their bicycles, some to get from one side to the other, some to stand and gawk at the medieval town of Heidelberg, the ruins of the castle above it, and the busy river traffic on the Neckar below. It would be easy to get lost in the crowd, Tom thought, especially on a Saturday at noontime. He caught sight of a sign on the north side of the river that read, Philosophenweg, Philosopher's Walk, that pointed in the direction of the wooded hillside above. Yes, here would be the perfect place to take the Creep, tomorrow.

Tom caught the streetcar going back to Schwetzingen. This time the car was crowded, he had to stand in the middle section and hold on to a strap. About halfway along, at the suburb of Eppelheim, he noticed a commotion on the town square, people crowding around the back of a truck off which something was being sold. What did the crude handlettered flap over the backboard say.

"Streikbrecher Fahrrad! Hier!" Strikebreaker Bicycle? Of course!

Acting instantly, Tom barely made it off the already moving streetcar, running along until his jump had expended itself, and continuing his trot towards the truck. They were selling bicycles all right, a team of swarthy men one of whom, in the back of the truck, would hold up a bike on a muscular arm, another would ask in strangely accented German, how much was bid for it. Two hundred? Three hundred? A buyer would shout "two hundred"; the bike would be handed down to another man below who finished the transaction, and the buyer would move off quickly.

Tom asked a bystander what was going on. "Gypsies," he was told by the buxom woman, "from France; the bikes were probably stolen. The police should soon come and put an end to it."

She was probably right; Tom also knew immediately that a bicycle was exactly what he could use tomorrow for greater flexibility of moving about. He pushed through the crowd and made his bid on the next bike being held up, a man's model, with lights and a luggage rack. This one would not go cheap.

"Five hundred," he said to the man, and waved five bills.

Wild gesticulation between the three men, the bike was lowered to him, his money grabbed out of his hand, and Tom pushed off with it immediately. He made it to a small park near the main street and checked out his purchase. It was a good model, sturdy, French made, and seemed in good order. It even had a small tool kit attached to the back of the saddle, and an air pump clamped onto one part of the frame, a plastic water bottle onto another. Perfect.

Predictably, the tires needed air. He started pumping. He'd soon find out if the tubes were holding the air or not. In the meantime, he'd ride it. Taking off his jacket and tie and clamping them on the rack, he started pedaling away. All was well, the air in the tires held. The seat could be higher for his size, but to his great, almost boyish elation, his bicycle proved reliable all the way to Schwetzingen. During the ride, Tom had figured out what he would do with it. First, he would ride it to the car park, take the wheels off and try to fit the bike into the Audi's trunk, or if not there, then onto the back seat. Second, he would check out of the hotel in the morning, and leaving the car in Schwetzingen, would ride the bike to Heidelberg. Ideal for his purposes of quick and commonplace mobility. After he had dealt with the Creep, he'd make it back here, put the bike back into the trunk and hightail it to the airport outside Munich. There, on Sunday, he'd meet Cab. Cab would take the car, he would board the plane and be back in London on Sunday night. Perfect! He might even ship the bike, if they'd let him.

It was a tight fit, the handle bars had to be turned sideways, but the bike fit in the car trunk, with space to spare. Tom put tie and jacket back on and whistling, walked towards his hotel.

His euphoria was such that he decided to call London and speak to Bertie and of course to Betts and Pat. He looked at his watch; it was shortly after 6:00 P.M., too early for London time. He stopped at a pub and had a beer and a sandwich. The local paper was full of dire predictions as to what the strike would do to everybody. Tom was glad he'd be out of here before it would hit. One of those situations, he told himself, that you'd look back on as a lucky miss.

The restaurant had a phone booth. Tom first dialed Cab's number at the hotel. Cab was in his room; he said to hell with going down to Park Lane. "It's raining cats and dogs here, Bubba. Quickly. What's new?"

"Met El Creepo. Will meet again tomorrow. Then I'll be outa here."

"Looks good?"

"Yup. See you Sunday?"

"Okay. My ETA will be 7:40 P.M. Forgot to tell you that."

"Got it, Kiddo. Take care." He hung up. Tom and Cab had agreed that any conversation they would have over the telephone from "unsecure locations" would have to be for a minute or less. Cab had read somewhere that that was the time span during which tracings could not be made. Tom had laughed and said Cab had read too many books by Tom Clancy. Cab had replied, half seriously, that if it was from a Tom Clancy book he would be sure about it.

Throwing the one-minute theory to the wind, Tom got himself a handful of change and dialed Bettina's number. It rang just twice, and the "Hello" was Pat's. Tom guessed that they were in the kitchen, fixing high tea. "Hello, Pat?" he said. "It's Tom. How are you?"

"Tom?" He heard her shout to someone, "It's Tom! It's Tom! It's your Daddy!" When all the commotion had subsided, and Bettina had come in from feeding the dogs in the pantry, and Pat had asked if he was still in Northumberland (the postcard, Tom told himself, you've sent a postcard from Newcastle, don't forget!), and he told her no; he was on his way back to London, Bettina finally had her say.

"It's really quite extraordinary, Tom, that you should keep us in such a muddle about you! I don't wish to go into it here but when you are back, we must have a word!"

"Absolutely, Betts. We shall. Now, how is Bertie? May I speak with him, please?"

The request was granted, and Tom had one of those conversations with his son where nothing substantial was said but much communing was achieved. He told Bertie that in a couple of days, Monday morning probably, he'd be back, and that he looked forward to that very much, and that he loved him.

It was with a sharp pang—of longing? of guilt?—that he hung up the phone. It would be a long night if he didn't pull himself together. In the lobby of his hotel he bought the only English-language paperback on the rack, Rosamunde Pilcher's September. Surprisingly, he found himself hooked by it, fully engrossed in the long-winded tale until well past midnight, when his eyes gave out.

He had breakfast in his room, and after his shower attached the latest of Cab's electronic miracles to his body—a miniature tape recorder with small sensitive microphones taped to strategic places. Cab had argued, and Tom concurred, that they would have to have evidence that the Creep had done the deed. If it could not be obtained, or in the unlikely event that the Creep was not the Creep, Tom was not to proceed further.

That done, Tom dressed lightly in his newly acquired togs and stuffed everything else in his bag. He checked out paying cash and walked back to his car. He drove out of the lot and on his way towards Heidelberg looked for a more secure parking facility. He found one next to a cemetery, where all-day parking was ten mark for which he was given a ticket to put on the dashboard. He put the car in the shade of a willow tree, where he reassembled his bicycle and put the insulin kit into the carrier bag. He used the plastic envelope that had hung from the rearview mirror, removed the driving and safety instructions in order to insert his money and his passport, then fastened the thin pack to a cord which he tied around his undershorts. Wearing the baseball cap and sunglasses and clamping the windbreaker onto the carrier, he took off in the direction of Heidelberg. It was shortly after ten in the morning.

On his way into town he stopped at a bicycle shop to make a few more purchases. He bought some high-caloric drink to fill into the bike's plastic bottle, a chain lock, a tire repair kit and a rain poncho. Just being prudent. He'd rather not have a minor occurrence become a major problem, and besides, it did look a bit cloudy towards the south.

He reached the Theodor-Heuss bridge in plenty of time to lock his bike in a city-owned Fahrradstand. With the poncho in the carrier bag and the insulin kit now in his pocket, he began hanging around the pedestrian walkway to the bridge. He didn't quite know, after they had had their talk, when and where he would administer the insulin. But he knew how: with a quick jab deep into the Creep's gluteus maximus. It was not an overdose, nor would it do much harm; but as far as the Creep was concerned, he would be told that he had been injected with hepatitis-B serum which would kill him in the long run. The idea was for the Creep to frighten himself to death. This final scenario was the best Tom and Cab had been able conjure up, short of wringing the Creep's neck or shooting the bastard. It had the added advantage of being uniquely unbloody and swift. Trite and anticlimactic though it was, it was the best they had been able to come up with. Besides, it was the taped confession that would clinch the deal.

As Tom stood musing, staring into the distance, he felt a tap on his shoulder. "You are very punctual, Herr Major!" The Creep. The tone of his voice was not wary and subdued like yesterday's. Now, it was fresh and cocky.

Tom turned around. "Yes. Hello Doctor Ullmer. I see you are rushing the summer!" Tom cast a bemused glance over the way the Creep was turned out. Shorts that fitted tightly from his fat thighs to his ample girth, colorful stockings that came up to his round knees, a blouse—not a shirt, but a blouse—with short puffed sleeves and unbuttoned just to the beginning of a cleavage and no hat but a kerchief knotted around his curly head. The guy, if such he was, looked like a joke and Tom was half embarrassed to be seen with him. On the other hand, the thin cloth straining against the Creep's buns would not pose a problem for the syringe's needle; Tom had worried about that. "It's a nice day, why don't we go for a walk?" he said, pointing to the wooded hillside.

"Oh no!" Ullmer gave a merry cackle. "Look down there," he led him to the bridge railing and nodded towards the Bootsverleih. "It's a nice day for a boat ride! You can row, can't you, Herr Major?"

There were quite a few boats spread out along the sides of the river, and the traffic in the middle was full with pleasure craft, too. Yes, a row boat would do. "Fine with me, doctor. Let's go." Inside his pants pocket, he flipped the microphone switch to "on." With a running time of one hundred and eighty minutes, the micro-device should serve its purpose, Tom hoped.

The rental was for a minimum of one hour and required a cash deposit of triple the hourly rate. A gnarled spidery man took a pair of oars from a rack behind him and walked out to the floating dock ahead of Tom and Ullmer.

"Here," he rasped and handed Tom the oars. "You get in, I'll hold the boat for the young lady." When they were both seated, he unknotted the line and gave the boat a push. Then he turned and stalked back to his boathouse.

Tom locked the oars in and began rowing. "Young lady, huh?" He gave a false smile. "Are you a young lady, Doctor Ullmer?"

In a snippy tone, Ullmer replied, "I don't see where that is any of your business, Major, but just to satisfy your curiosity, yes, I am undergoing treatment to correct a birth defect. And that is all I will say about it."

"Hey, no offense. It's your body, and your business, as you say." Tom pulled the boat out onto more open water where the fringes of the river current began to tuck against the hull. He needed only to row gently against it to stay pretty much in place.

Ullmer was sitting against the stern, holding fast to the seat board. He didn't look at Tom but rather past him, turning his head this way or that, as if he were wondering where they were going.

Tom decided it was time to get to the nitty-gritty. Adopting a matter-of-fact attitude, he said, "Doctor Ullmer, I am here to ascertain the sequence of events that took place on Friday, the 25th of June of last year, on the premises of Goleta Research Laboratories in Santa Barbara, California. A certain Doctor Olaf Runge, a German national, injected, accidentally or intentionally, a fellow researcher with a highly virulent substance. The temporary work contract of Runge expired at the end of that week and Runge departed, leaving the United States via Western Canada to return to Europe. The research worker, a veterinary doctor by the name of Natalie Campe, succumbed to the virus infection a week later. The incident has been investigated and found to have international ramifications in that the prestigious animal rights organization ALARM was the putative employer of said Doctor Runge." Tom paused. "What has been further ascertained," he said, looking straight at Ullmer, "is that the identity of said Doctor Runge was phony, made up for use by people such as you. Would you care to comment, Doctor Ullmer?"

Ullmer, with a smirk, said, "No, I would not. This is preposterous."

Tom nodded. "Under recognized national and international legal standards, the case is also criminal. Count one, gaining access to work in the United States under misrepresentations. Count two, gaining employment with an American research organization for the purpose of industrial espionage and sabotage. Count three, to cause the death of a fellow worker by injection of a lethal substance, a charge of murder that, if found to be willful and premeditated, could result in the death penalty under California law." Tom recited the legalese hoping that it at least sounded convincing; back in London he and Cab had worked hard on it, Tom never entirely comfortable with the results of the exercise.

Ullmer's smirk had not left his fleshy lips. "This is Germany, not California. And I am Ullmer, not Runge. You have no authority over me, Herr American Major!"

There was anger and disgust rising steadily in Tom, and it took all his self-control not to lunge at the weirdo across from him. He feared that if he did, he would not stop until he had killed him. And killing the Creep outright was the one step that Tom and Cab had sworn they would not take; it would have meant putting themselves down on the same miserable level of cant and cunning that was the dwelling place of the Creep and his handlers.

Worse yet, Tom began to realize that he had not yet wrangled out of the Creep any admission of complicity, let alone guilt; and he needed that.

He decided to change his tactic. "You are quite right, Doctor Ullmer. We are in Germany, not the U.S., and I am not a process server." This was another impressive word he just picked out of the blue; he hoped the Creep would be as vague about its meaning as he himself. "That is why we are here, talking to each other, instead of you being taken into custody and extradited to the United States. In other words, you have a one-time opportunity to set the record straight. Did you, for whatever reason, inject Doctor Natalie Campe with the Ebola virus back in June of last year?"

"Why should I tell you that?"

"Because at this point, Doctor Ullmer, this is not yet an official criminal case. In view of the gravity of all viral dissemination, it is in the best interests of the world scientific community as well as the animal rights organizations to keep your case from becoming public knowledge. Do you understand what I am telling you?"

"Yes."

"Therefore, to close the case we need to know, at your own volition, whether you gave that lethal injection to Doctor Campe. Did you?"

Ullmer stared at his shoes, then looked around as if someone was there to overhear him. There were boats in the vicinity, with people in them shouting and laughing, splashing each other with the oars, or rowing for the exercise of it, one in particular that Tom had seen coming in their general direction with a steady pull.

Ullmer finally spoke, with some urgency, "I had to do it. Had to! The bitch was getting on to me, she would have, what is the word, entlarvt?"

"Exposed?"

"Yes, exposed me! Not just me but the whole organization! I could not let that happen! The organization knows that; they are protecting me!" He worked up a triumphant expression, nodding with each emphasis.

Tom felt a chill run down his spine. So it was true. He was sitting across from Nettie's murderer! There was no doubt anymore! Now what was he to do? How could he go on pretending . . . ?

He pulled the oars in and rested his arms on them. Should he get up and jab the bastard, or should he wait until they had reached the dock when Ullmer was climbing out of the boat? Yeah, the latter, he'd be an easier target.

"Halli-hallo! What do we have here, then? Old friends?" The rower with the steady pull had reached their boat. It took Tom a moment before he recognized him. It was Fred, the Duke of Cumberland's chauffeur and gofer!

Tom realized immediately that with Fred's sudden appearance the balance had been altered, perhaps decisively so, in favor of the Creep. When he saw Ullmer's relieved grin, he realized further that this was not a chance meeting, that in fact he, Tom, had been had. Why else would a totally unathletic Ullmer have suggested an outing by boat, or put another way, Fred must have been the one who suggested it, which meant that there had been prior contact between the two; which made sense, considering it was the Duke who had fingered Ullmer to Tom.

A set-up, a classic, get-the-sucker set-up.

"Herr Major, oh pardon, I must speak English with you." Fred bleated merrily as if this was indeed a meeting of old friends. "You have a good conversation with our Doktorchen here, yah? Was he a good boy, or should I say girl, ha-ha-ha!" He reached over the two boats that were bobbing side by side to pat Ullmer on the back. "Was the Major good to you, Ulli, yah?"

Ullmer gave a false grin and replied, "Yah-yah, but I did not say much." In German he added quickly, "Of course I didn't tell him anything, Fred."

"Naturlich nicht!" Fred nodded; he seemed to find this very amusing. To Tom he said, "I will relieve you of the company of this Doktor Ullmer now, Herr Major. Those are my instructions. And you will promise to let the matter rest. Case closed. Yah? Agreed?"

The way Fred looked at him, steel-blue eyes totally without emotion, Tom knew that right here, right now, he had no choice. "Yes," he said. "Agreed."

"Did you hear that, Ulli? The Major agrees. Sache erledigt." With a very toothy grin, Fred said in German, "Come over here, Ullichen, into my boat." He leaned half over to assist Ullmer, who got up shakily and quickly steadied himself by holding on to Tom's boat, then to Fred's, his head turning this way and that, anxiously checking for open water between the two boats that kept bumping against each other. A wind had come up, and dark clouds were hanging low over the top of the hills. Tom held the side of his boat firmly to Fred's. Rummaging for something on the bottom of his boat, Fred seemed unaware that it was drifting apart by a foot, maybe two, with Ullmer now bridging the gap with his plump body. "Fred!" he bleated, "Fred, don't let me fall!"

Fred looked up, grinning. "Not to worry, little one, we will hold you fast. Here!" In one quick motion he slipped a rope over Ullmer's outstretched head. Uncomprehending, Tom saw that the rope had a hangman's knot that rested like a pony tail on Ullmer's neck.

"Fred!" Ullmer's voice was quavering. "Fred . . . help me . . ."

"Yah. Right now." Fred slid sideways on his bench, making the boat list lower. Ullmer lost his tenuous grip and plunged into the water with a plop. At that moment Fred pulled the rope tight around Ullmer's neck, then he bent down and with both hands lifted up a black gym bag from the planks. Tom saw that the bag had a rope around its handles, and that it must be heavy, for Fred grunted as he heaved it overboard. The bag hit the water with a splash, and as it sank and the rope played out, Ullmer's head was yanked into the water, his body following like a seal diving for fish. Bubbles came to the surface, then nothing. Ullmer had disappeared in the murky darkness of the Neckar River.

Tom sat stunned. It had all taken only a few seconds. He stared at Fred.

"You drowned Ullmer, Fred!" he shouted. "You drowned him!" Tom gripped his oars, letting go of the other boat. "Why did you do that?"

Fred nodded, with an oafish grin that was almost self-congratulatory.

"Yah, I told you. Case closed." He grabbed the side of Tom's boat before it drifted away. "That is what you want, Herr Major, isn't it?"

Tom, who was now keenly aware that he was wired, spoke with some vehemence, "We wanted justice! What you just did, Fred, was an execution!"

Fred's grin turned nasty. "That is good for you, it is good for us, and this little Hanswurst," he pointed in the direction of the water, "got what he deserved. He stepped out of line. He paid for it. Sache erledigt."

Tom decided there was no point in arguing. He dipped his oars, anxious to get away, but Fred held on to the bow of the boat. "You and I are not finished yet. You have to sign a statement, Herr Major. Where are you parked?"

Thinking fast, Tom said, "In Heidelberg, at the parkhaus for Herte's." Herte was a large department store.

"Herte's. Good. What level?"

"Ground."

"What kind of car, Herr Major?"

"A VW Passat."

"Color?"

"Dark-green."

"License number?"

"I have no idea, it's a rental. Look, Fred, this has gone far enough."

Fred cut him off. "You sign. Those are my orders." He added, unnecessarily, "And I always follow orders."

"All right." It was beginning to rain, big drops were splashing down from thick dark clouds, heralding a thundershower. "I have to bring the boat back first. We both do that, and you can give me a ride across the bridge."

Fred seemed pacified by that answer. "My boat comes from the other side. You will have to take the streetcar across." He looked at his watch. "I meet you at your car in forty-five minutes. That should be time enough." He let go of the boat.

"Let's make it an hour, to be on the safe side," Tom said, and began rowing. Before he pulled away, he shouted, "Does the Duke know about this?"

"His Highness never knows about anything!" Fred shouted back, grinning.

It was raining hard by the time Tom reached the dock. He tied the boat to it, grabbed the oars and ran in the direction of the Bootsverleih office. There were several people ahead of him trying to get their deposits back from the old geezer, and when it was Tom's turn he was refunded an hour's worth.

Immediately Tom raced out into the rain, discarding the insulin kit in a trash can that he was passing. He also switched off the mike. He hoped it had done its job. And what a job it had been!

His bike was still at the stand where he had left it. He quickly pulled the poncho out of the side bag, putting it over himself including the hood over his head. He unlocked the bike, mounted it and pedaled away in the direction of the other bridge farther away. Looking at his watch, he had less than a half hour to get out of Heidelberg.

The image of Ullmer being dragged to his watery grave did not leave Tom's mind. An anger was building up in him that focused not entirely on Fred, the Duke's henchman, but on the wretched Duke himself and his organization. How dare they execute the Creep in front of his eyes, when it was Tom, and Tom alone, who had the moral right to render judgment! And what power over life and death did they dare assume, from the reckless sabotage of the laboratory in Santa Barbara to the agony of Nettie and the drowning of Ullmer! Tom was half tempted to stop off at the Herte parking garage and have it out with Fred when he realized that that was the worst mistake he could make. It would only compound the problem and in the end lead to his own demise, for even if Fred did not cause him bodily harm, the organization would surely hound him down and destroy him. No, he had to be smarter than that, smarter than them, by removing the mythical Major Nemo from the scene and extinguishing all his footprints. A truce would prevail. Tom was under no illusion that his true persona was, or soon would be, known to the security elements of the ALARM people. The pretensions were mutual, as were the benefits. A Mephistophelean deal if ever there was one, of which his son Bertram was the only innocent beneficiary, as Nettie had wished it to be with her dying breath.

It was with sad realization that Tom directed his bike's path away from the town center of Heidelberg, away from where Fred, his last link to the Nemo chapter, would be lurking in the parking structure near someone's dark-green VW; good luck and good riddance. Tom increased his speed, splashing through puddles and on to the suburb where he had left his car.

He found it to be the only car still on the lot by the cemetery. The rain had become a steady downpour, and the young green leaves of the willow tree gave little protection from it. Tom dismounted and began taking the wheels off the bicycle. Crouching down to do so, he noticed a small animal underneath the car, its little black snout poking this way and that.

A rat, Tom thought, and clapped his hands to shoo it away. The animal dropped on its haunches and gave a whispery whimper. Tom bent down more and looked. This was no rat, not with a furry tail that was wagging a bit now, and not with those floppy ears. A cat? He went down flat on the soggy gravel and reached with his arm under the car, snapping his fingers. "Here, kitty-kitty!" he said. More whimper, but no meow. No cat, either. And no raccoon, they don't have them here. With a determined lunge he grabbed the animal by the scruff of its neck and pulled it out. A dog! A wee little one, probably a pup. Son of a gun! A dog.

Tom sat up and cradled the dog in his arm. Its light-brown curly fur was sopping wet, and its brown eyes looked scared. Spasmodic shivers ran over its entire body. "Easy now, little guy," Tom tried to soothe it, stroking its pelt. "Who let you out in this rain? Or did you run away?" Tom looked around. There was no other person anywhere near.

Tom unlocked the car door and sat on the front seat, still holding the dog. He took the hand towel he had swiped from the hotel and gently rubbed the worst of the wetness out of the fur. What a little guy, weighing only a couple of pounds, its skin on the belly pink, and the penis tiny.

"What we have here," he told the dog, "is a male puppy, of as yet undetermined breed and age, who has lost his mama. Are you hungry, guy, huh?" He put his thumb against the pup's snout, and sure enough, it began to lick and suck. "Well," Tom said, "we can do something about that, but not right away. Let me stash the bike away first, okay? And you stay here, warm and dry." He wrapped the towel around the dog and nestled it down on the other seat.

When he had put the bike away he checked the immediate area around where his car was parked. There were no houses within a block of the parking lot. The cemetery gates were closed and locked, and the guard hut where he had paid the parking fee was shuttered. The rain was steady, there were no people in the vicinity, certainly no one who was looking for a lost pet.

He returned to the car. "Well," he said as he slammed the door shut. He touched the dog on its head. "Here we are, just the two of us. Common cause. Joining forces. I look after you, and when you are bigger and smarter, you return the favor. Deal?"

Em

As he would look back on it later, the appearance of that little puppy, just at the time when his search for the Creep had come to such an unexpected end, would acquire an almost mythical significance for Tom. Where had it's home been, why was it underneath his car—had it run away, or worse, had it been abandoned? And what if he had not bought that bike and therefore had no need to stop and stoop and notice, but rather had jumped into the car to get out of the rain and driven off—was it not entirely possible that the wheels could have crushed the little creature? Without Tom ever knowing?

It caused him to shudder.

At the moment of driving away from the parking lot, those thoughts were far in the back of Tom's mind. Of more immediate concern was the feeding of the pup, heaven knows when it had last suckled—or had it been weaned yet? Tom looked around as he slowly drove through the narrow streets, but all the stores were shuttered tight. He cursed the confounded German closing laws, it would be this way now until Monday morning.

Then he remembered that the Autobahn service stations were always open, and that most of them had fast-food eateries and some even motels and restaurants on their premises. That was the way to go.

He made his way back onto the same superhighway that he had come up on, and stopped at the first filling station. Traffic was at a crawl, and the car would need the gas tank topped off under the circumstances. He went into the snack shop and made a sack full of purchases—milk, beer, sandwiches, hot dogs, bananas and apples. Back in the car, he noticed that the pup was curled up sleeping, still wrapped in the towel on the seat. It would be best to leave him undisturbed and pull in at a motel soon. It had been a full day!

It was early evening when he checked into a motel on the outskirts of Stuttgart, about one-third of the way to Munich. That would do, the next day, even at a snail's pace, he would reach Munich, or rather Freising, the new airport northeast of it, in plenty of time for Cab's arrival.

He praised his luck for getting the room, not only because as a corner room it was more private, but also because it seemed it was the last vacancy. Beyond the motel grounds was a small forest where he could set the little dog down for a pee or a poo—it was never too early to house-train a pup.

When he had brought in all his gear from the car he first tended to the dog. He guessed it was about eight to twelve weeks old, the way it was wobbling about on paws much too big as yet for its little body. Tom poured some milk into an ashtray but the pup did not try to raise its snout over the rim. Rummaging in the first aid kit he had bought at the drugstore in Baden-Baden, Tom found what he was looking for: a small plastic ear syringe. Filling it up some with milk, he put the nozzle end into the side of the dog's mouth and began pumping. "All right, guy!" Tom cheered when he saw the slurping and sucking that ensued. "You got it!" He actually had to refill the bulb before the pup turned its head away.

"Okay, that was just for starters. Dinner comes later. Meat! Hot dog!"

He stopped and looked at the puppy in sudden recognition. "Speaking of hot dogs, you wouldn't be a dachshund, by any chance, would you?" The long tapered face, the flopped-down ears, the straight sturdy tail—but what of the coat, so coarse and curly now that it had dried, and what of those tufts of blond hair on top of its head? Not to mention the beginnings of a beard, and those bushy eyebrows! "You are quite a guy, you know that, young feller?"

Tom saw an ornamental flower basket on the dresser and took it down, emptying it of the imitation greenery. He made a bed of it for the dog, with the shoeshine cloth and the face towel as blankets. Then he gently lifted the dog with his hand under its belly and placed it into the basket. The puppy sniffed and turned around a couple of times, then curled up with a sigh. When Tom looked down on the floor where it had been, he saw a small puddle. He took some tissue paper and wiped it up. "We'll work on this tomorrow, guy. Hey, how about calling you Guy, huh? Any objection?" There being none, Tom nodded. "Okay. Guy, it is." The so-named Guy was already asleep.

For himself, Tom was busy for a while. He stripped, and peeled the tape recorder, microphone and lines off his body. He took out the contact lenses and bathed his eyes. Aaah, relief. While he was having a hot shower, he went over the events of the past twelve hours, considering carefully what he should and reasonably could do to erase any traces of his presence at the Neckar drowning.

It was possible that he and that henchman had been observed, but after weighing all the aspects of that question he considered it unlikely. There was a storm coming up, the people in the boats were busy heading for shore and shelter, and inasmuch as the actual disappearance of Ullmer was a matter of just a few seconds, it was reasonable to assume that the event, or the significance of the two-boat encounter, indeed went unobserved.

More worrisome was the fact that he, Tom, had been at Ullmer's workplace the day before, Ullmer would likely be missed, but not much earlier than the end of next week, allowing for the probable confusion of a strike in which even some institute employees might be involved. Eventually, someone would check, and Ullmer would be noted as missing from his rooms. Unless, of course, and this was more likely to be the case, the Duke's people had taken care of that with some phony story. After all, it was not in their interest to have Ullmer become notorious for his absence.

But Ullmer, or traces of him, might turn up eventually: His body might not be found for a while longer, but gradual decomposition would sever it from the head. Would it then float downstream? There were canals and a series of locks and gates downriver towards the Rhine that in the aggregate could well dispose of Ullmer's remains forever. An added factor was that business of his known weirdness, his sex-change operations. There would be speculation of his desire for starting a new life, of not wanting to return to the former self. Shoulders would be shrugged, and Ullmer soon forgotten.

No, Ullmer posed no urgent threat, and Tom figured that he himself would not enter into the equation inasmuch as the Major Neimow character would disappear also. Without a trace, in fact. The clothes he had been wearing to the outing with Ullmer—the T-shirt, the cap and the windbreaker—he would dispose of right here and now, in a couple of the autobahn trash cans. Of the microphone system, he would save only the tape, the rest he would smash and cut into small pieces and flush down the toilet. The tape casette he would wrap in plastic and hide somewhere, maybe in his shaving kit. In any case, he would be careful to preserve its existence, as it recorded the whole sequence of events on the river. All the while hoping, of course, that there would never arise a need to produce it as evidence.

Again, Tom did not think that he was at risk. The whole sad and sorry episode was over, this chasing after the villain a chapter of his past that was now closed. It was time for turning to the future, his and Bertie's.

During the night he was awakened by the little dog's persistent and pitiful whimpering. Tom sat up and felt for the puppy. It was not in its basket. The sound came from somewhere under the bed: there it was, cowering against the wall as Tom saw when he trained his flashlight on it. He went flat down on the floor, pulled it out and carried it back to bed, laying himself on his back and putting the pup on his chest, stroking it and murmuring soothing sounds. It worked, for both of them. The dog curled up, cradled by Tom's hands as Tom dropped off into a half-sleep in which he had the most bizarre dream. In it, Nettie was floating about in his semiconsciousness, smiling and nodding and hovering over him, and when he longed to reach out to her she dissolved into a silent ethereal void, leaving him feeling so cleansed, so pure that he wanted to weep with joy.

Tom must have shed real tears, for he awoke from a wetness on his cheeks and on the pillow around his face. He let it be. As his consciousness returned he realized he had received a form of purification of his soul, of absolution. His own life was being given back to him, at last.

The airport in Munchen-Freising, with a reputation as Europe's most modern and most automated, was on this day also one of its most crowded and confusing. Tom chose to cruise around looking for a temporary parking spot, not wanting to go through the turnstiles in the underground garages where he feared becoming stuck if there were no personnel in the toll booths if he wanted to exit. He found a spot near the car rental center and wedged his Audi into it. It would be a while before someone would question its presence there.

He was wearing a business suit again, the one in which he had left the hotel room in Baden-Baden, and the same dress shirt, too. Slung over his shoulder he wore a canvas bag with a round Mercedes Auto crest embroidered on it, which he had bought at the novelty shop in the motel lobby. Inside the unclosed bag, nicely cushioned, resided the puppy, now much more at ease and sated from sharing bits and pieces of Tom's breakfast and lunch. Earlier that morning, it had been keenly pleased for being taken on a wobbly walk in the woods behind the motel. Life was looking up for Guy, too.

The airport buildings jutted out in a long line of protuberances, terminals A through D according to the location map Tom was studying, each agleam in steel and glass and aluminum. He was in Terminal A, he found out, Domestic Arrivals and Departures. What he wanted—International/Europe—was in Terminal D, at exactly the other end. Tom sighed, it never failed. He briefly considered and rejected returning to the car to drive there. It would not save much time, and who knows if he would find another parking spot. Besides, walking Cab back to the car would give them a chance to talk, to fill each other in with what they needed to know.

Tom entered the terminal, and almost instantly regretted his decision.

There were crowds of people wafting like ants at a picnic from one end of the terminal to the other and to the next and back again. Line-ups were snaking in tight coils at every airline counter. Announcements were blaring in German, French, English, Italian, indistinguishable one from the other. The arrival and departure signs were changing their digital output constantly, none of them saying "on time." He had to push his way through the crowds, the puppy bag clutched close to his chest, to get on the moving sidewalk to the next terminal. As he glided past a bunch of people clustered around a man who seemed to be a shuttlebus driver for nearby hotels, he thought he saw a familiar face, a woman's, a brimless fur cap askew on her head. He craned his neck to get a better view but too late, the people cluster was moving out the door.

Terminals B and C proved less crowded. Tom could walk briskly, making better time on the checkerboard square floor than on the moving sidewalks.

Terminal D was Terminal A all over again, except that here, in European Arrivals and Departures, the mood of the crowd was more outraged, more voluble and multilingual. Families with children, businessmen with briefcases, youths with backpacks were milling around in the lounge areas, talking and eating, sleeping and smoking. It was a mess.

Tom searched in vain for Cab's British Air flight, it was now well past 8:00 P.M. and it should have arrived. One harried British Air person he could corral seemed as confused as he was. He had no idea when the flight would land, if in fact it had taken off in London, and even less of an idea if it would make it for the return leg that Tom was supposed to be on. The strike, you know, everything would shut down at midnight. Sorry.

On the small chance that Cab might still be at the Hilton in London, Tom picked up a phone, but the moment he had put money in, the dial tone changed to "busy" and that was that, no matter how many times he tried.

It became increasingly obvious that Cab's plane had not taken off at all in London. Tom managed to leave word with a British Air representative—a very blond German woman—that if a Mr. Charles Blumenfeld should inquire he should be advised to hang around the vicinity of the British Air booth as he, "Doctor Thomas," would make periodic forays into the terminal hall, looking for him. The woman gave him a pitying smile about his naiveté and stuck his message into a folder. Tom left, now thoroughly pissed, as he growled to himself, about "those striking assholes." It was dark outside when he came back to where he had left his car. Nothing more could be done for the moment. He would come back early in the morning to see what the situation was then.

He drove into Freising and straight to the one hotel he had seen advertised all over the airport as a "Preferred Airline Hotel," presumably the small town did not have many other choices, and besides, it was getting too late to drive into Munich. He saw a parking lot adjacent to the hotel and drove onto it, pulling a ticket from the gate machine. There were several empty spots and he took one near a tree-lined hedge.

Entering the lobby of the hotel was almost like being back at the airport terminal. It was thick with people, and there was a sort of queue snaking towards the registration desk. He had no desire to waste his time with that and was about to turn back when he saw the woman with the fur cap again, and this time he knew who she was.

"Miss Dessauer!" he called out. "Miss Dessauer! Here, over here!" He waved his arm.

The woman was standing near the lift area. It took her a moment to react and then she looked with an uncertain frown to where the sound had come from. Tom waved his arm more vigorously, while he was pushing his way through to her. "Hello!" he said. "Miss Dessauer, I presume," and smiled.

Recognition: "Oh my God! Doctor Watson . . . uh, I mean . . . "

"Campe. Tom Campe. How do you do?" His smile was broadening.

"Yes, of course—Doctor Campe. Oh my God." She shook her head.

"Call me Tom, please. What brings you here?"

"Hi, Tom." She shook his hand, smiling now, too. "And Emily, please. I got a room, at long last." She nodded towards the lift doors. "That is, if and when the elevator arrives. Are you registered here, too?"

"No, I'm not even going to try, the way it looks."

"You'd probably have to share one. I do, with an elderly Swiss lady."

Tom shrugged his shoulders. "Never mind." He said, "What brings you to Munich, Emily?"

"They told me in Berlin that I would be able to catch a plane to London from here."

"To London? I'm waiting for that flight, too! Couldn't you fly direct from Berlin?"

"No, they were all sold out because of the strike. Berlin-Munich-London was all I could get."

"Been in Berlin long?"

"Actually—I flew in from St. Petersburg." She sighed. "Don't ask why. It's a long story."

"Yeah. Mine, too." Tom looked at her. She was a bit disheveled, tired around the eyes. "I have a car," he said quickly, "and you are welcome to go back to the airport with me tomorrow morning."

"Oh—that would be great!"

"Early, though. Six A.M.? Here in the lobby?"

"Fine! Thanks, Tom!" She pointed to the bag over his shoulder. "What's in there? It seems to be moving!"

"It's Guy, my puppy dog." Tom opened the top of the bag and let Emily take a peek. He smiled. "My faithful companion."

"How cute! Look at him!" She touched the dog's head. "Hi sweetie!"

There was the ping of the elevator cars arriving, all three of them at the same time.

"I better not miss this one," Emily said. "See you in the morning."

"For sure!" Tom called after her. "Six A.M.!"

From the back of the packed elevator car Tom saw an arm rising, waving a fur cap.

As he made his way back to the parking lot Tom became aware that he was seized by a strange sense of elation. Strange, because his circumstances did not exactly call for buoyancy of the spirit, but "Oh my God!" in the words of Emily, what luck! To run into her here, of all places, and more luck, to see her again in the morning, and to drive her to the airport and perhaps flying to London with her! Unbelievable.

He made a bed for himself in the car by putting the sleeping bag to use, stretching out over the back seat and a lowered front seat, the dog on the floor below him. Sleep, however, would not come for some time. Jumbled thoughts were flitting through his head, none very sensible and nearly all connected to the presence of "Em," as he dubbed her, in that building just behind him, and that he would see her again in the morning.

Emily was already there when Tom, intending to use the hotel washroom, came through the door at half past five. She was sitting on one of the few empty chairs in the lobby, the others being occupied by weary travelers who had spent the night unable to get a room.

"Hi!" Tom said, surprised, "Emily."

"Good morning!" She waved a hand. "I woke up early."

"Great! Good morning to you, too. Look, I thought I'd use the bathroom here, quick shave and stuff," he pointed to the kit under his arm.

"Take your time," she said. "Where's your little companion?"

"Guarding the car," Tom winked. When he returned to her a few minutes later, she was sipping from a plastic cup. "Coffee!" she said. I got you one, too. Cream and sugar, whether that's how you take it or not. I figure we'll need the energy."

Tom gulped it down. He asked to fetch her luggage to take to the car.

"I have none. This is it!" She held up her handbag.

"You checked your baggage through to London?"

She shook her head. "It's probably still on Aeroflot. If I'm lucky." She grimaced and rolled her eyes at the mention of Aeroflot.

Tom laughed. "Okay, then, let's go!"

A man came running after them as they reached the car. "Sir!" he called out breathlessly. "Wait. You take me to the airport, and I will take over your car. Pay all the rental fees!" He was a thin dark-haired man speaking heavy-accented German. Tom was instantly wary. He had seen him lurking around the hotel entrance, almost mistaking him for the doorman.

"I'm sorry," Tom took a defensive posture in front of Emily who was standing still, an expression of fear on her face. "This is not a rental car. It's my private property."

"I buy from you, you tell me how much." The man pulled out a wad of dollar bills and made them riffle.

"Sorry, no sale." Tom unlocked the door and made Emily get in.

"You name the price—I pay! American dollars!" The man stood his ground, Tom could not back out the car if he did not move.

"Look," Tom held up both hands and approached him. "You are talking to the wrong party. This car is not for sale. But someone else may be happy to make a deal with you." He patted the man on the shoulder before he would try to push him out of the way.

The man put his money away, but quick as a flash his hand came up again, holding a switchblade.

Suddenly Tom became so enraged, he deflected the man's wrist with his left arm while hitting him hard on the chin with his right fist. The man stumbled back a few steps. Tom followed through with a barrage of pummeling blows that made the man sink to his knees. For good measure Tom kicked him in the guts, hard, grabbed him by the scruff of his neck and sent him packing, pushing him in the back again and again. Then he turned, entered and locked the car, started it, put it in reverse backing out in a sweeping arc, then shifted to forward and revved up the engine driving past the empty toll booth, making the lowered gate splinter like matchsticks.

"Wow!" Emily gasped.

It had all been a matter of a few minutes.

When they were on the main street, feeding into the sparse traffic, dawn breaking over the city roofs, Emily said in a throaty voice: "My God, are you all right, Tom?"

"I'm fine," he replied, his heart still pounding. "You okay?"

"Yes. The dog and I are okay." She had taken the pup on her lap.

"I'm sorry this had to happen. I don't know what came over me. I am not normally a violent person."

"You were magnificent," Emily whispered. "You have no idea how this all hits home with me, this attacking you and all. I was scared to death."

"It's over. Let's make sure we get the hell out of here."

They had gained access to the main highway leading to the airport. The huge complex came into sight, bathed in light, and as they turned off onto the central airport avenue it became apparent that nothing had changed from the night before. Worse, no aircraft were visible on either of the two runways.

Tom said, "Let me tell you why I am here," and told Emily of his proposed meeting with his friend Charles who would fly in from London, take over the car, and Tom would return to London. "I don't think the flight ever left Heathrow. And with the strike now in full swing, I doubt that any flight will be taking off, either. That affects both you and me, Emily."

"Tom!" There was alarm in her voice. "You are bleeding!"

"What? Where?" And then he saw it: the left sleeve of his jacket was dark-wet, and as he touched it, he knew it was blood. His blood.

"Damn," he said.

"You've got to see a doctor, Tom!"

"I am a doctor, remember?" With a suppressed curse he said, "We gotta stop somewhere; I have a first-aid kit in the trunk. We'll fix this."

They made an illegal left turn and drove back out of the airport area.

Emily groaned.

"Emily, I'm sorry."

"No, no, no. I am sorry, for you."

"Okay, we are both sorry. That doesn't help any, though, does it? Let's find a spot where we can park and take care of this. I'm sure it's just a flesh wound from that bastard's knife. Doesn't even hurt." As an afterthought he asked, "Are you squeamish, Emily? Be honest!"

"No, I am not," came the quick reply. "I'll help, if that's what you mean."

"That's what I mean. I'll need your two hands."

They were on the highway that eventually would feed into the Autobahn to Munich. When an opportunity to turn off onto a rural lane presented itself, Tom took it. There were open fields on either side, and no traffic that early in the morning. A little ways down, a wind hedge of poplar trees and mulberry bushes provided the privacy Tom was looking for. He backed the car off the road and across the grassy shoulder, making the trunk open towards the hedge.

They got out. Tom was dripping blood when he lowered his left arm.

"Let me help you with the jacket," Emily said. As Tom wrestled out of it she got hold of the sleeve ends and pulled, letting it fall to the ground. "You can't wear this anymore, Tom. And look—there are blood drops on your pants, too! And your shirt's a goner. You might as well get rid of it and change clothes." She looked into the trunk. "That's your suitcase?"

Tom said, "Actually, there's just a sleeping bag in it. I wouldn't have needed clothes if Cab had arrived as planned."

"What cab?"

"Oh, Cab is my friend's nickname, from his initials C-A-B." He added, "We have known each other since boarding school," as if that explained everything. "So, we've got to work with what we've got." He wished now he had kept the slacks and the windbreaker he had thrown away the night before. Bending over the open trunk, he pulled out the plastic shopping bag from the Adler Apotheke. The stuff would come in handy now, after all.

First, he took the scissors and asked Emily to cut off his shirtsleeve. It revealed a long cut that ran from below his elbow to his wristwatch. Blood was oozing out of it, but not gushing, Tom noted. He asked Emily to open the alcohol and the iodine bottles and to soak cotton balls with each, then hand them to him one at a time. He had to clench his teeth not to cry out in pain, but he managed to cleanse the wound.

"A clean cut, epidermal. A scalpel couldn't have done better," he said. "One other thing: it runs lengthwise, not across. Bit of luck there."

"Won't you need stitches?" Emily asked. She craned her neck, not the least put off by the bloody mess.

Squeamish she was not, Tom observed with satisfaction. "Yes. Stitches would be nice, but I don't have suturing material here. We'll clean the cut, then press it together with surgical tape."

Again, Emily was of assistance, under Tom's direction doing all that could be done to dress and bandage the wound. Tom held his left arm up to the open trunk lid, to lessen the bleeding. Not yet closing the trunk, he said, "We've got to talk, get our bearings right, Emily."

She nodded, "We have to drive into Munich, buy you some new clothes."

"That's not what I mean. It's you I am concerned about. The way this shapes up, you have two choices. I can drive you back to the airport, to join the people who are stranded here, like you. My guess is that all the major airlines, British Air included, will make an effort to get their passengers out of Munich, probably by bussing them to Vienna, or Prague, and flying them out of there. It may take some time, a day or two lost, but you'll end up in London. Where, by the way, I would ask you to let my sister know about me."

Emily said, "Your sister, Bettina, right? I thought at first she was your wife, what with that little boy of yours peeking down on us through the banister rails. So I told her I had met her husband, and it took a while to get the confusion sorted out. Where were you that evening, Tom?"

"Doing part of the preparations for this trip." He looked into her eyes. "If I had known you were coming . . . "

"You'd have baked a cake. Yeah. So what's my other choice?"

"Not quite that simple, and possibly not nearly as attractive, except for me, if I may put it that way."

"You may. Tell me about that not-so-simple, unattractive choice."

"Well," he gave a brief laugh, "first, under the changed circumstances I feel that I must return to Baden-Baden, where I left Cab's girlfriend who should be told that Cab is not coming."

"You could phone her!"

"It's not that simple. I have an obligation to take her out of Germany and into France, to make sure she gets back on a plane to New York."

"Good," Emily nodded.

"In that sense, that would be your other choice, coming along with me and Freddie."

"Who's Freddie?"

"Cab's girl. Frederica Lindenstromberg. And as the name might imply, she is young, blond, Swedish, beautiful. I say that to ward off future surprises. Freddie and I came down here together, to Baden-Baden, as the touristy Mr. and Mrs. Charles Blumenfeld. Cab stayed in London, assuming my identity."

Emily squinted at him. "Intriguing! I won't ask the why of it, not yet, anyway. What I am hearing you say is, that you took your pal's girlfriend to a nice spa resort in Germany—I have been to Baden-Baden, as a kid, with my parents. I know the place. Ritzy, upscale, right? With you two acting as husband and wife. I know it's indelicate, but I've got to ask you, did you sleep together?"

"Yes. No excuses, no explanations."

"Of course. Young, blond, Swedish. And both of you unmarried." Emily shot him a mischievous glance, "And your friend Cab—he knows?"

"He is not married to her. Not engaged, either, Emily."

She held up her hand, "No excuses, no explanations. Your words, Tom. And I apologize for asking, though I appreciate your honesty."

They were silent for a while, until Tom removed his arm from the trunk lid, grimacing.

"Are you in pain, Tom?" Emily asked.

"A bit. Natural, under the circumstances."

"Anything in your surgical kit here, like a painkiller?"

"I'm afraid not. And aspirin I can't use, because it works against blood clotting. I'll be all right. It'll pass."

"I've got another kind of painkiller in my purse." She rummaged around until she found the little bottle. "Will this do?"

Tom checked the label, "That'll do. Yes. Thank you." Tom swallowed two of the pills. "You have been a great help, Emily. Well done."

"So," she smiled, "am I going to meet your Freddie or not?"

"It's up to you."

"No, it's up to you, too. Do you want me to come?"

Tom looked away, then found her eyes and held them, "If I said no, it would be a lie. If I said no, I would never see you again. And that would be the worst thing that could happen to me."

Emily stood silent, an earnest look on her face. Then she said slowly, "You better give me the keys. I'll do the driving for a while."

It actually worked out pretty well, Emily driving and Tom being the copilot. He had fashioned a sling from his tie, to keep his arm immobile and slightly elevated. The pain had receded to a dull throbbing, soon forgotten.

Tom worked the radio, which was full of strike news, especially gridlock horror stories on the autobahnen. They chose to use regular highways and it was up to Tom to read the map and match it to the road signs. The dog had the whole back seat to himself, which worked out to everyone's satisfaction.

By mid-morning they reached a small town on the banks of the Danube, which Emily decided they should stop at. "Ginzburg, you see? That was my father's mother's maiden name. A good omen."

"I see," Tom smiled. "And what do we stop for?"

"For a pee break. For food and gas and for clothes for you, Doctor Baron Vonder Campe, sir."

"Okay, but I'm no Baron."

"You are the brother of the Baroness Vonder Campe?"

"Betts is my half-sister, and she inherited a title from her mother's side. Nothing to do with me, sorry."

Emily smiled back as she coaxed the car into a metered parking spot. She said, "There is a department store, see? Come along, we'll go shopping."

"In this condition?" He pointed to his arm. "People will be wondering."

"They won't wonder. You speak German, don't you?"

"Fluently."

"Just tell them you just flew in to Munich, and your luggage is still on the plane. You need new everything and you want to wear it right away. You tell them that, and I'll wave my plastic. Platinum works, even in Russia."

"Actually," Tom said, "I have money. Thanks, though. Let's go."

There was a very eager clerk in the men's haberdashery department. Tom gave himself over to him, and a half hour later he was outfitted anew from top to bottom. Suit—on sale yet—extra pants, windbreaker, shirts, socks, tie, underwear, walking shoes. Emily turned up with a soft-leather satchel for herself, "A real bargain, Tom!" And she had bought a few things, too, including a sweatsuit and running shoes, and "raiding the cosmetics counter. God, it's great to be back in civilization! Even the toilet flushed!"

They found a cafe nearby that had not yet opened for mittagessen but was willing to cook up omelets and toast for them, with hot coffee. They felt so revived, they couldn't stop grinning at each other across the table.

"I should make a phone call to Freddie," Tom said. "If she is still there, she needs to know that we are coming. If she has left, we can alter course and drive straight to Strasbourg."

"Go!" Emily said.

There was a phone near the bar. Tom remembered the number of the hotel in Baden-Baden, and dialed. "Mrs. Blumenfeld, please. Room 406."

He waited anxiously, hearing the phone ring three times, "Hello?"

Freddie's voice! So she's still there! "Hello, Freddie! It's Tom. Gosh, I'm glad to hear your voice!"

"Thomas! Where are you?"

"Somewhere near Ulm, I think. About a half day's drive from you, the way it's going. How are you, Freddie? Everything all right?"

"It is now, that you have called! Are you coming back here? I hope you are! I missed you!"

She sounded genuinely touched. It made Tom squirm a bit. "Look, Freddie, Charles did not come down from London because of the strike, you know? So I am coming back to pick you up, and we'll drive to France, take it from there."

"Drive? Do you have a car?"

"Yes, I do. Have you heard from Charles, by any chance?"

"Not a word! I've been so worried, Thomas!"

"Everything's okay. Freddie, listen carefully. I want you to make a call to Charles' office in New York, tell him, or his machine more likely, that the Major will drive you to France, to Paris probably, and to wait for further messages from there. Please? Would you?"

"Yes, Thomas. What time will you arrive here?"

"Oh, the way traffic is, by evening for sure. And Freddie, one more thing. I am bringing another guest, a woman, who also got stuck at the Munich airport and we knew each other from the States. Her name is Emily. Okay?"

Slight pause. "Yes. Emily, huh? Sure. Just get here as fast as you can."

"I promise. And Freddie, we probably won't be leaving tonight anymore. Ask the hotel to move a rollaway bed into our suite, will you?"

"Yes, Thomas. Anything else?"

"Uh, yeah. I'm also bringing a little puppy dog, but I don't want the hotel to know about that."

"Thomas!" A slight laugh at last. "I don't know what to say!"

"Save it, shweetheart." He made like Humphrey Bogart. "So long!"

When he got back to the table he said, "Freddie is still there. She was terribly worried, poor kid. We'll spend the night at the hotel, leave the next morning. Everything's all set." He gave the thumbs-up sign to Emily.

"Did you tell her about me?"

"Of course! She looks forward to meeting you."

"Sure," Emily smiled. "I look forward to meeting her, too."

They had about two hundred fifty kilometers ahead of them using secondary roads, bypassing the major traffic hubs of Ulm, Stuttgart and Karlsruhe which, under normal conditions using the autobahn, would have brought them to Baden-Baden within two hours, saving about fifty kilometers to boot. The news on the radio was so bad, however, nightmarish gridlocks making the autobahn one huge parking lot, that they stuck to their original plan of grinding along in low gear on two-lane highways, where the traffic was at least moving, as it was snaking from city to town to village to city at an average speed of 35 kph and with frequent stops at traffic lights.

There were other stops, too, to top off the gas tank, to buy some snacks and coffee, to walk the dog—Emily bought a cute little halter and leash for the puppy—and to use the washrooms.

At one of those stops, in Freudenstadt at the foot of the Black Forest, Emily came back into the car and said, climbing into the passenger seat, "I've had it. You drive, Tom. Think you're up to it?"

"Of course." He had offered to take the wheel more than once. "You all right, Emily?" He gave her a scrutinizing look. She had shadows under her eyes as she had had the night before, when he met her in the hotel lobby.

"Yes. I think I'm getting my period, though." She grimaced. "Everything is out o' whack in my life."

"Still having headaches?" He touched her forehead. No temperature.

"No, doctor." Her eyes lit up when she smiled. "I took your advice and saw a specialist. He took me off the pill. Worked like a charm."

"I'm glad," he said. "Now, ahead of us is the Black Forest ridge road. Lot of curves, and some climbing. Lean back, relax. You've done enough, Emily. It shouldn't be more than an hour to Baden-Baden from here." He went to the trunk to stuff all the medical paraphernalia into the leather bag. His arm felt dry to the touch, the bleeding had probably stopped, but he would need to rebandage the wound later.

It was dusk when they arrived at the hotel. Tom slipped the doorman a tip to allow him to self-park the car in the hotel parking area, so that it would be readily available in the early morning. Emily adjusted his tie and put his suit jacket over his shoulders. He carried the suitcase, she the "doggy bag" as they had dubbed it, slung over her shoulder, and so they marched through the doors held open for them. Tom barely stopped at the reception desk, except for leaving an order, "Please have our bill ready for us later tonight. Blumenfeld, four-oh-six We have to leave ahead of time, regrettably. The strike, you know."

"Yes, Mr. Blumenfeld." The elderly clerk nodded. "We are very sorry."

Tom said he was sorry, too, and took Emily by the arm walking to the elevators. "Shouldn't I register?" she whispered to him.

"Take a look at our suite, then decide," he replied. "There is plenty of room, and Freddie has ordered a rollaway. We can call the desk from upstairs."

The desk had already called Freddie, when they came off the elevator there she was, standing by her door, in a dress but barelegged and barefoot, her hair up in a bun. The aquamarine hung low from her neck.

"Thomas!" She ran to him and gave him a warm hug. "You're back!" Then, without waiting for an introduction, she smiled and said, "You must be Emily! I'm Freddie. Welcome."

"Thank you," Emily said. "Hope I'm not too much of a bother."

"Not at all. Let's go inside," and she led them into the room.

Tom noticed a folded-up bed in the suite, standing at the ready against the wall but otherwise the place looked as he remembered it. Quietly elegant. There was even an ice bucket again, with a bottle of champagne under wraps.

The awkwardness of the next few minutes was overcome by the presence of Guy, the little dog obviously glad to be out and about, and to be petted to the ooing and cooing of the two women. Tom sat down in a chair and watched the scene for a while, until he asked for attention.

"We have to let the desk know how we want to handle this. I propose that I take the rollaway, sleeping in the entrance hall right there. It's really like a separate room. I'll take care of the dog, too."

"Of course!" Freddie agreed immediately. "Look at the huge double bed, Emily. It's actually two beds pushed together. You take the one on the right!"

Emily hesitated, glancing at Tom and then at Freddie. "I don't know. I'd love to stay here, but I think I should take the rollaway bed."

Tom disagreed. "It's only for this one night. You and Freddie should take the beds. I'm the soldier, I'm used to cots. Okay? I'll call the desk, have them charge us for the extra person. Then I'll call room service, order us something to eat. What'd you like?"

They settled for salads and cold cuts. "We can take some along as sandwiches tomorrow!" Freddie suggested.

Emily put her bag down on the bed, and peeked into the bathroom. "Look at this! Gorgeous! Does anyone mind if I have a bath, and wash my hair? I feel I really need it!"

Of course nobody minded. When Emily was behind the closed door, and the water was running into the tub, Freddie said, "Tell me what happened, Tom."

Tom went to the bar and poured himself a scotch. He nodded, "You are entitled to know all I can tell you, Freddie. The mission that Cab and I were working on was fully successful, although I was not the one who completed it. Cab is still in London, I presume, and we should hear from him eventually, if he got your message, Freddie."

She gave him a long look. "That's not entirely what I meant with my question. I would like to know all you can tell me, Thomas, about this classy woman you brought along, and that bandage on your arm."

"Oh, that?" Tom shrugged. "It's nothing. A cut. Some wild man in Munich wanted my rental car, and when I said I still needed it, he got nasty before I got rid of him. He had a knife. It's okay, just a superficial cut."

"Let's hope so. And Emily? Where does she come in?"

"Oh, we have met twice before in the States, and there she was at that same airport, stuck the same way I was, and when we ran into each other I offered to take her with us to France."

"With us? You told her about me?"

"When I told her why I wanted to stop off in Baden-Baden, yes."

"What did you tell her about me?"

"Well, not all that much. It was not germane."

"Did you tell her we slept together?"

Tom gave a brief laugh, "Damn! She asked me the same question!"

"And? What did you say?"

"I said that we had made love. Yes."

"You did. So, why would someone you have met only twice before be interested in that? Isn't that rather personal?"

"Yes, it is. In fact, Emily apologized for asking that question."

"And yet, you freely supplied the answer. People only do that when there is a lot at stake. Such as when they are very close. Are you two that close, Thomas?"

He put his glass down and walked over to the window. The park below was dark, except for the lighted pathways. When he turned back he said slowly, "I honestly don't know, Freddie, if we are mutually close. For my part, I wish we were. I don't know about her. Also, I believe she is engaged."

"You wish you were." Freddie got up and walked over to him. "You wish you were!" She put her head on his shoulder.

He held her with his good arm, stroked her back. When she looked up at him, he kissed her hair. "Freddie."

She freed herself, shook her head, and turned away from him.

The room service cart was a welcome interruption. The chambermaid came and turned down the bed, including the rollaway, brought new towels and left chocolate-glazed strawberries on the pillows. And Emily emerged, all pink and warm in the fluffy hotel bathrobe, her wet hair in a towel around her head.

"That was wonderful! I feel so clean!" She eyed the table, "And oh, look at the food! Yummy!"

When there was no real answer forthcoming, she looked at Tom, and then at Freddie, and said, "You have been talking, haven't you. About me?"

Tom nodded, and Freddie said, "Yes, we have, Emily. I asked Tom how he felt about you."

"And? What did Tom say?"

"The question wasn't really put quite that way," Tom cut in. "Freddie asked if we are close, Emily, and I said I honestly didn't know but I wish we were."

"Really!" Emily plunked herself down into a chair. "Close! What do you mean by close? We have not been intimate!" She said that to Freddie, with emphasis on *close* and *we*, which was not lost on Freddie.

But before she could answer Tom spoke again, "May I suggest that we leave this discussion for another time and another place? We all have to be fit early tomorrow morning, and it's going to be a tough drive, if we want to make Paris by nightfall."

"In that case," Freddie rose abruptly, "I will have a bath now, too." She stepped into the bedroom area and began to undress. When she was bare she walked to the bathroom and closed the door behind her.

Emily, watching her, turned to Tom. "Well, you weren't exaggerating when you said young and blond and beautiful. Wow!"

"It's her way of being natural, among friends."

"Or intimates. I see." She bent down and picked up the dog, holding him on her lap. "Guy here is wondering what you meant by us being close."

"Is he!" Tom smiled. "Tell him, Ein Herz und eine Seele."

"I bet you think I don't know what that means. But I have studied music a while back, see? German Romantics, like Schumann, Clara and Robert, One Heart and One Soul. Do you think we are like Clara and Robert, Tom?"

"God, I hope not like them. He went crazy, as you know."

"But not before he had fathered seven children."

"Or was it because?" Tom laughed. "How about a drink?"

"Yes! None of that bubbly stuff. I need something more honest."

"Scotch?"

"Perfect. On the rocks, please."

Tom got up to make her drink and to freshen up his own. When he handed her the glass he touched his to hers, "To closeness?"

Emily nodded. "I'll drink to that."

They agreed on an early departure of six o'clock, which meant packing ahead of time, and closing off the hotel account. It turned out that "Herr Blumenfeld" had a credit balance, which he had to accept in cash, American dollars because the prepayment had been in that currency. Tom pocketed close to a thousand dollars. He'd have to sit down with Cab in New York and work out who owed what to whom, overall.

Freddie made sandwiches of their leftover cold cuts and raided the mini-bar for anything drinkable and edible, to carry as a picnic in one of the bags supplied in the room. It caused Tom to call back to the desk to arrange for payment of the mini-bar use, but he was told not to worry, the hotel was sorry to see such esteemed guests having to leave early, and to hurry back when things were normal again. Tom thanked them and put his appreciation in an envelope on the writing desk. A hundred bucks would do it, he thought.

He had a restless night on the cot in the hall, not because it was uncomfortable but because so many things were on his mind. Emily, mostly. He was convinced that they were meant for each other, whatever that meant, which caused him to worry how that still so very fragile relationship could be nurtured to blossom out, to bear fruit—and he castigated himself for his flowery choice of words, including "relationship" which he and Nettie had always ridiculed as "pop-psych," which conjured up Nettie again and made him fret how she would feel about Emily, which was futile because Emily would not exist for him if she still did.

And why was the dog restless, and yelping in a high-pitched sort of way as if he was learning to bark? Wrong time for that, kiddo, Tom grabbed the pup and put him on the bed with him. And so they both did fall asleep.

His watch showed 4:30 A.M. when he awoke, curiously refreshed. He tip-toed into the bathroom, clutching his shaving gear and the first aid kit.

He had just turned on the light and put his things down when the door went and Emily stepped inside. She was in one of Freddie's nightgowns, which showed, under gossamer fabric, much bosom and pink panties. She said, "Hi!" and combed her hair back with her fingers, but cascades of copper-brown strands, cut to frame her face, kept falling down obscuring her eyes and making them reappear even more luminous in their light gray-green way when she finally locked her hair behind her ears. Tom stood entranced.

"Emily! Hope I didn't wake you. It's still early."

She shook her head. "It's okay. I'm awake." She came closer and took his left arm, inspecting it. "I thought you might need some help redoing the bandage?" She seemed uncertain when she looked at him.

"Yes! I do, as a matter of fact. Very thoughtful of you."

Busy cutting the now blood-caked old gauze off carefully, and equally so replacing the butterfly tapes after Tom had applied an antibiotic cream to the edges of the cut, their heads were so close together that he could smell the warmth of her body. When she was finished winding new gauze around his arm, he impulsively took her face in his hands and kissed her lightly on the lips. She did not return the kiss, and he dropped his hands.

"May I stick around while you shave?" Emily asked.

Tom said, "I was going to take a shower."

"You better be careful. Don't get your arm wet." She smiled. "The tub's better for you. For now."

"Right." Tom started getting his things ready around the rim of the sink. "While I scrape my face, why don't you tell me about your St. Petersburg job. What's it like up there?"

"It's over, that what it's like." Emily found the chaise and sat down, pulling up her legs and clasping her hands around her knees. "I quit. On the day I left. Which was the day when a mob of street kids ganged up on me, pinned my arms to my side and took my briefcase, my laptop and my purse, and yanked my necklace off me. That took place on a busy morning, on a brief walk on Nevsky Prospekt where my hotel is, to Fontanka street where my bank is. At that point I had had it."

"Good Lord!" Tom, who had brushed his teeth, spit out into the sink. "Did you call the police?"

"You're kidding! The four weeks I've been there, I've been stolen from at work and in my hotel room, watch, calculator, micro-recorder, blue jeans, a sweater, even underwear and heaven-knows-what-else. I reported it to my bank manager, who just shrugged and suggested I move to a more secure hotel, which I did at three times the per-diem allowance out of my pocket. He also told me to dress less provocatively, when I had already dressed down compared to London standards. And so on and so forth." Emily threw her head back. "No. The street robbery was the last straw for me. I went back to the hotel, packed, and took the hotel shuttle to Pulkhovo-Two, the international flights airport. The first available flight out was an Aeroflot to Berlin. I took it." She gave an ironic laugh. "I've no idea where my luggage went. What's more, I don't care! I'm out."

"Well," Tom was working up a lather on his cheeks and chin, "what now?"

"I'm going to London and put in my resignation. High time for me to get out of the rat race anyway. Too much stuff happening to me."

"I'm sorry. What are you going to do instead?"

"Get married, have kids. Lead a normal life for a change."

"Hmm." Tom turned back to the mirror. He was tempted to ask if she would marry him, but fortunately the inanity of the question at this time dawned on him before it could slip off his tongue. And he remembered that not too long ago, this very question had popped into his mind with regard to Frederica Lindenstromberg—and how did she spell her name, anyhow, with a "c" or a "k"? And was it -berg or -burg? A woman he knew so fleetingly he wasn't even sure how she spelled her name? Marry her because she was a good lay? Good grief, Tom, he scolded himself, get real!

He grimaced at her through the mirror. "You did have a run of back luck."

"You don't know the half of it," Emily said.

"I'm willing to listen."

"It'd take longer than your shave." She got up. "I better go now, see if Freddie will lend me some clean clothes." She smiled. "Think her bra would fit me? Don't answer that. Let me know when the john is free."

It was free when Tom stepped back into the room. Freddie, it turned out, had gone downstairs to the fitness center and used the facilities there. She had also ordered some coffee and rolls which came just when they were dressing. The puppy was walked on the balcony and did his thing.

They were ready, in the car and pulling out of the hotel driveway, when it was not yet six o'clock.

They had a headstart on the day. Paris, here we come.

Coppet

Their first attempt to cross the border, at Kehl to Strasbourg, did not work out, even before they had reached the Rhine Bridge it was clear that lining up with all the trucks, vans and cars would mean a wait of not just an hour or two but possibly more. The three of them were unanimous in opting for another try further down, to Colmar, and again were appalled at the heavy traffic. By now, they had spent close to three hours in the car. Freddie, who sat up front in the passenger seat, was dishing out sandwiches, fruit bars and apple juice, en lieu of stopping for breakfast.

Emily had volunteered to sit in the back with the puppy, she declined food but took some juice. "I'm not ready for those ham-and-cheese things so early in the morning," she said. Tom glanced at her in the rearview mirror. He thought, as he had yesterday, that she looked kind of peaked around the eyes and mouth, and wondered if she traveled well, at the next stop, he would ask.

Luck was with them at last, at the triangle where several major roads met to cross the Rhine towards Mulhouse. They came to the smaller of the bridges just when all non-commercial traffic was being waved through. Within minutes thereafter they found themselves on the Autoroute that would lead past Dijon direct to Paris.

Alas, traffic on this main artery, spilled over from Germany, also moved at a crawl. They pulled into a service area. While the women went to the restroom and gas was pumped into the car, Tom consulted the map.

He spoke to them when the women got back, "Look," he said and spread the map out on the hood. "We are here, close to Besançon, and Paris is there, still some four hundred or more kilometers away. If past experience is any guide, we'll be lucky to make it there by nightfall. Possibly later. On the other hand, Geneva is only a hundred fifty kilometers away. And I doubt that orderly, sober Switzerland will give us as much trouble as France or Germany, and even if it does, it is still closer by two-thirds. I propose we change course for Geneva. What do you say?"

"By one-third," Emily said, with a languid gesture.

"Beg pardon?"

"It is two-thirds longer to Paris, and one-third shorter to Geneva."

"I opt for Geneva," Freddie said quickly.

"Of course," Emily murmured. "I didn't mean to nit-pick."

They climbed back into the car. They found an exit that said "Pontarlier-Lausanne" and took it. It was definitely easier going, although the road became mountainous and required reduced speeds to negotiate the many turns and climbs. But the Pontarlier stretch was less than forty kilometers long.

Emily was heard lowing to herself in the back seat.

Tom became concerned, "You all right, Emily?"

"Not entirely. Tom, maybe at the next stop I should get something from the pharmacy."

"Have you been known to suffer from motion sickness, Em?" Tom asked.

"Not so far but in this crazy year almost anything is possible with me."

"Do you want to change seats?" Freddie offered.

"No, thank you. I actually like stretching out a bit here."

"Well," Tom said, "in a couple of hours we should be in Geneva."

But that was not to be. A little while later Emily cried out, "Stop! Stop the car! I have to go!"

Tom saw in the mirror that Emily was clutching her stomach and was bent over. "Okay!" he shouted. "Hang on. I'm going to find a spot." He searched for a suitable layover off the mountain highway and settled for a wood-cutters lane that presented itself. He made a sharp right turn. The car bumped along for a few yards before it stopped. They were at the rim of a forest with dense undergrowth. Emily grabbed her bag, pushed open her door and bolted for a clump of bushes ahead.

Puzzled, Freddie asked, "Something she ate? We all had the same. I feel all right. How about you?"

"I'm okay, too. She may have picked up a bug in Russia." Tom watched where Emily had disappeared. "Freddie, would you go and check on her?"

"Sure." Freddie climbed out of the car, as did Tom, but he stayed behind, watching Freddie round the clump of bushes.

A moment later there was a shout. "Tom?" Freddie's voice. "Come here, please, quick!"

"Coming!" He closed the car door and hurried over. The clump of bushes were atop a slight gradient, so when he pushed himself through he saw Freddie kneeling and holding a pale, faint-looking Emily whose head was inclined against her shoulder. Not far from where the women were crouching, Tom observed a puddle of dark red blood.

He jumped down and knelt by Emily's other side. "Emily?" He turned her face to his. "Emily! Can you hear me?" He squeezed her cheeks a bit.

She barely opened her eyes. "Yes."

"What happened? Did you vomit? Emily, you must tell me!"

"She lost blood from her period," Freddie said and nodded at the puddle.

"I want her to talk," Tom said tersely. He took Emily's wrist. The pulse was weak and fast, her hand cold.

"Freddie, I need your help. We have to take her to a hospital, ASAP. You can help me carry her to the car. Please."

They put Emily's arms around their shoulders and dragged her to the car.

Tom noticed that her skirt was still askew, and that drops of blood were dripping steadily to the ground.

"You carry tampons or pads, don't you, Freddie?" he asked. "Help her place a couple tight against her vulva, and make her cross her legs. I'm going to fetch the sleeping bag from the trunk. We've got to keep her warm." As he did so and threw the sleeping bag to Freddie, he saw in the trunk a small folding spade that was attached to the road emergency kit the Audi carried. He took it, grabbed a plastic shopping bag by dumping its contents, and raced back to the spot where Emily had been. Very carefully, he scooped up the blood from the bed of leaves on which it rested, and dropped it into the bag. When he returned to the car, Freddie had done her job already.

"I couldn't zip her into the sleeping bag," she half apologized, "but I put it all around her." Emily was on the back seat, a pale mummy.

"You did right." Tom leaned into the car. "Emily? We are taking you to a doctor. You'll be okay."

Her eyes were closed, but she mumbled something about being "so very sorry . . ."

"Don't be. Don't worry. Everything's going to be all right."

He and Freddie jumped in, and he backed the car out onto the road, then sped off into light, mostly downhill traffic towards Pontarlier. They reached the outskirts of town ten minutes later. They were still on the N-67 which fed into the city's main street. The moment he saw a policeman, he stopped, honked the horn to hail him over, and in his school French asked where the nearest hospital was, and that they had an emergency, pointing to Emily.

The police officer took one look and motioned them to follow him. His motorbike's lights flashing and his siren blaring at each intersection. Tom following closely, they roared down the street and across the river Doubs, where they turned into the emergency entrance of the large district hospital of St. Etienne. Tom jumped out of the car, thanked the cop with a salute, and strode into the reception area. He grabbed the first green-smocked doctor who went by him, said that he, Tom, was a medecin Americain and that he had a patient in shock in the car outside. "Vite, vite!" he pleaded, "depechons-nous, docteur!" not caring if he was choosing the right words.

The man understood immediately, barked some orders that brought two orderlies running with a gurney. Tom led them outside, they put Emily on it and she was wheeled inside and into a curtained cubicle, where the French doctor, a bear of a man with a walrus mustache, was awaiting them.

"Alors, Monsieur le docteur," he said, and gave Tom a steely-eyed look, "tell me what is wrong with Madame."

"Je crois . . . " Tom fumbled for the correct French in vain, "spontaneous abortion."

"Fausse couche," the Frenchman nodded.

Emily's eyes were now open, and she followed the exchange with an anxious look. Tom bent over her. "It's okay now, Em," he soothed her. "I say so because I know so. Hmm?" He stroked her cheek.

In response, she reached out and pulled his head down to her, kissing him. "I owed you this one," she whispered. Tom squeezed her hand and gave her a reassuring look. Then, at the wave of the French doctor's hand, he left the cubicle.

Freddie was still standing at the car when Tom came out. He told her briefly what had gone on inside, then remembered that the plastic bag with the blood he had collected was still in the trunk. He took it out. He asked if Freddie would park the car for him, and she said she would. They would meet in the reception area. Tom brought the bag to where he had left the doctor, but the cubicle was empty. The patient had been moved, he was told. Tom said that the specimen was the patient's, and that the doctor should be told about it.

His request was looked after, but not until after Tom had filled out a lengthy form where he was asked to put down Emily's vital statistics. He sweated over most of the questions, making up her date of birth, using the address of her London bank as her address in the U.K., and that of his own mother as her New York home address. When it came to marital status, he ticked off "married" because he might be called upon to give consent in case of an emergency, he also used his own name as that of her husband, although he wrote in "Dessauer" as Emily's last name. For method of payment, he made the notation of "US$."

All of this had taken some time. When he returned to the lobby, Freddie was not there. He figured she would not have an easy time finding a parking spot in a strange town, although there should be a parking lot close to the hospital, but knowing her, she would probably give the puppy a little walk as well. As it happened, Freddie turned up a short while later.

She had found parking. She gave Tom the keys and told him that she had given the pup a walk and some water. Then she said, a bit hesitantly, "May I talk with you, in a personal way, Thomas?"

"Of course!"

She heaved a sigh. "I hope this will not be misunderstood by you, because I really believe it is best for all of us, or I wouldn't have done it."

"Done what, Freddie?"

Another sigh. "I drove to the railway station, which is close by on the other side of the river. I bought a ticket to Paris. I was lucky to get one even though I had to take first class. It puts me into Paris later in the afternoon. The local feeder train leaves in about an hour from now." Freddie breathed out. "Okay, that's it. It's been on my mind since we've arrived in France. There is no strike here, the bad traffic is just a spillover from the German situation but French trains are running. So why not go by rail?"

Tom had followed her reasoning. "You are absolutely right, Freddie."

"You are not just saying that, are you? Or are mad at me? Or feel hurt?"

"No! Not at all." In fact, as he thought about it, this was going to make things a lot easier now that Emily had become a patient. He knew the procedure: There would probably be a D and C involved, some anesthesia, possibly more. His own role would be one of a care-giver to Emily, with Freddie increasingly left out of the picture. He meant it when he said, "You did the right thing. Which is not to say that we won't miss you. You have been an absolutely marvelous friend, Freddie. I am indebted to you." He came over and gave her a hug.

Freddie hugged him back, hurriedly, averting her face.

Practical considerations took over. Freddie needed her suitcases, Tom had to be shown where the car was parked, and Freddie had to take a taxi to the station. She insisted that Tom stay at the hospital. They rushed about to do all that. And Freddie promised she would bring Charles up to speed. Tom said he would be in touch via Cab's New York office.

When Tom returned to the hospital lobby, the realization set in that he and Emily were now truly on their own, and that with the exception of Freddie on her train, nobody knew where they were, or where they were going. Or rather, where they would have to be going, because undoubtedly there would be a post-op period where Emily would require bed rest and recuperative care for several days before she could travel again. And he could not see that happening here at this provincial French hospital, if in fact they had a bed for her at all. He would have to find a place, out in the country somewhere, for them to hole up for a couple of days, in peace and quiet.

The Swiss border was just down the road. Why not in Switzerland?

Instantly that rang a bell. Bettina! Didn't she have a place in Coppet where she went every year on holiday? Call Bettina, now, for more than one reason. Somebody, someone quite trustworthy, ought to know where they were not to mention that he longed to know how Bertie was.

He rushed to exchange some money, went to the telephone in the lobby and placed a call to Bettina's business number, it was not yet noon in London.

It took a bit of wrangling to persuade Bettina's secretary to interrupt an editorial conference, but Bettina did come to the phone, breathless.

"Tom! For heaven's sake, how are you? And where have you been? Surely not in Norfolk or wherever you pretended to be. Where are you calling from?"

Tom tried to quieten her down, by giving her a thumbnail sketch of the past few days activities, mentioning of course that he had been in Germany all along, on important private business—which he would explain later. It had been interrupted by the strike and they, he and Emily Dessauer, had made it into France.

"Emily Dessauer? Isn't she the young woman I met when we had our party, whilst you were in absentia?"

"The very one."

"And she was in Germany with you?"

"Not with me, Betts. We met there, quite by coincidence, and decided to make it back to London together. Unfortunately, Emily has come down with a sudden bout of ill health, requiring a bit of surgery, just as we were passing through Pontarlier. That's a town just north of Switzerland, Betts."

"I know where Pontarlier is. In the French Jura. Is that where you are calling from?"

"Yes. The hospital of St. Etienne."

"Oh dear. Nothing serious, I hope?"

"No, but requiring a couple of days bed rest. Absolutely essential. I was wondering, now that we practically are in Switzerland, if you could let us use your chalet in Coppet for a few days."

"Well, first of all, it's not a chalet but an auberge. Secondly, I don't own it in toto, you know, just a sixth of it, together with other investors, and most of the time it is making money for us as an inn, renting rooms to tourists. But yes, I could call and see if they have a vacancy. It's a lovely place, overlooking Lac Leman, just the right spot to gather back one's strength. Give me the number where you can be reached."

"Thank you, Betts." He gave her the number on the phone. "Do call back either way. I want to know about Bertie. Is he all right?"

"Doing very well, thank you. If you keep up your meandering ways, I don't know if we shall give him back to you. Now, stay where you are."

Bettina called back in five minutes. "You are in luck. Or rather, we are, for you shall pay for your room and board, of course, and we shall make some money. It's been a slow spring so far." She gave him the address— "L'Auberge au Soleil," Madame Evangeline Auger the manager—and the phone number. They talked a little while longer, Tom promising to call from Coppet to speak to Bertie the very next day. "And good luck to your Emily, Tom!"

"My Emily, Bettina? That's a bit farfetched as yet, I'm afraid."

"Oh, but she shall be. I have no doubt. No doubt at all."

Tom switched the subject to Bertie, and was regaled with wondrous stories of the lad's latest achievements, which included riding a pony. "He'll soon want one for his own, I shouldn't wonder! You started him on it, haven't you?" All in all, it was clear that Bertie was no cause for concern at the moment.

Emily, on the other hand, was. Tom was called into consultation with the gynecologist who had done the procedure: the curettage had gone well, but the loss of blood overall had been considerable. Emily was currently on a drip infusion which contained nutrients, but a blood transfusion was preferable. The husband's consent was required.

"Why not the patient's?" Tom asked, and was told that she was still in post-op recovery, and not yet out of anesthesia. Tom replied that they would have to wait until she regained consciousness and then ask her directly. In the meantime, he asked to see the lab report.

It was an interesting document. Pathology reported an "embryonic tissue indicating a fetal age of six to seven weeks," the blood panel showed lowered values consistent with recent blood loss but not to such a degree that a blood transfusion was of vital necessity. Of course, a transfusion would bring up the values immediately, but in Tom's opinion, the risks of using someone else's blood were too great for such a routine application. He would advise Emily to decline it.

This she did, tired but alert, about an hour later when he saw her in the recovery room. Tom made the point that it would require a period of rest and recuperation, preferably now and here instead of later in the States. He told her how he had contacted his sister who happened to be a co-owner of an inn right on the shores of Lake Geneva, that being about an hour's drive from where they were now. Would that place not be just right for her to regain her strength and build up her blood again? He was talking to her in a low voice, sitting by her bed and holding her hand.

"And you?" She whispered back. "Where would you be, Tom?"

He smiled, "Right there, with you. Your personal attending physician."

She squeezed his hand, "Let's go! Oh please, let's, Tom!"

It was a bit of a wrangle to make the hospital doctors agree to her immediate discharge and to allow her transport to Switzerland by car. Emily had to use her fluent French to make her position clear, and Tom had to supply the name and number of the gerante de l'auberge, the innkeeper, confirming that a room would indeed be at the ready for them, although he insisted that the true cause of Emily's surgical procedure be treated with complete confidence and not be disclosed to anyone without her express consent. The hospital doctors, no fools themselves, agreed. The travel documents, for transport across the border, listed Emily's condition as "removal of intrauterine growth." When it came to paying the bill, Tom's Baden-Baden dollars, minus a professional courtesy discount, were more than adequate to settle the account.

By late afternoon, Emily resting comfortably on the lowered passenger seat, wrapped and cushioned by hospital blankets and pillows, Tom steered the car cautiously out of the hospital driveway and onto the south-bound N-67. The Swiss border at Vallorbe was only a half hour down the road. And Vallorbe was already in the same Canton as Coppet.

At Swiss customs, the two U.S. passports and the Audi's Wagenpapiere were barely looked at. The medical certificate was scrutinized and the declared destination confirmed by a phone call to the auberge. They were waved on their way. Tom's anxiety about the name in his passport—Campe— that it would not match the name of the lessee in the car lease—Blumenfeld—proved groundless. He was gratified for the prime concern from now on would be Emily. It was in this context as well that he had explained the absence of Freddie, her departure by train, Emily took the news without any comment, as if that had been predictable.

The L'Auberge au Soleil proved to be not only easy to find, just off Coppet's arcaded main street down a tree-shaded country road, but harmoniously situated in a garden-like setting, a verdant meadow sloping down from it to the waters of the lake shimmering in the late afternoon sun.

Emily, who had not talked much on the short ride from the border, was enthralled by the sight of the place, which, unlike most of the Swiss buildings with their heavy, low-slung roofs and gables, was almost Mediterranean in style. "Look!" she pointed ahead excitedly. "The red tiles, the white-washed walls, the terrace! The balconies! This could be on the Riviera!"

Tom agreed. "Beautiful. The South of France. The French border runs along the middle of the lake. They've got vineyards on either side."

They pulled up in front of the entrance. Tom went inside to register, and made the acquaintance of Madame Auger, who was a matron of dignified bearing, her alert brown eyes inscrutable when Tom tried to explain the special situation. He had decided that nothing but the truth would do. He and Mademoiselle Dessauer were not married, but after her unfortunate operation he felt called upon to be her personal physician. They would require a common room with two beds. He hoped that Madame Auger would understand and approve and provide such accommodation for them.

A smile began to play over Madame's severe features. She had heard from La Baroness Campe that such would be the case. If Monsieur le docteur would follow her and inspect the room she thought suitable.

It was more than suitable, a large room on the ground floor, towards the other side off the common room of the inn. It had two canopied beds separated by a night table, and French doors to a private patio where the lake and the distant Alps provided an almost theatrical backdrop.

"C'est bon," he said. "Mercí Madame," and hurried out back to the car.

He opened the door, "Put your arms around my neck, Emily," he commanded and lifted her up. "I'll carry you across the threshold of the Kuleana."

She did as she was told and inclined her head to his shoulder. "I hope you'll explain that word to me," she whispered into his ear.

"That and more," he promised, "in Hawaii."

"Hawaii . . . ?" She gave him a wan smile.

He brought his head close to hers: "Ku-le-ana. Meaning 'your own turf, your private haven.' My next prescription for you: R-and-R in Hawaii." He felt her hand squeeze his shoulder.

There was a final problem to overcome—the presence of the puppy. Here Emily's French, her pleading with great emotional flourish for Madame Auger's indulgence of her cherie petit chien, did the trick. The puppy was allowed to stay in their room, especially when Tom offered to pay a surcharge to defray the costs of extra cleaning, et cetera.

When evening fell they had a light supper brought to their room, of which Emily ate very little, except for the bouillon into which she dunked some bread. Tom ventured the suggestion that they turn in soon, and how should they handle their "cohabitation," as he termed it jokingly.

They agreed there would be a strict observance of privacy. If Emily at any time felt uncomfortable with his presence, she needed only to say so and he would seek other accommodations, and no hard feelings.

"Uncomfortable with your presence!" Emily raised her eyebrows. "Why would I be? I am damn lucky to have you with me, my personal attending physician, as you put it. And besides, aren't we friends?"

"Well, I'm glad you feel that way. And yes, we are friends but we are also man and woman. The situation precludes any temptation of intimacy, but I think you should know that I have carried a torch for you since I first saw you. It's only fair to mention that up front, even though it will have no practical consequences, as yet. My main concern will be to restore you to your good health and well-being." He smiled. "Perhaps, at the end, you will have become thoroughly bored with me."

Emily sat silent, giving him one of her searching looks. "D'accord," she nodded at last. "Except I shall never be bored with you."

They agreed on one other thing—that they would not be foolishly coy in their living together, no silly acts of false modesty, they would, however, respect a certain intimate privacy.

They went to bed—their respective beds—shortly after dark fell. It had been a long and trying day, they said as they wished each other a good night's sleep.

Emily's voice floated into the darkness once more, drowsily, "Tom, I thank you, so much. Tomorrow will be a better day for me . . . we'll talk."

Talk they did, the next morning, the next day, the day after that. Talk, it turned out, would be the essence of their time together at the inn by the shores of Lake Geneva. Emily was seemingly insatiable about all the things she wanted to know and say, with Tom seldom at loss for an answer, a reply, an explanation, and always ready to lend an ear.

The first morning, Tom had slipped into the bathroom and showered, shaved and dressed before Emily awoke, and Emily would probably have slept longer had not the service girl knocked, opened the curtains and set the breakfast down on the patio table. The rays of the morning sun slanted into the room, and a warm breeze wafted through the French doors.

Tom came to her bed, wished her a good morning and said it looked as if she had a good night. Then he took her hand to feel her pulse.

Emily gave him a sly look. "Doctor Campe at work, already?"

"Well, we want to establish a certain routine," he smiled back, and put a thermometer into her mouth.

Both readings were normal. "May I get up now, doctor?" she asked.

"Certainly. But do not bathe, yet. Just a sponge bath. Easy's the word."

Emily nodded, and as she walked to the bathroom she pulled the nightgown over her head and flung it to the floor. A moment later she poked her head back into the room. "Freddie's," she grimaced. "I don't ever want to wear it again. Dump it, Tom."

Later, at breakfast, Tom said, "I guess I'll have to buy new nightclothes for you. Do you prefer pajamas?"

Spooning up her soft-boiled eggs from a glass that Tom had ordered for her as "a regular feature of your diet, until further notice," Emily asked, "Why would you want to buy that for me? I can do that myself!"

"Yes, but not just yet. Not today."

"I'm not an invalid, Tom!" She sounded a bit tetchy.

"No, you are not."

"Then please don't treat me like one." Her nostrils quivered.

Tom said nothing more, and they returned to their breakfast. Over the last of the coffee poured from the can, Emily having regained her composure, she said, "I'm sorry. Perhaps this is as good a time as any for you to tell me what's going on with me. Medically speaking?"

Tom joined her on the cushioned bench. "All right," he agreed, "let's do that. And let's begin with the present, and work back. If I am out of line with my statements or questions, say so. The purpose of all this is to help you, not to hurt you more that you already have been."

"What do you mean 'more than I already have been'?"

"Emily, you have had a curettage, a reaming out, to use a drastic word, of the lining of your uterus. The need for that arose when your pregnancy suddenly proved not viable." He paused, eyeing her with concern. "We can stop right here. There is plenty of time to take this up later."

Emily shook her head. "No. We talk now."

Tom leaned forward, took her hand and held it. "Were you aware that you were pregnant?"

Again, she shook her head, looking down at their hands.

"The lab report says it was a six to seven week embryo." He stroked the back of her hand with his thumb. "That puts it roughly into the beginning of March, end of February. Think back."

Slowly, her head sank to his shoulder. "Nick," she whispered.

He stroked her hair. "Shhh," he soothed, "we can take this up some other time."

He felt her head shaking: "No." She straightened up and fumbled for a tissue, blew her nose. "I am not a sissy. I face facts. I am good at that." She crumpled the tissue and got a new one. "What happened was, I had flown to Los Angeles in February. The January earthquake had destroyed the apartment house I had just moved into, after I had lost my house in Malibu to the fire in October. Pretty good so far, huh?" She blew her nose again, more noisily.

"You lost your house, in the Malibu fire?"

"Yeah. Spectacular event. I'll tell you about it another time." She snorted a laugh. "My house? Just the evening before I had given a housewarming party for my friends. Boy, did it get warm."

Tom looked at her aghast. "Holy Moses, Emily!"

She nodded. "Afterwards, I needed a place to stay. Where would I move to? That apartment house in Santa Monica. Why that one? Well, as it happens, it was owned by Nick's family trust, a nice building, half-timbered in fake Tudor style but with a gorgeous view of the mountains. Come the quake, and it was a complete loss, and I mean complete. Zilch, zero, nada. I had bought a new Steinway, an upright, beautiful tone—crash-boom, gone. So here I am, standing on that meridian on San Vicente Boulevard, and I am looking at that piece of earth where my other home had been, now just a plot, perfectly graded, wire fence around it, as if nothing on it had never existed. It floored me. For the second time in a couple of months, I had lost everything to the elements. What was going on here? Huh?" She tried another brief laugh.

"Anyway, Nick had wanted me to fly down to L.A., filing for the insurance and FEMA and what not, so I had come. I actually didn't want to see it. The remnants of my home. Once is plenty enough, know what I mean?"

"I do. From a different perspective. Go on."

"Well, Nick had put me up at a Santa Monica hotel, and of course he tried to get into my knickers. He always does. And sometimes I let him. In this case, for instance. I felt kind of weepy-creepy, and Nick was so nice . . . Except I forgot I was no longer on the pill. Remember, my headaches? Well, it sure looks like I traded it in for an even bigger one!" The tone of her voice was edgy, belying the humor of her words.

"Nick, I take it, is your fiancee?"

"Oh," she nodded. "Yes. Nicholas Grady, Esquire. Lawyer, former Marine, played tight end for USC at the Rose Bowl. Great guy. BMOC, forever." Emily needed another tissue.

"All right," Tom said, "so that's when fertilization occurred."

"Must have been. I'm not like Freddie, I don't flaunt it and get it." She stopped. "Sorry. But I bet she's on the pill!"

"Implants," Tom grinned. "Six of them, right up here." He pointed to the inside of his arm.

"Oh, you checked, did you? Never mind. I'm not a fun girl, like her. Maybe I should be. Maybe I'm missing something." This time the tears were coming, and she pulled furiously at the box of tissues.

"I think that's enough for now," Tom said and got up. "I am going into town, I want to buy some medication for you that'll build up your blood a little faster. What about those pajamas?"

"All right." She was trying to smile. "Size ten. Twelve, if in doubt. And bring me a box of pads, maximum strength. Oh, and puppy food. Guy's hungry." She picked up the pup and cradled it in her arms. "We'll wait here for you."

Tom had to drive all the way to Nyon, six miles up the road, to find a pharmacy that would carry a large enough stock to accommodate his wishes. He picked high-potency vitamins, complex Bs, especially B-12, C and E, and an iron product that he thought would be less hard on the stomach. By and large, that was all he felt could be done for Emily, along with proper food intake and rest. Her being up and around wouldn't hurt as long as she did not overexert herself. Not just physically, but also emotionally. He was shocked at what he had heard her tell him. Losing her home, twice in a row, to natural disasters? And then the St. Petersburg thing, the German strike, and worse yet, a miscarriage? How would she be able to cope? His heart went out to her. Not, he told himself, that it didn't, anyhow . . .

He bought her pajamas, a sensible Swiss cotton outfit that would do the job, and he didn't forget about the pads and the puppy food.

It was nearly lunchtime when he returned with his purchases. Emily was on the patio, stretched out on a liegestuhl, her eyes closed, taking in the sun. She was dressed in the gym suit she had bought in Bavaria. The puppy, curled up beside her, stirred and tried his squeaky bark, and that woke her up. "Tom! There you are, back already?" She blinked. "What time is it?"

"About noon. How are you feeling?"

"Fine! I tried to read, but my eyes kept shutting on me."

"Well, I brought some vitamins to pep you up. Build up your hemoglobin, too. You are a bit on the low side there."

"Yes, doctor." She smiled. "Whatever you say, I'll do."

"Gosh, you're easy!" Tom smiled back.

"Not in every respect. But for you," she splayed her hands, "I'll make an exception."

He unpacked the pajamas. "Think these will fit you?"

She laughed. "Where'd you get 'em? Grandmere style. Madame Auger would approve. They'll certainly protect me."

"And me," Tom grinned.

Emily ignored that. "Your sister called," she said.

"Oh? Bettina? When?"

"About an hour ago. Wanted to know how we were doing, if the accommodations were satisfactory. I said fine, to both."

"Did she ask about me, that I should call back?"

Emily shook her head. "We had a pretty long chat, but you came up only once. I said you were in town, buying some things we needed. The rest of the time we were talking about Bertie, who is also fine, and about me and her, what we are doing and so on. Girl talk. She's very nice. I like her."

"I'm glad."

"She's lesbian, isn't she?"

"Yes."

"Not that I mind. She and her friend Pat, whom I also met at her party, they seem to have things pretty well figured out for themselves, how to live their lives and such."

"But that's not the life for you?"

"Heavens, no! I need a man in my life. My father was my greatest influence there. Wish you could have met him."

"Past tense?"

"He died, two weeks before my nineteenth birthday. I was crushed."

"So, Nick is the new father figure?" Tom bit his tongue when he said that. "Sorry."

"Hah! My father would have sent him packing."

"Then why—if you don't mind my asking—are you marrying him?"

"Because he's so persistent, like this puppy dog here." She laughed. "Always wagging his tail!"

"And you can't say no to a lovable, tail-wagging puppy dog. I understand."

"No, you don't. Let me tell you something." She sat up. "There comes a time in a girl's life when it's sink or swim, shit or get off the pot, if she wants to get married and have a family. All about that clock running down. And a girl could do a helluva lot worse than Nicholas Grady."

Tom gave her a serious look. "We'll let that go, for the moment."

They took a walk in the afternoon, the pup on the leash half pulled, half carried, down to the waterfront. They found a bench and sat down.

Across from the footpath, the lake lapped quietly over shiny pebbles. The sun was beginning to touch the ridges of the distant mountains. The air was calm, fragrant with the scent of blossoms of cherry trees and lilac bushes.

Emily was leaning her head against Tom's "good" arm that was straddling the back of the bench. "Aah." she breathed, "just being here is therapeutic."

"It's heaven," Tom said.

"Tom? Exactly why didn't I stay pregnant, was it something I did or didn't do?"

"Well, for one thing, you didn't even know that you were pregnant."

She shook her head vehemently. "Never crossed my mind! I just thought I was late, due to all that stress of the St. Petersburg situation."

"That stress may well have been a contributing factor."

"Contributing to my losing the baby, you mean?"

"Look," he pulled his arm back and turned to face her. "That wasn't a baby you lost, let's get our terminology straight. It would have become a baby if you had carried it into the third trimester. In your case, the fertilized egg, the embryo, traveling down the tube into your uterus, somehow failed to achieve complete nidation."

"Whoa, whoa, hold it. Complete what?"

"Nesting, anchoring itself to the tissue, for nourishment and growth. So it eventually came loose, and had to be surgically removed. That's what happened. Now, you may well ask if your transfer to Russia caused this malfunction. After all, if you had known you were pregnant, you would probably not have gone there but taken special care of yourself, and so on."

Emily nodded. "Probably."

"Then again, it might not have made any difference. Spontaneous first-trimester losses can be self-corrective. I mean, statistics show that from one-third to over one-half of them were caused by glitches in the embryonic development. In other words, Mother Nature looks after young mothers and stops what would otherwise not work out well. Perhaps you ought to be glad, Emily."

She leaned her head back against his shoulder. "Tell me more."

"That's it, essentially."

"You are telling me I could have had a defective baby."

"Hmm. Could have, yes."

"Whose fault would that have been? Mine, because I didn't take care of myself? Or if it would have happened anyhow, was it genetic?"

"You are a healthy young woman, and women have been able to carry all the way to term even under the most harrowing circumstances. So I would question the stressfulness of your job as being the cause. As for genetic, who knows? Now, if you were to repeatedly abort early, and given the same sperm donor, then it could be argued that genetic defects play a role."

"Whose defect, mine or the man's?"

Tom shrugged. "Hard to tell."

"Oh no, you're not going to get off that easy, Tom!" She sat up to face him squarely. "What if a different donor, as you so delicately put it, were involved, and I delivered a fine healthy baby: That would absolve my genetics, wouldn't it? And what, to prove my point, if I chose a donor with a proven capacity to father a healthy child. My odds would improve, wouldn't they, Tom?"

Tom protested, "You know that this is an inherently unfair question, Emily. If I say yes to it, it would be patently self-serving, because I have fathered a healthy child, and you know that I have."

"I don't see where that is unfair. Unfair to whom?"

"To your fiancee. He might stand wrongly indicted."

"Don't let that worry you. Nick is my business. I'll take care of it."

Later, that night, in bed, Emily's voice rose in the darkness.

"Tom? Are you awake?"

"Ha-ha. Funny question."

"What did you mean, when you said that you were carrying a torch for me? I wasn't exactly the image of female pulchritude when we first met."

"I had seen you before."

"You had? When? You must tell me!"

He hesitated. How could he possibly explain. "Well," he said, "it's more of an image I've had of you."

"Tell me," her voice was husky, a whisper almost that barely carried across the room to his bed.

"It was last July, in the airline lounge at Los Angeles airport. You happened to sit down across from me, waiting for your flight."

"More, tell me more."

"I was struck by your whole appearance . . . smart, elegant, beautiful . . . totally struck . . . and I felt awful about that, because it was just a week after my wife's death, but I couldn't get you out of my mind."

"What did I do?"

"Nothing, leafing through a magazine. I stared at you across the top of my newspaper. Couldn't get my eyes off you. I fantasized we would be on the same flight, perhaps even seated together, what I would say to you. Then your flight was called, to New York, not to Washington, like mine. And you got up and left."

"That's true, I was in Santa Barbara in July, at my mother's. And I took a Sunday flight back to New York. My God, why didn't I notice you! You know, we are so trained in New York to avoid eye contact."

"It's okay. We did meet, after all."

After a while, she spoke again. "Tom? Come over to my bed, for a while? I want you closer to me." When he complied, padding through the darkness until he bumped against her bed and she lifted the covers for him, she said, "I am inaccessible as a woman, for the time being, but that doesn't have to mean we can't be close and caring. Does it, Tom?"

He didn't answer, just lied down beside her, sideways, his injured arm across her midriff. When she turned her head their lips met and they kissed, very tenderly, just for a moment. With a sigh, Emily said, "Tom, there is so much I want to ask. You mustn't mind."

He shook his head.

"Tell me about your wife. Would you? Could you? Please."

He nodded.

"What was her name?"

"Natalie Goldsmith . . . Nettie . . . a California girl, she went to UC Davis for her vet degree, but we met at a horse show in Virginia."

"Love at first sight?"

"Yes. And we went to bed on the second date."

"What'd she look like?"

"Oh, hard to describe . . . quite beautiful."

"Try. What film actress did she most resemble?"

He searched for the answer, until he said, "Greta Scacchi."

"Really!" Emily seemed to have an immediate image. "I know her, I mean—I have met her! At a party when the film 'The Player' came out in New York! I actually talked with her, someone had annoyed her, and she made a remark about him under her breath, in French, and I replied in French, agreeing with her. We talked for a while, and we kind of both liked each other. I can't believe you said Greta Scacchi! This is weird, Tom, because she is not that big a star! You could've picked, oh, like any one of the really big movie stars."

"Like Madonna."

"Yech! Get outta here!"

"Is that an order?"

"Not just yet. I want you to make me a promise, though—that we will discuss Nettie in a nice, normal manner, whenever her name comes up, so she doesn't hang like a ghost over us in our life. Because Nettie is dead, Tom."

"I know. And yes, I agree, we must be able to talk about Nettie without qualms. I know she is dead, believe me I know. One day I will tell you how she died. And why I am here in Europe, and how that all hangs together." He leaned over and kissed her. "You have no idea what this talk means to me. The words, the way you have expressed yourself. It gives me great hope. G'night, Em. Sweet dreams. See you in the morning." He left her side and went back to bed.

He heard the phone ring while he was shaving, a shrill, old-fashioned bell-ringing tone until Emily picked it up. A brief response by her, and then she poked her head into the bathroom. "It's for you, Tom. Your friend Charles. The one you missed in Munich? Tax, or whatever you call him?"

Tom laughed. "Cab! Thanks." He wiped the lather off his face and went to the phone. "Hiya, Kiddo! Finally. How goes it?"

"Finally, my foot! I had to get your sister involved to track you down. We missed each other on Sunday. This is Thursday, what gives?"

"The strike, Cab. And more. I'll be back in London probably Saturday or Sunday. I'll e-mail you from there. I take it you are back in New York."

"Yes. Give it to me in a nutshell. Mission accomplished?"

"It was, but not the way we figured it. The Creep's dead. The Duke's guy did it. I have it all on tape."

"Geez, Tom, this is an open line!"

"I don't care. We didn't do anything illegal, Cab. Remember that."

"Who's the broad in the room with you? I know it's not Freddie. She left messages on my tape, twice."

"Haven't you talked to Freddie? She was with us until we crossed into France."

"She had to fly home, to Seattle. Something to do with her father." Cab sighed. "I guess you're not going to tell me why you are in Switzerland, and with whom. Huh?"

"Sure I am. Emily Dessauer. My mother's account executive at MetroBank? She was stuck at the Munich airport, too. We picked up Freddie in Baden-Baden and drove into France trying to get to Paris. Emily had an accident—a minor operation. Freddie went on to Paris, and I took Emily to my sister's time-share place here in Coppet, at Lake Geneva, for her to recuperate."

There was a moment's silence at the other end. "I can't believe what I'm hearing, Tom. We gotta talk. As soon as you are back."

Emily, who had followed Tom's responses with increasing curiosity, asked, "Let me talk to him?" and when Tom handed over the receiver, said, "Mr. Blumenfeld? This is Emily Dessauer."

"Yes? Hi!"

"Would you say that you are Tom's best friend, Mr. Blumenfeld?"

"Absolutely. Best and oldest."

"Good. I'd like to meet you when I'm back in the States."

"Glad to! I'd like to meet you too, Miss Dessauer."

"We'd be talking business, Mr. Blumenfeld."

"Of course," he replied, but it was Tom who caught that, Emily had given the phone back to him.

"Cab?" he said. "I hope you gave me a good reference!"

"Hey, let's stop kidding around. She's the woman, right?"

"Right." Tom grinned silently and pointed to the phone in his hand, but Emily had left the room.

"Right. We'll take it from there when you get back. When will that be, after London? Give me a timetable."

"Oh, I would hope by the weekend following. Early May. I'll call you."

They both said good-bye and hung up.

When he went looking for Emily he found her on the patio, hunkered down feeding the puppy bits of dog food. She looked up. "I thought it was my mother when the phone rang. I had called her yesterday to tell her where I was." She straightened up. "Naturally, she wanted to know the whys and wherefors."

"Naturally," Tom nodded. "Let me finish shaving, and you can have the bathroom."

Emily raised her eyebrows. "Don't you want to know what I told her?"

"Only if you want to tell me."

"I told her I was being robbed blind in St. Petersburg, that I was quitting the bank, that I met you in Munich, that I fell ill in France, that you are a doctor and took care of me, that we are now at your sister's place in Coppet. And I gave her the auberge phone number and address."

"You didn't mention the miscarriage?"

"No! That has to remain confidential between us, Tom!"

"No problem. Who did you say I was, other than a doctor?"

"A friend. That we had met in New York, bumped into each other again at the airport in Munich. About the strike, that you had a car, how we were trying to drive to Paris—the works. With certain deletions. Such as Freddie."

"You must have had quite a talk!"

"My mother, Angelique, she never stops asking questions. Tom, I want to tell you about her. There are certain things you should know."

Tom put his arm around her waist. "Come with me. Use the shower while I shave, and talk to me." When she looked at him a bit doubtfully, he said, "If you need rinsing off, call on me. I've been trained by an expert—Freddie."

"Freddie!" Emily protested. "That's no recommendation!"

"No, but it's the truth. Part of my incredible journey."

They were both pleasantly surprised, without saying so, that they felt natural in their almost-bareness together. Tom finished shaving and combing his hair before Emily was out of the tub. Wrapped in a towel, he sat on the closed toilet seat and said to Emily, who was wringing out her hair, "Do you still want to talk, or shall I leave you for the moment?"

"Bring me a towel, would you?" She turned off the water.

Tom held a bath towel open for her and let her wrap herself in it. Then he held her close to him. "Maybe I should start. I love you, Emily. Deeply. From my heart."

She put her arms around his neck. "I love you, too. No bull. Honest."

He gave her a quick kiss, and laughed. "There! We talked! That wasn't so hard, now, was it?"

She was serious. "The hard part is still to come. Why don't you go and get dressed, order breakfast. I'll be out soon. Then drive me somewhere where it's truly beautiful and we will remember it forever, and we'll talk."

Tom consulted a guide he found in the reception room and suggested they drive along the lake to Morges, which proclaimed itself the "wine-growing center of the Vaud Coast." It'd be only a half hour away if they took the toll road, and not much more if they meandered along the old coastal highway.

They chose the latter. Emily, the dog on her lap, her complexion rosy, her eyes sparkling, proclaimed herself "much, much better." She said she was ready to do some serious shopping. "Clothes, Tom! I have hardly anything to wear, except this stylish, steel-gray Bavarian jogging suit!"

They stopped in Nyon, and while Tom went to buy a camera—ending up with one of those disposable ones complete with film and flash—Emily went to a local couture shop. She came out in a simple, long dress that hugged her figure as much as it disguised it, and carrying parcels in each hand.

"Ta-da!" she exclaimed, spreading her arms.

Tom took a picture. "Marvelous!" he said, and took another one.

They drove leisurely along the lake, through one village after another, none of which seemed very rustic anymore but rather reminded Emily of the secluded "beach houses" in the Hamptons.

"Let's go down one of those lanes and see if the properties all go to the waterfront," she suggested. "And take some pictures."

"Why?" he asked. "Want to buy one?" He made a right turn.

"Who knows," she smiled.

There was nothing much to see when they reached the lake shore. But yes, the properties seemed to extend to the water. They pulled over and got out of the car. Emily wanted to take a closer look. There was a rusty gate on their left, it creaked when they pushed it open. A much overgrown footpath snaked down to a dock with a boat shack on shore. There was not a soul around. Up to their left they could see a house, half hidden by large trees.

"We are trespassing!" Tom said.

"It's beautiful! Isn't it? Look at those mountains across the lake! What are they?"

"Those would be the Savoy Alps," Tom guessed.

"Let's take a picture of us. First you, then me." They took several.

"Come," Emily said then, and walked on down to the dock. Tom followed.

At the shack Emily tried the door and it, too, gave way. There was the hull of a small sailboat leaning against one wall. The sails lay folded on the planks of the shack. There was utter quiet, except for the faint sound of water lapping underneath the floor boards. The air was warm and dank.

Emily turned to Tom. "Now tell me again that you love me, Tom."

He took her in his arms. "I love you, Emily." His voice grew husky.

They kissed, tentatively at first, their lips touching and parting, then more urgently. "I love you, Tom," she breathed, "I love you, I love you."

They could not explain, later, what they had done, and how they had done it. They had made love, right down there on the sails that they covered with Emily's new dress, having both shed all their clothing, clinging to each other as they moaned and shuddered, trying to avoid penetration. They sat up, half dazed, smiled a silly smile, kissed, got up and dressed. Holding hands, they made their way back to the car, climbed in, turned it around and drove off.

At the end of the lane, Emily decided that the pup needed a walk. She sneaked around to the front gate with him, and made a note of the address. "You were right," she said coming back, "I may want to buy it. Our Swiss retreat."

In Morges they found a restaurant, vine-covered and half empty, where they took lunch. Tom ordered a hearty local red wine to go with the roast beef. "It'll help build up your blood, Emily. Here's to your health."

They clinked glasses. "And to yours. It goes together."

"Like a horse and carriage?" he smiled.

She nodded. "You know the next line. Do you think it will work for us, love and marriage?"

"Do you doubt it?"

"I don't doubt it. I fear it might possibly not come about."

"Why?"

Emily twisted the stem of her glass around. "Because of what you don't know about me—facts that might turn you off."

Tom stopped her fiddling and took her hands in his. "Tell me."

She sighed. "For starters, I am Jewish."

Tom couldn't help a short laugh, "So what else is new?"

"You don't understand. I was brought up Catholic, but secretly my father and I had me bat mitzvahed. When my mother found out about it, she was terribly hurt. She was a simple French-Alsatian country girl who was hired as a nanny to my father's two small sons when his first wife was dying. He ended up marrying her, and as he told me, one of the promises he made her was that she wouldn't have to convert and that I, her daughter, wouldn't, either. But I did it, to please my father. If nothing else, that'll give you an insight into my character. I don't think my mother has really trusted me ever since."

Tom said nothing, and she disengaged her hands. "Look at these!" She held them out. "Long fingers! I grew up training to be a concert pianist. By age eighteen I placed fifth at the Cliburn piano competition. My mother was ecstatic. Then I decided I wanted to study business, learn from my father, and attend Stanford and Harvard. Get an MBA. My father was pleased." She took a sip from her wine. "He died, while I was still in my freshman year."

"I am sorry for you, Em," Tom said. "I lost my father, too, when I was still a kid."

"Then you know," she said. They turned to the food that was being served, and ate quietly.

Over coffee, Tom smiled and said, "Well, I survived your two secrets, Emily."

But she was still in a serious mood, "Oh, that wasn't all! Here's the kicker. My father, the daredevil RCAF pilot from World War Two and penniless immigrant from Montreal, had made a lot of money, mostly in the construction field and later as a movie financier. He left each of his children a multi-million dollar trust fund, and to my mother he left twice that, plus his business. Now, it doesn't take a genius to figure out that if all you do is invest in the DJIA, you'd have tripled or quadrupled your money in the last ten to twelve years. Just off her money, my mother earns about three hundred thousand dollars a month."

Tom had to laugh, "That's about five times what I earned as an Army doctor, in a year."

"Right! You get the point. She built herself a twenty thousand square foot chateau right on the ocean in Santa Barbara. She has started a new venture, a profit-making symphony orchestra of all things, and she always gets her way. Right now, she wants me to marry Nick, because he's suitable, in every respect. Also, his firm looks after her legal matters. It suits Angelique that I marry him. And up to now I couldn't think of a better choice, myself."

"Up until now, as you say. Until you and I connected, by chance or by providence," Tom said. "So I don't see what your mother's wealth has to do with us, the two of us living our life."

"Have you ever had a lot of money, I mean really a lot?"

"No."

"Then you don't know what I am talking about. It distorts everything, it makes everything too easy, and in the end worthless. It's awful. And it's nice, too. For instance, I could buy that house at the lake we've just been to, just like that." She snapped her fingers.

Tom caught her hands again. "Emily, listen. I can see where that's a problem for you, which would make it mine as well. I have no easy answer. We'll just have to work with it or around it. There'll be other problems. I have one, right now. It has to do with knowledge I have to withhold from you at this point, because you're better off not knowing than knowing all."

"What do you mean?"

"My wife's death. She didn't die by accident, she was murdered."

Emily's eyes widened. "Murdered! Good Lord, Tom!"

"Yes. Cab and I have been on the trail of the culprit."

"Is that the creep you mentioned on the phone this morning?"

"Oh, you heard. There you go. That is what we have to guard against, that you don't become involved unwittingly. The matter is essentially resolved. We have to let some grass grow over the thing. Then, when it's safe, and you are my wife, I'll tell you the whole story."

"I can wait," she said and sent him a kiss with her finger. Then she added, "I thought your main concern was whether I would get along with your son. I don't think you need to worry about that. I love kids, and I'll love him too. Not to mention that we might have kids of our own. Right?"

"That's it then," Tom said and leaned over to kiss her. "Glad you accepted my proposal, Emily, my love."

"Oh?" she winked at him. "I thought I was proposing to you!"

They toured a winery up on a hill, sampled some of the vintages and grew increasingly more relaxed. Back on the street in Morges, they happened to pass a veterinary office and instantly stepped inside, Emily carrying Guy.

A conversation in French ensued. The pup was examined, weighed, given shots and pronounced in good health. To their surprise, the doctor declared Guy to be a pure-bred wirehair dachshund, and so stated on the certificate he handed Emily, who was listed as the owner on Tom's insistence.

Outside again, Emily protested. "He is our dog, Tom, not just mine!"

Tom shook his head. "He will be ours when we are together. Meantime, he's yours. If you want him?"

She cuddled the dog to her chest. "Do I!"

It was late afternoon when they returned to the auberge. Tom took the parcels and walked towards the entrance while Emily grabbed the puppy, who was making a game of it, from the back seat. Tom pushed through the door with his back and held it open with his foot. A stately flaxen-haired woman was standing at the reception desk talking animatedly in French to Madame Auger, then turned around when Madame Auger said something and pointed in Tom's direction.

Emily came through the door and Tom withdrew his foot to let it close.

"Mother!" Emily shrieked.

The older woman smiled broadly and approached arms open. "Emily, cherie," she said and the two women embraced, with Emily bending forward to protect the dog. Madame Auger wore the beatific expression of a Murillo duena.

He packed his few things immediately. He rang for Madame Auger to settle his bill, but was told that the account had been taken care of. Angelique, of course. He went to the Audi.

Within minutes, he was on the National-1 throughway and gunned the car to one hundred fifty. He was past Lausanne as he fiddled with the radio until he found some music he wanted—piano, Mendelssohn—and his heart ached. Em! He had now driven past Montreux, next, Bern. After midnight he connected with the N-2 and made the environs of Basel. In the city center he found a parkhaus near the railway station and put the Audi in there. The keys and the parking stub he locked into the trunk, the lease papers he took with him. He would phone Auto-Hansli from London and tell Manfred where he could pick up the car.

There was a train from the station to the airport, as he had expected. The Euro-Airport Basel/Mulhouse was located across the border in France. The train took twenty minutes to get there. He marched straight to the British Air counter and bought himself a ticket on the early morning flight to London. He had less than five hours to kill, which he spent in the frequent-flyer lounge of the airline, drinking coffee and reading newspapers. The German strike was over, everything would be back to normal in a few days. He said a quiet prayer of thanks for the strike. Without it, he and Emily would not have met. The miracle would not have happened. Or would it have, anyhow?

And by morning, he would knock on Bettina's door, and probably take Bertie to school. It was only Friday.

A new day was dawning when he hurried to the gate for his flight home.

The T-Factor

Within a week after Tom's return to London it became clear that Tom would not return to the States right away. There were a couple of good reasons for not rushing it, one concerning Bertie, the other Emily.

Bertie had done so well in his pre-school class, had matured so much in his speech and social skills that Bettina's argument to leave the boy be until Tom had found a permanent home somewhere had made sense. After all, it wouldn't do the boy any good to move back in with his grandmother Watson in New York, nor with his Aunt Laura if they went straight to Southern California.

Emily had weighed in with the proposition that the next time Bertie was relocated it should be with his own family, his Dad and his Dad's new wife who would also be the kid's new mother. In any case, Emily would be looking for a house for them to lease. There would be no need to rush home until mid-June.

"And what about all those preparations for our wedding? Shouldn't I be involved in some way?" Tom had asked. They were talking on the phone almost daily since Emily's return to Santa Barbara with her mother.

Emily had laughed. "What preparations? My mother has hired a professional company to look after all that. Just keep the seventeenth of June clear on your calendar, if we want a rehearsal dinner, and be sure you be here on the eighteenth when I walk down the aisle! Promise?"

"Cross my heart. Bertie and I will take the red-eye from London."

That conversation took place exactly a week to the day they had parted in Coppet. Tom was still amazed at the speed with which things were changing in his life, and in hers, too, considering that Emily had to break off her engagement to Nick, after she had convinced her mother that the one and only man she wanted to marry was that disheveled medic last seen lying drunk on the lobby sofa of the L'Auberge du Soleil. It had, or so Tom surmised from the tone of Emily's voice, been a battle royal until Angelique gave in. In perfect follow-up, Emily pushed for a middle of June wedding date. Then she flew to New York to terminate her employment with MetroBank.

Cab was none too pleased, either, with Tom's late return to the States. Using their e-mail system, he badgered him to at least take a weekend off and fly to New York for "a debriefing." "I am getting some money back from your pal Manfred at Auto Hansli—as well I should, seeing that the car wasn't used for more than a week. That would pay for your airfare. By the way, did you know there was a bike in the trunk?"

"Yes," Tom hit on the keys. "I'll explain at the debriefing. Which we'll have to do via the information highway, Cab, because I'm not leaving Bertie again. I was going to put all the stuff on a floppy, anyway, for the record."

"Okay," Cab replied, and signed off. Earlier, when Tom had asked him, he had agreed to be his best man. "I guess that's the only way I'll meet the bride, before she becomes Mrs. Vonder Campe!"

As it turned out, Cab was wrong on that point. The following Monday he received a telephone call from Emily who told him she was in New York for a few days, and would there be a chance to get together.

"Of course!" Cab was delighted. "When? Where? You name it!"

They settled on lunch, the next day, at the Hotel Plaza Athenee where Emily was staying.

Cab was floored when he saw her. Her quiet elegance, her natural beauty, and her self-assured manner won him over immediately.

"I must say, Miss Dessauer," he said when they were seated, "of all the women I have met, you are top echelon. Tom is one lucky feller."

Emily laughed. "I've never been called an echelon before. Thank you, Mr. Blumenfeld, for this first!"

Over aperitifs, Emily came straight to the point. Based, she said, on the complete confidence her future husband had in him, she would like to acquaint him with a problem that she would want to prevent from becoming a stumbling block in the future. The problem, she said, was money, the fact that she had a lot, and that Tom, as far as she knew, had little.

"None, is more accurate to say." Cab shook his head. "Is that the business you wanted to discuss with me when we talked on the phone while you were still in Switzerland?"

Emily nodded. "Yes."

"Are we talking—let me be blunt—prenuptial agreement?"

"Yes. Except the other way around. I want you to explore the possibilities that may exist for Tom to become involved in my holdings, without it becoming a huge tax problem. Could you do that, Cab? May I call you Cab? That's what we call you anyway, when Tom and I talk. And of course, I'm Emily."

"Sure, Emily. Yes. But why would you want to do that? Why not just move along gradually, California being a community property state, half of what you own and earn accrues to your husband."

She nodded, "But I want him to have discretion over some of my funds now, in case of an emergency, for instance. And also, I think Tom is not too interested in money."

"You are right there. He isn't. He is very frugal. And when he has some money, he spends it, mostly on others."

"Well, there you are. That's what I am getting at. I want to hire your expertise. I need someone who is intimately familiar with my future family's business affairs, someone we can always come to for advice."

"I am flattered that you, a financial expert yourself, should think that way of me. I'm signing on!" He handed her a couple of his business cards.

Smiling, she took them, and they shook hands across the table. A fee was never mentioned, although it was implicit in their understanding.

Over rare roast beef the question came up of what Tom had been up to in Europe. She said that she knew that Cab, himself, had also been involved. But Cab declined to discuss it, on the grounds that he was bound to a confidentiality agreement with Tom.

That frustrated Emily. "Don't you think that I am entitled to know?" she asked.

"Yes, you are. But the when and how is up to Tom. Meantime, it'd probably be best to let some grass grow over it, Emily."

"Exactly the phrase Tom used!" she grimaced. "What grass, and over what? That's what I want to know!"

On the way out of the dining room, she asked, making it sound casual, "How is Freddie doing? All right?"

"You know," Cab said, "I haven't seen or talked to her since she got back! She had to fly home to Seattle, according to the message she left on my phone. Something to do with her family."

"Well," Emily gave him a sly look, "I slept with her, too, in a manner of speaking, in Baden-Baden!"

"Did you!" Cab half smiled and stopped. They were in the lobby and they kept their voices low.

"Yes. That makes three of us. Sort of binds us together, you and Tom and me. Don't you think?"

Cab's voice was calm but there was a glint in his eyes. "No, I don't, Emily. Freddie is my girlfriend, so we don't just send out for Chinese and watch Letterman when we are together. Freddie volunteered to work with me, on the basis of very limited knowledge, in getting Tom's problem solved over there. I suspect, as you do, that when she and Tom shared that room, she may have persuaded him to make love to her. She is a very natural girl, and Tom has been living a celibate life since Nettie died. Bear in mind, that was before Tom had any idea he would meet you. Do you wish to blame him or her?"

Emily blushed. "No, I don't. I am sorry I brought it up." She touched his arm. "I see I can expect to get good advice from you, Cab. Bye for now. I'll call you, okay?" She turned quickly and walked to the elevators.

Cab shook his head as he walked out on 64th Street. That woman would take some getting used to.

Emily plunked her briefcase on the bed when she reached her room. It was bloody frustrating, she grumbled to herself, that neither of the "boys," as she called Tom and Cab, would talk to her about what had gone on in Europe, and inasmuch as Tom had already said that it had to do with Nettie's death, and that she had been murdered, which was shocking enough in itself, she didn't see why she couldn't be told the rest of it.

She resolved to insist on it, next time she was face to face with her intended, although, she had to smile, that might not be the first thing they'd get into, right then . . .

She zipped open her briefcase and took out her computer, a new one with a better system and more power than the one stolen from her in Russia. The bank had been very generous in replacing what she had lost, as well as in matters relating to her leaving employment. They were negotiating a long-term leave of absence, that would restore her the same standing if and when she should decide to reenter full-time employment. Emily liked that idea. From her father she had learned never to burn all her bridges, in case she had to recross one some day. She considered it totally inconceivable that she would recross one of them, though—the Nicholas Grady bridge. That one she burned with a vengeance. She did not say so, but in her heart of hearts she could not forgive Nick that he had made her pregnant, and left her ignorant about it.

There was a sheaf of messages she had taken with her from the office, she would call back from her room, that being more private than whatever place the bank had to offer her. Plus, she could kick off her shoes and slouch while talking. And later, by 4:00 P.M., she would call Tom in London. They had last talked on Saturday. She missed hearing his voice.

The first calls were dully routine. The insurance carrier, regarding her baggage loss claim, the airline—still diddling about the unused portion of her ticket, the pension department of MetroBank in Stamford, and so on. She was getting bored. Just in time, she remembered that she had promised Tom to call his mother. She had called Mrs. Watson often in the past, when she was still her account manager. It would be weird to talk to her now as her future daughter-in-law. Tom had already told his mother about them, and had reported no adverse reaction. Still, she had a funny feeling in her stomach when she dialed the Watson residence number. What if the Yankee aristocrat did not like her as a member of her family?

She need not have worried. With a genuinely warm and cordial voice, Mrs. Watson welcomed her back. She invited her to come over "for tea, for dinner, for breakfast—any or all, you pick, Emily dear!" They settled for dinner the next evening. Whew!

More cheerfully, she picked the next message. It was from a June Wild, and a 202 area code. That was Washington, D.C. She knew nobody by the name June or Wild. Most likely someone's secretary. She remembered that the Sol Pasternak estate, the heirs of which had been "orphaned" to her account service, had a D.C. law firm. There was no point in calling back from her hotel room, in the office tomorrow, she'd go to the file and at the same time transfer it to her hard disk.

Come to think of it, she stuffed the remaining messages back into her briefcase, she might as well do all the others in the morning. Right now she would do what she had become accustomed to doing since her return from Coppet—lie down for an afternoon nap. Her overriding ambition was to become well, so well that she would conceive and carry a healthy baby to full term. In ten days she had an appointment with Dr. Fallon, soon after she'd expect her period to return. And in mid-June she'd be married. She sighed and sank into the pillows. They would not have a traditional honeymoon. She and Tom had agreed that they had outgrown the turtle-dove aspect of it, just as they wouldn't leave the wedding party with tin cans tied to the car bumper. Instead, with Bertie in tow, they would go away for two weeks as a family, probably to Hawaii. They would learn to live with each other, and love each other as husband and wife, and Mom and Dad and kid, and Mom and baby-to-be.

At four o'clock her order for tea was brought to the room. Emily poured herself a sweet cup and bit into a croissant as she dialed London. It would be past Bertie's bedtime there.

It was Bettina who picked up the phone, and they had a nice chat, mostly about the wedding. Bettina asked Emily what she really, truly wished as a wedding gift.

Emily laughed, "Your brother, Bettina! And your sisterly love!"

"But you have that already, Emily! Think of a truly memorable gift, this side of the crown jewels."

"How about the Blarney stone?"

Tom cut in from the upstairs extension. "Hello, sweatheart!"

"Hello, Tom!" the women mocked in unison. Bettina hung up, laughing.

"All right. Hi, Em. I miss you. Let me tell you what I think is the most attractive part of your body."

"Tom!"

"Your face. Especially the part that goes from the tip of your nose to your chin. Your lower mandible pushes slightly forward, which causes your mouth, when you smile, to curve upward in the most endearing way. Other parts are in close competition, but we won't discuss those today. So, what's new?"

"Oh geez, Tom. I'm all alone here, in a New York hotel room, with a view of 64th Street. Don't do this to me!" Then she told him of her meeting with Cab and that she hired him as her financial advisor. "I want him, as time goes by, to trust me the same way he trusts you, and vice versa. And by the way, he hasn't heard from or seen Freddie at all since she got back. Can you imagine? She's said to be with her family in Seattle. Have you heard from her?"

Tom said he hadn't, and not to worry. Freddie was a free spirit, and she would turn up again one day, or not. Either way, it wouldn't matter to them.

Emily went on to tell him of having been invited to dinner the next evening with Mrs. Watson, and Tom said she'd better practice saying "Mother" to her. The conversation turned to the latest on Bertie, and a bonus mention of Guy both of whom, thank-the-Lord, seemed to be thriving. Before they rang off, Tom promised he'd call tomorrow at his mother's place, and that he would be at his best behavior and not mention any of Emily's body parts. Emily said "Hah!" and sent him kisses over the phone.

In the office the next morning, Emily pulled the Pasternak file and dialed the Washington, D.C. number. To the switchboard voice she gave the extension number and was instantly put through.

"A.T., two section, June Wild speaking."

"Oh, hello. This is Emily Dessauer, of MetroBank. I am returning your call?"

"Miss Dessauer, thank you for calling back. I'll connect you now."

Emily heard some click-clack and then a male voice, "Miss Dessauer! Good of you to return my call. I hope you are not too surprised to hear from me!"

"May I ask with whom I am speaking?"

"Oh, I'm sorry. Didn't June mention it? I am Thad Montgomery. The A.T. dash two section head."

"Section head, what's the name of your firm?"

"Firm? Miss Dessauer, this is the Federal Bureau of Investigation. I am beginning to think you don't know that!"

"The FBI? Does this have to do with the Pasternak estate?" Dumb question, she cursed silently. The bank switchboard had resorted lately to just giving names and numbers on the message pads. The FBI!

"I'm sorry. Let me explain. I am the agent who has talked a couple of times with your future husband, Major Thomas Campe."

Tom? Tom has talked to the FBI? "I had no idea."

"No, of course not. That's as it should be, and that's why I am taking the initiative of contacting you. I want you to feel free to talk to me."

"Talk to you about what?" She felt her voice tightening up on her.

Montgomery cleared his throat. "Perhaps this conversation is a bit premature. I had presumed that you had some cursory knowledge of the circumstances of Natalie Campe's death."

Emily took a deep breath and forced herself to be calm. "Tom, my future husband, to use your phrase, has told me that his wife's death occurred under dubious circumstances, and that at a later date he'll tell me more. That's all right with me. We have other matters that are more pressing, such as preparations for our wedding next month, which will take place on June eighteenth in Los Angeles. After which we will vacation in Hawaii for two weeks. In case Tom hasn't told you that."

"Tom hasn't told me much of anything, Miss Dessauer."

"What? Then how did you get my name and number, Mr. Montgomery?"

"From Frederika Lindenstromberg. Freddie, as we all know her. It was her report that prompted me to contact you."

"Freddie!" Emily almost screamed that name. "Freddie reported to you?"

"Not directly. Her father is our bureau chief in Seattle. On her return from Europe she confided in him, because she thinks that there may be an unknown element of danger, both to you and to Tom. Her father forwarded the report to me. I consider her remarks to be prescient and in some areas congruent with our own findings. It was on that basis that I contacted you."

Emily held on for a few seconds, before she replied. "Mr. Montgomery, I will not continue this conversation with you. I will speak to my fiancee again tonight; he is still in London, which I am sure is not news to you—and we will see where we go from here. I, we, may wish to consult with counsel."

"Of course, Miss Dessauer. It would certainly be preferable if both of you could be present in our next discussion."

"Good-bye, Mr. Montgomery." She replaced the receiver, but her hand was shaking when she released her grip. Freddie the bitch—a snitch? Wow! Did Tom know that? Only one way to find out. She looked at her watch. It would be mid-afternoon in London. It was highly unlikely he'd be home. Usually he and Bertie spent time in the parks and playgrounds at this hour. She tried the phone anyhow, and predictably got the answering machine. She left the message that she had an important matter to discuss with him and that he should call her after 10:00 P.M. New York time, at her hotel. In his call to his mother earlier that evening, he should merely confirm that he would do so.

Then she thought of Cab. Freddie was Cab's girlfriend, had he lied when he said at lunch that he hadn't heard from Freddie? Were the two of them in cahoots, or was Cab duped, too? There was only one way to find out—confront him with what she had just learned. Immediately.

She took his business card out of her purse. His office was not far to hers. She would walk over and not even call first. Hit him with the facts, boom slam, and watch his reaction.

By the time she had pushed her way up Fifth Avenue and reached the Gump Tower her agitation had abated somewhat. Taking the escalator to the third level, the cool splashings of the giant waterfall sculpture helped to put her into a more serene mood. There was no point in presuming the worst about Cab. But she would be watching him and his reactions, closely.

From the outer office she rang and gave her name. The door was opened almost instantly, by a very surprised Cab, in shirtsleeves and silk suspenders and a glittering checkerboard tie. "Emily, you are here, already?" His astonishment was genuine, and quickly explained: He had left a message at her office suggesting that they have another meeting before she left for home.

"Another meeting? What about, Cab?" Emily asked as he ushered her into his private office

"About selling you some insurance!" Cab grinned. "No, really! It would make a lot of sense. You apply, say for a million of term. Would cost you less than a thou a year. I immediately acquire a data bank on you, on everything from your date of birth to your health and financial record. It also makes me your official agent, which can extend into other areas. And the commission, we'll blow it on dinner at Lutece."

"Cab," Emily said, looking straight at him. "Let me tell you why I am here. I had a call this morning, from a Mr. Montgomery in Washington. Does that name ring a bell?"

Cab's smile disappeared. "From the FBI?"

She nodded. "Apparently you know him."

"Not personally. I know that Tom had dealings with him."

"What kind of dealings?"

He squirmed a bit. "That gets us back to what you asked me yesterday. I cannot say more than what I said then, Emily. Try to understand."

"But you could tell Freddie. Freddie knows, doesn't she?"

"Not a hell of a lot, no! What's going on here, Emily?"

"Oh, nothing much." She made a hand gesture. "Since Freddie doesn't know a hell of a lot. So why worry, that she blabbed it all to the FBI?"

"What?" He grabbed her by the shoulders. "Freddie talked to the FBI?"

"Hah! Talked? She wrote a report to the FBI, about your goings-on in Europe. Wherein I appear, and certainly Tom, and probably you. Neat, huh?"

Cab released her and sat against the edge of his desk. "I can't believe this. Why would Freddie do that?" He seemed genuinely baffled, even shocked.

"Well, for one thing, because her dad is the FBI chief in Seattle. You knew that, didn't you? Data bank? You must have sold her some insurance!"

"No, to both of your questions." He shook his head. "I'm not going to ask you if you believe me or not. You've got to make up your own mind about that." He gave her a searching look. "You may leave now, Emily, with your doubts and anger and I wouldn't blame you. Or you stick around a while, and we'll try to figure out what's going on here. Your choice."

She sighed. "There's no point in my leaving. And almost no point in my staying, either, as long as you are bound to your confidentiality oath, or whatever. Don't you see? I am in it with you but I know nothing! Even the FBI guy was surprised about that!"

"What did he want from you?"

"I think he wanted to find out what I knew. And he wanted to slip it to me that Freddie had talked. He accomplished his mission."

"How did you leave it?"

"That I would talk no further, that I would take the matter up with Tom, that I would want counsel present the next time."

"Good girl!" Cab straightened up and went around to the phone on his desk. "Let's call Tom, right now."

"He's not home. I tried."

"When?"

She looked at her wristwatch, "A little over an hour ago."

"He may be home now. It's close to Bertie's tea time." Cab pressed some buttons on his phone. Soon they heard the ringing on the other side. To their relief, it was Tom's voice that said, "Vonder Campe residence. Hello?"

"Tom! It's Cab. Listen, Emily is here with me. She's had a call today, from Montgomery. He wanted to talk with her, but Emily refused. Also, Freddie sang. Her dad's FBI, too, which I didn't know."

"Geez!" Tom was heard exclaiming.

"May I tell Emily what I know? It's essential now."

"Em, darling," Tom's voice. "I was going to tell you, okay. Cab, tell her."

"Thanks. Good decision. Talk to you later, Tom." Cab terminated the call. "Wow," he said, pointing to the digital clock on his phone. "Twenty seconds to spare." To Emily he said, "I don't know if it still works, but under a minute calls are hard to trace." He came back from behind his desk. "You heard the man. I will tell you what I know. Afterwards, you and I are going to have a strong drink, and lunch at Lutece."

With a faint smile Emily said, "Shouldn't I sign for the insurance now? I will, you know!"

On the first Sunday in June Tom and Bertie left London, after a tearful farewell from Bettina and Pat, made a bit less so because of the prospect of all of them seeing each other again soon at the wedding in Los Angeles. Also, there was a diversion—throngs of people at the airport, most of them arriving for the fiftieth anniversary celebrations of D-Day, being greeted with fanfare and whoops and signs, which Tom explained to his wide-eyed son. It was astonishing to Tom how much Bertie had improved during his stay in London, the boy now spoke intelligently in coherent sentences—amusingly, with a slight English accent—and had learned to count to twenty. It was proof to Tom, if such was needed, that the presence of intelligent, caring adults was utterly essential to the development of a child in the crucial early years. He was grateful to Betts and Pat for how much of that they had provided. And he was even more grateful to Emily, who had stated flatly that there would be no honeymoon but that they would take Bertie and go on a two-week family vacation. "No more separations," was the motto, and that meant all three of them.

As usual, Cab picked them up at the airport in his limo, although the driver had changed, Fernand had been drafted as an interpreter for the soon-to-be American invasion of Haiti. His replacement was a squat, surly white man against whom Cab raised the inside window as soon as they were seated.

"So," Cab said, after he had play-wrestled with Bertie for calling him "sir." "It's Uncle Charles to you, my boy! There's plenty of lollipops involved for getting it right!"

"We've outgrown lollipops, too," Tom smiled.

"Not my kind, you haven't," Cab said, and produced a package from FAO Schwartz. "Welcome home, kid!" Under his breath he said, "You and I have to talk, Tom. As soon as possible."

"Yes. We will. You are staying for dinner at my mother's house, Cab. No argument, she expects you. And I'll give you a little package that I want you to check out before we get together at your office tomorrow morning."

"Another hollow scientific tome, containing moola?" Cab asked.

"Better. Our tape."

Cab whistled, and nodded.

They got together at ten the next morning, in Cab's office.

"I have run the tape. It's a bit rough at times, but when I enhanced the sound it came through. It's dynamite, Tom."

"Yes. Turn on your recorder, I want my first report, verbal or otherwise, to be like a deposition."

"A sworn statement." Cab nodded. "Good idea, Tom. Let me set it up, and you start, in your own words, that what you are about to say is the truth, so help you God."

"Or the Grand Architect of the Universe . . ."

"For godsake, Tom, don't be flippant about it! It'd kill it, right off. Speak clearly, don't be afraid of emotions, stumble now and again if you must, but get it out, straight from the heart, and fresh from your memory. Okay?"

"Sorry. You are right. Let's go."

The conference room of the Blumenfeld insurance office was equipped with a table model of a high-fidelity sound recorder. Cab and Tom sat opposite each other. Cab started the tapes running, the machine being on a dual system that could produce a second copy simultaneously. Cab identified the speakers, himself as the operator, giving the date and time, and Tom as the narrator who would speak for himself, or both of them would talk, as the narrative demanded. Interspersed would be other documented evidence, such as a minitape recording of certain events as they happened at the time when the narrator was "miked," and the reading of a statement from a computer disk.

And then Tom began. He started with the events of that fateful July Fourth, when he witnessed the agony of his wife's death throes, until the explosion which he termed a probable suicide by his wife whose mind and body had been fatally damaged, the force of which, however, was totally underestimated in that it very nearly killed him, too. Tom stated that he recognized the nature of his wife's symptoms because as a research scientist he had studied the earlier Marburg eruption at the German pharmaceutical company's laboratories. She had contracted a massive infection by a highly lethal agent, a filovirus. Employees of labs such as Nettie's, where research animals were kept had been trained in the detection of viral outbreaks and in the recognition of symptoms. Nettie knew that there was no cure for her, and she also knew that all her bodily fluids and excretions would be highly contagious. Tom, his voice breaking, praised his wife's actions as hugely courageous, in that she separated herself from all human contact when her symptoms had become acute, which at that point also meant that they were irreversible. She realized that she was doomed, but that once the virus had run its course and had failed to infect the next living organism, it would die with the host body. In the frantic hours before his wife's death, when their boat was drifting away from human habitation, Tom reasoned that his wife had to have been infected at her place of work, either accidentally or intentionally, by herself or by a person or persons unknown. In her dying agony, his wife had tried to communicate to him frenziedly that she had left something for him, which he could not understand at that time. Weeks later he would find it to be a statement of hers on one of her computer game disks. He would come back to that in due course.

Tom then spent some time explaining why he had reported the explosion as accidental, and why he did not disclose his wife's infection. He said he was certain that such a claim would have met with skepticism, as indeed had happened with the much simpler accident report. But even if taken seriously by more sophisticated authorities later on, it would have led to media involvement he considered harmful to his child and contrary to his wife's last wish. He emphatically rejected the notion of his wife infecting herself, he believed that she was de facto murdered, and that the party who did this to her intended to sabotage the animal population of the laboratory. Where, he asked, could a live virus have come to a healthy monkey population but from willful introduction from the outside? He could only speculate as to how that was done, and by what interest groups. Such outside forces would have powers beyond the ordinary legal recourse he could have taken. He feared that if he had made himself the accuser, it would have exposed his son and himself to probable retribution. Adding to his anxiety as a possibly not unintended move against him by the invisible enemy was the suspicion raised by the military that he could have murdered his wife. When he was exonerated, other methods were tried to keep him quiet. One early proof that such reasoning was correct was the anonymous, covert "gift" to him of one hundred thousand dollars in cash, with a note of condolence for his wife's death attached to it. It only served to strengthen his resolve to go it alone in trying to bring the actual culprit to justice. At this point, he added, it seemed futile for him to engage official channels in this quest.

Cab broke in here and stated that he was contacted by Tom in strict confidentiality. He declared the remnants of the cash package to be exhibit one, and the floppy disk with Natalie Campe's statement exhibit two, both of which were kept in his office safe. He then read Nettie's words off the computer screen into the recorder. He said he at first counseled Tom to go to the authorities, before he wholeheartedly joined his old friend in the endeavor to uncover the conspiracy, or to disprove there was one if such were the case. From this point on, he declared, the actions taken were planned and executed as a joint effort. He wanted this to be understood.

Tom now elaborated on what transpired further, especially in England and in Germany. He gave names and dates of contacts leading to the suspects, and described the actions in detail. By silent agreement between the two of them, Tom selectively omitted certain facts he regarded as unessential, such as the story Thea had told about her mother's death, although he did mention Thea as a "forensic consultant," assuming that her name had come up in Freddie's report, anyway. Likewise, he chose not to bring Pat into the narrative, by stating only that the Duke was reached through his sister's social contacts. The episode with Phyllis remained locked in his heart, forever, he hoped. As for Emily, he would only say that a sudden "illness" forced their detour into Switzerland. To him, privacy had certain well defined parameters.

He then came to the description of the detection and pursuit of "The Creep," hereafter "T.C." He stated that despite his urge for bloody revenge on the murderer of his wife, he was counseled to moderation by his friend. They devised a scheme that had to have two components: a prerequisite confession made directly to Tom (he described how he was "wired") and, point two, would be followed by a phony injection of insulin, but proclaimed to be tainted hepatitis-B serum whereby "T.C." would be left in doubt whether he would die of a viral infection himself, a self-inflicted scare and torture for the rest of his life. Tom went into some detail on how that was to be accomplished, at which point Cab played the recording of the tape, with the dramatic moments of "T.C.'s" drowning. Tom closed by describing the coincidental effects of the German transport strike which prevented Cab from joining him as planned from England.

Tom signed off, "In your memory, Nettie, with love." Cab stated the time—they had been at it for nearly two hours—and stopped the machine.

Tom mopped perspiration from his forehead. "I feel half sick," he said.

Cab nodded. "What we need is a stiff drink. Let's go over to the Waldorf and have a double scotch."

On the street, Tom said, "I wonder sometimes what the Duke is saying now. His henchman had wanted me to sign that release. Of course, I got away from him. D'you think they will come after me here?"

"I doubt it, Tom. It's past history for everybody now."

"You hope," Tom said.

When the first swallow of whisky hit his gullet, Tom shuddered. "I'm worried, Cab. About what I'm doing to Emily. Is it fair to make her marry me?"

"Now that you have told her everything, and she hasn't recanted her commitment to you, I would say you both have nothing to worry about."

Tom nodded, "I want her to have knowledge of the recording we did today. And I want her agreement that we send a copy of that tape to Montgomery."

Cab narrowed his eyes. "I didn't know that's what you had in mind."

"I hadn't, until now. But I think we must. Any objections?"

"Let's discuss it. Okay? It's not an easy step to take, getting the Feds into the act. It might open a whole can of worms."

"It's our can, and there are no worms. We are innocent of any wrong-doings."

"As a lawyer, let me tell you that you could get an indictment even of Mother Theresa, these days, for practicing medicine without a license. Montgomery may be okay, but if the stuff falls into wrong hands, there's no telling what might happen. Particularly if there is a conspiracy to sabotage, and if big corporate entities are involved, either as targets or as plotters."

"But you, as my agent, my lawyer, and my friend, could go to Montgomery and tell him that you have something for him, if he can give us immunity?"

"Immunity implies wrongdoing exists. Protection, is a better word."

"You are the mouthpiece. You'll find the right words. Call him, Cab."

Two days later Tom and Bertie flew on to Los Angeles. Tom's mother would follow in a week's time, her daily presence at her ailing husband's bedside should not be interrupted any longer than necessary. Also a week later would come the arrivals of Bettina and Pat from London, and of Cab from New York.

Tom and Bertie moved in with Al and Laura again, in their newly rechimneyed Santa Monica house. Laura appeared not to be pregnant, but was curiously radiant about all she said and did—all, that is, except to answer Al's question if it "took." They had been to a fertility clinic for some months now.

Emily had chosen to remain with her mother in Santa Barbara. She had suggested, and Tom had agreed, that they would find excessive prenuptial mingling too trying. She would come to Los Angeles on Sunday, to attend the wedding of her friend Steffie to an English lord. "Yes, a real one, Tom! He doesn't have a lord's name because he is the eldest son of the eldest son of the present lord. Ask Betts about it. She'll tell you." They were talking several times a day on the telephone.

"Guess what," Emily said a short time later in another call, "We could rent Steffie's house! She's going to England with Philip, but doesn't want to sell her house here because the market is so bad. Three bedrooms, two baths. Real cute. Large yard, too. For Bertie, and Guy? We could have it for six months, she says. Furnished. What do you think?"

"Where is it located?"

"Brentwood. On Sunset Boulevard. Walking distance to St. Martin's Church, where Bertie can go back to pre-school."

"Nobody walks on Sunset Boulevard, Em. There aren't even sidewalks!"

"We'll drive him, natch. What do you think?"

"That settles it!" Tom laughed. "Can I come to the wedding?"

"Of course! You're the groom!"

"Thanks. How about to your friend's wedding?"

"On the invitation to me it says 'and escort.' Will you be my escort?"

"For the rest of your life."

"Then you are qualified. It's in Beverly Hills, by the way, in the famous Bistro Garden. Her father owns the place."

"Well, at least the food will be good."

The food was good, the ambiance California golden. The garden patio of the restaurant had been transformed into a magical grotto, with flowers, potted citrus trees and blooming bushes everywhere. The wedding party spilled over into the restaurant. Tom and Emily sat at a table in the back, close together. It was Tom's first opportunity to give Emily the present he had bought for her in London. It was a one-of-a-kind creation by a jewelry designer friend of Bettina's, consisting of a necklace and matching earrings, employing a variety of stones. It looked at once festive and informally modern.

Emily loved it. She kissed him. She made him help her put it on. And she kissed him again. It made Tom blush with desire. Later, when they were dancing, she whispered, "I'm okay, you know . . . in every way."

"Tell me again a week from now," Tom whispered back, "in Hawaii."

Emily moved into the Sunset house that same evening. The bridal couple had retreated for the night to the Peninsula Hotel, prior to leaving the next morning for the Bahamas where His Lordship owned "a pad and a boat." Emily was thinking about that as she left early Monday morning, driving down to the supermarket. Steffie's pantry and fridge were almost bare of anything edible, she took all her meals at her father's Bistro where she was the bookkeeper.

On the winding road to West Los Angeles, she had to slow down as she passed a number of police cars and vans parked curbside to her right. Emily craned her neck. Nothing to see, no banged-up cars, no ambulances. Just a whole lot of police activity, on the sidewalk and the house behind it. On her way back she had to slow down, the road had narrowed with more police vehicles parked on the opposite curb, too. She leaned out to ask a policeman who directed traffic, "What was going on?"

The policeman asked her if she lived in the neighborhood?

She told him she lived on Sunset and again asked him what had happened. He told her that some people got killed last night. He asked her when she last had driven down the street. She told him less than an hour earlier, on her way to the market.

The policeman waved her on. She turned up her car radio, and before she reached the house she learned what was going on. O.J. Simpson's ex-wife and her male friend had been brutally slain that night, on her townhouse steps, right by that spot Emily had passed. O.J. himself was in Chicago, now flying back to deal with the tragedy at home.

O.J.'s home was just a few blocks up Sunset Boulevard and around the corner from where Emily lived now. The police car sirens were howling. From her front window she saw huge trucks with antennas atop rumbling by. The media arriving in full force. To cover O.J. at his house.

Emily shuddered and turned away. Her wedding would take place on this street this week. Would that gruesome homicide cast a shadow on it?

She mentioned it to Tom when he called in the afternoon. He and Bertie had been to the Galleria to find a store where they sold tuxes, matching ones for father and son. Tom laughed when she told him of her fear. "It'll blow over in a day or two. The media are voracious, they'll need new news to feed on by then. By the way, Laura says for you to come over, we're having pineapple pizza. You know, pineapple? Hawaii?"

But it didn't blow over, on the contrary, it got worse. By Wednesday the streets around O.J.'s house were clogged with media and police vehicles, reporters by the dozens were camping out on lawns and sidewalks, the murder scene was roped off to throngs of gawkers, traffic around the area was crawling with sightseers, and all the news, fit to print or not, was about O.J., O.J., O.J.. And about O.J.'s ex-wife, and O.J.'s ex-wife's friend, the hapless waiter who had brought a pair of forgotten eyeglasses to O.J.'s ex-wife's townhouse, and was slashed to death along with O.J.'s ex-wife. O.J. looked suitably pained, surrounded by celebrity lawyers.

On Thursday, O.J.'s ex-wife's (henceforth known universally as Nicole) was eulogized at her church on Sunset Boulevard, with O.J. attending. Her church was none other than St. Martin's, where Emily and Tom were to be married. More throngs, more cars, more police. Emily, near tears, had to cancel her rehearsal, the Monsignor suggested a week's postponement.

"Postpone the wedding?" Tom took Emily in his arms. "Like hell we will!"

Emily's eyes were brimming. "You got a better idea?"

"Yes," he said, and kissed her. "Let's talk about it in the car." They were driving to the airport to pick up Cab and Tom's mother who were traveling together on the same plane, when Tom ventured a suggestion. To his great surprise, Emily agreed immediately. For the moment, though, they would keep it to themselves. The new arrivals had to be delivered to their hotel, and Tom's mother's comfort especially had to be seen to. Cab wanted to talk, with some seeming urgency, but Tom waved him off. "Later. After dinner, Cab. Please." There was a message from Al, Laura said when they came to her house to pick up Bertie. Tom was to call him at the office, immediately; it was urgent.

Tom took the phone when Laura had punched in Al's number. "Hi, Al!"

"Finally. I've been trying to reach you for hours! Did you pick up your friend from the airport? Good. He's at the hotel now, right? I'll call him. You come over to my office, Tom, right now. Okay? Don't argue."

The phone went dead. Tom said, "Al wants to see me, now."

"About what?" Laura and Emily asked, almost in unison.

"I don't know. It sounded important. I better go. You three may want to get yourselves ready for dinner."

Emily shook her head, "I'll go with you, Tom. I'm already dressed. You drop me off at the hotel, I want to be there when my mother drives up."

In the car, Emily wanted to know what the meeting with Al was all about, but Tom said he didn't know, it just sounded urgent, and that Cab would be there, too.

Well, Emily mused, if he was there, and Al, and Tom—chances are it'd be about the wedding, right? Tom said he really didn't know, but the only way to find out would be for Em to come along and ask Al. Then she could make up her mind if she wanted to stay or walk over to the hotel, which was close by.

Al's office, suffused with the burnished red of a glorious sunset, was empty. His secretary, about to go home, said that Mr. Becker was awaiting them in the conference room.

They trudged along the corridor and opened the door to the conference room, which had no outside windows. The indirect lighting from the ceiling cast a sterile white brightness on everything. Al was sitting at the highly polished oval table, and so was Cab. When they saw Emily, they got up. Her presence was almost daunting, smart and willowy looking, dressed in a long beige jacket over a short black skirt that sensuously accented her well shaped legs down to her low-heeled black leather pumps. When Emily greeted Cab and Al, she gave them a smile and a handshake. And, a bit flustered, they smiled back. Later, they would find that a trace of her perfume had lingered on their palms.

Tom said that Emily would leave if the matter that Al wanted to discuss did not concern her, such as, perhaps, the bachelor party slated for Friday. Anything else—she would stay, if she wanted to.

Al squirmed a bit when he answered. "I don't know if she should."

"Nonsense." Cab was firm about that. "I think you should stay, Emily."

Tom said, "I have no idea what this is about, but I think it's time you told us."

Cab spoke again, "Al's got a summons for you, Tom. I got one, too, in New York. It's from our pal, Montgomery."

Al splayed his hands. "Sit down, sit down, both of you. You make me nervous, standing there."

Tom pulled up a chair for Emily and she sat down, her legs mercifully disappearing under the conference table.

"What kind of summons?" Tom asked as he took his place next to Emily. "A subpoena?"

"No, no," Al said irritably. "Let's not get off on the wrong foot here. It's not a subpoena, and it's not exactly a summons, either."

"May I explain?" Cab asked. "Whatever you call it, it's the result of my sending your stuff to agent Montgomery, Tom."

"What stuff?" Al demanded to know. "Montgomery is FBI. You sent stuff to the FBI? I'm your lawyer, Tom. How come I don't know about it?"

"If it's any consolation to you, Al," Emily said, putting her hand on his arm, "I didn't know about it, either, until very recently. These two boys have cooked up a private scheme to unravel the mystery of Nettie's death. The FBI got interested in that. You take it from there, Tom, Cab."

Tom nodded, and began to tell Al the story, with apologies for not having kept him up to date as the successive revelations occurred. Cab gave a corollary report, stressing the need for absolute confidentiality that the case required as it developed. The fewer in the know, the better and safer.

"Except," Emily broke in, "that your girlfriend was an FBI stoolie, Cab. No hard feelings, but it has to be mentioned somewhere along the line."

"I was coming to that," Cab said testily.

"Holy malony," Al groaned. "This isn't going right. I want everything laid out to me now, chapter and verse. The FBI guy is coming in tomorrow. My license may be on the line, quite apart from my looking stupid. I don't like to lose my license, and I am not stupid. So, now we start from the beginning."

Cab said, "Hold your horses. I brought a copy of the tape I sent to Montgomery. With your permission, Tom, I'd like to give it to Al."

"Of course," Tom nodded. "You go over it, at your leisure, Al. It's yours anyway, for your files. It'll take about an hour or so listening to it, which you will want to do before tomorrow's visit. Meantime," he looked at his watch, "we have to go to the hotel. We have guests there."

"What time is Montgomery coming to your office, Al?" Emily asked.

"The afternoon. I'm supposed to call him, at the local FBI office in the Federal Building. He's probably here for the Simpson case."

Emily said, looking at everyone around the table: "My father told me once that the mark of an intelligent person is the ability to cope with the unexpected. As you say, Al, you are not stupid, and neither are we. So, gentlemen, I have a suggestion to make." Turning to Tom, she said, "It's a slight variation from what we discussed in the car. May I?"

"You go right ahead, Em," Tom nodded.

It didn't take Emily long to make her suggestion, and she got no objections when she had finished. Al said he'd listen to the tape, but first he had to make a couple of phone calls. The others left together, saying they'd see him at the hotel.

The meeting with Montgomery was set for 4:00 P.M., the earliest that Al said he could get him to commit. Cab was at Al's office on time, while Tom and Emily were a few minutes late. It didn't matter, Montgomery wasn't there yet. When he did arrive, the FBI man was politely apologetic for being a half hour beyond his promised time. "It's absolute bedlam at the local office. O.J. did not surrender to the police this noon, and has now been declared a wanted murder suspect. I'm glad it's not my case."

"Agent Montgomery," Tom said, greeting him, "allow me to introduce my brother-in-law and my attorney, Al Becker. "My old friend and my insurance agent, Charles Blumenfeld." The men shook hands. "And I am pleased to introduce my wife, Emily."

Montgomery said to Emily, "We spoke on the phone, didn't we. I'm sorry to bust in on your wedding plans, Miss Dessauer."

Al, who was still standing behind his desk, held up a document. "Miss Emily Dessauer and Mr. Thomas Vonder Campe were wed this morning, in Superior Court Judge Wilton Snyder's chambers, Mr. Montgomery."

Montgomery didn't bat an eyelash. "Well, allow me to congratulate you both." He smiled and shook hands with Emily and with Tom.

Al invited everyone to sit down around the low table of the seating corner. He buzzed his secretary, who came in carrying a tray with a small coffee urn and cups. They all busied themselves pouring coffee, and leaned back into the seat cushions, stirring their cups. Nobody talked.

Montgomery cleared his throat. "Thank you for accepting my invitation, on short notice, too. We should all benefit from this meeting." He pulled his lanky frame up and rested his elbows on his knees. "Now, I don't want to be palsy-walsy here, but if you would permit me in this discussion to call you by your first names I'd be grateful. I'm Thad."

"Sure, Thad," Al said quickly. "It's a lot easier that way." The others nodded their consent.

"Next," Montgomery continued, looking thoughtfully at Emily, "I wonder if you'd want to excuse yourself. It has really nothing to do with you personally, and this being your wedding day, I worry that what I'll have to say may be disquieting to you."

Emily, who sat close to Tom whose arm was over her shoulder, replied in a measured tone: "Disquieting. What a nice, understated term you use there, Thad." With her hand she reached up and held Tom's fingers. "Let me tell you about disquieting. A year ago, Tom lost his wife under the most cruel of circumstances. For a while, he was suspected of murdering her. Very disquieting. Now, take me. Several months ago I lost my home in the Malibu fire, barely escaping with my life. Then, following the earthquake, I learned that my new home had been totally destroyed. Next, in Russia, I was mobbed and robbed. And afterwards, I had to deal with a medical emergency. Talk about disquieting."

Montgomery nodded, unruffled. "I know. My empathy was purposely understated, Emily. I do not want to add to your burden."

"My burden, as you put it, Thad, has already been added to by the sad spectacle of the brutal murder of a young man and woman in the very vicinity of our new home, and the church where we were to be married has been the site of her funeral. Not to mention the media frenzy around the house of the suspect, also nearby. Disquieting, indeed. We live in interesting times, Thad." She pressed Tom's fingers and looked up at him. Tom pulled her closer to him.

Montgomery drained his cup and put it on the table. "In China, to live in interesting times is a curse. I see, Emily, that you seem to have a grasp of the reality of the present. I have no objection to your staying."

"What exactly is your purpose here, Thad?" Al asked. "Is this an official inquiry by the Federal Bureau of Investigation? If so, in what matter?"

"A fair question," Montgomery glanced at each of them, "and one I must first answer again with generalities. With the end of the Cold War has come an explosive growth of terrorist activities, mostly centered abroad and some of them directed against the United States and individual citizens of this country. We call it the T-Factor, and we are taking it very seriously.

I am with the Anti-Terrorism section of the FBI, which has several subheadings, mine being the office that deals with terrorist acts committed by introduction or dissemination of infectious agents or poisonous substances, into the population or food supply chain. Unfortunately, it is a growing field, we are only now gearing up to meet the challenge to prevent or deflect these threats against our society and institutions."

"What's it got to do with us, specifically?" Cab asked.

"With you personally, very little, Charles. But knowingly or not, you have been a player in this game, from the time your friend came to you for help, up to the moment you contacted me and sent me the interview tape. I repeat now what I told you then. I appreciate your cooperation. I would add, though, that I would like to have the original of the Mac disk by Natalie Campe, and the audio tape of the Ullmer conversations and the drowning. We need them to verify their authenticity."

"They're in my safe in New York. Tom?" Cab raised his eyebrows.

Tom nodded. "Hand it over, Cab, when you are back."

"Thank you." Montgomery continued, turning to Tom: "We have independently confirmed your suspicions, Tom, that Natalie was willfully infected with a filovirus. It may interest you to know how that was accomplished. One day I hope I'll be able to give you the details, but briefly, they transported the virus in the bodies of live marmosets, primates as you know, some of them not larger than a mouse, that were smuggled in from Victoria, Canada. Ullmer's job was to infect the monkey population of the laboratory. Your wife got on to him, somehow, although probably not nearly as deeply as Ullmer suspected. Nevertheless, she had to be eliminated. Where Ullmer went wrong was the method he employed, instead of reporting his suspicions first to his handlers, he lashed out on his own. By the time he did report it, the damage was done. So, Ullmer was tainted, but he could still be marginally useful under a new identity, as he was anxious to undergo a sex change. Except, that you came in, Tom. You, and you too, Charles, were two very effective investigators. You set our own sights in a direction we had not initially pursued. I might add, that when you refused to confide in me, Tom, we decided to let you run with it and see where it took us. You had us worried for a while, though, for going way out on a limb. That Heidelberg thing could have gone wrong, you know."

Tom shook his head. "How did you find out about us?"

Montgomery allowed himself a thin smile. "We are patrolling the information highway ourselves. Including the road to and from Vaduz, Liechtenstein."

"Oh, no," Cab groaned. "That, plus Freddie—"

"Frederika had no role in it, I want to assure you, except afterwards in reporting her fears to her father, who relayed the information to me. Freddie was just confirming what we already knew."

"So," Al said, visibly relieved. "That's it, huh? No charges?"

"No charges." Montgomery shook his head. "Still, you must be wondering why I took the trouble to come all the way out here to talk to you. Don't guess, let me tell you. There is an aftermath to be considered." Here he turned to Emily. "I am glad that you are here, now that I know that you are strong. The thing that worries us, and that you should be prepared for, is the revenge factor from the other side. It is only a matter of time before they have figured out that you were freelancing, Tom, at which point they have two options. They may be relieved the episode is over and let it go at that. On the other hand, they may consider you a potential threat to them in the future, and decide to eliminate you. That may not necessarily mean Mafia-style revenge, but they could easily ruin you professionally. In any case, you two should be alert to the possibility."

Cab sounded worried now. "He could change his name, and move away with his family, couldn't he? Husband, wife, small boy—easy camouflage."

"Yes. He could do that. Or he could confirm what they suspected from the start—that you acted as an agent of the United States government." Montgomery paused, looking around at everyone before he rested his eyes on Tom. "You remember when you fooled the Duke in London with your Major Nemo charade? Of course he never really bought it, but he believed you were working for us. We still command a healthy respect in some quarters. And so he delivered the culprit to you." He smiled. "I am authorized to make you an offer, Major Campe. The Bureau has established a biomedical research laboratory that concerns itself exclusively with the threat, global and local, of viral and mutated bacterial infectious onslaughts. We are woefully short of experienced personnel, and would welcome you and your expertise. As a job, it isn't much as pay goes, compared to private industry, but it is still a cut or two above what you were making in the Army."

There was silence when Montgomery finished. All were looking at Tom.

"It would mean moving to Washington, wouldn't it?" Tom asked, casting a glance at Emily.

"Yes," Montgomery nodded.

Emily broke in. "Before anyone says what you may privately think, I'm not a problem wife. When I agreed to marry Tom, it was for love. It still is. It always will be. If Tom wants to go to Washington, I go with him. No sweat."

Al said, no way did he think that, and Cab said he'd never doubt her. Tom gave his bride a hug, and whispered something in her ear. To Montgomery, he said, "Let me think about it, Thad, okay?"

Montgomery said, "Sure. Only tell me how it sits with you, at first hearing it, right now. Does it sound attractive to you?"

"Yes." Tom nodded.

"On a scale of mildly to very, how do you rate it?"

Tom hesitated a moment. "Very," he said solemnly.

Emily said, "We are going on a two-week vacation to Hawaii. When we come back, and it's still very, I predict you got a deal, Thad."

"That's great. That's really great." Montgomery allowed himself a broad grin now. "Thank you, Tom. Look forward to hearing from you. And thank you, Emily. You're great, too." He shook hands with both of them.

Tom said, "We're having a small bachelor party this evening, just a half a dozen guys having a steak and a drink. You are invited to join us, Thad."

Montgomery hesitated, saying that he had a plane to catch, but when it turned out to be a red-eye, and when Cab and Al joined in the invitation, he agreed to join them. Al said he could stick around at the office, freshen up a bit, and drive with him to the Beach Club by 7:00 P.M. Emily excused herself, saying she had some last-minute changes to attend to. Cab and Tom would walk back to the hotel together, to meet Emily's half-brothers and their families who were flying in for the wedding. They would then take the brothers to the bachelor party. Including Montgomery, there'd be six around the dinner table. The invitation list was deliberately kept small—it topped out at forty-two.

Al and Montgomery were already there when the other four men arrived, as they noticed when they entered the lounge of the Beach Club. Clusters of people were hanging around the two television sets that were mounted high in the corners of the bar. There was hooting and hollering at times, and Cab was wondering aloud which important game he was missing.

"No game," Al shouted at them, "it's O.J. They got O.J., on the freeway! See the white bronco? He's in there, his old Bills pal Cowling is driving him. The cops caught up with him in Orange County and they are driving north on the San Diego Freeway!"

Tom felt a wave of annoyance sweep over him. Not O.J., again! Would this sordid story never end? He looked at the TV screen: There it was, the white car, chased in almost respectful distance by a dozen or more police cars and motorcycles. The news anchors reporting "this still developing story" were urging O.J. to pick up his cellular phone and call ahead for his surrender, while at the same time, in a gloomy voice, expressing the hope that O.J. would not use the gun he was holding, not on himself or anyone else.

It was bizarre, grown men and women glued to the TV screens watching an almost stately procession along the northbound freeway, all rush hour traffic swept aside, and now, as "The White Bronco" was passing through the southern suburbs of the metropolis, there were people crowding onto the traffic lanes, leaning from the overpasses and standing on the tops of their cars, cheering O.J. on! The bartender handed out frothy glasses of beer from the tap to everyone in the bar, courtesy of an anonymous member. And still the chase went on, up the wide expanse of the Sepulveda pass. It became clear that the caravan was headed to Sunset Boulevard, no doubt to O.J.'s Brentwood home.

"This is disgusting," Tom said.

Montgomery just nodded, with a faint smile.

"Why aren't the cops blocking his car and taking him into custody?" Cab was almost sneering.

Al looked at him in disbelief: "You're kidding. And have another riot?"

"Shit," Cab said. "Well, I'm hosting this dinner, and I am asking you all to come into the dining room with me."

When they were seated, there was still no escape from the action on the TV screens. The sound came from everywhere, it seemed, from the lobby, from the crowd in the bar, and even from the kitchen. It was annoying, and it stifled any attempts to make the stag dinner the fun event it was intended to be.

Halfway through the main course, the waiter came to Cab and whispered something to him. Cab thanked him, and turned to Tom. "There is a phone call for you. You can take it in the library. It ought to be quiet there."

It was Emily. In a tense, high-pitched torrent of words she told Tom that she could not get into her house on Sunset Boulevard because her driveway was blocked by a huge TV news van and a couple of smaller cars. She said it was like that up and down the street ever since the O.J. caravan had returned to the O.J. house. Why? Because O.J. hadn't surrendered yet, and he had a gun, and so the police had cleared O.J.'s neighborhood of all media vehicles and reporters, citing public safety. "There are helicopters buzzing around, with their cameras and lightbeams, Tom. It's like a war zone!" There was an edge of hysteria to her voice.

"Easy, Emily!" Tom spoke soothingly. "Where are you now? Are you safe?"

He heard her take a deep breath. "I'm five blocks from my house, in my car, calling you on my cellular phone. Yes, I'm safe. That's not the problem."

"Drive over to the hotel. I'll meet you there. The dinner is a dud, anyway."

"That's just the point, Tom! This O.J. thing is continuing to throw a monkey wrench into our wedding, what's left of it! There's no way the media circus is going away tomorrow, and besides, the lookiloos are already arriving!"

"Emily, get a grip on yourself. This is not the end of the world."

"No, but it sure seems that I am jinxed here in L.A.! Fire, earthquake, and now this! Is Montgomery still there?"

"Yes."

"You better tell him we're taking him up on his offer. I want out of here. I've had it. I want a nice little house with a yard, in Virginia."

"Emily, remember what you just told us earlier, about what your father had said? How did it go? The mark of the intelligent person is the ability to cope with the unexpected? Well, this is certainly unexpected. How are we going to cope with it?"

There was a moment's pause, before she answered: "You're right. We can cope with this. As a matter of fact, I have an idea. Tom? Are you there?"

"I'm listening, Em."

"We're going to move the wedding to another venue. Come to think of it, this opens a new vista. We're going to have the ceremony and the dinner at the same time and place! Remember Steffie, my friend, whose house I'm renting? Okay. Her father gave her the wedding at his restaurant in Beverly Hills. He can do the same for us, even on short notice. He's a nice man, he knows me, and we'll pay him so he won't have any losses because of us."

"There you go!"

"And you know what? This would get us around the Monsignor. We are already legally married, aren't we? I'll ask the young priest at St. Martin's to come and bless our union, and that's that. What do you think?"

"I think, Emily, loving you will be an exciting adventure."

She laughed. "Likewise! I can't wait for Hawaii. And Virginia."